Reynolds Dodson was born in [illegible] He has spent much of his adult life as a magazine editor. He is co-author of *Beyond Valium*, a book about brain chemistry, and co-creator of the critically acclaimed comic strip *Splitsville*. Another strip he writes, *The Loner*, appears regularly in *Playboy*.

Reynolds Dodson

URBAN RENEWAL

Penguin Books

Penguin Books Ltd, Harmondsworth, Middlesex, England
Viking Penguin Inc., 40 West 23rd Street, New York, New York 10010, U.S.A.
Penguin Books Australia Ltd, Ringwood, Victoria, Australia
Penguin Books Canada Ltd, 2801 John Street, Markham, Ontario, Canada L3R 1B4
Penguin Books (N.Z.) Ltd, 182–190 Wairau Road, Auckland 10, New Zealand

First published in the U.S.A. by Doubleday & Company, Inc. 1984
First published in Great Britain by Viking 1984
Published in Penguin Books 1985

Reproduced, printed and bound in Great Britain by
Hazell Watson & Viney Limited,
Member of the BPCC Group,
Aylesbury, Bucks

To my wife, Susan

Part One

1

A commuter was down in the Pan Am Building. Alex Gronsky, having picked up a *Post* and now on his way to catch the five thirty-seven, first became aware of it outside of Charlie Brown's restaurant when he felt something soft under the sole of his cordovan. It was a man's hat, a tan fedora. He caught only a glimpse of it, then it was gone—crushed and trampled under the stampede of Florsheims shuffling in lockstep toward the Grand Central escalator bank. My God! he thought. He felt a lump in his stomach. The crowd surged forward, parted like a river. He saw a splayed foot, an open attaché case, an outstretched hand turned palm-up against the marble. "Hey, wait!" he shouted, or at least wanted to shout. Afterward, it was not clear whether he had really said anything. But his impulse was to say, "Stop! There's a man down here! Wait! Can't you see him? Watch out—you're stepping on him!" The crowd kept moving. It was like some vast tide of fabric—worsted, double-knit, gabardine, flannel—a mindless torrent of chalk stripe and tweed funneling inexorably toward the teeth of the escalator. Over the heads of the men next to him he could see a security guard approaching. He was trying to cut crosscurrent against the unyielding tide. He had a walkie-talkie and was trying to talk into it, but the aerial had become snagged in somebody's shoulder bag. The crowd pressed forward. Gronsky's foot touched something. With horror, he realized it was an empty shoe. In another couple of seconds he had reached the escalator tread, and with relief he descended into the cool of Grand Central.

Ex-marine, ex-Midwesterner, ex-small college football player, Alexander A. Gronsky lived in horror of this: to end one's life in a New York rush hour, strewing memos and sales reports all over the thoroughfare. What a meaningless surrender! You'd feel so helpless. "Did you see that back there?" he said to the man next to him. But the man didn't answer. He was looking at his wristwatch. Gronsky pulled out a handkerchief and dabbed at his forehead with it.

Whether it was Gronsky's imagination, or whether it was simply a stage he was in, being almost forty-three and moderately successful, it seemed to him that in the past several months he had had an unusual number of disquieting experiences. Like the other day at Fifty-first and Madison. He had been waiting for a walk light when he had felt a tap on his shoulder. Out of the corner of his eye he had seen a disheveled man behind him—a beggar, he supposed, one of the city's soft-touch artists.

"Get lost," said Gronsky.

"Wha?" The man stared at him.

"You heard me, get lost! Get the hell out of here!"

The man stepped back, began to wail like a siren. He was flapping his arms. His eyes rolled excitedly.

Gradually, obliquely, the truth began to dawn that the man was not a panhandler at all—he was a retarded messenger with a package to deliver and who simply wanted to know where 480 Madison was. "Whaaa?" the man cried, turning to the other pedestrians. In his hand was a slip with the address scrawled in pencil. The pedestrians had scowled, looked at Gronsky with disgust, as if to say, "What's the matter with you? Have you no humanity?"

There had been another incident last week up at Townsend's. Townsend's was a hideaway near Rockefeller Center. Gronsky sometimes went there alone at noon hour and sat at the bar drinking vodka gibsons. He looked forward to those times. It was his special retreat. It was the one place where Eastman, his father-in-law, couldn't find him. Sometimes he would spend the entire afternoon there, slowly sinking into a delicious stupor.

"Excuse me . . ." said a woman suddenly appearing at his elbow.

"Not interested," he had said—and he had turned his back on her.

The woman began to scream. "Whaddaya mean, 'not interested'? You're sitting on my coat, and you say you're not interested, damn you?"

So it had come to that. After seventeen years, he had assumed the likeness of a typical New Yorker. Ask him a favor, he would slip you a shiv. The maimed, the handicapped—no one was safe from him.

As he strode past the orange-juice stand in the Upper Level waiting room, two black kids approached carrying a large box radio. The sound grew in volume, a kind of cacophonous mayhem. Gronsky's jaw grew taut. His eyes hardened to chalcedony.

He and Martin had discussed this on the train up to Westchester—blacks and transistors, the modern white man's burden—and they had devised ingenious methods by which to take their revenge: jamming devices, squirt guns with acid in them. Martin was a shirt buyer for the Brooks Brothers clothing chain. He was a stout, dapper man with a touch of the *artiste* about him: patterned suspenders, bright flowing handkerchiefs, suits made of cashmere, raw silk, fine wool materials. For the past seven years they had been smoking-car seat partners—third row from the rear, across the aisle from the poker foursome. It never varied. It was one of nature's rare constants. Few worlds were so disciplined as Conrail during rush hour. And Martin had proposed that the killing of a radio player should come under the heading of justifiable homicide. "It's no worse," he had said, "than killing a burglar or dope addict. In fact, maybe it's better. It would help pick up the tourist trade."

Gronsky looked forward to seeing Bob Martin now as he loped down the ramp at Gate Forty-two, his glen plaid suit coat like a tent over his body, his elephant-skin briefcase properly scuff-marked and handle-worn. The five thirty-seven lay groaning in its burrow. A pre-Diesel haze seemed to hang in the atmosphere. Gronsky smiled, nodded curtly to Sam, the conductor, then entered the smoker, with its acrid tobacco smell.

In the number of years he had been commuting on this railroad Gronsky had never sat in any car forward of the smoker. There was a reason for this—it had to do with his automobile, which was parked in Mount Kisco near the most southerly lot exit. The older he got, the more habit seemed to dictate. Friendships, parking lots, time schedules, mortgage payments—they were all like cogs in some diurnal machine which, if one piece was missing, might have clattered to a standstill. He was friends with Bob Martin because of the train car he sat in. He sat in that train car because of the positioning of his automobile. He positioned his automobile so that he could get home faster, so that he could eat dinner sooner, so that he could be with his son longer. God knows, it was not a very interesting pattern, but he felt as compelled to follow it as a dog to dig bone holes. It was what one did. You didn't examine it. It was as natural as mating or the migration of waterfowl.

Bob Martin was late. Gronsky looked at his wristwatch. It would be the perfect end of the perfect day if, on top of all his other problems, his seat partner would fail to show up by departure time. That would mean that he would have to travel alone. Worse, he might have to sit next to a stranger—some foreigner, some black, some female, God forbid!—someone so untutored as to upset the scheme of things.

Under his arm he was carrying his copy of the *Post*, which he now unfolded, glancing at the headline. Since that Australian had taken over, the *Post* had become a scandal sheet, but, through force of habit, he continued to look at it. Like everything else, it was part of the routine. The crossword puzzle was also part of it. It was his and Martin's custom to work the New York *Times* crossword puzzle, livening the action by using an indelible ballpoint.

Strange how relationships like this become sanctified. Bob Martin was an unknown beyond the parameters of Conrail. They had never socialized, had never had lunch together, yet for two hours a day they had an important bond between them. It was doubtful that they really had anything in common—a shirt buyer from Brooks Brothers and a Sunday-supplement space salesman—but they enjoyed each other, perhaps enjoyed their differences. Maybe it was because there was so little at stake between them.

Across the aisle from Gronsky, where the poker players sat, was a competitor he recognized named Angelo Karpeghian. A shark in man's clothing, a human torpedo, a man who, it was said, would sell his own grandmother. "Stay away from that guy" —that's what Eastman had warned him once. "He's the kind of guy, Alex, who would eat you for breakfast. A put-down artist, and not all that honest. What he brings away in overrides would make Croesus look saintly." Of course, the magazine business was full of Karpeghians. The world in which they moved was a refuge for predators—hawking, huckstering, glad-handing, bad-mouthing . . . sometimes Gronsky wondered how there had come to be so many of them.

"How ya doin?" said Gronsky.

Karpeghian saluted. He had a dark, beaky face and hair like a Brillo pad. "How's Revlon?" he said.

"Same old shit," said Gronsky. He smiled, turned away, tried to push down the tingling feeling.

What had happened was that Revlon had run an ad in *Focus* and somebody had inserted the wrong kind of paper stock. The ad for Charlie had come out too thin, and there was a see-through from a page showing an ad for mouse repellant. The net result was that the Charlie model seemed to be flaunting her wares for an oversized rodent. It was a horrible goof, and he, Gronsky, got blamed for it. It was the third time that year he had taken flak from the Revlon agency.

"Look, Alex," his father-in-law had told him last Thursday, "I can't keep fronting for you. I'm out of excuses. Family or not, you're going to have to produce. Charm's not enough. We also need follow-through." It was what Eastman called one of his "Dutch uncle chats." Everybody got them—Gronsky wasn't the only one. The problem was that Eastman was a pipeline to Mandy, and that meant everything that happened became fodder for dinner discussion. "Hear you had some problems with Revlon," she would say. "Daddy said it was because of a mistake in your insertion order. You know, he's trying to be fair, Alex, he really is, but if you don't make an effort then you can't expect him to." It was one of the drawbacks of marrying the boss's daughter. And presumably, God help him, it worked in reverse. Every argument, every failure, every letdown in his homelife was lodged and registered in some corporate ledger book.

Well, Gronsky wasn't worried. He got along with Darryl Eastman, and he was still the magazine's top-earning space rep. With commissions and bonuses he had made seventy grand last year. Not bad for a boy who had once used his head for a battering ram.

As he perused "Page Six," then turned to the sports section, again his mind went back to that escalator scene. The memory haunted him. It had some special significance. He wished Martin were there so that they could hash out the meaning of it.

Among Bob Martin's various peccadilloes, two stood out in sharp relief: one was his fastidiousness and snobbishness toward clothes, the other was his obsession with punctuality. In a way, Gronsky thought, the two traits dovetailed—like two clear overlays which, when joined, form a caricature. Could you really imagine an employee for Brooks Brothers who would be negligent or carefree in the conducting of his private life? Often he would explain the fine points of haberdashery, sometimes going so far as to pull out his shirttail. "Note the double stitching and reinforcing here," he would say. "You don't get that with an Arrow or Hathaway, Alex." And Gronsky would nod; he supposed you didn't. "Listen, Alex, don't buy ready-to-wear stuff. Buy made-to-measure. Those cuffs are too short for you. Your body has eccentricities you aren't even aware of, fella." These lectures were delivered with such enthusiasm that it never occurred to Gronsky to take affront at them. On the contrary, he considered them painlessly educational. His last three shirts he had bought in the custom department.

Martin's neurosis about time was a little harder to assimilate. It was a subject on which he rose to the mystical. It was as if he could feel the rhythms of the earth rising and falling in measured increments. Every Sunday afternoon, between two and three, when other men in Westchester were playing golf or lawn-mowing, he would sit at home listening to a shortwave radio that provided Eastern Standard Time to within a hundredth of a millisecond. "It's a Canadian frequency. You need a scanner to find it. But it's a damn sight more accurate than they provide in Washington. We Americans don't care. We're totally undependable. I suspect that's probably why NATO's so skeptical of us." Having found his frequency, he synchronized all timepieces—his watch to his clocks, his clocks to his radio-alarm. "It's the digitals that are tough. They drive me crazy. I can't rest until I've got them all turning simultaneously."

Gronsky didn't know what to make of these confessions. Were they serious or not? It was hard to interpret. There was a drollery about Martin that Gronsky found elusive. He himself was so straight, so head-on, so flat-footed.

The conductor growled something, a brake valve hissed, and there was a scraping on the platform as the rear door clanged shut. Gronsky's body registered a sense of momentum. With dismay he realized that the train was moving.

"Whew, just made it!" said Martin, suddenly appearing out of nowhere. His face was flushed, and he was breathing heavily. "Got tied up with the manager, thought I'd never get out. Thinks I've got all night to sit around and gab with him."

Martin, like Gronsky, was somewhat overweight. Not so muscular, perhaps—more endomorphic. His heart-shaped face was split by a widow's peak, and when he laughed his eyes looked like two gnarled walnuts.

"Can I get you a drink?"

"Double vodka," said Gronsky.

Martin took out a handkerchief and blew his nose in it.

"Vermouth?"

"Just rocks."

"No respect for commuters. Thinks we're all like him, can take an A train to Riverdale."

As Martin walked forward toward the makeshift bar setup, Gronsky leaned back and lit up a cigarette. By now the train was crawling through Harlem. Graffiti-scrawled bricks shouted meaningless messages at him.

His mind was still dwelling on that escalator incident. It was like a whiff of mortality that clung to his coat lapels. The longer he thought about it, the clearer it became, the details coming through as if submerged in developing fluid. The victim, it now occurred to him, would have a wife who was waiting for him. They probably lived in Rye, or Larchmont, or Bronxville maybe, and there'd be children involved, perhaps they were college age, and later tonight they'd get a call from the police department . . . Where all this was coming from, Gronsky wasn't sure, because the fact of the matter was, he knew nothing about the man. Nevertheless, it was as if he had known him. It was like looking in a mirror and seeing a skeleton.

To his right, the card game was now in full swing. Karpeghian was dealing for seven-card draw. A gold cap twinkled in the corner of his smile, and he was wearing coin-silver cuff links that scraped on the game board. It was inevitable that Karpeghian would have heard about Revlon. Madison Avenue is like a small-town social club. Everyone knows who's giving, who's receiving, who's up, who's down, who's been getting the shaft that day. For some men such knowledge was an all-consuming passion. They collected bad news like pennies in a jar. Karpeghian was like that —a connoisseur of weakness. He would hoard such knowledge and try to cash in on it.

Well, let him try. Gronsky wasn't worried. After all, he was married to the publisher's daughter. By next year at this time, he'd be *Focus*'s ad director. Not even a Karpeghian could tamper with nepotism.

By the time Bob Martin returned with the drinks, Gronsky had almost forgotten the man by the escalators. It was only when he saw Martin's florid face that his mind slipped back to its previous morbidity.

"I saw something happen on my way to the train," he said.

"Cheers," said Martin. He handed him his vodka.

"A man collapsed in the lobby of the Pan Am Building. Nobody stopped. We all just stepped over him."

Martin leaned back. "Poor devil," he muttered.

Gronsky nodded. "His wife's still waiting for him."

Yes, that's what he dreaded: to die in New York, while at home, unknowing, your family sat waiting for you.

2

For Ted Shaughnessy, six was the worst time of day. It seemed to weigh heavily between the stays of his discipline. Too late to work and too early to drink, it was like being in a time warp where everything moved slower somehow. To compensate for this Shaughnessy went to McBurney's, an old red-bricked Y down on West Twenty-third Street. There, he would run ten miles, do fifty push-ups, and spend an hour or so in the weight and exercise room. It was a kind of penance, a novena of the pulmonary system. He had been doing it religiously for the past seven months now. The results were finally beginning to show. He examined himself furtively in the mirror by the urinal basins.

Furtively, it is emphasized, because, although Shaughnessy was vain, it was the kind of vanity that denied acknowledgment. His self-image was one of casualness and neglect—as if, in a moment of insouciance, God had created a masterpiece. Furtively also because Shaughnessy was straight and two thirds of the men in this locker room were gay—the kind who preened and talked about deltoids. He had no wish to be confused with *those* people.

Head lowered, self-absorbed, he slouched back to his locker to put on his "uniform"—a jockstrap, a pair of sweat-stained running shorts, a pair of dirty white Etonics that looked like a rat had chewed on them. The serious athlete. The man who defied ad images. The dedicated masochist whose motives were impeccable. He tackled these activities with a kind of solipsistic grimness, as if he alone knew the task that awaited him.

Ted Shaughnessy's notion of civilized behavior was as firm and inflexible as any living mortal's—which is not to say that it was in all ways consistent, since it was riddled with paradox and myopic nonsense. Homosexuals were bad. Alcohol was good. Roller-skating in the street was an affront to humanity. Feminism was silly. Psychoanalysis was decadent. All things Californian were vulgar and ridiculous. Sometimes he would express his philosophies in public. He would announce, for example, that abortion was immoral; or that the Third Reich had many fine governmental virtues, and that if Israel weren't so paranoid there would be a lot less fuss in the world. These opinions inevitably incurred listeners' wrath, many of whom, until then, had been perfect strangers to him. There would be heated exchanges, sometimes punches were thrown. Once a cab driver had pursued him on foot with a tire iron.

None of which made any difference to Shaughnessy, but, on the contrary, tended to confirm his weltanschauung: that something, somewhere, was crazy in humanity, and that we are living on a planet that is doomed to absurdity.

Having laced up his shoes and trudged off toward the elevator, for a moment he wondered whether he had locked his clothes locker. Last month he had forgotten and his billfold was stolen—thirty-eight bucks and his American Express Card. He was sure he had remembered, and he leaned on the up button. Not that locking his locker offered that much security. Sometimes they simply came right through the metal. Sometimes they smashed through the tops with sledgehammers.

Shaughnessy's father, Larry Shaughnessy, was a Boston ward heeler who had once been indicted on a fraudulent real estate scheme. His mother, Mary, was an alcoholic. The parents had been separated since his earliest memory. Shaughnessy's memory of his childhood was that it was lonely and unhappy. He lived with his mother in an apartment in Southie. Sometimes the woman stayed in bed for weeks. Often she just sat there and stared at the television. In a way, objectively, Ted Shaughnessy felt sorry for her—she had loved and lost the only man she had cared about—but her whining self-pity and her depressive languor served to instill in Shaughnessy a contempt for all womankind.

The elevator arrived, and he stepped inside. Like everything at McBurney's, it reeked of body odor. There were several other runners already on board, and Shaughnessy kept his head bowed lest he be forced to speak with them.

"Shaughnessy, you remind me of a crustacean," said Lee Schoenstein, creative director of the Caduceus Agency. This was a firm that specialized in drug ads, and it was where Shaughnessy was employed as associate art director. "You know what that is? It's a thing without a spinal column. It derives its strength from its outside skeletal structure. Take away the shell, the whole thing collapses. You're a fucking lobster, a prisoner of your support systems." To which Shaughnessy had just shrugged—it was an apt enough description. Besides, Lee Schoenstein, as his friend, had the right to say such things. It was all part and parcel of the Shaughnessy charisma—good-natured fecklessness within a Jesuit's straitjacket.

On the seventh floor the elevator opened and disgorged its contents onto the platform by the running track—women in sweat suits, blacks in white knee socks, gays and health freaks and young IBM executives. Shaughnessy exited and turned to the right. Over his blond curly hair he wore a blue and white sweatband. The overall effect was of a golden Comanche—something raw and undisciplined, fueled by ferociousness.

The McBurney Y running track at six in the evening almost defies the power of narrative description—it is as if, on cue, every misfit in New York has suddenly become an Olympic marathoner. Track shorts, sweat shirts, warm-up suits, ballet leotards, sweating, panting, floor-pounding, lap-ticking, a ragamuffin carrousel of cellulite and hamstrings circling round and round over a dingy gray cityscape. Shaughnessy looked at them and inwardly cursed. He should have done this this morning, or taken a longer lunch hour. He ought to just quit his job and become a full-time marathoner; at least then he wouldn't feel as if he were part of a lemming migration.

The track was suspended over an echoing basketball court in a high-ceilinged room with a cathedral dome on top. Tall metal-cased windows looked out over rooftops, the dark water towers so endemic to Chelsea. It took twenty laps to complete one mile. You alternated directions according to the days in the week. Today was Monday, which meant counterclockwise. It was an understood ritual having to do with calf development.

Of the various rites of manhood Shaughnessy felt cheated out of, the two he regretted most were the army and the football scrimmage. The first he had avoided because of his marital status, the second avoided him because his mother wouldn't allow it. During the Vietnam War, of course, the army was unpopular, and Shaughnessy's deferment was socially justifiable. But now that that was over, he felt that he had been cheated; it was a badge of masculinity that had been denied him by circumstance. As for football, he might have stood up to his mother, but the fact of the matter was, he was not that coordinated. In his junior and senior years he had been his high school team's manager—which was a euphemistic term for go-fer and water carrier.

Now, at thirty-seven, Shaughnessy was getting his revenge. His body had filled out, he was free from maternalism. It was a revenge against his mother, his ex-wife, all feminization, and he embraced it heartily, like a soldier in a bayonet charge.

He entered the track at about a seven-minute-mile pace, counting his footsteps as he approached the embankment. For some reason it was his habit to count every other footfall, measuring his paces against some nebulous absolute. He usually kept this up for about the first ten laps, then the count became irregular and finally nonexistent. By three quarters of a mile he had surrendered to the monotony, and from that point on he was aware only of the laps completed.

By now he had assessed most of the other runners. There were a couple on the track that he could not hope to compete with. They moved gazelle-like in long fluid curves, their torsos relaxed and cutting the air like bowsprits. There were four or five others at Shaughnessy's level. They stayed about even, neither gaining nor losing on him. One in particular, wearing dirty mauve track shorts, seemed to be using Shaughnessy as his reference, his pacesetter.

There is an etiquette at McBurney's, not always adhered to,

that the slower runners stick close to the railing. This allows the faster runners to take the outside lane, swerving up like race cars when rounding the curve embankments. Most runners respect this, a few do not. Inevitably there are women who use the track for coffee klatches. Inevitably some dolt will hog the top of the embankment, forcing the faster runners down into the slower rail position. Nothing was so irritating to a man like Shaughnessy. As he passed he would glower at them, sometimes swear at them. They were just one more instance of random chaos, a decadent perversity unleashed within the scheme of things.

Strange the memories that assault the distance man; they're not so much memories as ghosts and phantasms—bits and pieces of a fragmented past that swirl through the mind like jagged pottery shards. Sarah, his ex-wife . . . Jaime, his daughter . . . the house in Bay Ridge where he had struggled to meet mortgage payments—they all came back in dreamlike distortion, a series of images with no continuity between them. He remembered Sarah's mouth. Why, he didn't know. He particularly remembered the line where her lips met. There was a funny crease there caused by some occlusion of her dental structure that reminded him of a monkey's face, something primitive yet appealing to him. Sarah, it occurred to him, was in some ways a fantasy figure—not a fantasy of the groin, but a fantasy of the cortex. She was the high-minded embodiment of what a man was supposed to want—intelligence, good taste, a certain Betty Crocker sex appeal. Well, so much for high-mindedness. He'd have been happier with a bombshell. He'd have been happier with a tart who swabbed her cleavage with animal oils. In matters of sex, high-mindedness meant nothing. It was just another chimera that grew fragile and crumbled on you.

He had spotted one offender: a stringy-haired blond girl, who, like some run-amok satellite, kept varying her orbit. Twice she had blocked him while he was trying to pass her, first in the high lane, then again in the rail position. Shaughnessy cursed. It was one of the inanities of our times that the YMCA should allow female membership. She should stick to Elaine Powers, take aerobic dance exercises. She had no right coming here and interfering with his activities.

Shaughnessy's daughter, Jaime, was another matter. Already, at eleven, she was burgeoning with sensuousness. She had the beginnings of breasts, the legs of a thoroughbred, and soft auburn hair styled to look like a fashion model's. Last summer he had taken her to a beach in Westhampton and had been startled when she had appeared wearing a scant bikini. She was a magnet of sex, an undiscovered Lolita, and he had a nagging suspicion that there would be no end of trouble in store for her.

Of course the marriage had been rotten. Even the memories depressed him. They had married too young, too poor, too problem-ridden. He had been an instructor at Northeastern University, and they had met on Cape Cod, and she had ended up pregnant by him. Incredibly, she was only his third experience. Three lousy lays, three meaningless orgasms, and he winds up saddled with a lifelong albatross that even today tended to drag his existence down. What with the problems of breadwinning, studying, and child-raising, things had quickly deteriorated into a bone-wearying doldrum. Their sex was infrequent and on occasion self-masturbatory. If she had felt any pleasure, she had done a good job concealing it from him.

And yet there was something about Sarah that still appealed to Shaughnessy—her straightforward manner, her unabashed honesty. Sometimes he wondered whether he could ever replace her—or, even if he could, whether he was capable of living with it. At thirty-seven, Ted Shaughnessy was crumbling. He had been deprived of purpose, ambition, integrity. His only buttresses were alcohol and body-building—and a kind of raging hostility in the face of all social change.

Whether he had allowed himself to slip into reverie, or whether his brain was still clouded from last night's drinking, he was suddenly startled to hear footsteps behind him and the heavy breath of somebody gaining on him. He glanced around. It was the runner in mauve. Suddenly there was no more than a body length separating them. He quickened his pace, began to add a sprint kick. "Son of a bitch," he muttered, "you ain't gonna get around this mother!"

If running, as has been said, is a kind of Western man's Zen, a physical attainment of spiritual tranquility, that concept was clearly lost on Ted Shaughnessy, for whom, if anything, running was the equivalent of warfare. You could see it in his rhythm—contorted, at odds with itself. He was a man in contention with the forces of gravity. The speed he attained he attained through exertion, a tremendous will to make his muscles work harder for him. At the beginning of his regimen, when he had first started jogging, he had been soundly defeated by a female dance instructor. She had left him gasping at the one-and-a-half-mile mark, and he had ended up vomiting in a corner of the locker room. It was an embarrassing experience. He had never told anyone. To be beaten by a woman! He had felt so humiliated! From that day on he had doubled his exercise program, until now, if not a champion, he was clearly in the men's class.

At the turn he encountered a clot of slow runners piled in twos and threes against the inside rail. Ahead of him was a woman who had just entered the track, and who, fresh from the locker room, was going for the outside. His only chance was to squeeze between them. He had to get there before his enemy caught up with him. If he was lucky the gap would close behind him, leaving the man in mauve hemmed in at the straightaway.

He poured on the steam. He was almost in a sprint now, traveling far too fast to complete the allotted ten miles, but that made no difference, he was in a race for his life, and the runner in mauve seemed to have sensed his competitiveness. He approached the curve. It was a calculated gamble. If the woman swung too low, he would be right on top of her. The runner in mauve could take the higher trajectory, then come down at an angle and cut him off at the straightaway. He gritted his teeth. The floorboards flew by. As he went for the gap, he knew it was too close. As he passed the woman, he brushed her shoulder, not a forceful blow, but rude and unsettling.

"Hey . . . !" she cried.

The word trailed off. He was approaching the straightaway,

where there was less congestion. "Sorry," he muttered, or at least attempted to mutter. It came out as a sibilant, a kind of harsh respiration sound.

"You asshole!" he heard. It made no difference. To his amazement he realized that his enemy was still closing on him. He had taken advantage of Shaughnessy's blocking and had spurted through after him, like a Ferrari in draft position.

Hot September. Heat on the concrete. The playing field brown and grass-bare from August. The grueling preseason for the South Boston varsity, their white practice uniforms showing the first scars of body contact. Young Ted Shaughnessy stood by the bench with the backfield coach. Cradled in his arm was a laminated clipboard. The team roster fluttered in the afternoon breeze, and his throat felt parched from hot air and lime dust.

"Mark forty-two," the backfield coach growled at him. "His right knee's too low and he's hunched too far forward. He gets hit from the side, he's gonna land on his pecker. Check forty-seven. His shoes look too big for him."

Shaughnessy obeyed. Against the ramshackle bleachers, the linemen grunted, drove their weight against tackling dummies. At the far end, by the goal, two quarterbacks played catch, while the rest of the backfield worked on running and ball-handling. Oh God, to be allowed just to put on a uniform! To feel the ball slapped hard in midsection. To take off full gallop, cutting, straight-arming, causing confused admiration among an army of linebackers! He was capable of that. He had stamina, power. In softball, during gym class, he had once hit a triple. Why not this? Why not in shoulder pads? Why not with spectators and pretty girls cheering for you?

"Becaz!" cried his mother. She was sitting in the kitchen, a half glass of sherry on the table in front of her. Her hair was loose, her eyes looked sullen, and he could see her bra through the V in her house jacket. "Jiss becaz!" she said, and she turned away from him. "You got any idea what I shelled out in dental bills for you? You wanna leave your teeth all over some gaddamn football field, over my dead bady, you're jiss like your fatha, Teddy."

The memory came back like a bitter aftertaste as he moved to the inside and tried to cut off his pursuer. He could hear the sound of feet at his elbow, the rhythmic breathing through outflared nostrils. His opponent was strong, much stronger than he had estimated. He was also younger, more wiry, more long-legged. He was also smoother and better coordinated. He was also, thought Shaughnessy, a homosexual.

How Shaughnessy arrived at this last conclusion was a matter of intuition that bordered on mysticism. He had a sort of sixth sense, an endogenous Geiger counter, something implanted in the genes of his heritage. Whether in Greenwich Village, the bars on First Avenue, the Art Deco corridors on the first floor of Bloomingdale's, he could spot "those people" like a pointer spots game birds, regardless of wardrobe, posture, or speech patterns. The eyes, perhaps? Were they a little too eager? The nape of the neck? Something in the thigh region? He didn't know. He couldn't explain. But he knew that the runner in mauve was an immoralist.

A strong immoralist. A *fast* immoralist! An immoralist who defied the laws of nature! How the hell did a gay get so powerful as to outrun an Irishman from the slums of Massachusetts?

"I really don't like to say this to you, because I know it's silly and probably just bitchiness, but Sarah once said the reason she left you is because she suspected you were probably a latent homo." The speaker was Snooky, Sarah's erstwhile roommate, a tall, black-haired girl with a Modigliani spinal cord. It was a month or so following the legal divorce, and they were having drinks together at a table in Kitty Hawk's. The words struck home. Ted Shaughnessy went pale. "Well, now don't blow a gasket!" said Snooky sarcastically. "Even if you are, that's not so bad. Besides, that's an ex-wife's fallback—impugn his sexuality."

He remembered that now as they neared the far turn, and he also remembered what he had done to refute it. He had taken Snooky home and practically raped her, tearing her blouse as she tried to flee from him. Women! he thought. You can't trust any of them! He could not remember one female who had ever been just to him—not his mother, not Sarah, not the floozies he had bedded, and certainly not Snooky, who later ran off with a piano player.

And now this, the spread of feminization, the encroachment of estrogen into the XY chromosome structure, a girl in man's track shorts, a competitive android, pulling alongside and threatening to surpass him! It was more than he could bear. He closed his eyes. His entire body ached from starvation of oxygen. He was going to fail! This man was beating him! Theodore Francis Shaughnessy was doomed to oblivion!

On the far straightaway, there were four runners abreast, four weekend joggers, four candidates for the fat farm. Shaughnessy and his rival were barreling down on them, two high-speed trains in a congested switch yard. "Watch it!" cried somebody. Shaughnessy brushed one. It was a painful sideswipe, and he was momentarily staggered by it. But he kept on going, he was into the secondary, he could hear the crowd roaring as he headed toward victory.

The runner in mauve had had to slacken his pace. The runner who was hit had veered in front of him. But he was back in the race, only a half step off stride, and Shaughnessy could feel his breath, the heat from his body exertion.

What happened next was a defiance of physics. It ignored the laws of all civilized orderliness. Worse than that, it ignored McBurney's laws—which, to Shaughnessy's way of thinking, were synonymous with godliness. As they sped down the straightaway, crossing the halfway mark, shoulder to shoulder, running on will power, the stringy-haired girl whom Shaughnessy had noted earlier got halfway through the turn, then began doubling back on herself. Shaughnessy saw it, but he couldn't believe it. She was waddling at a pace of about three miles an hour, eyes closed, totally oblivious, and *in the opposite direction from the way the arrow was pointing!*

Both runners saw her, but it was too late to swerve. Besides, it was impossible to predict her reactions. She was not only running clockwise, she was also running diagonally, apparently in an attempt to get to the exit gate.

"Shit!" muttered Shaughnessy. "Jesus Christ!" he heard next

to him. They were barreling down on her with all their muscle power. The girl veered one way, then the other. Shaughnessy lowered his head—

And hit her square in the midsection.

Later he would question the propriety of that. Had it actually been necessary to put his head down? Was it acceptable etiquette, even within the bounds of McBurney's, to lower one's shoulder into a female's pelvic region? Somehow he doubted it. An embrace would have been preferable—a masculine bear hug and a brief pirouette. She would have probably been winded, but at least she would have been conscious, rather than sprawled, as she was now, like a discarded laundry bag.

But that was in retrospect—cheap Monday-morning quarterbacking. The reality of the moment was that she had gotten what she had asked for. Moreover, the impact had thrown him off stride and allowed the runner in mauve to gain a full-step lead on him.

There were shouts from around the track—were they cheers? Were they protests? Whatever they were, Shaughnessy ignored them. He was in hot pursuit of the runner in mauve, who had broken through safety and had nothing but daylight in front of him. The man was too fast. His legs were like animal's legs. Shaughnessy could see the hocks, the tapered calf muscles. The mauve nylon shorts flared out at the sides, and Shaughnessy was angrily aware of the developed thigh tendons.

Shaughnessy tried to sprint, but he had no power left. His right knee ached, and he had a cramp in his rib cage. Failure welled up like a ghost from a grave and he saw the shrouds of defeat rushing to embrace him.

There was only one thing to do—and that's what he did. He angled himself over into the wake of his victor. He aimed his right foot at the other man's achilles, took one final stride, and caught the other man's running shoe.

It was not so much a stumble as a dive. The man in mauve seemed to float in the air. His body was extended parallel to the floor, and when he landed he skidded, his arms out in front of him. Shaughnessy stumbled, caromed off a railing. On the rebound, he toppled another runner. Where once there was a track there was now a battlefield, a corpse-strewn oval full of Adidas and Puma merchandise.

Smirking, glowering, Shaughnessy ran for the exit. He ran through the shouts of alarm and the curse words. He ran through the cries of "Stop that guy" that circled the ceiling like wounded barn swallows. He ran from the track. He ran down the stairway. He ran past weight lifters, past Exercyclists, past yoga masters. He ran past the shower room and straight to the locker room—only to find, to his dismay, that he had not locked his clothes locker.

3

"Target heading west on West Eighty-ninth Street. Dark brown hair, navy-blue sport jacket. About five-foot-seven, one hundred and twenty pounds. Background unknown, possibly of Semitic origin."

Don Pelligrew paused until the woman was well past him. He was hidden from view on the south side of the street. She was on the north side, heading toward Columbus, and there was a line of parked cars that prevented her from seeing him. He lowered the antenna on his walkie-talkie and crossed the street behind a Boar's Head meat truck. The girl rounded the corner and disappeared from view. Taking giant strides, he hurried to catch up with her.

Ever since he had been a kid in Hagerstown, Maryland, Pelligrew's main ambition had been to be a detective. Or, if not a detective, something equally clandestine—a CIA agent, a narc, an intelligence officer. As a kid, he had sported a long black cape that his grandmother had made out of leftover chair upholstery. It had a collar that could either lie flat (like Captain Marvel's) or, if stays were inserted, stand up (like a Dracula outfit). Wearing a Lone Ranger's mask, a pair of black gym shoes, carrying a mail-order replica of a German Luger, he would creep through the streets with his billowing black cape on, collecting secret information against the enemies of democracy. In the fifth and sixth grades he had headed the Detective Club. It was not a big club, having only one member, but through it he learned about fingerprints and lie detection and had an astonishing knowledge of forensic pathology. On occasion he had put his expertise to practice. Once ninety-three cents had been stolen from the "treasury"—a cigar box kept in the teacher's top desk drawer in which monies were accumulated for field trips and birthday parties. Pelligrew on the scene. They were dealing with a felony. Donning his crusader's cape and his black Lone Ranger's mask, he took a solemn oath to bring the culprit to justice. "Truth will out," he swore, "or else I am not—

"THE BLACK PHANTOM!"

"Hello, Jerry?" he said.

"This is Jerry's mother."

"Is Jerry home?"

"Who's calling, please?"

"Tell him it's a friend. It's very important. It involves a certain matter concerning Mrs. Ashton's class treasury."

Shades drawn, room cast in darkness, The Phantom sat hunched over his parents' extension phone. The mouthpiece was covered with a Boy Scout neckerchief, which would give his voice a muffled unreal quality.

"Hello?" said the earpiece.

"Is this Jerry Bixton?"

"Yeah—who's this?"

"It's . . . The Blaaack Phantom!"

"The *who?*" said the earpiece.

"The Blaaack Phantom! The Avenger of Truth and Democratic Principles!"

When The Phantom spoke it was with the resonance of authority—a husky growl on the lower edge of alto. He pointed his Luger at the holes in the mouthpiece and hunched up his cloak to conceal his identity.

"Pelligrew, is that you?"

"It's The Blaaack Phantom! Put back the money, or face the consequences! The Phantom knows! You cannot escape! Pay ninety-three cents, or you shall pay—with your blood!"

And with that he hung up and lay back on the bedspread. Downstairs he could hear his parents watching television. He would wait five minutes, then call again. The Phantom was nothing if not inexorable.

But the beautiful part was that three days later, when Mrs.

Ashton was looking for her Art Gum eraser, in another box, under rubber bands and paper clips, what should appear but the missing lucre! Proving once again that evil cannot win, that the enemies of society must repent or perish; that, although by day he was an innocent-looking schoolboy, in the world of darkness The Phantom was invincible!

Unfortunately, fate has a way of thwarting superheroes. It was Pelligrew's misfortune to have been born into affluence. His parents, rather than setting him up with a detective license, had compromised his principles and sent him to Yale and Georgetown. It was a political expedient for which he had never forgiven them. They had deprived the world of its last chance for purity. He had repaid them for it by getting mediocre grades and running off to Canada with a girl named Jennifer.

Now, at thirty-nine, divorced, near bankruptcy, he was finally getting a chance to fulfill his destiny. He raised the antenna on his walkie-talkie and radioed his position to Control at Headquarters.

"Target pausing, stopping near bookstore. Make a note: This could be the rendezvous. If she chooses Sartre, we're in like Flynn. If it's Krantz or Michener, no sense pursuing it."

He lowered the antenna and approached nonchalantly. The "target" was perusing a stall full of paperbacks. He picked up a book at the other end of the stall and leafed through the pages with studied casualness.

Pelligrew was the master of innocuous come-ons. Indeed, since his divorce, he had made something of a science out of it. He hit swiftly, subtly, unexpectedly, ensnaring his victim before she knew what was happening to her. He would approach his objectives in the most unlikely locations—in the middle of a crosswalk, on a bus, in a subway station—coming on with a line so seductively natural that only a hopeless paranoid could take any offense at it. He might say, "Pardon me, but where did you get that jacket? I've been thinking of getting one like it for my fiancée. The trouble is, I probably can't afford it. I saw one at Bendel's, but I was afraid to even ask about it." To which the victim might reply that she had bought it at Alexander's, or

Wilson's House of Leather, or on the Lower East Side somewhere, and he would say, "Really? They had one just like it at Bendel's. At least it looked sort of like it. Maybe not quite so understated."

At that point, most men would have reached an impasse. She had answered his question and she had acknowledged the compliment. And she had certainly caught the fact he was involved with somebody, which meant (a) that he was a winner, and (b) she was probably safe with him. The problem is, where do you go from there? How do you keep the conversation rolling? It was at this stage that Pelligrew bordered on brilliant, coming in with what he called the "old down-and-out slider" pitch.

"My jacket was free."

"Pardon?" she would say.

"It didn't cost anything. I found it in a rag pile."

"Uh-huh," she would say.

"The label says Paul Stuart, but I didn't get it there. I didn't pay anything for it."

Notice the subtlety, the elided non sequitur. One, he is implying that he may have no money. Two, he is name-dropping a prestigious haberdashery frequented by men who are in social ascendancy. Is he rich or impoverished? Is he a bum or an eccentric? And, most important, why is he saying this? Why is he divulging such a personal irrelevancy to a woman he has met only fifteen seconds ago?

"You're lucky," she would say, and she would keep on walking.

"I know. It looks new. Only it's not, it's used. I get all my stuff from secondhand stores. I don't believe in clothes. I don't find them interesting."

And all the while he would continue to keep pace with her, a gem of casualness in his pleated tweed slacks, his Ivy League cap perched jauntily on one brow, his lapel turned up as if he had dressed in a hurry that morning. The overall effect was of a daguerreotype hero—a Stephen Dedalus, with bolshevist overtones. Someone, in other words, different, mysterious, not quite what one finds among the usual cookie molds.

"Wanna coffee?" he would say.

She would hesitate, vacillating.

"One cup," he would say. "I just feel like talking. There are so few women in this city you can talk to. I mean, not about deep things. I mean little things, silly stuff." Spoken, of course, in a Maryland accent—flat, unthreatening, with a trace of southernness; an accent that said, "As unpredictable as I seem, I am one of the very few men in this world who is trustworthy." And persistent, too, because he was still at her elbow, although not in any way that would seem pesty or annoying, but more like someone who just happens to be moving parallel, and if she would like to cross over, that would be her decision.

There's no need to guess how these episodes turned out. What had she to lose? A cup of coffee, for God's sake! Was she so closed-minded that even this was forbidden to her? Was a Nedick's or a Squire's such a compromise of principles? So of course she would accede, and he would buy her a coffee, and the coffee would lead to a first-name acquaintance, and the acquaintance would lead to an exchange of phone numbers, and the phone numbers would lead, inevitably, to intercourse. By Pelligrew's reckoning, in the year since his divorce, he had succeeded in bedding more than six dozen women, all of them strangers, all of them different, a few of them even tolerable to be with. He had his preferences. He liked Jewish girls best. Jews were followed by Italians and Greeks. At the low end of the scale he put Irish girls and Latins, and at the very low end he put white Protestants like he was. He was particularly adept at the "BBQ" trade, girls who commuted from Bronx, Brooklyn, Queens, whom he would meet on the streets, seduce, take to bed, and provide subway fare home on the E or the LL lines. Sometimes, if pressed, he would travel to their turf. He would walk along the streets of Forest Hills or Kew Gardens. He would make love to a housewife while the planes roared into Kennedy or to a young divorcée while her son was watching television.

It was a doomed existence, and he hated himself for it—who would have thought The Phantom could ever sink to such depravity?—but he did it anyway, it was the only life he had, and he pursued it loathsomely, continuously, voraciously.

"Target has just entered bookstore," he muttered. "I'll wait two minutes, then follow discreetly. Upon closer examination, have reason to suspect rhinoplasty. This could confirm our previous assessment."

He lowered the antenna and pulled out his pocket watch. It was a gold antique Waltham that he had stolen from his father. The elegant black hands pointed to six twenty-three—which, he noted instinctively, was in New York's highest crime hour.

Bookstores, of course, are an ideal meeting place—he would put them right up there with art museums and supermarkets. They provided the prey with a false security—like the dun-colored shoal that covers the sand shark. In bookstores, girls talk. They exchange information. They'll discuss the vagaries of a Bellow or Auchincloss. You can trap them with ideas, with logic, with enthusiasm, and they'll surrender willingly, never questioning their destiny. Bars were less fruitful. They were the refuge of losers, and the girls who frequented them were defensive, neurosis-prone. Which is not to say that he didn't go to bars, but usually only later when he had exhausted the other veins.

It was a typical bookstore, overcrowded by half, the center aisle filled with best sellers and paperbacks, the walls piled high with art books and classics, the usual illiterate clerk at the cash register. He took his time. His prey was in the back. She was engrossed in something from the cooking section. This was perfect. He would pull the old pesto bit. "Pardon me, but do they have any books here with pesto recipes?"

He scowled distractedly as he browsed through the thriller section—Ambler, Goldman, Graham Greene, Robert Ludlum—through the history section—Durant, Van Doren—and on through medicine, theology, and sailboat maintenance. No question about it, his victim was delectable. She was in her early thirties and had dark, wiry tresses. Her only flaw was that goddamn nose job. He happened to like noses. They aroused the lust in him.

The girl moved on. Suddenly she was in science. That was annoying, because he had barely passed chemistry. "Excuse me, but could you tell me the structure of hydrocarbons and how they relate to Friedrich Kekulé's ring hypothesis?" He would have to resort to a more personal approach. He would smile, say "hello"—then drop something on her. He would steal her purse, then claim he had found it. He would read her statistics from the revised *Baseball Almanac.*

As he stood there deciding what course to take, leafing disinterestedly through one of Anais Nin's diaries, the girl moved on through art and literature and came to light in the puzzle and humor section. His mind skipped frantically. He knew nothing about crosswords and had no interest at all in "Garfield" or "Doonesbury." Maybe he should just go right up and tell her that if she was going to buy that stuff, he would wash his hands of her.

He was contemplating this when suddenly she turned and without so much as a glance walked right out of the store. It happened so quickly and on such rash impulse that for a moment he just stood there, unable to follow her. Outside on the street, he looked both ways. Which way had she gone? He seemed to have lost her. Then he saw her crossing Ninety-first Street and heading in the direction of D'Agostino's.

Wearing his pressed Calvin Klein jeans, his tailored tweed sport coat, his leather-thonged boating shoes from an L. L. Bean catalog, he crossed the street in the shadow of an Itkins van and emerged just in time to see her enter the supermarket. "Now we've got her," he radioed Control, having earned his black belt in the kosher and Goya departments; because if there was one place even more promising than bookstores, it was that sanctuary of desire, the New York supermarket.

Entering casually, picking up a basket, he scanned the aisles and saw her standing in the yogurt section. A Jewish American Princess who kept slim on Dannon and lolled around in bed reading cookbooks and science manuals! It would not be the first time he had experienced such exotica. One of his first New York conquests had been a Sephardic Valium junkie. She had stayed in his apartment for three and a half days, and he had finally had no choice but to call the cops on her. Far from feeling disgust or revulsion, the experience had appealed to his sense of adventure.

He was finally tasting the ethnicity of Manhattan, the infinite variety of the Naked City!

"Target now proceeding into meat and poultry. Seems to be lingering over Hebrew National. Could cause trouble. Could be too orthodox. May prefer men who are dentists or chiropractors."

The way Pelligrew figured—and he was experienced in these matters—she would be heading west through detergents and oven cleaners, east through canned goods, west through condiments, and back east again through health aids and paper products. He, meanwhile, would stroll east through baby foods, west through vegetables, doubling back through salad dressings, west through baked goods, east through kitchenware, and they would meet at the spice rack, where he would pull out his shopping list for her.

The only drawback—the "downside," if you will—was that you sometimes wound up with a bunch of dumb groceries. Once he had come home with three jars of gefiltefish which had looked so disgusting he had thrown them in the garbage chute. On another occasion he had spent a fortune on artichokes. What are you going to do with six containers of artichoke hearts? He had given them to a neighbor who was an ex-airline stewardess, and she had steamed them in butter and fed them to her cockapoo.

D'Agostino's at this hour, like most New York supermarkets, was catch-as-catch-can, overcrowded, inadequate. It was as if every item in the gross national product were battling for survival within a six-foot shelf area. He felt vaguely grateful that he did not have to shop there. Think of the poor souls who actually came here for sustenance! As far as Pelligrew was concerned, if it weren't for sex, there would be no reason even to set foot in a supermarket.

He spotted his prey rounding the bend at baked beans. God, she looked great! She was even sexier than he had thought. She was wearing these high-heeled shoes below tight French jeans that pitched her weight slightly forward, as if she were climbing an embankment.

His interest in these matters followed rhythmic patterns, peak-ing twice a year just after the equinox. The spring was logical, because that's when the sap rose, but the autumn, like now, was more attached to cerebral yearnings. It was the season of football, wool sweaters, and leaf burning. In New York it was also the season for clothes hawking, and there was something exciting about seeing women newly demure who had so recently been braless, suntanned, and raw-looking. He noted that she was wearing a fluffy white turtleneck under a pinch-waisted blazer with patches at the elbow. He would love to disrobe her layer by layer until he had arrived at the last fading glow of her sunbathing. It was like an autumn perfume that lingered in fantasy—Fire Island, the Hamptons, Puerto Rico, the Rockaways—each according to one's means and social level, but each deliciously revisited in nudity.

He felt a rush at his temples. Boy, this was terrific! This was the best time he had had since he was a kid back in Hagerstown! This was the best time he had had since he was eleven years old and had crawled through an air duct to spy on girls in the locker room! That, of course, was The Black Phantom's handiwork. It had been done out of necessity and in the service of his country. It was suspected that there might be a spy ring in there that was using the girls' gym facilities as a front for espionage. This had proved untrue. There was nothing in that locker room except a glimpse of underwear and some undeveloped mammary glands, but it was a daring adventure, dangerous in the extreme, particularly when his Luger got snagged in the ventilator.

The Phantom paused. He was well into baked goods now. If all went well, he would soon meet his quarry. "Pardon me," he would say, pulling out his shopping list, a yellowing piece of paper he had been carrying for months now.

He was anticipating this and examining rye bread labels when, much to his surprise, he was approached by a presence. He looked up briefly and there, bearing down on him, was none other than the girl who was the object of his surveillance!

"I DON'T KNOW QUITE HOW TO SAY THIS, YOU ASSHOLE"—that was lie number one; she was stating it quite eloquently—"BUT IF YOU DON'T STOP FOL-

LOWING ME I'M GOING TO CALL THE MANAGER AND THEY'RE GONNA THROW YOUR FUCKIN ASS IN THE HOOSEGOW!"

Pelligrew said nothing. He was too stunned to reply. The rye bread labels danced crazily in his vision. Was she talking to him? What had he done wrong? He tried to turn away, as if it had no relevance to him.

"You bastard!" she cried. "You're all alike!" She backed up her grocery cart and rammed at his knees with it. A carton of milk hopped out of the basket and fell to the floor, like a thing with white blood in it. "You been followin me for the past half hour! Don't deny it! I got eyes, I saw it! You followed me in the bookstore, you followed me here . . . Whaddaya think I am, some goddamn prostitute?"

Pelligrew tried to speak, but nothing came out. The girl was in a rage that bordered on hysteria. She backed up her cart and rammed him again. Her face was red. Her lips had foam on them.

A small crowd had gathered, mostly elderly and food-stamp candidates, a few Hispanics with eyes like mud puddles, gawking, curious, absorbing the drama, yet with all the involvement of cats watching dogs piddle. From the front end of the store a security guard was approaching. He was a scarecrow-looking kid carrying a club in a holster. From around cartons of soup cans peered the eyes of young stock boys; a hard hat smiled over a display case of marshmallows.

"Y-you got the wrong guy . . ."

"Like hell, you fucker! He's been followin me around and talkin to his hand! He's been holdin his hand up with his finger stickin out. What do you think you've got there, a two-way radio?"

He held his hand up. "This?" he said, blushing.

"See, what did I tell you? The guy's a fruitcake! He's been followin me around talkin to the palm of his hand! He thinks he's Dick Tracy! He's a goddamn loony-tune!"

"Okay, break it up." It was the security guard talking. The girl was still using her cart as a battering ram. "Let's all calm down and cool it, shall we? And you," he said, "—out!" He waved his thumb at Pelligrew.

"I want him arrested! I want him in jail!" cried the girl. "He's a menace to women! He's a fucking loony-tune! They're gonna get you!" she shouted. "They're gonna cut your damn balls off! If I ever see you again, you better have a good lawyer with you!"

Pelligrew retreated, pallid, quaking. He stumbled through the express line, dropping his basket on the counter. Now other women were screaming: "HEY! I WAS HERE FIRST! WHERE DYA THINK YOU'RE GOIN! END OF THE LINE, YOU TURKEY!" He took off in a run. The electric door was broken, and he practically ran through it in his quest for freedom. He ran out on the sidewalk. He ran up Columbus. He didn't stop running until he had reached Ninety-seventh Street.

And the thing about it was, the girl was so irrational! So beautiful on the outside and so screwed up internally! Like saying that the next time he'd better have an attorney with him. Hell, that was a laugh! What did she think *he* was?

4

It was always dark by the time Gronsky got home. No matter what season of the year it was, by the time he pulled into the gravel driveway the house was colorless, obscured by shadows. In the walk to the front door there was a bicycle tipped over. He lifted it one-handed and set it on its stand. "Damn kid," he muttered, brushing off his pants leg. At the top of his cuff there was a smudge mark of sprocket oil.

Bobby was nine and the image of his mother: blond hair, green eyes, a tendency toward pudginess. The only time Gronsky got to spend much time with him was on Saturday mornings during football and Little League practice. If Bobby didn't grow up to become an athlete, it would not be for Gronsky's lack of trying. "You gotta set, *then* throw," he would tell the youngster. "Try to throw on the run, you're gonna land in the woods somewhere."

The reason that this was so important to Gronsky was that it was the keeping of a promise he himself had reneged on; he had made a rendezvous with athletic greatness and, through weakness or misfortune, had failed to show up for it. After a spectacular career at Steubenville High School, his play in college had steadily deteriorated. He had started at fullback, been switched to tackle, and finally wound up playing second-string nose guard. It was one of the bitterest memories of his middle-aged life. Somehow he had failed—his body had betrayed him. By the time he had graduated he was suffering from knee injuries, and the pros had shrugged and washed their hands of him.

In the foyer, which was dark, he encountered three shopping bags. One said OHRBACH'S, the other two Bloomingdale's.

They seemed to be stuffed with rags and old clothing. He shoved them aside and went into the living room.

In the early years, before Bobby was born, Mandy, Gronsky's wife, had been a scrupulous housekeeper. A place for everything, everything in its place: ashtrays emptied, silverware glistening. Then came Bobby, born relatively late, and somehow things had begun to unravel—minutely at first, then more and more noticeably, until finally the house had become intolerable.

"I need a maid"—this was from Mandy—"someone to help with the cooking and housecleaning. It would be money well spent, because she could also be governess, and that would save sending Bobby to day care."

At first, Gronsky had resisted this notion, because he couldn't even see why day care was necessary, but later he had accepted it on the simplistic premise that a woman's unhappiness stems directly from housecleaning.

"I'm afraid," the man had said at the employment agency, "that the help in this country has deteriorated badly. We find most of our clients prefer foreign servants. Not Italian, of course, but Dutch, Scandinavian."

"Norwegian?" said Gronsky.

"Norwegian, Swedish. Of course there's not the demand that there was ten years ago. Nevertheless, we have certain candidates who are willing to tolerate our lower living standards."

So a maid it was. He had filled out the documents, had plunked down money for plane fare and travel expenses, had even gone so far as to send off a letter introducing his family via words and Polaroids. "You will find," he wrote, "we are typically American. Bobby is nine and likes race cars and football games. My wife, Mrs. Gronsky, has taken up tennis. We are very informal. We all love smorgasbords."

In reply, he had received a letter from Stockholm, signed by somebody named Ingrid Olafsen, saying "how delighted I be to come to your country and so look forward to exchange of philosophies."

This latter had begun from the moment she had arrived, climbing off the plane wearing sandals and dungarees, her earthly possessions all stuffed in a rucksack, her neck weighed down by cameras and lens attachments. She was pretty in a way, having long tawny hair, a willowy body like an emaciated schoolboy's, but there are girls in whom youth is mistaken for beauty, and needle-jawed Ingrid was probably one of them.

Now, as he made his way into the kitchen, it was this same Ingrid Olafsen whose anatomy introduced itself: suntanned legs, breasts like sea pods, a flat hipless torso swathed in a tennis outfit.

"Oh, Alex!" said Mandy. "Come in, come in!" She was sitting across from Ingrid at the kitchen table. She, too, was wearing a white sleeveless tennis dress. On the table was an ice tray and a half-empty vodka bottle. "Come in, sit down. We were just talking about you. Ingrid here has the most marvelous idea. Pour yourself a drink and let me tell you. I think we've found the solution to everything."

Mandy, Gronsky's wife, was a fair-complexioned blonde whose plump schoolgirl figure had thickened with maturity. Her hair was straight and trimmed in a pageboy, and her round moon-shaped face had a laughing-sad quality. Ingrid, on the other hand, was built like a doe. Her most positive virtues were her long wobbly legs. When dressed like now, naked to the flanks, there was something alluring, even sexually arousing, in her.

"What I'm about to say may come as a surprise," said Mandy, "but I certainly hope you won't take it personally. Ingrid's afraid you might take it personally. Give me your word—we're going to discuss this objectively."

Gronsky gave nothing. This kitchen was a mess. There were coffee cups, egg shells, tea bags with ooze in them. The skillet from breakfast was still on the stove burner. What on earth had these two women been doing all day?

"We have decided," said Mandy, "upon a trial separation. A few weeks maybe. Maybe till Christmas. Nothing permanent, nothing irrevocable, just a little time away so we can all get our heads together."

"Who?" said Gronsky.

"Ingrid and me. That is, you and me. It was Ingrid's suggestion. She pointed out that after seventeen years, we should take some time to reevaluate."

Gronsky just stood there. His mind reeled backward—back to that day of Ingrid's arrival, she with her umlauts, her mispronounced anglicisms, her cool Nordic eyes full of self-possessed skepticism. It had begun fairly well, Ingrid doing the housework, picking up Bobby from the bus every day, whipping up dinners somewhat heavy on fish oil, talking like a therapist in a Bergman psychodrama. In the evening they would sit and "exchange philosophies." Ingrid's, it would seem, was distressingly enlightened. She did not hesitate to talk about sex, including an abortion she had had and a child out of wedlock.

"A child?" said Gronsky.

"Yah, last December. I had it a month, then I gave it to Karl. He vants a baby, let him take care of it. I am a vagabond. Babies don't interest me."

"You know," said Gronsky when they had retired for the evening and he and Mandy were alone in their bedroom, "I've heard what they say about Swedish women, but that girl's attitude seems unbiological."

"Oh, I don't know." Mandy had just shrugged. She was sitting at her vanity applying cold cream. "You have to remember she's terribly young, Alex. Perhaps she's right. In a way, I admire her for it."

Admire her for it. Gronsky had said nothing. It was one of those innocuous exchanges that take place in a marriage—a fin that rises, breaks the surface, circles once, then disappears again.

The first untoward incident had happened one evening when Gronsky, in pajamas, on his way to the bathroom, had happened to walk past Ingrid's room, where she was lying in bed smoking a marijuana cigarette. "If you don't mind," he said, "I'd rather you wouldn't. We don't approve of drugs in this house. I realize some people might not object, but there's a nine-year-old boy here, and we should set an example for him."

"Oh, shoor," said Ingrid, and she had put out the cigarette. And that, it would seem, had put an end to the incident. But he continued to smell pot in the most unlikely places—the garage, the laundry, coming out of the vegetable crisper . . .

"She's a junkie," he told Mandy.

"Oh, come on, don't be silly."

"For all I know, she's probably a dealer. I read that once in an article in *Time.* The users are the dealers. It's called 'the vicious drug cycle.' "

"Well, in the first place," said Mandy, "it is not a drug. It's marijuana, and it's not that bad for you. And in the second place, she's never smoked it around Bobby, so I don't think we should make a big federal case out of it."

All right, he wouldn't, but this was surprise number two, because he had distinctly remembered only seven or eight years ago this same Mandy Gronsky holding forth at a cocktail party that kids who smoke pot ought to be sent up for life somewhere.

The second incident was somewhat more jarring. He had come home one day on an earlier train to find Bobby downstairs watching an "Afterschool Special" and a young man upstairs whom he had never seen before.

"Who are you?" said Gronsky.

The young man just grinned. His misbuttoned shirt said Perrin's Tree Service.

"Are you the guy I called who was supposed to spray for gypsy moths?"

The young man nodded. He was fiddling with his pants zipper.

"Ooooh, hi," said Ingrid, emerging from the bathroom. Her dress was unzipped and pulled sideways on her torso. "I vasn't expecting you home so early. I vas just showing ziss man how the trees hit the vindow panes."

"Like hell!" said Gronsky, struggling to keep his voice down as he and Mandy were getting ready for bed that evening. "They were screwing, damn it. It was plain as day. His pants were unzipped and the bedspread had wrinkles in it."

"I'm sure there's an explanation," said Mandy.

"Of course there is. It's the one I just gave you. I tell you, the girl's a nymphomaniac. And our own son's downstairs watching a movie about sheep herding."

Mandy agreed to have a "chat" with Ingrid. The next day, she sat her down over coffee. Mandy gave her views, then Ingrid gave her views. In the end they agreed: American men were Victorian.

"Victorian!" cried Gronsky.

"Well, I know you can't help it, darling. It's the way you were raised. It's your midwestern upbringing. But you have to remember, this is 1980. We have the pill and the vote now. It's a whole new ball game."

A whole new ball game. Well, maybe it was, but it did not have to be played on top of his bedspread, and he did not think maids were entitled to a sex life, but if they were entitled, they should clean up afterward.

The next misfortune was in some ways the strangest, and it came to his attention in the most innocuous manner. He was sitting one night watching the eleven o'clock news when he happened to notice some discarded photographs.

"What are these?" he said. They were lying on the coffee table. He recognized them as coming from Ingrid's Hasselblad. Her camera was Ingrid's proudest possession, and, to give her credit, she was a talented photographer.

"They're pictures," said Mandy.

"I know they're pictures. But who are these people? What are they looking at?" He held the photos up to the light. Try as he may, he couldn't decipher them.

What they were were snapshots, developed from color slides, of a typical-looking office building in Midtown Manhattan, each picture focused on a different window, behind which a small crowd of men had congregated. The men were smiling. Some were waving. One had his hand clasped comically to his crotch. They were all staring straight into the lens of the camera, which seemed to be stationed on an opposing window sill.

"By the way," he said when they had turned off the television and Ingrid had come in to say good night, "I see you took some pictures last week. They're very interesting. Modern, but interesting."

"They're men," said Ingrid.

"I see that, yes."

"I am planning to send them to my boy friend, Karl. He vill be glad to see the men I am meeting and that there is plenty in America to keep me occupied."

"I don't understand," said Gronsky a little later as he was lying in bed, Mandy beside him. "Why would she take pictures of men in an office building? And why were they all gawking and acting like idiots?"

"It's her age," said Mandy. "She's young. She's mischievous."

"Mischievous," said Gronsky. "Psychotic's more like it."

"Well, when a girl is young she likes to show off her body. It's silly, probably, but understandable."

Gronsky lay there pondering this statement. He pondered it after the clock had struck twelve. He pondered it long after Mandy had rolled over and her breathing had slowed to a rhythmic sleep pattern.

"Are you saying," he said finally, "that she had no clothes on?"

"Go to sleep," said Mandy. "It's not important."

"Are you saying she was exhibiting herself to a bunch of strangers and taking pictures of their reactions to send to her boy friend?"

There might be many virtues that pertained to this Gronsky, but a steel-trap mind was certainly not one of them. Everything had to be ground and sifted, falling into place after laborious scrutiny. He was particularly puzzled by moral conundrums. Everything was approached through head-on collision. The bizarre, the quirky, the neurotically devious were areas of behavior that remained unintelligible to him.

"Don't you think," he had said over breakfast the next morning, "that maybe we ought to find a new governess?"

"Why?" said Mandy. "Because Ingrid's liberated? Grow up, Alex. These are the 1980s."

"Well, I know," he said, "but I think it's strange."

"The trouble with you, you're a product of the fifties. Frankly, I find Ingrid very refreshing. I only wish I had had her honesty."

Honesty, thought Gronsky. The honesty to fornicate. The honesty to lie around stoned in your bedroom. Well, it was all beyond him, he didn't understand it, but at least the house was reasonably tidy now.

Then:

"I've been thinking," said Mandy. "We're spending too much money."

"I agree," said Gronsky.

"I think I should give up my tennis lessons. You know, Ingrid plays tennis. She's really excellent. Why don't we buy her a restricted membership?"

"A *what?*" said Gronsky.

"Now don't be elitist, Alex. Think of her more as a cultural exchange student. It's true we pay her, and she does our housework, but that doesn't mean she is in any way inferior to us."

"I didn't say that."

"Not in so many words, maybe, but it's obvious that unconsciously you are influenced by class structure. The thought that your wife might play tennis with a servant poses a serious threat to your fragile value system."

Well, Jesus Christ, thought Gronsky the next Saturday as he drove over to the club to buy Ingrid her membership, since when is it considered an act of oppression if your maid doesn't belong to the Croton Hills Country Club? A thousand smackers! And that was tourist-class. What if they decided to take up golf lessons? What if they decided, on top of greens fees and cart rentals, that it would be nice to have lunch there, maybe go to the beauty parlor?

That was in August. Now it was October. Tennis had been abandoned for something more seasonal. Now they were spending their days playing paddle tennis and having cozy tête-à-têtes during the afternoon cocktail hour. In the meantime, unfortunately, the house was suffering. Nothing major at first, just minor annoyances, like not being able to find his laundry and having to look at the television through the legs of an ironing board.

"Where are my socks?" he would say, staring in his sock drawer, which had all his life been the repository for footwear, to which Mandy would reply, "Downstairs in the basement. Ingrid didn't have time to do all the sorting yesterday." Okay, fair enough. So he would go to the laundry room, and there he would find his socks, his underwear, and he would sort them out and brush off the lint and carry them upstairs with the bath towels and bed linens. No big deal. No cause for hysteria. But there was something about it that augured revisionism. It was as if, whatever the contract they had previously lived by, it was being rewritten, and he had no understanding of it.

So now as he stood there in that dish-cluttered kitchen, his tie unfastened, his briefcase still hanging from him, here was yet another proposal being submitted for discussion, only this one was worse, because there was no place for him in it.

"What do you mean, 'separation'?"

"Now, Alex, you promised."

Gronsky blinked. He was beginning to look agitated.

"It's no big deal. Just a little time away. Just a few months apart so we can all get our heads together."

It has been said that all meaning can be defined by omission, as when a chisel strikes stone and a statue emerges. The statue has meaning, but the stone is reality, and the difference between them is what falls on the refuse pile. A similar metaphor might apply to this instance, for if the angle had been different, it might have been Mandy's tale. These past several years had not been easy for her, and if she had had them to relive, she might have done them quite differently.

Mandy, as it happened, was of a disenfranchised age group. Too young for the fifties and too old for the sixties, she had graduated from college during a transitional era that still chose to follow a conventional morality. And she had not been unhappy. She had never been a brave soul. She was perfectly content to lead the life of a housewife. But as the world began to change, she had begun to feel cheated. She had married too young. She had walled herself in too much.

Gronsky understood this—he was not insensitive. He too had

felt the lure of freedom, variety. Only it would never have occurred to him to give up his home for it. His home was—well, *home!* That was a man's way of viewing things.

"You want a divorce."

"That is *not* what I said, Alex."

"I mean, don't try to tell me about trial separations, damn it. They're never just trial. That's not how that works. You want a divorce. You want to throw over everything."

He was beginning to perspire. His jaw muscles twitched. He went over to the refrigerator and set down his sales case. He straightened back up and glanced around the room. He put one foot forward as if he were about to charge at them.

From another part of the house he could hear the television playing. There was a sound of shots, the roar of a car chase. That would be Bobby watching "The Dukes of Hazzard." Or maybe it was "CHiPs." Something subliterate.

"No, no," said Gronsky, "I just want to know what we're talking about. Are we talking about sex? Is that the discussion here? Because, if so, those surveys about frequency of intercourse are grossly exaggerated. That's common knowledge, Mandy."

"We're not talking about that."

"I mean, three times a week. Where the hell does Kinsey come up with that bullshit? Once a week, twice maybe . . . the rest is bravado. I'm forty-two years old. What the hell do you want from me?"

"We're not talking about sex."

"I work hard. I'm tired. Of course I guess in Sweden they screw all the time, don't they? Here in America we've got an economy to run. We gotta keep up our military just to protect their damn welfare paradise."

"Alex," said Mandy, "if you'll just calm down . . ."

"Inadequate sex life. All right, what else is there? I suppose I'm also a failure as a provider. I'm an incompetent businessman. That's what your father tells you."

By now hysteria was beginning to grab hold of him. From his pocket he withdrew a small leather-bound diary. He went over to the table and took out a pencil. His hand was trembling. He was fumbling with the lead ejector.

"We've got sexual inadequacy, incompetent businessman . . . I suppose we'll want to talk about unfaithfulness. The fact that I didn't come home a few evenings, had too much to drink, pinched a secretary's ass or two . . ."

"I have never questioned your faithfulness, Alex."

"I mean, it makes no difference that none of them meant anything. Not even Maureen . . . God, that was a tragedy . . . but she didn't mean anything. It was a strictly emotional thing."

He was fumbling with the diary. October nineteenth. That was tomorrow. It said "Daily Reminder." He had an eleven o'clock appointment at Needham Harper & Steers, after which, he now noted, he should improve his sex performance.

"We've got sexual inadequacy, poor provider, adulterous philanderer who gets smashed during office hours. How 'bout lousy father? That's always a good one. The guy who makes promises and never lives up to them."

"I sink," said Ingrid, "he iss taking ziss personally."

"Alex," said Mandy, "I wish you'd stop talking."

"No, no," said Gronsky, "I'm just trying to be rational. I am writing it all down so we don't lose track of anything."

By now Mandy was beginning to cry. They were not really tears so much as the precursors of tears. Her head was bowed and she was holding her temples. Gronsky kept writing. The lead kept breaking on him.

"We've got drunken sot, inadequate father . . . Oh, yes, Victorian—I believe that was your word, Ingrid. We have a benighted American with materialistic values who believes that a maid should at least sort his socks for him."

"Alex," said Mandy, and now she really was crying, her face contorted in ugly paroxysms, "I'm not talking about that. I am talking about me. I am talking about Ingrid. Must I spell it all out for you?"

Gronsky blinked. The room seemed to tilt. His body caught it before his mind could acknowledge it. It was like a blow to the midsection—breathtaking, paralyzing. His mouth kept moving, but he had no control of himself.

"We've got inadequate father . . ."

"Stop it!" cried Mandy.

"We've got a washed-up ex-football player who was no good anyway . . ."

"Alex, stop it! Don't shut me out! I need your help! I need us to talk about it!"

Gronsky stood up. The room was still spinning. From beyond the kitchen came the sound of the television. He had some vague idea that if he could just make it to that television, he would be all right, it would all go away somehow.

"Iss best," said Ingrid.

"No!" said Mandy. "Alex, come back. Can't you see what you're doing? All I wanted was to discuss this rationally. I wanted to be positive. I wanted to be fair about it."

In the den, which was dark, he could see the television. It seemed to be glowing with an unnatural hue. It was a color set, but it had no tint to it. Everything seemed bathed in a sea of cobalt.

"H'lo," said Bobby.

Gronsky didn't answer. He was standing in the doorway like a baffled dinosaur. He would give anything right now to be able to scream—to cry, to wail, to take revenge on something.

Bobby was lying with his feet up on the sofa. He was wearing gym shoes, corduroys, and a Miami U. football jersey. His father's appearance seemed hardly to register on him. He lifted his head, then put it back down again.

"I know," said Bobby. "I got a C in social studies. I gotta do better or they'll be sending home notes again. Dumb ole Miss Kilgour—'How the Eskimos Build Igloos.' But if you're gonna play football, you gotta keep up your grade average."

It was droned as a litany. Gronsky's total legacy: "Set before you throw" and "keep up your grade average." Was that all there was? After all these years? Would that be chiseled on the grave of their relationship?

"Alex . . ." said Mandy. She had followed him from the

kitchen. The sound of her sneakers made squeaks against the hardwood. "Alex, listen. I have to explain. You owe me that much. Don't just run off this way."

"I'll need some clothes." He turned away from her.

"Alex, be reasonable."

"A couple of suits. I can pick up the rest next week—whenever. Some shirts, some underwear—a coupla neckties."

He broke her grasp and went into the living room. He was suddenly like a thing adrift, directionless. No wife, no son, no house, no anchorage. Everything seemed strange. It had no relation to him.

"Goddamn you," said Mandy.

He paused by the armoire. This house—they had bought it for fifty thousand dollars. Now they were saying it was worth four times that much. It wasn't even his, it was just a place where he stayed sometimes.

"Alex," said Mandy.

He turned toward the kitchen. He had built that back deck himself out of redwood. Could have used pine, but it wouldn't have been right. *"Let's do it right—it'll last us a lifetime, Mandy . . ."*

"Oh, Alex," said Mandy.

Gronsky didn't answer.

"I suppose it sounds silly, but I really do care about you. We've had seventeen years. I don't want to lose them. But I've got to explore. I've got to find out, Alex."

He walked toward the foyer. Mandy was following him. "I'm thirty-nine years old. I've lived my life in a cocoon. Ingrid's just twenty. She's young. She's exciting. I'm no pioneer. I've never been brave, Alex."

In the foyer, on the floor, there were three crumpled shopping bags. He supposed he should have guessed when he came in what was in them. He opened them now and examined the contents. His best blue chalk stripe . . . his old gray herringbone . . .

"I'm sorry," said Mandy. "I couldn't keep hiding it. After all these years, I'm no good at hiding, Alex. I know what you think

—you think it's disgusting. And maybe it is. But I've got to find out, Alex . . ."

Gronsky picked up the shopping bags and headed toward the door. Outside, in the driveway, stood their two-year-old Volvo. It needed a tune-up, but it was in fairly good running order. He'd leave them the Volkswagen. He would not be a martyr about it.

A half-moon shone down through the half-barren tree limbs. The night was chill, and he turned up his coat collar. These leaves needed raking. They should put up the storm windows. There were all these little things that suddenly needed to be done here.

"Funny thing," he said. He looked up at the porch light. The bulb was yellow and somehow strangely out of focus to him. "On my way to the train I saw a man die tonight. He was lying on the floor. There was nothing I could do for him."

"Oh, Alex," said Mandy.

"Tell Bobby I'll talk to him. I got tickets to the game. I'll pick him up Sunday." He started toward the car. "Just lying on the floor. I had the feeling I knew him. His wife's still waiting for him."

5

From the White Horse Tavern to Shaughnessy's apartment was three and a half blocks if you walked it soberly, but since this was something he had never tried, it made the trip a bit more circuitous. Here came Shaughnessy, hands in pockets, head bowed hangdog and clouded with alcohol, lurching, staggering, slaloming lampposts, cutting across corners oblivious to traffic patterns. To Mr. Poukos, the Greek who ran the glass shop on Twelfth Street, it was a singular example of American providence. "He must be saint. He must have God's blessing. No mere mortal could do that and live through it."

Tonight had been particularly depressing for Shaughnessy. This being a Monday, the White Horse was moribund. He had been forced to sit for three and a half hours downing scotch after scotch and staring at the television. But that wasn't the worst part. The worst part came later when they gave him the tab and he reached for his billfold. Because he had no billfold. It had been swiped from his gym locker. No cash, no cards, no wristwatch, no driver's license.

Fortunately, the White Horse was a neighborhood hangout, and Shaughnessy, being a regular, was grudgingly tolerated. Besides, this was hardly the first time this had happened. He was always being robbed. "The gays got it in for me," he told them. So they had totaled his bill—some seventeen dollars worth—and added it to his tab, which was now in the hundreds, and he had staggered out feeling physically nauseated. He paused at the corner and looked blearily northward.

The apartment Shaughnessy lived in was on the second floor. It was a run-down building, devoid of luxury. A rusty old fire escape hung over the glass shop and zigzagged its way up the dirty gray brickface. From adjoining rooftops the building was vulnerable. It was constantly being assaulted by dope fiends and cat burglars. They would descend like spiders, break through the windows, and clean out everything that was reasonably portable. Shaughnessy himself had been ripped off three times: They had taken his stereo, his TV, his typewriter. About the only thing left was his furniture and appliances—and that was because they didn't fit through the window frame.

"Ev'nin," said Poukos.

"Fu shi," muttered Shaughnessy. He was struggling with a packing crate full of ironstone dinner plates. Mr. Poukos came over and helped him move it. It was a routine procedure—sort of a ritual of homecoming.

There were several possible ways of entering this building, one of which, as noted, involved grappling hooks and rope ladders. A more conventional way was through a dingy black door between Mr. Poukos's glass shop and the corner pizzeria. Unfortunately, this door was usually kept locked. Equally unfortunately, Shaughnessy had no key to it. Or rather he had one, but he could never find it, probably because it was still upstairs in his apartment somewhere.

"Careful," said Poukos.

"Unh," said Shaughnessy. The crate tipped sideways under the weight of his running shoe. Mr. Poukos reached up and steadied his hips. Shaughnessy's legs were like rubber. He was wobbling precariously.

This meant, in order to get into his apartment, yet another means of entry had to be subjugated. Which, in fact, was what Shaughnessy was doing right now. It was an aerial act fit for the Flying Wallendas.

"You a friend of his?" Poukos had said one day when Lee Schoenstein, Shaughnessy's boss, had dropped by. Since the intercom was broken and the doorbell had been vandalized, Schoenstein was standing on the street throwing rocks at the windowpane.

"You might say that. We work together."

"Ah?" said Poukos, nodding incredulously. It had not occurred to him that Shaughnessy might work, and certainly not in a job that required contact with normal people.

" 'Mazin fella," said Poukos.

"That he is," said Schoenstein.

"He flies through the air. I seen him do it."

"Wouldn't surprise me if he did," said Schoenstein. "After a couple of drinks he can do most anything."

By now Shaughnessy was standing on top of the packing crate. His arms were extended like the arms of a cliff diver. There was a good eighteen inches between his fingers and the fire escape, and if he didn't make it he would land on the wine decanters.

Had it been sleep alone that motivated Shaughnessy, had he sought nothing more than a place to lie down, it would have been as comfortable and safe curling up outside as in that house of horrors he called his domicile. When he had first moved in, like most reborn bachelors, he had had elaborate fantasies of elegant soirées. The ladies would arrive, succumb to the ambiance, and promptly retire to get screwed in the bedchamber. Unfortunately, in reality this was not the case. In the first place, the living room had about wiped him out. By the time he got through paying for the sofa and end tables, he was too broke even to go on a movie date. He had also discovered that, fantasies notwithstanding, his sexual encounters had been less than ecstatic. He began to realize that, given his druthers, he would prefer to sit in a bar and drink Cutty Sark. So, despite his intentions, when it came to decorating, it had all just stopped at his Bon Marche living room, beyond which was an ungovernable quagmire of refuse that could be contained only by slamming the doors on it.

Nevertheless, the apartment did have its virtues. It was the only place nobody would dare come to look for him. It was also a place where he could enjoy his last nightcap before slipping into a coma on the couch with the lights still burning.

It was this that now impelled him upward, sailing through the air with his fingers bent clawlike, catching and holding on the grate of the fire escape, swinging madly like a drunken orangutan. It was an incredible feat, even for a man who was sober. Mr. Poukos just stood there and watched with wonder. The rickety old fire escape groaned and clattered. Loose pieces of mortar fell down on the wine decanters.

"I've heard of Black Irishmen, but you take the cake," said Schoenstein, as they had sat after work one day at the Copter Club. Shaughnessy had already downed three scotches. Schoenstein was still on his first and only Dubonnet. "You know what my mother used to say about alcohol? She used to say, 'Levi, liquor is the gentile's psychiatrist. You feel lonely or sad, better you should go to a head doctor. It's just as cheap, and you'll feel a whole lot better for it.' " Shaughnessy had just shrugged. It was an irrelevant insight. Maybe his drinking was self-therapy. Maybe most of the alkies in New York were simply amateur practitioners of psychopharmacology. But reason didn't matter. It was the hurt that dictated. The hurt that had been created by his parents, by Sarah. His hurt for Jaime. His hurt for himself. He absorbed them all like fists to the solar plexus.

When he and Sarah had first gotten married, his father, Larry Shaughnessy, had come to the reception. He was a short, stocky man with handsome white sideburns and pale liquid eyes the color of Wedgwood. He pulled Shaughnessy aside and gave him an envelope. Inside was cash—ten thousand dollars worth. "Take it," he said. "It's the best I can do for ya. But that's all there'll be. This squares our account, Teddy."

Ten thousand dollars, probably skimmed off some slush fund, or given as a kickback by some sleazy contractor, and Shaughnessy had taken it, murmuring gratitude, although remembering the days when there had been no food in the refrigerator.

They had moved to New York, bought a small house in Brooklyn. Five thousand down, the remainder on mortgage. He had taken a job as a paste-up artist and enrolled at Pratt in a graduate night course. When the baby came, he had to give up the night course. He earned a hundred and ten a week gluing paper to cardboard. Within less than a year all their cash was gone, and Sarah had to work as a part-time secretary.

My God, the weight! The bone-crunching weariness! Each

day he had traveled to Midtown by subway. Each night he had returned, his steps growing slower, the youth and vitality being slowly drained out of him. They ate frozen dinners. The baby was colicky. They had had no money even to pay for a baby-sitter. They had watched TV. They had hidden from each other. At night, in bed, they had lain there and suffocated.

Finally, neither had been able to continue, and the divorce became final on the sixteenth of January. He had moved to the Village, begun roaming the gin mills. His drinking and his running were all that were left for him.

By now he had a fairly firm grasp on the fire escape and was clambering up, his lips uttering grunting sounds. "God in Heaven!" said Mr. Poukos, watching admiringly. Shaughnessy's foot swung up and caught the balustrade.

Once on the fire escape, which adjoined his living room, there was still the problem of getting through the window. Although the lock was broken, so were the sash cords, and one entered at the risk of being decapitated. Besides which, the railing was almost severed. One false move and it could be your last. He crept toward the window, using the wall to balance himself. Now if he could just feel with his hand that chink in the window putty . . .

In an out-of-the-way cabinet by the grease-splattered stove, concealed by a skillet and a grimy percolator, stood a half-empty pint of emergency Cutty Sark that could be used, like now, in place of a sleeping pill. Shaughnessy didn't believe in the use of sleeping pills. He didn't even believe in vitamins or aspirins. It's true, he made his living designing ads for drug companies, but the use of their products was morally abhorrent to him. Nor did he believe in keeping alcohol in volume. He never kept liters, half gallons, or quarts. Only pints. Pints were self-limiting. Whatever was around, he was certain to guzzle it.

Now, as he half-climbed, half-fell over the windowsill, knocking off an ashtray that he had left on the radiator, all he could think of was that half pint of Cutty Sark. It beckoned invisibly like a buoy in a night channel.

He made his way toward the unlit kitchen. He patted his

pockets. He wanted a cigarette. Damn, now he remembered. He had run out of cigarettes. "Christ," he muttered, "what else can go wrong tonight?"

At the threshold of the kitchen he reached for the light switch. His hand drew back. Something felt strange to him. Because instead of plastic, the light switch felt fleshy. My God, he thought, this apartment's turned humanoid!

"Move on," said a voice. "This apartment's taken."

Shaughnessy said nothing. There was a heavy breathing sound.

"Ain't nuttin here. No teevee, no stereo. Try someplace else. This fucker's a lunatic."

Shaughnessy was stymied. His mind reeled crazily. Was he suffering from delusions, or was there somebody in here with him? He pulled at the light switch, this time more forcefully—

And found himself staring into the blade of a straight razor.

6

"Hello?" said Pelligrew.

"Hello, Don?" said the voice. It sounded vaguely familiar, but he couldn't quite place it. He raised himself up with one elbow on the pillow and looked vacantly, almost quizzically, at his bedside telephone.

"Don, this is Emmy. I suppose you've heard."

Pelligrew stared. He hadn't heard anything.

"He's dead," said the voice. "Last night. Massive hemorrhage. I'm going to need your help. I'm coming right over there."

In the grim aftermath of the supermarket debacle, sitting alone in his West Side apartment, it had occurred to Pelligrew that celibacy was a virtue and that the pursuit of sex was a misuse of resources. So enrapt had he become with this Zen-like hypothesis that he had decided to go out and test its validity. He had decided to go down to this place called Ruelles and stare at the women and not pick up any of them. This had worked pretty well for the first two hours, then somehow the theory had begun to reverse itself. It was not the pursuit that was the misuse of resources, it was the sitting there frustrated and not being rewarded for it.

He sat up in bed. He couldn't think. Who had he just slept with? Some secretary named Ruthie. But who was Emmy? And why was she coming here? Damn all these women. He was going to have to change his phone again.

In the past couple of years, since he and his ex-wife had separated, he had changed his phone number six different times. He kept getting calls from these hysterical women accusing him of the most outrageous injustices. There was one girl particularly—

some crazy named Leonore—who had tracked and hounded him through four different phone exchanges. She would curse or weep, as circumstance dictated, and he had finally had to resort to buying an answering machine. Even that didn't stop her. She would plead with the Code-a-Phone. She went through those tapes like a shark through whale fat. Finally he had gotten an unlisted phone number, which he shared only with clients and business contacts.

So whoever Emmy was, she was apparently business, or the wife of business, or some lapse in his security system. Maybe she was some target he had pursued through a Sloan's and, instead of his shopping list, he had shown his phone number to her.

From the bathroom, off the hall, there was the sound of water. A toilet flushed—then a latch was turned. Now he could hear the sound of feet. They were heading away from him, toward his office-living room.

Pelligrew's apartment was a modest walk-up that he had purchased primarily for the size of the living room. It allowed him to keep a desk and two filing cabinets, plus the mandatory cases full of reviews and legal precedents. It also allowed for an oversized sofa whose cushions concealed a fold-down hide-a-bed, and it was here, on weekends, his ex-wife permitting, that the one important person in his life could cohabit with him.

Jeremy was eight and a younger version of his father. He had dark tousled hair and unseparated eyebrows. When he talked, his eyes seemed to recede into his head until there were no whites at all, just smoky black irises. "Tell me," he would say, "about the mask and the cape." He had inherited at least some of his father's romanticism. He never tired of hearing stories about The Phantom, which he seemed literally to absorb through his cavernous dark eye sockets. "Well, it was a really great cape," his father would tell him, "because when you ran it flew out like a vampire's wing. I used to jump from my bedroom and land in the tulip garden. You never quite knew where The Phantom might strike, you see." "Tell me about the time you broke the flagpole." "Oh, I didn't do that, that was Sandy Miller. All I did was provide the alibi. I told the teacher it was done by a poltergeist." "What's that?" said Jeremy. "Who knows? Some spirit. The important thing is, it's always invisible. It flew in through the window, erased all the blackboards, knocked over the waste can, and splintered the flagpole."

Jeremy would scowl—then suddenly he would laugh. There was a ridge of gum where his front teeth should be. "That must have been the stupidest teacher in the world!" he would say, and Pelligrew would nod, and the two of them would grin at each other.

As it happened, Jeremy had been there last weekend. They had rented bicycles and ridden through the park. Afterward, Pelligrew had gotten out his motorcycle, and they had gone for a drive down the abandoned West Side Highway. Elizabeth, Pelligrew's ex, would inevitably get furious. "What are you trying to do, get him killed?" she would holler. That's the trouble with women—they didn't understand. There are priorities in life, but life itself was not one of them.

Nevertheless, since Jeremy had been staying there, there were inevitably signs of unlawyerly activity: a Nerf ball half-hidden by the skirt of the sofa, a paper airplane stuck in the window valance. They didn't bother Pelligrew. In fact, he liked them. They seemed to add something to his office's decor. Like houseplants, maybe, or a bowl of goldfish. Subtle reminders of life's asymmetry.

Only now, in addition to subtle reminders, there was something unsubtle prowling the premises. What the hell was her name? He was sure it was Ruthie something. It was either Ruthie or Mary. Or maybe it was Joanna somebody.

"Got a heyabrush?" came the voice. It was a tremulous sound, nasal, metallic, Flatbush or Bensonhurst, with elliptical *r*'s, misplaced *w*'s, and other strange patterns that seemed to have been learned on Ellis Island sometime. "I'm lookin for a heyabrush—sump'n to comb my heya with!" He could hear her rifling through the papers in his mail basket. Every so often she would walk across the room. The thud of her feet rattled the glass in the picture frames.

Pelligrew sat up, placed his hand on his head. Was he sure it was Ruthie? Maybe it was Roseanna somebody. No, Roseanna was the Italian he had met at the Frick last Friday. This girl was Polish. Or she could be Ukrainian, possibly.

Through some unknown mechanism, too circuitous to analyze, a face suddenly emerged through the wine in his brain pan. It flickered briefly, swam back down, then rose again and lay there smiling at him. "Hello," it said, "my name is Emmy." A hand reached out as if to touch his coat sleeve. "This is my husband. He's so anxious to talk to you. He's on the advisory board of the Seventy-eighth Street Rehab Center." Yes, now he remembered: a short, swarthy man. "I'm very concerned about addiction," he told Pelligrew. "I suppose you might say it's a matter of conscience. We owe something to these people who get hung up on the pills we sell." Yes, that was it, only it had been so long ago, and he seemed to remember that it involved some estate plan, and he had gone to their apartment on East Fifty-seventh Street and they had reviewed the man's will, and the wife sat there smiling at him . . .

"Hey, what's dis?" said the voice.

Pelligrew didn't answer. Why did these women always insist on sleep-overs? Why couldn't they just fuck and get the hell out of there? He was not a believer in extended afterplay.

"You got kids or sump'n?"

Still didn't answer. Emmy Shinespun! No, it wasn't Shinespun. Dark, liquid eyes . . . shoulder-length hairdo . . . A little old, perhaps, but he wouldn't hold that against her.

"Hey, Dwonnie?" came the voice—and now it was approaching—he could hear the thud of the feet in the hallway. "Hey, Dwonnie, what's dis? You didn't tell me you was married. Not that it makes no difference, but you could at least let me know or sump'n."

Pelligrew turned, and now it was confronting him, all five-foot-three, one hundred and twelve pounds of it, the thing that had looked so enticing last night but which now just looked naked and no different from other women.

"What are you talking about?"

She was holding some notepaper. She couldn't have been

more than nineteen or twenty. She had puffed, sleep-filled eyes and underdeveloped breasts. Her fingernails were painted a ghoulish dark brown color.

"Dis," she said. She sat down on the bed. She unwrinkled the paper and began to read from it. Through the fiber's transparency he could see the typing. It was random, illiterate, some hunt-and-peck exercise.

"daddy," it began . . .

"Give me that," said Pelligrew.

"Who's Jeremy?" she asked.

"None of your business."

"I couldn't help seein it."

"It's a personal letter. There are laws against that. It's a violation of the postal act."

The girl just shrugged and gave him the letter. Pelligrew scowled. Goddamn her, anyway. The girl got up and went back toward the hallway. It was as if, having read it, she had somehow cheapened it.

Actually, there was a drawer full of letters from Jeremy—some typed, some printed, some scribbled in Crayola—exhortations to get up, to make breakfast, to go somewhere, many with drawings or snatches of alphabet on them. He could never part with them. They were there every Monday. He would find them stuck in the roller of his typewriter, and he would pull them out, read them carefully, then put them in a drawer with the puzzles and the Monopoly set. Sometimes, alone, he would open that drawer. He would sit with a drink and read over the contents. A strange sensation would rise in his adenoids, and he would slam the drawer shut with a curse against womankind.

"Got a toothbrush?" called Ruthie.

Pelligrew said nothing.

"Oh, wow, look at dat! Another pimple!"

Still said nothing. Picked up the notepaper. It read, *iI love you daddy. DadaDdaddy.*

"You know, last night," said the girl, calling in from the bathroom, her words deflected off her face in the medicine chest, "I was sittin in dat bar and I was sayin to myself, I says, 'Yous bettuh be careful. Dis guy's got a wife somewheah.' . . ."

I love you daddy. do yOu love me?

"That was silly of me, right? I mean, it makes no difference. Like I knew right away we was gonna go home togethuh. But I couldn't help thinkin, He's got a house out in Joisey or sump'n."

There was a moment's lull as she turned on the tap water. Pelligrew sat stone-faced, his muscles tensing. *it's time to get up. upupupUp. if you love me getup. lovelovelove jJeremy.*

"Course it don't bother me if you're married or not," she was saying. "I mean it's not like I'm ready to get tied down or nuthin. But if you are, you should say so. It'd help prepare me. I been hoit befoah, I don't need no second time."

Pelligrew folded the note.

"I'm divorced," he said, finally.

Silence from the bathroom. Then: "Yeah, well, that's different. I was wonderin that too. I said, 'Maybe he's divwossed. Married or divwossed—he's gotta be one of em.' "

Emmy Weintraub! No, that wasn't it. But it was something like Weintraub, and he remembered being attracted to her. She had translucent skin and small conical breasts. There was something about her that radiated energy.

"Got a kid?" said Ruthie.

Pelligrew didn't answer.

"Is Jeremy your kid? Does he come to visit?"

Still didn't answer. Just sat there ruminating. Shinespun . . . Weintraub . . . Gildenblatt . . . Silverstein . . .

From the bathroom again the sound of water, and this time the sound of teeth being brushed. "Hope you don't mind, I'm usin your toofbrush!" she shouted. The words gurgled out through a mouthful of foam at him.

Pelligrew looked up. Wait a minute! Hold it! Now he remembered—it was about a week after the will signing, and he had run into her at Saks, or maybe it was Bergdorf's, and they had gone out and had a drink at the St. Regis Hotel together. And he remembered her smile, the feel of her body heat, and he remembered walking her home toward dusk and the slight feeling of self-consciousness as they passed the doorman and she said "My husband's out of town" as they got on the elevator . . .

"Got a razuh?" said Ruthie.

It was all coming back to him.

"I just wanna take a few strokes at my awmpits. As you may have noticed, I got very hairy awmpits. My fathah says he thinks I got monkey blood in me."

Pelligrew said nothing. It was all coming back to him. They had gone up in the elevator and he had unlocked the door for her and she had worn a lavender turban held in place by a stickpin and she had smiled suggestively and said, "You're very persuasive, aren't you?"

"Hey, Dwonnie?" said Ruthie.

Pelligrew's heart was pounding.

"Hey, Dwonnie, you don't happen to got any Tampax, do ya? I can't be sure, but I think it's my period startin. I thought maybe if yous got one, I'd take it along wid me."

Because now he remembered that he had stayed there that evening and they had made love on the floor with the window open, and afterward, as he was getting ready to leave, he had seen a picture of a girl who looked vaguely familiar to him . . .

"Dwonnie?" said Ruthie.

Pelligrew just stared.

"You think maybe I could borrow one of your hankies or sump'n? I thought maybe if I wore it or pinned it on somewheah, it'd make me look different, like I'd maybe gone home last evenin."

"Oh, no!" cried Pelligrew.

"How come?" said Ruthie.

"OH, NO!" he cried, because *now* he remembered, because Emmy had turned and there was tension in the air, and she had said, "She's too young for you, Don. She was sixteen last February."

"Oh, my God," he muttered, grabbing at his underwear, searching frantically for his socks and trousers, because now he remembered that the girl was her daughter and, unbeknownst to Emmy, he had already made love to her!

"Hurry up," he said. "We gotta get out of here."

"I was thinkin—maybe if I could borrow a necktie . . ."

"Borrow anything you want. Take the whole damn closet. We got three and a half minutes—then it's good-bye everything!"

He was hopping on one leg, trying to get his pants on. Somehow his shirt had gotten caught in his zipper teeth. No time for that. He grabbed for his shoes. "I'm going to ask my daughter to come with us," she had said to him.

At the rear of his apartment, beyond a gray metal door, there was an unused fire stairs that led to the roof. At the top of the stairs there was a door with a burglar alarm that could easily be silenced with some putty and a screwdriver. He knew how to do that. He had done it often. Then he would run across the roof to the adjoining rooftop, climb down the drain spout, vault over a fence, and land in some trash barrels in an alley off Amsterdam. When you're The Phantom, you do that. You have various escape routes. You never quite know when they might come after you. Why, there was this secretary once, this crazy named Leonore, who had spent two whole days parked downstairs in the reception area . . .

"Whatsamatter?" said Ruthie.

"Stay away from the windows!"

"You mad or sump'n?"

"Don't use the telephone!"

"If you're mad, just say so. I'll put it all back. It's just that I thought it'd go well with my eyelinah . . ."

They were heading through the living room, approaching the kitchen, and he was remembering again how he had stared at that photograph. The girl's name was Lilah, and she was absolutely gorgeous, and whatever else she was, she was *not* too young for him . . .

"Dwonnie," said Ruthie, "you tryin to get rid of me?" He was struggling to open the steel-encased fire door. Ruthie, dumbstruck, was standing behind him. She had on one of his handkerchiefs and a Countess Mara necktie.

The buzzer rang.

"Whozzat?" said Ruthie.

For God's sake, where had he hidden the key? The damn door was locked! He was trapped in his burrow! He could feel the estrogen slowly closing on him! . . .

"Hey, Dwonnie?" said Ruthie. He was rummaging through the cabinets. "Dwonnie, listen. I think someone's buzzin ya." You should always keep the key within easy access . . . "You want I should go and maybe open the door for them?"

Pelligrew turned. There was a note of panic. "Ruthie, listen. My life is in danger. That woman at the door is a homicidal maniac. She has some paranoid suspicion that I've done some injustice to her."

The buzzer again.

"Like what?" said Ruthie.

Pelligrew scowled. He peered through the window shade. Was it just his imagination, or was there a girl on that roof over there? And what was in that truck turning right on Amsterdam? . . .

All of Pelligrew's life he had been pursued by these crazies. Neurotics, psychotics, moonstruck ingenues, they would call him up, write nasty letters, accuse him of callousness, of trying to manipulate them. And it was all a lie! How was he to know? He had spotted this girl in the Museum of Modern Art. A little young, perhaps, but with breasts like cantaloupes, and he had engaged her, quite innocently, in a discussion of the Bauhaus School . . .

"Don," came the voice, *"I know you're in there!"*

"Dwonnie?" said Ruthie.

Pelligrew turned. "Goddamn it!" he cried. "What the hell do you want from me! Leave me alone! I never hurt anybody!"

Ruthie stared.

"You're just like Elizabeth! You expect me to live like some goddamn Trappist? I am not an angel! I'm a man! I got sex drives! What am I supposed to do, just stay home and masturbate?"

Ruthie stared. "I dunno whatchous talkin about."

"Big deal!" he said. "So we discussed the Bauhaus School. And afterward we happened to go get some coffee, and afterward she happened to get smashed on some gin I gave her. How was I to know? I don't ask to see driver's licenses! For all I know, you could be sixteen yourself! For all I know, you could be my half sister! How do I know what the hell my old man was doing?"

Ruthie just stared. It had begun so innocently. Last night she had gone out with her girl friend Lisa. She always went out with Lisa on Mondays. They did Xenon . . . Roxy's . . . perhaps made the Village scene . . .

"I have never done anything against anybody's will!" cried Pelligrew. By now his eyes had begun to roll. "And I can tell you this—I was not her first! She may have been young, but she was not inexperienced, damn it!"

The buzzer again.

Pelligrew picked up a knife.

"I refuse to be made into some feminist scapegoat!"

He took the knife—and plunged it in the door lock. There was a metallic snap—and it came back with no point on it.

"Aw, fuck!" he cried. He shoved past Ruthie. "Okay! I surrender! Bring on the death penalty! I stand accused of being led by my hormones! Do what you will! Life has no more meaning to me!"

Ruthie just stared. It had begun so innocently. They had happened to stop in this great place, Ruelles. There was this man sitting there. He had seemed so romantic. He had told her his work was highly classified . . .

"Do you know what it's like being a man?" cried Pelligrew. "Come here, I'll show you!" He was standing in the living room. He went over to his desk phone and began unscrewing the mouthpiece. "I'll show you something that is rarely talked about!"

There was a pound at the door.

"Don!" cried the voice.

He unscrewed the mouthpiece and pulled out the disk inside. "The staff of *Ms.* magazine has been listening for months!" he shouted. "You didn't know that! They don't like to advertise it!"

He threw down the telephone.

"I'm coming!" he shouted. He wheeled on Ruthie. "And *you*

—" he said menacingly. "You have the unmitigated gall to take the clothes from a dead man! That's a fifty-dollar necktie. I hope you appreciate that!"

He headed toward the door. Ruthie stood thunderstruck. Her friend Lisa had warned, "You be real cayaful, Ruthie. Gimme a cwall. You never know. Remembuh Diane Keaton in *Lookin fwa Mistuh Goodbwah* . . ."

Pelligrew fumbled with the chain. It all passed before his eyes: his night with Emmy, his night with Lilah. Until he had seen that picture he had had no way of knowing that his sperm had already swum in such a similar gene pool. In the next few minutes, that would all come out. Emmy would be standing there, and behind her her daughter, and Lilah would say, "Hey, wait a minute! I know you! But you told me your name was Christy Mathewson!" And Ruthie, behind him, would be totally confused, because he had told her his name was Donald Larson, and Emmy, who had known him by his real name, Pelligrew, would not be amused by this affinity for baseball pitchers. And in one horrible moment it would all come down on him, they would descend on his carcass like shrieking harpies, a JAP, her mother, and some Polack from Bensonhurst, ripping, snarling, chewing the flesh off him.

He threw back the bolt.

"God help me," he muttered.

He opened the door.

He tried to smile.

"Sorry," he said. "I was a bit inconvenienced. Emmy, this is Ruthie. Ruthie, Emmy Schoenstein."

7

The thing he didn't understand about this—the thing that made him hike up his reading glasses—was that nothing squared with the way he remembered it or the framework his mind had constructed around it. AD EXEC DIES IN PAN AM BLDG. That's the way the New York *Times* was playing it. It was buried at the bottom of page twenty-eight under a run-over column on co-op interest rates. AD EXEC DIES IN PAN AM BLDG. Make that: AUTOMATON MALFUNCTIONS ON WAY TO TRN STA. Or: MAN SUCCUMBS TO LIFE OF ABSDTY, IS TRAMPLED TO DEATH BY HUMAN BFLOES. "A man collapsed of an apparent hemorrhage in the Pan Am Building at the height of the rush hour. He was pronounced dead on arrival at Bellevue Hospital, where he was tentatively identified as Levi F. Schoenstein." Gronsky scowled, bit into a croissant. The newspaper lay to the right of his grapefruit. His tortoise-shell glasses had slipped down his nose, and with his index finger he pushed them back up again. "Mr. Schoenstein, who lived on East 57th Street, was creative director of Caduceus Advertising. He is survived by his wife, Emmy, and his daughter, Lilah. A memorial is being planned at the Sutton Place Synagogue."

The Edwardian Room at this hour was filled with businessmen, many sitting alone, at separate tables, all of them dressed as neatly as Gronsky in his gray banker's suit and his shirt with the monogram on it. They, too, were reading their morning newspapers—the New York *Times*, *The Wall Street Journal*—absently sipping their second Sankas before sallying out into the gray world of empire-building. The only difference between them and

Gronsky was that they still viewed their existence as meaningful. They had not yet confronted the black hole of nothingness through which all living matter must pass and be negated.

Gronsky picked at an egg as he reread the article. He was thinking of writing a letter to the editor. "Dear Editor," he would say, "You are full of shit. I ought to know, because I was a witness to it." He would describe how this commuter, whose wife was still waiting for him, had surrendered himself to the Florsheim Shoe Company. "I personally obliged him by stepping on his hat. He could have been saved, but we decided to sacrifice him."

The reason all this was so important to Gronsky, besides the fact that it had touched him spiritually, was that, slow as he might be in matters of intellect, he was very good at subliminal impressionism. This had been true even as a child back in Steubenville. "Heavens, how that boy does remember!" said his mother. "I swear he remembers the day he was born! You'd think he'd do better when it came to algebra!" Their '34 Nash, the voice of Russ Columbo, the hauling of scrap iron to take to the movies—all these things were indelibly printed on him: even today he could remember his father's old union card number. And what he remembered about this person Schoenstein was that he was a commuter like himself and he was heading toward the train station. Why, he even thought maybe he had seen the man's face. It was not a Jew's face; it was fair; it was ruddy even . . .

AD EXEC DIES IN PAN AM BLDG. Let's take this through to its logical conclusion. Why should this man have even been in that building if he had not been en route to the rotunda of the train station? The answer: he shouldn't—not during rush hour—not if he lived on East Fifty-seventh Street. It was obviously an error, of logic if not typesetting, and it would not surprise Gronsky if it resulted in lawsuits.

"More coffee?" said the waiter.

Gronsky shook his head. The waiter wrote out a check and placed it by the saucer: fourteen dollars and sixty cents for two eggs and a grapefruit. Yes, error, thought Gronsky. There is error everywhere.

Once upon a time there was a young man named Alex who lived in a town called Steubenville, Ohio. It was a poor little town, black with coal dust, and there was no way out for anyone who lived there. One day Alex met a mysterious stranger. "Alex," said the stranger, "I'm going to give you a key. It is a magical key that will unlock the gate. For the rest of your life you will have riches and happiness."

Five dollars, six dollars, seven dollars, eight dollars . . . There was no sense paying for this bill in cash. He could charge it on Visa, American Express. It would come to the house. Let Mandy pay for it . . . .

So Alex took the key and went up to the gate. The gate was oiled with pain and injury. When it swung, it roared like a million spectators. On the walls by the gate were brass bands and pom-pom girls.

"Is anything wrong, sir?"

Gronsky didn't answer. He was staring vacantly at the cards in his wallet.

"Can I get you something else?"

"No. No, that'll be fine." He pulled out a pen and signed his room number.

Actually, there were things that he was supposed to be doing today, although he hoped that none of them would be at the office. "You Can't Make Sales If You Sit in the Office"—it was an axiom of Eastman's that had been engraved on his forehead. "You Can't Plug the Holes If You Don't Move Forward"—this was what the line coach in college used to tell him. "Once They Get to the Line of Scrimmage, You're as Good as Dead! You Gotta Nail 'Em!" "But coach, I'm tired. I've got all this gravity!" "It's in your mind, boy! We're talkin about Attitude!" "I'm hurt! I'm sick!" "You're a goddamn pantywaist! Hell, this is Football! This is Life, buster!"

On the adjoining chair sat his elephant-skin sales case. Crouch & Fitzgerald. Three hundred smackers. "Daddy says sales is all in the appearance, Alex. Think of it as capital. It's a kind of investment, actually . . ." Only now, for some reason, that case was looking heavier. He imagined it as filled with cement, lead ingots. "Do I gotta, coach?" "You disgust me, Gronsky! You and your whining . . . you and your 'injuries' . . ."

Before leaving the hotel, he went up to the desk clerk. "Pardon me," he said. "Perhaps you can help me. My name's Gronsky—Room 1121. I wonder if you can tell me how much I owe you."

"You're checking out?"

"No—I'm just curious."

The clerk looked it up, came back with the answer. "For one night," he said, "that's two hundred and sixty dollars. Plus tax, of course. And whatever meal charges."

Two hundred and sixty. Plus tax and meal charges. All in all, that seemed very reasonable. Gronsky turned and went out onto East Fifty-ninth Street, his eyeballs aching in the morning sunlight.

"A salesman's place is out on the street," said Eastman. "It's calling on the media buyers at J. Walter Thompson. It's hitting those account men at Doyle Dane Bernbach. It's telling McCann Erickson, 'Hey! We got a message for you!' " Go get 'em, Gronsky. Go hit 'em in the midsection. Go open those holes for our fleet-footed editors. Go tell 'em why *Focus* is better than *Parade*, why it's better than the *Digest*, better even than television. The name of this game is The Big Score, Gronsky. Your commission goes up on the scoreboard in lights. The crowd goes wild. The band plays the fight song. Those cute little cheerleaders all waggle their tushes for you . . .

He looked at his watch. Now he remembered. He had an eleven o'clock appointment at Needham Harper & Steers. Some new breakfast cereal that tasted like marshmallows. He was going to be late. He needed a taxicab.

As he walked, the elephant-skin sales case got heavier. He imagined it as a permanent extension of his arm. "And this, ladies and gentlemen, is the American salesman. Notice that he belongs to the marsupial family . . ."

Of course, the objections: "Tell me, Mr. Gronsky—how many

of *Focus*'s readers are men? How many belong to that accidental gender who might have been women were it not for testosterone?" "Men, you say? *Men*, sir? We got seven million men, sir—all of them rich, and all of them cereal eaters! Builders of democracy! Defenders of society! And all of them just love the taste of marshmallows!" "But how many of these men do the *buying*, Mr. Gronsky? How many actually go to the supermarket? Why should my client waste his precious fortune on seven million readers who are as dead as dinosaurs?" "But that's not true, sir. These men have input. At *Focus* we call it 'the power of dual readership.' It's the women who buy, but it's the men who eat. No, men are important. You can't live without them, sir!"

By now he was crossing Fifty-sixth and Park. He was five minutes late. He had a catch in his windpipe. Ahead and to the right glinted the mirrored walls of Citicorp. The sunlight bounced off like the Great Star of Bethlehem.

"This is bullshit, Mr. Gronsky. Men are irrelevant. The American economy runs on its women. What do men care what their kids eat for breakfast? What do men care if they pig out on dog turds?" "Not true, sir—not true. We're men, but we care, sir. I love my family, I always took care of them. Have you seen my son, Bobby? I just happen to have a picture here. Look at those shoulders. He's going to be a great football player . . ."

The agency where he was headed was at Fifty-fourth and Third. By now the old limp was beginning to show. His right leg was stiff and he was favoring his left. His body was lopsided. He was scuttling crablike.

"I love my family. I've always loved them. It's all a mistake, a misunderstanding."

"It's your mistake, Gronsky. Nobody needs you. Even Marshmallow Crunchies wants nothing to do with you."

Whether it was his knee, his chest, the pain in his eyeballs, the remembered inflictions of a million past injuries, suddenly the sidewalk seemed to yawn in front of him, and he stopped and leaned panting against the window of Conran's.

"BUT I LOVED THEM!" he cried.

Pedestrians turned. The Citicorp Building rose like a guillotine. His eyes filled up with exquisite hopelessness. To Steubenville's chagrin, Alex Gronsky was blubbering.

"Well, look at it this way," said Shaughnessy sardonically as he reached into his pocket and pulled out a Kleenex. "At least you still got your goddamn wristwatch. I had an Omega wristwatch. It had an alligator band on it."

Gronsky turned. His eyes still had tears in them.

"Shhh! Don't say anything. This is a major embarrassment to me. There's a woman over there, she thinks you're a queer. Keep looking at your feet. Try not to acknowledge me."

They were standing on the corner of Fifty-fourth and Third. Ahead and to the left was the FDR Post Office. Shaughnessy was still dressed in his outfit of last evening. His jacket was torn and had coagulated bloodstains on it.

"Don't talk. Just listen. First they rob me at the Y. Last night I come home, there's a guy in my apartment. He thinks I'm a burglar. I say, 'Hell, you're the burglar!' He pulls out a razor, he gets mad, he starts slashing at me . . ."

"Do I know you?"

"He practically kills me! I go to the hospital. They put seventeen stitches in me. This morning, in the office, I learn my boss has dropped dead. Cerebral hemorrhage. They're holding a funeral service . . ."

Gronsky said nothing. He blinked myopically. Shaughnessy kept talking. He was staring straight ahead. By now they had reached the southeast corner and were preparing to cross in the direction of the post office.

"Hold it," said Gronsky.

"Shhh! Keep your head down. You're six-foot-three, you stand out like an elephant. If you won't think of me, at least think of yourself. Straighten your tie. You look like an imbecile."

"Ted Shaughnessy!" cried Gronsky.

"O God, take pity . . ."

"Fuckin Theodore F. Shaughnessy, you goddamn bastard!"

"Mother o' Mercy, make him be quiet. I don't know him, lady. I never laid eyes on him."

And now the shock of male recognition, the grins, the oaths, the bone-crushing handshakes, the raucous howls hurled against the canyons where such chance encounters are a daily commonplace.

"You used to have a moustache!"

"I shaved it off."

"But I haven't seen you—"

"—since they fired me from Grey."

"Goddamn!" cried Gronsky. "Those pantyhose layouts—"

"I ripped them all up and told my boss to go fuck himself!"

Like sirens' wails, like the howling of wolf cubs, like overgrown spaniels newly freed from captivity, they laughed, they pawed, they grew red in the temples, they exhausted themselves while pedestrians stared at them.

"Hey, look," said Gronsky, "I gotta go to this meeting—"

"The hell you do. You look like an idiot."

"You should talk!"

"Hey, this is high fashion. I just bought this outfit. Don't make fun of it."

"No, seriously, Ted—"

"I am being serious. We'll call 'em up. We'll tell 'em you died or sump'n. We're holding a wake at P. J. Clarke's. If they want to commune, they can bring a communion bottle."

Gronsky smiled. His cheeks were still puffed. "Well, I don't know . . ."

"I do," said Shaughnessy.

Gronsky laughed. "What the hell!" he shouted—and through his tears shone the glimmer of resurrection.

8

The Sutton Place Synagogue is on East Fifty-first Street; P. J. Clarke's is four blocks north. Each has its own way of mourning the dead, depending on one's beliefs and ethnic origins. Shaughnessy's way was with a deluge of Cutty. "Easy on the water—put the ice on the side," he ordered. He had never believed much in funerals anyway. Wakes were his forte. They were so much more masculine.

"So tell me," he said, "what you've been doing with yourself."

"Same old stuff. Still work for *Focus.*"

"Still married?" said Shaughnessy.

"More or less. And you?"

" 'fraid not," said Shaughnessy. "Don't say you feel sorry for me."

They were sitting up front near the end of the bar. The lunchtime crowd was already arriving. Soon they would be lined four deep by the beer taps—noisy, conspicuous, predominantly masculine. Gronsky felt better. In fact, he felt buoyant. A little boy's grin was stamped on his face. He downed one vodka, ordered another. He beamed at Shaughnessy. The fire was kindling.

"Remember that time we got plastered at lunch," he said, "and you went back to the office and got on the intercom?"

"Oh, hell, don't remind me. I almost got canned for that. I saw Pierson yesterday. They're all still talking about it."

"What was that you said?"

" 'Paging Connie Lingus.' "

Gronsky hooted. " 'Miss Connie Lingus!' "

" 'Mr. Phil Fellatio paging Connie Lingus. Would Miss Lingus please report to the men's room?' "

Gronsky laughed. The fire grew warmer. It was as if some terrible burden were being lifted. Mandy and Ingrid seemed to recede in the distance. He took another drink. His breathing grew easier.

By now it was the peak of the lunchtime rush hour. The roar grew steadily in a raucous crescendo. From the back there was the sound of forks against dinner plates. Aproned waiters growled out their bar orders.

Shaughnessy scowled. He had grown morose.

"Goddamn Sarah," he said. "She called me up yesterday. She wants two hundred dollars for Jaime for ski lessons. Two hundred dollars! I mean, what does she want from me?"

"Must be tough," said Gronsky.

"Listen, I'll tell you. If you're married, stay married. Consider yourself lucky. I'm so goddamn horny I can hardly see straight. And I get a call from Jaime's school that she's having emotional problems . . ."

Gronsky just nodded. If you're married, stay married. A distant memory flickered ethereally: a warm spring day . . . Mandy laughing . . . himself and Bobby trying to unsnarl a kite string . . .

"Listen, Gronk," said Shaughnessy, "let me tell you about women. Women are currency. They're like shiny gold pieces. You walk down the street, it's like fuckin' Sotheby's. 'Look at me!' they're all saying. 'How much would you bid for me?' "

Gronsky said nothing. The fire was hot now. Mandy laughing . . . Bobby looking up at him . . . He knit his brows, stared at his vodka glass. A blonde in the corner seemed to laugh derisively.

". . . So after I got canned, I was out of work," said Shaughnessy. "I couldn't even afford the goddamn child support. What does Sarah do? She takes me to court. I gotta go down there and plead like a welfare mother." He took a sip. His eyes were heavy. "That bitch," he said. "It's ignominious. Finally I pick up a job with Caduceus. It's boring as hell, but at least I can live on it."

"Caduceus," said Gronsky. "That sounds familiar."

"Pharmaceutical agency. Park Avenue South. I sit there and

grind out layouts for miracle drugs. If it weren't for running, I'd have probably collapsed by now."

Gronsky said nothing. His mind was dimming. He could still see the smile on Mandy's face. What had he done wrong? Why was it gone now? What the hell's become of all our golden-haired cheerleaders, Ted?

Shaughnessy leaned back. He was the epitome of casualness. Even the bloodstains looked oddly appropriate. With his jeans, his Etonics, his unruly hair, everything about him had a take-it-or-leave-it quality.

"Hey, Gronk, look at that! No, the one in the jumpsuit. Now that's what I call a nice pair of buns. Since I've been working out, I've got a whole new perspective. I've sworn off tits. I'm into hard thigh muscles."

Gronsky looked. He wasn't interested. Why did Caduceus sound so familiar to him? Something he had read . . . something he had seen . . . A man on the floor . . . A shoe with no foot in it . . .

"Goddamn!" cried Shaughnessy. His face contorted. "The bastard's dead! I can't believe it! I was just with him yesterday. We were going to have lunch today. He was a good man, Alex. It shouldn't have been like that."

"I know what you mean." Now Gronsky looked sobered. "Reminds me of something that happened yesterday. I was heading toward the train and I saw this body. He was just lying on the floor. We all stepped over him."

"A toast," said Shaughnessy, "to the dear departed."

"To the dear departed."

"May they rest in peace. May there be no more women to make them miserable."

"Amen," said Gronsky.

That was a heaven worth drinking to.

"Oh, no," said Emmy.

"What's the matter?" said Pelligrew.

"That man over there. I think I know him. Let's see if we can find a table in the back. He used to work with Levi. An obnoxious Irishman."

By now it was well after 2 P.M. and the first shift at P.J.'s had begun to evacuate. Pelligrew threaded his way through the bar crowd and held up three fingers to a man wearing a bow tie.

Nothing that morning had gone predictably, starting with the moment he had opened the door. "Don," Emmy had said, "I'd like you to meet my daughter"—and there stood Lilah, just as he remembered her. Only something was strange, because instead of screaming, or instead of saying "You told me your name was Mathewson!" she had just nodded politely and said, "Glad to meet you," and held out her hand without any recognition of him!

He had barely had time to recover from that one (Ruthie had fled wearing half his wardrobe) when the next thing he knew he was in the back of a taxicab and they were heading down to the medical examiner's. Drab, scuff-marked walls. Composite floor tiles. The body laid out behind a plate-glass viewing screen. When they were outside again, the air smelled blasphemous. They hailed another cab and drove up to the synagogue.

And all the while, Pelligrew's mind was racing: What was going on? What did they want from him? Why was Emmy so keen on sticking with him, and why, above all, wasn't Lilah acknowledging him?

The service over, they lingered on the sidewalk. "I think we could all stand a brandy," said Emmy. He had followed them dutifully up to P. J. Clarke's, morbidly entranced by their coolness, their callousness.

It had started with a will—that much he remembered. Emmy's husband had wanted to attach a codicil. More precisely, he had wanted to divert ten thousand dollars from Lilah's trust to the Seventy-eighth Street Rehab Center. "As I see it," he had said, "it's a matter of conscience. Do you know how many people get addicted on tranquilizers? And that's not counting all the uppers and other drugs. I help sell those pills. I owe it to the community." So a clause was drawn up on a separate piece of paper, a neighbor had witnessed it and Schoenstein had signed it, and Pelligrew had stapled it to the existing will, with a separate dateline and appropriate notary seal.

That will, at present, was in Emmy's pocketbook. He had seen it earlier when she had searched for some eye makeup. "Remind me," she said, "to discuss this with you"—then she had shoved it back down under car keys and facial tissues.

Thin, almost too thin, an aging ex-mannequin, Emmy Schoenstein had the skin of a well-preserved olive. She had short black hair, a sensuous nose, and her smile revealed the hint of an overbite. Lilah, her daughter, was a reflection of Emmy, only she had not yet succumbed to diet pills and health spas. She had black, unplucked brows and a voluptuous bosom. When she sat down he could see that she had no bra on.

"Now, Donald," said Emmy when the drinks had been ordered and the crumbs of their predecessors had been hastily disposed of, "I do hope the two of us can still remain friends. I'd hate to be thought of as a manipulative female."

Pelligrew said nothing. He looked at Lilah. My God, she was gorgeous! She was his ideal sex fantasy. Everything about her suggested passion and dirt. Let the Jews yearn for shiksas; he would take her, thank you.

"Now, it's about this codicil," said Emmy officiously. "I know it's legal and it's the way he wanted it, but really, Donald, it is a bit galling. That was Lilah's money. I mean, to give it to drug addicts."

Pelligrew just shrugged. He studied her bemusedly. She was holding the will between her lacquered talons. Was it his imagination, or had she had her face lifted? Probably so. It had the texture of candle wax.

"Tell Donald, Lilah, about your classmate at Dalton—the one who had such a horrible experience. Listen to this, Don. This is unbelievable. You will not believe there could be such cruelty."

Lilah smiled. "Her name was Leonore."

"Leonore Stillman. A beautiful girl, Donald. A little high-strung, but absolutely gorgeous. Spectacular bone structure. Go on with your story, darling . . ."

"Well, Leonore met a man at a Central Park rock concert . . ."

"An older man, Donald—that's important to the story. Of course she didn't know how much older at the time. He had told her thirty, but he was obviously lying to her."

Pelligrew said nothing. He stared at his brandy snifter. The lines crept forward. They were approaching a locus. In another minute he would see how they met: the "classmate" named Leonore and the ten-grand codicil.

"Leonore and this man went home to his apartment," said Lilah. "He told her his name was Walter Johnson. They went to bed, and it was her first experience. She fell hopelessly in love. She was absolutely wild about him."

"This is Leonore," said Pelligrew.

"Yes. Leonore Stillman."

"I mean, it couldn't be we're talking about anyone more personal. Sometimes I notice people get things confused. They'll say Walter Johnson when they mean Christy Mathewson."

"No," said Lilah.

"Unh-unh," said Emmy.

"Okay." He shrugged. He smiled perplexedly. Whatever this was about, he knew he wouldn't like it. Two smoldering eyes stared out of the brandy at him.

"Now listen to this, Donald, because this is the strange part, because later this Leonore tried to get hold of him, only it was as if Walter Johnson had never existed. He had changed his name, his mailbox, his phone number."

Pelligrew squirmed. His stomach was churning. There was some animal, some rodent, nibbling his shinbone. He reached down to swat it—only it wasn't an animal. It was a female foot. It had no shoe on it.

"And the thing was," said Lilah, "she had to contact him, because the week before she had been to a doctor. She had missed her period, and now she was pregnant. She was sixteen years old. Can you imagine how scared she was?"

Pelligrew stood up.

"Where are you going?" said Emmy.

"I gotta pee."

"No, you don't. Sit down. Waiter, bring this man another brandy. We haven't gotten around to the point of our discussion, Donald."

Pelligrew sat down. He was like a hypnotized cobra. On one side sat Lilah, youthful, seductive; on the other sat Emmy, mature, self-confident—and from one of them a foot crawling up his trouser leg!

"Well, at that point," said Lilah, "poor Leonore went crazy. She bribed a supervisor at the telephone company. She called his new number, only he had bought an answering machine. She went to his apartment and camped out in the reception area."

"Can you believe this, Donald?"

"With difficulty," said Pelligrew.

"She finally had an abortion, and she talked to me about it. We looked up Walter Johnson in an encyclopedia, and guess what we found? He was an old-time baseball pitcher."

Pelligrew just sat there. The lines were converging. He felt like something being trapped in a spider web. At the center was himself—himself and that codicil. He could hardly wait to see how they all tied together somehow.

"Interesting," he said.

"Yes, isn't it?" said Emmy.

"Because I used to know a Leonore Stillman. Only she didn't go to Dalton, she worked in the garment district, and she wore a contraceptive, so that couldn't have happened to her."

"It might have," said Emmy.

"Yes, it might have," said Lilah.

"No. No way."

"But it *might* have," said Emmy. "And think what a frightening experience that would be. To be sixteen years old and having to go to an abortion clinic."

Pelligrew thought. It did not seem frightening. What really seemed frightening was Leonore Stillman. That crazy neurotic, she had driven him bananas. He seemed to remember that she had called when Lilah was there . . .

"At any rate," he said, "this has nothing to do—"

"You're right," said Emmy. "It's just an interesting story. It shows what it's like living in a jungle of penises. That's what I tell Lilah, 'They're all led by their genitals, darling' . . ."

She smiled at him saccharinely and pulled out the codicil. It was a simple typed paragraph on a piece of onion skin. She rolled it up into a paper log. From her purse she withdrew a gold cigarette lighter.

"Now how much would you say is just compensation, Donald? Ten thousand dollars? At least that, isn't it? How much would it be worth not to tell that girl's mother? They're still very upset. They could make quite a fuss over it."

"Leonore's mother."

"Who else would we be talking about? I want to make it clear, this is all hypothetical. How much would it be worth to a man like 'Walter Johnson' if Leonore's mother would just forget the whole incident?"

Pelligrew said nothing. Emmy flicked the lighter.

"Of course it's not your money—it belongs to Lilah. Or it was going to, anyway, before my husband got charitable. It belongs more to her than to a bunch of drug addicts."

Pelligrew sat spellbound. The flame grew closer. But what fascinated him more was the foot in his trouser leg. Whose foot was it? It could have been either woman's. He felt himself surrounded by the forces of estrogen . . .

"Hold it," he said. He leaned across the table. "If we're going to be criminals, let's at least be clever ones." He took the lighter and blew out the flame. "Perhaps there are other things you'd like to see changed in there."

Emmy smiled. "Now you're talking." She picked up the will and began thumbing the pages. "As a matter of fact, I wasn't going to mention it, but there is one clause that's always bothered me . . ."

Pelligrew leaned back. His cheeks were smarting. He looked at Lilah, who smiled at him innocently. You bitch, he thought. *Fuck you,* she mouthed at him. His heart skipped a beat. Oh, God, she was wonderful!

"Ah, here it is," said Emmy. "Section two, paragraph one. It says here that the estate shall have two executrices. One is myself, the other is Lilah. Now it seems to me that's very impractical."

"Why?" said Lilah.

"Well, because it just is, darling. Take my word—you're too inexperienced. I think I know better how these funds should be allocated. And I am your mother. I don't want to fight over it."

There was an abrupt change in weather. Lilah grew petulant. "I don't see where age has anything to do with it."

"Well, it certainly does, sweetie. Ask Donald, he'll tell you. Now we've gotten you your money; let Mommy have hers, darling."

Pelligrew sat staring at them. This was absolutely fascinating. Not the fact that they were greedy, but that they were so damned civilized. He also noticed that the invisible foot was back. In fact, now there were two feet—one in each trouser leg.

"Explain to her, Donald."

"Explain what?" said Pelligrew.

"Explain why she's entirely too young to be executrix. It's just a minuscule change. It could be done with an ink blot. And it's not as if there's any question of cheating her."

"That's right," said Pelligrew.

"It is not," said Lilah.

The foot on Emmy's side grew more affectionate. The foot on Lilah's side was beginning to hurt. The blade of the toenail was gouging his ankle bone.

"On the other hand—" he said, and suddenly both feet stopped. They poised like animals on the edge of a clearing. "On the other hand," he said, "maybe both of you are right. Maybe there's a way that will benefit all of us."

The feet hung fire. They seemed to be waiting.

"Like what?" said Emmy.

"I don't know. Let me think about it."

"I want to be executrix!"

"I don't know. Let me think about it. I'll discuss it with each of you. On alternate evenings, preferably."

There was a moment's hesitation while the women evaluated.

Both feet had scuttled back to wherever they had come from. Pelligrew reached down and rubbed his shinbone. Somebody around here could sure stand a good pedicure.

"Now if you'll excuse me," he said, "I really do have to pee." He slid back his chair and stood up from the table. "If you see our waiter, ask for the check. I'll be back in a moment. This is all very interesting."

Oh, hot diggity! he thought as he advanced toward the bar section, his psyche reeling with lust and intrigue—this had all the elements of an old James M. Cain novel: incest . . . perversion . . . a touch of larceny . . . He went into the men's room. His nerve ends were tingling. The only problem was, he had no control of things. That would have to be changed. They were dealing with The Phantom, and when you deal with The Phantom, you're playing with dynamite.

"You know, someday," Elizabeth, his ex-wife, had told him once, "you're going to run into a female who's even nastier than you are. And when you do, I just hope I'm around to see it. I hope she hands you your balls, you are such a first-class son of a bitch." The Phantom had just smiled. Let them rail and rant. He was used to living on the knife edge of danger. There wasn't a woman alive who could get the better of him. He was cool. He was cunning. He was also not urinating straight.

He zipped up his fly and exited the men's room. His shins were still smarting from where the toenails had gouged him. He was also still bruised from that woman with her shopping cart. Sex can be fun, but it takes a lot out of you.

"Excuse me," he said. He pointed to a barstool. Instead of turning right, he had turned to the left. Emmy and Lilah were still sitting in the back. He could just make them out over the heads of the beer drinkers. "This taken?" he said.

Shaughnessy turned. "No, take it," he muttered.

Pelligrew sat down. He nodded to Gronsky, then grinned at Shaughnessy. "Interesting place. Masculine atmosphere."

By now the other two were pretty well crocked—or at least Shaughnessy was, Gronsky didn't show it. Shaughnessy had begun to list to the right. His eyelids drooped. He had a hard time focusing.

The bartender approached.

"I'll have a Glenlivet," said Pelligrew. "You can put it on the check of those two ladies in the back. Give these two a drink and put them on there, too. It's turnabout day. The girls pay for everything."

Shaughnessy squinted. "What girls?" he said.

Pelligrew pointed. "Those two back there. The older one's celebrating the death of her husband. It's an old ethnic custom. They buy drinks for everyone."

By now the clock was approaching three. The crowd had thinned, leaving a haze of cigar smoke. Shaughnessy leaned forward and peered through the mist. Between elbows and beer mugs he could see Emmy's hairdo.

"I know her," he said. "That's Emmy Schoenstein."

"Hmmmm," said Pelligrew. "The one with her's her daughter."

"She's a cunt," said Shaughnessy. "I know all about her. Lee used to tell me. She made him miserable."

Gronsky was still polishing his memory of yesterday. For some reason or other, he couldn't get rid of it. Whenever the rest of his mind went dormant, he remembered that body and the article he had read about it.

"Schoenstein?" he said.

"My late boss's widow. First-class bitch. An amoral golddigger. I had dinner with them once, she tried to put the make on me. I was never so embarrassed. I had to get the hell out of there."

Pelligrew grinned. Oh, this was going to be perfect! His mind raced forward in anticipation. Try to play games with The Phantom, would they? They would soon find out they were toying with a mastermind!

Shaughnessy scowled. His head nodded slightly. "Tell her," he said, "I don't want her damn alcohol. The man was my friend. He was the best friend I had. I consider her behavior immoral and nauseating."

"Schoenstein," said Gronsky. "That sounds familiar . . ."

"I agree," said Pelligrew. "She's a terrible woman. She's back there right now divvying up the inheritance. It's a disgusting scene. I wanted no part of it."

"Cunt," snarled Shaughnessy.

"Schoenstein," said Gronsky. "There was an obituary this morning in the New York *Times* . . ."

"Hey, bartender," said Pelligrew. "Give us another one. And make that guy's vodka a Stolichnaya."

The fire grew hotter. The minutes passed. Pelligrew squirmed. He could hardly wait. Eventually those women would have to come out of there, and the only exit was right past his lookout post.

"Let me tell you," said Shaughnessy, "what I think of that bitch. I may be many things, sir, but I am not disloyal. Lee Schoenstein was a man of consummate integrity. It is unseemly and uncivilized to desecrate his memory."

"There was an obituary," said Gronsky, "in the New York-*Times* . . ."

"That's the one," said Pelligrew. "Cerebral hemorrhage."

"And I saw that happen! He was lying on the floor. It was a terrible thing. We all stepped over him . . ."

Pelligrew nodded. He looked at his watch. They certainly were taking their sweet old time back there. How long did they think it would take him to urinate? He'd teach them a thing or two about upmanship.

The clock jumped forward. Now there was movement. They were rising from the table and gathering their wraps. Emmy had apparently settled with the waiter. Pelligrew turned and leaned his back against the bar rail.

"In fact," said Shaughnessy, "say what you like, sir, but I do not accept liquor from *any* woman! I'll go further than that. Say what you will, sir, but I do not believe women should be allowed in this atmosphere!"

Emmy and Lilah were now approaching them. They were cutting the mist like two angry schooners. Having no alternative but to pass through the bar, they heaved to starboard and ran a collision course.

"I suppose," said Emmy, "you think that was cute."

Pelligrew smiled. "I believe you two know each other."

"H'lo, Ted," said Emmy.

"Ng," grunted Shaughnessy.

"I must say, Donald, that was typically childish of you."

"Eshcuse me," said Shaughnessy. He was beginning to slur now.

"We're leaving," said Emmy. "Are you coming with us?"

"I can't," said Pelligrew. "I just ordered a drink."

"So I see," said Emmy. "And made me pay for it."

"Eshcuse me!" said Shaughnessy. He was raising his voice now. He turned and stared blearily at Emmy's left shoulder. "No impertinence or what-have-you intended, madam, but I have never asked a woman to pay for anything!"

Emmy looked at him. "You're drunk," she said.

"The man was my friend. I will not have him desecrated. Bartender!" he cried. "I refuse this drink! Dump it all out! It is against my principles!"

"I must say," said Emmy, "you choose lovely friends, Don."

Pelligrew smiled. The thought appealed to him.

"A drunken Irishman and whoever this other one is. If Levi were here, he would not appreciate it."

"If Levi were here"—it was Shaughnessy speaking; he was staring strabismically at the drink being poured for him—"if Levi were here, I would be forced to speak plainly! Enough said on that. Now we know where we stand, madam!"

"Pardon me," said Gronsky, who up to now had just gawked at them. He stood up briefly, offering his barstool. Emmy glowered at him, and he sat back down again. "I'm sorry," he said. "I had nothing against the man."

"Good for you."

"I didn't mean to kick him. If it weren't for the crowd, I would have tried to do something. You know what that's like—it's like a stampede of buffalo. And I had had a bad day because of Revlon and mouse repellant . . ."

Emmy looked at Pelligrew. "Who the hell is this idiot?"

"Alex," said Gronsky. "Alex Gronsky. Only I still don't know why he was in the lobby of the Pan Am Building. Why should he be there unless he was catching a commuter train?"

Emmy turned to Lilah. "Come on, dear, we're leaving."

"Wait a minute," said Pelligrew, "you haven't answered his question. It's a simple question. I see nothing wrong with it. What was he doing in the lobby of wherever-it-was?"

Gronsky scowled. "See, it's a long crazy story—a mistake, of course, a misunderstanding—but I was telling Bob Martin how I stepped on his hat, and then I got worried because his wife might be waiting for him." He blinked at Lilah. "Pleased to meet you," he said. "See, a man works all day, he gets locked into doing things. Then suddenly he discovers that nobody cares. I don't understand how you women can think that way."

"What way?" said Emmy.

"That's what I'd like to know," said Shaughnessy. He had his drink now and he was dropping in ice cubes. "All those hours I spent on the subway. She didn't care. She had no conception of it."

"Mother," said Lilah, "what are they talking about?"

"I have no idea."

"About women," said Pelligrew. "It's perfectly obvious. We're talking about women. Hang around bars and you're likely to hear such topics."

Emmy looked at him. "You've really got chutzpah, don't you?"

"See, I figured," said Gronsky, "that if he was taking the subway . . ."

"Well, he wasn't," said Shaughnessy. "I know where he was going. He was going to the bakery. There's a bakery in the train station."

"A bakery?" said Gronsky.

"Donald, we're leaving."

"But why would he go to a bakery in the train station?"

"To pick up some bagels for these two grateful ladies. There, I've said it. Make what you will of it."

Emmy sighed. "I feel nauseous," she muttered.

"Have a sip," said Pelligrew. "Might as well, you paid for it. You, too, Lilah. It's called Glenlivet. It's entirely different. It's got a kind of a peaty odor . . ."

Pelligrew was delirious. Oh, this was fantastic! Try to blackmail him into changing a will, would they? He had the advantage, and now he was pressing it. His sexual desire grew angry and lethal-edged.

"I thought," said Emmy, "we had reached an agreement."

"We have," said Pelligrew. "Our sex has been persecuted. We've agreed that women have no understanding of us. Don't ask me. I have no explanation for it."

"You bastard," snarled Lilah, who up to now had remained sidelined, her eyes flashing out in a stiletto fury. "Just who the hell do you think you are? Do you think you can fuck everybody and get away with it?"

Pelligrew just smiled. It was the strangest feeling. It had started as a joke, but now it was more than that. His lust had hardened into something frightening. He wanted to hurt them. He wanted to humiliate them.

"Who, me?" he said, shrugging.

"Well, you can't, goddamn it! Christy Mathewson! That didn't fool me! I happen to have been on the Dalton softball team! I knew who he was. I knew you were lying to me!"

There was a moment's lull. The bar crowd turned. Lilah, shouting, was flushed in the cheeks. "You'll stick your prick into anything that moves! You've had your fun, now you can damn well pay for it!"

"Hey, hey," said the bartender, "we'll have no more of that talk . . ."

"This son of a bitch owes me ten thousand dollars! He's screwed my mother, he's screwed half of New York. It's the least he can do. A bargain's a bargain, damn it!"

"Calm down," said Emmy.

"I will not calm down!"

"There'll be no solicitations in this bar," said the bartender.

"Solicitation! Is that what you call it? He's a goddamn bastard! I want him to pay for it!"

Pelligrew just stood there. It was the weirdest phenomenon. Later he would liken it to a shifting of platelets. He was a man and among men. These women were aliens. They were hostile invaders. He had nothing in common with them.

"Well, if you know so damn much about baseball . . ." he said.

Lilah shrieked. "I'm not talking about baseball!"

"What was Walter Johnson's lifetime won-lost record? Who did he play for? What hand did he throw with?"

"For that matter," said Gronsky, "who did Mathewson play for?"

"I don't know," cried Lilah, "and I frankly don't give a shit!"

"Well, then don't try to pass yourself off as an expert," said Pelligrew. "This is a men's saloon. You better watch what you say in here."

The men exchanged looks. It was like a spark of combustion. It was like a flash of lightning between poles of a generator. They had something in common! They had *themselves* in common! An invisible bond! A secret fraternity!

Lilah glowered. "I hate your guts."

"You didn't seem to hate them when you were playing footsie with me."

"That's a lie!" said Lilah.

"Then it must have been your mother."

"That's a lie!" said Emmy.

"You're a very sick man, Donald."

"To sickness!" cried Shaughnessy.

"This is outrageous . . ."

"To sickness and death! Long may they prosper!"

"I used to think I could call you my friend, Donald. Now I see otherwise. I just feel sorry for you."

Pelligrew shrugged. "Walter Johnson," he said. "Walter 'Big Train' Johnson of the Washington Senators. Four hundred and fourteen lifetime major-league victories. I don't know about you, but I'd feel honored to be screwed by him."

"Come on, Lilah . . ."

"And what about Christy Mathewson? Hell, he was a legend—the inventor of the screwball! Poisoned by nerve gas in World War One. You ought to be ashamed. He gave his life for you!"

The women retreated.

"You're sick!" cried Lilah.

"To sickness!" cried Shaughnessy.

"This whole goddamn bar's sick!"

The door opened and closed. There was a swirl of cigar smoke. The men leaned back. They had never felt happier.

Part Two

9

"Alex? Is that you?"

Gronsky nodded. It was one of those old wooden phone booths with the glass-panel doors in it. He had tried to close them, but the rollers were off. The bar noise competed with the voice on the telephone line.

"Where are you calling from? I've been trying to reach you."

"How ya doin?" he said.

"I left three messages for you. Daddy called. He's not very happy, Alex. You missed two appointments and an important client meeting."

O'Lunney's at this hour was like a crate of asparagus. There was no lateral freedom, all energy was vertical. On a makeshift stage there was a band playing hillbilly music. Through the spider-webbed glass he could see Shaughnessy gesturing to him.

"How ya doin?" he shouted.

"What do you mean, how am I doing? Alex, where are you? Do you know what time it is? Daddy called. Do you hear what I'm telling you? The account man at Needham's is absolutely furious with you."

Gronsky said nothing. It was like being gnawed in a wolf's jaw. Shaughnessy had his nose pressed flat against the door panel. One hand was outspread like a ganglion with suction cups. He was moving his lips in a contortion of guppy spasms.

"Where's Bobby?" said Gronsky.

"What do you mean, 'Where's Bobby?' "

"I gotta talk to him. Iss estremely important, Mandy."

"Alex, are you drunk?"

"We're gonna go to the game on Sunday. Giants an' Steelers. Iss important discuss it with him."

This was the sixth bar they had been to in the past seven hours. They had started at Clarke's and worked their way southward. It was not a quick drunk, but it was a sure and cumulative one. Shaughnessy, on wine, was becoming increasingly unmanageable.

"Look, Alex—" said Mandy.

"I wanna talk to my son, Mandy."

"It's ten after eleven. Let's try to be reasonable, shall we?"

"I am being reasonable. I haven't seen him since yesserday. Jiss put him on the phone. I gotta tell him whass happenin down here."

Up until now, the evening had been glorious—spectacular. How long since they had known the company of men together? The acerbity of wit. The exchange of insults. The ability to see humor in the most unlikely subject matter. Gronsky, transported, was reminded of his college days—feet stained with alum, the wet snap of shower towels . . . That's the trouble with women—they have no sense of irony. If you tease them, they cry. They take things so literally.

"Listen, Alex," said Mandy, "it is ten after eleven. I've got to get up. I've got a busy day tomorrow. Mrs. Lawrence is sick, and I've got to take Bobby to his den meeting. I've got an appointment at nine. I've got to go down to White Plains sometime . . ."

Gronsky squinted. Images arose. Instead of listening, he was peering through a keyhole at her. He could see her face. He could picture their bedroom. He could imagine the sweet smell of cologne from her nightgown bodice.

"Where's Ingrid?" he said.

"I beg your pardon?"

"You heard me. Where's Ingrid? She around? Can I talk to her?"

"Alex, be reasonable."

"I am bein reasonable. I jiss wanna know. No need to get mad about it."

Earlier that evening, in yet another gin mill, he had regaled Pelligrew and Shaughnessy about this incredible maid he had hired. Her name was Ingrid, and she was absolutely beautiful. She was better than beautiful—she was a liberated Swedish girl!

"Look, Alex," said Mandy, "I refuse to discuss this with you. Last night when you came home I tried to be reasonable about it. What did you do? You ran off like a crazy person. Now I'm not going to sit here and be degraded by you."

Gronsky said nothing. His throat seemed to tighten. He shifted his weight on the tiny phone booth stool. More images arose, only now they were ugly images: legs and hair and hot liquid tongues darting . . .

"I jiss wanna know . . ."

"I'm going to hang up, Alex."

"I jiss wanna know if she's in our damn bedroom, Mandy! I'll tell you sump'n—she is very untrustworthy. She's a dishonest bitch. She goes down on tree surgeons . . ."

Oh God, this was the last thing he had wanted to get involved in. All he had really wanted to do was hear the sound of her voice again. He hunched his back, cupped his hand around the mouthpiece. A gorge of fear rose up from his solar plexus.

"I am going to hang up . . ."

"She goes down on tree surgeons . . . She goes down on niggers, on children, on donkeys probably . . . She doesn't care about you. All she cares about's Marxism. She told me herself. I refused to listen to it . . ."

There was a click, then a hum. Gronsky stared at the telephone. "Hello? . . . Hello? . . ." Had she hung up? Apparently. He reached in his pocket. He had six quarters, two dimes left. The phone rang three times. She was back on the line again.

"You said come to New York. Okay, I came to New York, Mandy. I took the motherfuckin job at that motherfuckin magazine. What did it get me? It made me a toady, damn it! 'I'd like you to meet Alex. He was with the old Woody Hayes outfit . . .' "

"Alex, are you through?"

"Thass what your father says! 'This is my son-in-law. He was with the old Woody Hayes outfit.' Shit! I was a washout nose guard at Miami University, Mandy! It was Hayes's alma mater, but about thirty years earlier, thass all . . ."

There was another click. Now there was a man's voice.

"I'm sorry," it said. *"To continue speaking . . ."*

Gronsky rooted through his pockets. He had seventy cents left. He dropped in fifty. The receiver made belching noises.

"I do hope you're through . . ."

"I went through two years at Quantico, Mandy!"

"I do hope you're through—I'd like to tell you how I feel . . ."

"I wasn't called up, but I knew plenty who were, and the Swedes are over there calling us fascists and war mongers . . ."

From New York to Mount Kisco is about thirty-five miles. The phone lines parallel the tracks of the commuter system. Two souls ran counter through the twisted wire cabling, like two express trains on a head-on collision course.

"I feel absolutely nothing. Do you hear what I'm saying, Alex?"

"And who the hell's Sweden? What did they ever do?" cried Gronsky.

"Zero. Zilch. I don't even feel angry with you . . ."

"—besides roll over for Hitler . . ."

"All I do is feel sorry for you!"

Gronsky sat grimacing. His windpipe was clotted. He fumbled through his pockets. He pulled out a Viceroy. He tried to light it, but his hands were trembling. In fumbling with the matches, he almost dropped the phone receiver.

"Seventeen years! That's how long we've been married, Alex. You want me to be the bad guy? Okay, I'll play bad guy for you. I am thirty-nine years old. Do you know what that means, Alex? Maybe it's chemical. Maybe it's a medical problem . . ."

"Iss not—" said Gronsky. His head was spinning.

"The age-old cop-out—women and their hormone problems . . . But whatever it is, it is real, and I am living with it. I can't go on being an obedient nonentity to you."

There was another click. The man's voice came back.

"I'm sorry . . ." it said.
"Jesus Christ!" cried Gronsky.
"To continue speaking . . ."
"I DON'T HAVE ANY MONEY LEFT! ALL I GOT'S TWENTY CENTS! GET OFF THE GODDAMN LINE, YOU IDIOT!"
"You want to blame this on Ingrid? Okay, go ahead. If that's what you're after, I'll admit I'm attracted to her. But it's more than that. It's like a whole new life out there. There's no law that says we have to sit in our cells forever . . ."
"You're not in a cell—"
"It's like a goddamn cell, Alex!"
"I'm sorry . . ." said the voice.
"It's like a goddamn prison cell! What am I supposed to do, just curl up and die somewhere? My God, I'm a woman! I'm young and I'm a woman, damn it!"
Gronsky just sat there. His eyes were clamped shut. His lips were parted, and there was a strand of saliva on them. The only world he knew was what was coming through that phone line, and in another few seconds it would all be cut off from him.
"I'll make it up . . ."
"You wouldn't know how, Alex."
"I'll take you to Florida. We could stop and see Disney World . . ."
"Oh, Jesus, Alex! This is really beyond you, isn't it? Let's call it a night. I've got to get up tomorrow . . ."
"No, wait! Please don't . . ."
"I'm sorry . . ." said the voice.
"For Christ's sake!" cried Gronsky.
"To continue speaking . . ."
"What am I supposed to do? Where am I supposed to go, Mandy? I can't stay here. You got my house, you got my child with you . . ."
There was another click.
"I WANNA COME HOME, MANDY!"
Armatures closing—then a void—then a dial tone.

Gronsky just sat there. The hum was deafening. In the background the band was playing an old Hank Williams number.

"Forgive me," said Shaughnessy, reaching for a cigarette. The package was empty, and he threw it on the floor. He patted his pockets, but he was totally out. He helped himself to one of Gronsky's Viceroys. "Forgive me," he said, "but you're gonna have to revise it, Alex. Iss a good idea, but iss already been done before. Fediddle the margins. Rerun it through the typewriter. As it is, I'm sorry, but iss ole Woody Allen material."

The room in which they were sitting was on the eleventh floor. It was more than a room, it was a moderate-sized suite. To the north it looked out over lower Central Park, which at this time of night looked ink-splotched and guerrilla-infested. Gronsky said nothing. He hadn't quite caught it. Three pairs of feet merged like spokes on the coffee table. From the center of the hub rose an obelisk of alcohol. It had a sacred look, as if it had been left by a Druid colony.

"Whaddaya mean?" said Gronsky.

"Iss too derivative. 'My wife has left me for another woman.' No, no, no, thass a line out of whaddayacallit. Iss a seventies cliché. You'll have to make it a horse or sump'n."

How long had they been there? It seemed like hours. They had left O'Lunney's and walked back up to Weston's, and from there they had stopped in for a drink at the St. Regis, and by one they were meandering north up Fifth Avenue. "You kidding?" said Pelligrew. "You got a room at the Plaza?" Well, no, admitted Gronsky, it was not really *his* room, but he sometimes used it as a pied-à-terre. You know how it is—it gets late, there's a lady maybe . . . Oh, sure. Oh, sure, they knew how *that* was. Big Alex Gronsky, King of the Ass Bandits. So they had gone up to his room, ordered a bottle from room service, and now they were relaxing—living like gentlemen, thank you.

"You don't understand."

"I unnerstan perfectly. On a hot summer night Seventh Avenue's crawlin with em. They kiss on the street. Iss like a fuckin carnival. I saw a couple in the Riv, they were fondling their nipples together."

"That may be, but that has nothing to do—"

"You asked my opinion—okay, I gave it to you. Iss an old, old story. I'm tired of listening to it. Take my advice—change the maid to a horse or sump'n."

Dealing with Shaughnessy could be a difficult experience. Drinks three through six made him witty and affable. Drinks seven through ten made him gloomy and cynical, and anything beyond that led off into chaos somewhere. Tonight was worse because he had tried to be cautious. After five or six Cutties he had switched over to Almadén. After that he had had coffee, after that he had had Perrier, after that he had had brandy, and now he was back on the Cutty again.

"This is not a movie—"

"Don't tell me!" cried Shaughnessy. "They wouldn't accept it. They'd call in a rewrite man. You asked my opinion—okay, I gave it to you. Get rid of the maid. You gotta make her a horse or sump'n."

Through the damask-draped windows there was a glow on the horizon—a faint gradation, like the glare from a coke furnace. Gronsky leaned back and held his glass against his forehead. He would have liked to go to sleep, but the idea terrified him.

"What's her number?" said Pelligrew.

"Whose?" said Gronsky.

"You know. The maid. The one we were talking about."

"Whaddaya mean, whass her number?"

"I thought maybe I could talk to her. I could tell her I'm Swedish. I could get information from her."

"I'll say this," said Shaughnessy. "In a way, you're fortunate. At least when they're lesbians, you know where you stand with em. If Sarah had been a lesbian, it would have been a whole lot easier for me. Thass my trouble. She was too goddamn normal for me."

"They're not—" said Gronsky.

"Where she live?" said Pelligrew.

"Who?" said Gronsky.

"The maid. This Ingrid person."

"Whaddaya mean, where she live?"

"I was just wondering how far it is. How far is it? A half hour? An hour maybe?"

Gronsky stared at him.

"You're fortunate—" said Shaughnessy.

"It's in northern Westchester."

"Yeah, I know, but how far is it?"

"You're fortunate," said Shaughnessy. "I wish Sarah had been a lesbian. It would have made it all easier. It would have helped explain everything to me."

Know this about Pelligrew: It was the late nights that got him. He could go all day and be in reasonable control of himself, but when darkness fell and the loneliness set in, it was as if somebody had injected him with an extract of rhino horn.

"We could take a train . . ."

"We are not going up there."

"No, listen. I'm serious. What time do the trains stop running? We could be up there by three. You could say I was a friend or something. We could sit and have coffee. I could give you my assessment of it."

"I'm gonna tell you guys sump'n." Shaughnessy speaking. "Sometimes, toward the end, I couldn't even do it with her. You know what thass like? I'd try. It was miserable. It wouldn't get hard. I'd feel so goddamn guilty about it . . ."

"We are not going up there."

"Then give me her phone number."

"What are you gonna do? What are you gonna say to her?"

"I'm gonna ask where she's sleeping. I'm gonna ask what she's doing tomorrow. I don't know . . . I just know I'm in love with her, Alex."

Gronsky laughed. Well, in a way it was funny. After leaving O'Lunney's he had been so glum, so crestfallen, and when they had gotten to Weston's he had just sat there stone-faced, until finally they had asked, and it had just all poured out of him. He told them about the pot. He told them about the tree surgeon. He told them about the pictures he had found on the coffee table. Finally, begrudgingly, he had told them about Mandy. "I'm not sure," he said softly. "I suppose it's her age, maybe . . ."

Strange the effect that alcohol can have on you. Tired as he was, his mind was accelerating. Images, ideas, injustices, reveries —they all came back. It was like a fast-playing tape recorder.

"You know what it is? Iss this damn women's lib bullshit. I shoulduv seen it. I jiss wasn't prepared for it. We're s'posed to be a team. At least thass the way I figure. You got your line and your backfield. You can't change the rules, can you?"

Oh, God, he was tired. It was well after two now. Shaughnessy was nodding. He was on the verge of unconsciousness. He was sitting in a chair, holding a half glass of Cutty Sark. The floor around the chair was dappled with scotch splatters.

"You don't unnerstan. We're older," said Gronsky. "We got married out of college. We made all these big plans together. I was to come to New York, go to work for my father-in-law. We'd have a house, we'd have kids, it was the whole damn togetherness bit . . ." He leaned back in his seat. His head was aching. He dreaded tomorrow. Tomorrow he'd feel miserable. He'd go to the office, he'd stare at the walls, he'd confront his father-in-law, there'd be another "Dutch uncle" chat . . . "Hell, I didn't mind. It all looked good to me. You know what I'd have been? I'd have been a goddamn used-car salesman. I mean that, Don. I'd have been back in the coal mines, probably. What else was there? All I knew was the football field . . ." He poured another drink. His mind was caroming. Pelligrew sat listening. He too felt miserable. There was nothing but themselves—themselves and that night out there. Beyond those dark windows the boogeyman waited for them . . . "So I decided to marry her. That was right before the 'Nam business. I joined the Marines and spent two years in training camp. Two fuckin years! You know what I did there, Don? I drove the commandant's jeep and played interleague football for em . . ." By now it was three. Shaughnessy bestirred himself. Two bloodshot eyes stared wearily through the haze at them. Gronsky went on. Pelligrew sat stoically. It made no difference, he was talking to the ether now

. . . "I dunno. This is totally beyond me, damn it. All during the sixties I worked my goddamn rear end off for her. Clients, seminars—I wouldn't get home till midnight. The world was on drugs, everyone else was out screwing somewhere . . ." He emptied the bottle. The windows grew gray. "She used to agree. I remember we talked about it. 'Isn't this silly? Now they're burning their bras,' she'd tell me. 'What in the world's happened to virtue and motherhood, Alex?' . . ." Now Shaughnessy was leaving. He was putting on his jacket. Gronsky didn't notice. He had his head against the armrest. He had been drinking since morning, and still he was babbling. It was like trying to climb a hill, with the sand falling back on you . . . "Well, I'll tell you," he said, "she can do what she wants to, damn it. I'm not kidding. The whole idea nauseates me. You know whass gonna happen? She's gonna ask my forgiveness. Only I won't give it. She can ask, I won't give it, damn it . . ." And now there was just Pelligrew. Gronsky and Pelligrew. Pelligrew, who himself had his own kind of cross to bear. By the time he left, the sun was coming up. He would still like to know when the trains stopped running.

10

Shaughnessy had no car, had no money to rent one. He and Jaime had to get there from Brooklyn by subway train. Pelligrew had no car, but he did have a motorcycle. He drove over to Elizabeth's, perched Jeremy in the passenger's seat. Gronsky had a car. He had been keeping it at the Plaza. That, too, he had hoped could be buried in his expense account. He drove up to Mount Kisco, came back by the Saw Mill, crossed the Tappan Zee Bridge, and got lost near Hoboken.

Be that as it may, they were all there by game time. They met at the gate and ascended the ramp together—Bobby in his jersey, Jeremy with a helmet on, Jaime, in jeans, wearing a fake fur battle jacket.

"Now, you see," said Gronsky, when they had all gotten settled, the six of them in a row above the thirty-five-yard line, "the Giants won the toss, so they'll be electing to receive. You always receive, unless there's an unusual wind condition."

It was a bright, cloudless day—a paradigm of autumn. Pennants fluttered in a rhapsody of father sounds. Below them, the Astroturf unfurled like a billiard table; above them, a scoreboard flashed computerized "Charge!" signs at them.

The other night, when they were discussing their children, Pelligrew and Shaughnessy had begun arguing about parenthood. It was Shaughnessy's opinion that daughters were "different," and that men who had sons had it easier than he did. "That's bullshit," said Pelligrew. "Kids are just kids, Ted." "Forgive me," said Shaughnessy, "but a female has brain differences," and he had launched into some gobbledygook about cerebral hemispheres and an article he had read on South

American squirrel monkeys. He was good at such logic. He could totally astound you with it. "You take elbows," he would say. "You ever looked at a girl's elbows lately? They have an entirely different structure. They're for carrying water buckets. If you ever had a daughter, then you'd know what I'm talking about."

Now, next to Jaime, Shaughnessy seemed quieter than usual. It was as if he had no idea how to relate to her. She, for her part, seemed to idolize her father, but when she tried to engage him, he'd just turn his back on her.

Toward the end of the first quarter, Jeremy had to pee. "What else," sighed Pelligrew. "Excuse . . . coming through, please . . ." Then Bobby, then Jaime, then Shaughnessy, then Jeremy again, so that by the time the sides changed it had become a rotating traffic pattern. That was all right. Then Bobby wanted popcorn. "We'll have hot dogs," said Gronsky. Yeah, but Jeremy had a pretzel earlier. Well, all right, they'd buy popcorn, only he'd better not waste any, and he'd better not get sick, because you know how your mother feels . . .

By the time the half came, the kids were getting restless. There was a torrent of people funneling out toward the food concessions. Jeremy disappeared and Pelligrew went after him. Shaughnessy got up and took Bobby to the men's room with him.

"Well, whaddaya think?" This was Gronsky to Jaime now. It was the first time today he had had a chance to talk to her. Hands in pockets, she sat slouched in her bleachers seat. Her hair was swept back like an *au courant* movie star's.

" 'sokay," she said.

"We're eatin em up, huh?"

"Guess so," she said. "Where did my father go?"

"Men's room, somewhere . . . Hey, did you see what those Giants did? They used a triple formation. You don't see them do that much."

Had Picasso been present, some connoisseur of light, he might have noticed the way the shadows crisscrossed, bisecting Jaime's brow and running off toward her jawline, giving her small ovate face a sort of stained-glass madonna quality. Gronsky leaned back. Gosh, today had been wonderful! This morning, upon seeing Bobby, his heart had exploded. *"Dad!"* Bobby had shouted, and he had come running full tilt at him, his short stubby legs moving like rods in a steam engine.

When Bobby was first born, Gronsky had not felt much tenderness toward him. He was such a small little thing—what on earth could you do with him? Gronsky would pick him up, he'd burp him or diaper him, he'd pace back and forth, try to keep the kid's head from rolling. It got better later on. By three, he was cute. When Gronsky built their deck, Bobby had held all the nails for him. There was a kind of rivalry—a competitive mimicry. Whatever Gronsky did, Bobby was sure to imitate him. Now that too was gone—there was more independence there. It was at this stage that Gronsky really wanted to feel closer to him, but it was as if all those late hours, all that time spent on Conrail, had driven them apart, and only absence could join them again.

Jaime scowled. She sat fingering her charm bracelet. It was a small gold chain with a heart and a cross on it. The heart said "Jaime." The cross had a stone in it. She held up the cross, seemed to peer along the transept of it.

"You know what I do?"

"No, what?" said Gronsky.

"I live in the subways."

Gronsky smiled, looked benignly at her.

"I mean it. I do. I live in the subway system. I'm studying to be a rat. Ask me anything you want about it."

Gronsky said nothing. There was a half-time ceremony. One of the local high school bands was playing a medley of John Lennon numbers. A banner of The Beatles was strung out along the hash marks. Bass horns harumphed to the melody of "Yesterday."

"You don't believe me."

"I believe you," said Gronsky.

"I leave in the morning. I catch the Two or the Three train. I go to Times Square and cross over to the Flushing Line. I catch an eastbound Seven and ride clear out to Queens on it."

Gronsky nodded. Ah, the ceremonies of parenthood! He had seen it earlier between Pelligrew and Jeremy: Pelligrew bent sideways, his expression solicitous, listening attentively to whatever Jeremy was whispering to him.

"It takes an hour. I'm counting the waiting time. Then I come back on an F and get off at Forty-seventh Street. I cross over, get a D and go up to the Bronx, and I come back on a CC and take a Four down to Bleecker Street."

"Want a hot dog?" said Gronsky.

"You don't believe me."

"I believe you," said Gronsky. "C'mon, I'll buy you something."

"There's this guy in our school, he does it all on one subway token. Two hundred miles. It takes him a day and a night, he told me."

Down the steps, out through the portals, down the ramp into the echoing concourse, Gronsky following, Jaime in front of him, the Y of her legs auguring first signs of womanhood. "I tell you," said Shaughnessy (this was two days earlier; they were talking on the phone, which was becoming a habit with them; either Gronsky would call Shaughnessy, or Pelligrew would call Gronsky, and they would talk for hours like women at a hen party), "I tell you," he said, "she's beginning to scare me, Gronk. Last summer at the beach she had the lifeguards looking at her. What am I gonna do? She's too young to handle it. By the time she's twelve she'll be like a ewe in rutting season." And Gronsky had said nothing, because there was nothing he could say, because fathers always exaggerate their daughters' attractiveness, but now, beside her, standing at the food concession, he had to admit that such fears might be justified.

"Where'd you two meet?"

"Who's that?" said Gronsky.

"You and my father. How long have you known each other?"

"Oh, heck, we go back. Your old man's a character. I could tell you stories, only I'm afraid you're too young for them."

Jaime nodded. "Probably," her look said. Her jacket was unzipped and she was wearing a work shirt. The first three buttons were unbuttoned to the sternum. Shaughnessy was right. There were the beginnings of breast formation.

"You hang around bars?"

"Beg pardon?" said Gronsky.

"You and my father. He hangs around bars a lot. Mom says he's a drunk. I don't believe that. Besides, so what? He's got to do something, doesn't he?"

Gronsky bought her a hot dog. Now in line at the condiments counter, Gronsky trying to cope with a clog in the mustard spout, Jaime wanting relish, sucking the strands of her sauerkraut, dribbling the onions, getting mustard all over the place.

"My mom goes to bars. She goes on Wednesdays and Saturdays. Those are the biggies. I call em her 'nooky nights.' She's scared to death she's gonna run into my father there. I wish she would. That'd be funny, wouldn't it?"

Gronsky didn't answer.

"You pick up girls?"

"I beg your pardon?"

"When you hang around bars together."

"Well, no—I don't know . . . . We just talk. We just talk a lot . . . . Hey, watch what you're doing. You're getting relish all over you, Jaime."

When he was a kid back in Steubenville (this was in the late 1940s now) there had been a young girl named Laury who used to come to their football practices. By the time she was twelve, she was a walking marriage manual. She knew everything there was, and used to impart it all freely to him. Now, decades later, standing at that coffee counter, towering like a bear in his alpaca-lined car coat, it was as if the last thirty years had done nothing to educate him. The perversity of girls was an abiding enigma to him.

"My mom picks up men."

"Good for her," said Gronsky.

"She does it all the time. Particularly since Dad's been gone. There's this bartender, Tito—he's spent the last three nights with her. He's okay. Sorta dumb. I told her she oughta start chargin for it."

Gronsky said nothing. He looked at his wristwatch.

"One of these days I'm gonna just not come home," said Jaime. "I'm gonna get on a subway and ride off to eternity on it. You can do that, you know. You can turn into a skeleton on it."

A buzzer sounded.

"About finished?" said Gronsky.

"My father's all right. He's just a good ole Irish lad. In a coupla years I think I might move in with him. I told my mother. She just laughs. 'Go ahead!' she told me."

"Let's go," said Gronsky.

"She doesn't believe me. My father needs me. Have you seen where he's living lately? I could fix that up. We could paint it and wallpaper it. We'd get along great. I could cook all his dinners for him."

They began to move out.

"He's got room, he's got room," said Jaime. "Right now it's a mess, but I could move all my things in there. You just wait. I already discussed this with him. We've made big plans. It's just a matter of time, he told me."

By now the stadium was beginning to fill up again. They filed out through the portals and back up to the grandstand area. The band had left, the teams were returning. Was it Gronsky's imagination, or had it begun to cloud over somewhat?

"It's not the same."

"What do you mean?" said Gronsky.

"I mean just what I'm saying. She's a girl. She's built different."

"Aw, come on!" said Gronsky. "You know that's not true, Ted. She's a confused little kid. She needs a mother *and* a father, damn it."

They were heading west across the Brooklyn Bridge. It was beginning to get dark, and the cars had their headlights on. Beside him, Shaughnessy was fiddling with the radio dial. The spires of Manhattan rose like so many vacuum tubes.

When the game was over and they were out in the parking lot, "Don't be silly," said Gronsky, "—let me give you a lift, you two," and Shaughnessy and Jaime had gladly accepted, and they had driven up to Westchester to drop Bobby at his mother's house. Two hours later, they were back down in Brooklyn. Sarah, Shaughnessy's ex, lived in a brownstone on Henry Street. "Come on up," said Shaughnessy, motioning to Gronsky, and they had all gotten out and climbed the stairs up to Sarah's place.

It was a large apartment, spartanly furnished. There was an eat-in kitchen and a room with a skylight in it. Sarah smiled warmly and offered Gronsky some leftovers. He was genuinely impressed by both her wit and her sex appeal.

"Yeah, well don't let that fool you," was Shaughnessy's opinion when they were back in the car and turning left onto Fulton Street. "She may look like Betty Crocker, but, believe me, she's not. I have reason to suspect she's being pretty promiscuous."

Gronsky said nothing. He was thinking about Jaime. Something in that laugh, that pubescent bravado act. Finally, when they had turned and were on the bridge toward Manhattan, he took out a cigarette and confessed what was bothering him.

"You know, I was talking to Jaime. She thinks a lot of you, Ted."

Shaughnessy said nothing. He stared at the bridge cables.

"She doesn't seem happy. I think she needs you. I think maybe she'd like it if she could spend more time with you."

"Won't work," said Shaughnessy.

"What do you mean, it won't work?"

"Just won't. I know. She's an eleven-year-old girl, Alex. You've seen how I live. It's all a big fantasy to her. What am I gonna do, take her down to the White Horse with me?"

Gronsky shrugged. "I'm just trying to suggest—"

"It's not the same. She's a girl. She's built different. You don't know. You don't have the background for it. I'm talking fact. There's a difference in brain structure." And with that he was off, talking white mice and fetuses, raising academic questions about logic and space relations, mouthing garbled accounts of university studies showing microscopic differences in the bilateral hemispheres. Gronsky just sat there. It was totally inane. He hated it when Shaughnessy got into this science hokum. It was so obviously a smoke screen; it was an excuse for his lassitude. The fact was, Jaime was an unwanted burden to him.

"Let me tell you something," Pelligrew had said one evening as he and Gronsky were sitting alone watching a football game. "I spend about half my life in the Family Court Building. You ever been there? It's on the west side of Chinatown."

Gronsky shook his head. He had never been down there.

"Incredible place. It's like a big black Rubic's cube. And for every petitioner there's a broken promise. They're all other people's dreams who have been turned into nightmares." He propped up his feet. He emptied his beer can. "I'd say fifteen to twenty percent are ex-husband types. They're nice, normal guys whose ex-wives have been screwing them. They've run off with the kids. They've denied visitation to them." He took a swallow. "But that's the minority. In the majority of cases it's the guys who are the assholes. They've cut off support. They're threatening their families. The judges get mad and have to issue restraining orders." Gronsky said nothing. There was a pass interception. "But there's something I've noticed . . . I don't know, it's a theory," said Pelligrew. "In an amazing number of cases, those marriages were shotgun. The man's flaking out because he feels he got snookered somehow."

Now, as the Volvo headed west across Chambers Street, turned right onto Hudson, then back east on West Twelfth Street, Gronsky couldn't help remembering Pelligrew's hypothesis. Poor Jaime, he thought. Poor Shaughnessy. Poor everybody.

11

"Whose car is that?"

"What car?" said Jeremy.

Pelligrew pointed. It was a gray Mercedes. He banked to the left, made a turn in a driveway, circled back around and stopped in front of a neighbor's house.

Gronsky was right—this had been a wonderful day. The second half was even better than the first half, the Steelers roaring back on two fumbles and a punt return, the Giants finally winning on a spectacular aerial play. The men were ecstatic. Even the kids seemed infected. "We won! Did we win?" "Yeah, we won!" "Whoopee!" cried Jeremy—and he had begun jumping up and down and tossing his safety helmet, and on the way to the lot he and Bobby faked pass formations.

Pelligrew's motorcycle was an old BMW. Elizabeth always hated it when he took Jeremy for rides on it. "What are you trying to do, get him killed?" she'd shout at him. Pelligrew would just smile. He enjoyed tormenting her.

"He come here often?"

"Who?" said Jeremy.

"The man with the Mercedes."

"Oh, sure. He's Mom's friend," said Jeremy.

"What's his name?"

"I dunno. Ira something."

"Does he stay all night?"

"Sure. He's here all the time," said Jeremy.

It was a modest-size ranch-style in an upgraded neighborhood. It had an expansive flat lawn and two moderately large oak trees. Pelligrew had bought it back in the early seventies, and it was about the only thing of value Elizabeth had managed to get out of him.

Poor Elizabeth—she was a pretty enough woman, but she had patterned herself into such a stereotype. She was everything blond and proper and ambitious, and the banality of her yearnings had practically suffocated him. Carolina-born, dirt-poor, an orphan, she had met him in Washington during his last year at Georgetown. When he proposed, she accepted, because he was everything desirable. He had looks, he had wealth, he was on his way toward a law degree.

Little had she known that there was another side to Pelligrew—something wilder, brighter, more self-destructive. By the time she had found out they had already left Washington and were ensconced with child in New York's Turtle Bay neighborhood. From there they had moved to Greenwich Village, from Greenwich Village to an apartment in Queens, from Queens to Brooklyn, from Brooklyn to Yonkers, from Yonkers to this ranch-style on the outskirts of Paterson. All within the space of seventeen months! All within the time it took Pelligrew to "adjust." He had changed jobs four times, been dismissed from a fifth, and, in retribution, his parents had disowned him. Well, that was okay. Now he was himself. Now he was the loner, the champion of democracy. If only poor Elizabeth could have shared his enthusiasm, could have known the beauty of being penniless and persecuted!

"You know, it's funny," he was saying as he walked back toward where the car was parked. He opened the door and looked in on the passenger's side. Inside the burled-walnut glove compartment there was a packet with papers in it. The car was registered to a Dr. Ira S. Klimefogler. "It's a funny thing. I was talking to your mother, and she said, 'Don, what would you say if I decided to get married again?' Well, I didn't say anything. It was none of my business, really. She's a grown-up woman. 'You can do what you want,' I told her."

Jeremy said nothing. Pelligrew looked thoughtful.

"Of course, I had to admit there could be some complications to it. Like, 'Wouldn't it be nice if you discussed it with Jeremy first?' I thought that would be nice. I got sort of edgy with her."

Jeremy began scowling. Pelligrew nodded.

"It's a difficult problem. I have no easy answers to it. I mean, I suppose this guy Klimefogler could be a very good father to you. He'd be a good provider—that's what your mother told me."

Jeremy turned away. He was a bit small for his age. With his safety helmet on, he looked like a space creature. Under the glow of the streetlamp, his eyes were glistening. He went over to a fender and began fingering the car antenna.

"That's not true."

"What do you mean?" said Pelligrew.

Jeremy shook his head. "He's not a good father to me. You're my father. He's old. He's my mother's father. I don't like him. I'm not going to listen to him."

So far, so good. Of course he was at a distinct disadvantage here—he had only the weekends in which to exert his influence. The trick was to do it subtly, inconspicuously. He didn't want Elizabeth calling him up and shouting at him.

"Hey, well now look," he said, smiling, leaning back against the door handle, "we gotta face facts here. This is a very rich man, Jeremy. Just look at this car. You always wanted a mini-bike? Here's your chance. This guy could buy mini-bikes for you."

Jeremy pouted. "I don't care," he whimpered.

"Mini-bikes . . . go-carts . . . bicycles . . . computer games . . ."

"I DON'T CARE! I DON'T CARE!" He was beginning to cry now. He let go the antenna and put his head on the trunk lid.

Pelligrew just stood there. All in all, he felt satisfied. Every so often, it was good to test loyalty. Not that it would make that much difference in the long run, but it was nice to know that you still outranked video games.

"Hey, you got any paper?"

"What for?" sniffled Jeremy.

"I need something to write on. I want to try to explain something." He reopened the car door and reached back into the glove compartment. He took out the packet with the car registration in it.

Of course, in fairness to Klimefogler, Pelligrew had never laid eyes on him. For all Pelligrew knew, he was a paragon of saintliness. "I can tell you this—he's kind, he's sweet," said Elizabeth. "He's a compassionate man. That's a lot more than you are, Donald." To which Pelligrew had said nothing, because it was an irrelevant statement. They were talking about a man who was guilty of trespassing. They were talking about a "doctor" who was not really a doctor and who had been sticking his prong into what was rightfully Pelligrew's, damn it!

"Come here," he said. He walked back toward the streetlight. There was a guard rail there, and he plunked himself down on it. Jeremy came over and squatted down next to him. Pelligrew took out a pen and drew three points on the document packet.

"You see these?" he said.

Jeremy nodded.

"This is a triangle. It's a three-pointed triangle. This is the mommy point, and this is the daddy point. This third point is you. We'll call it The Phantom point."

Jeremy looked serious. "The Phantom's the fast point."

"Yeah, that's right." Pelligrew nodded. "We should give him some running shoes. He's a shadowy fellow. He can run like the wind, they tell me. I think he might fly. We'll put a black cape around him."

Jeremy sat spellbound. The crying had stopped now. In its place was a feeling of intrigue, curiosity. The points became embellished into crude little stick figures. One wore a dress. One had a cape around it.

"Now watch this," said Pelligrew. The ballpoint made scratching noises. He connected the figures so that they formed a pyramid. As he drew, he could feel Jeremy's cheek against his bicep. The paper fluttered under the moth-battered streetlight. "You see these lines? We call these connecting lines. There's a line up here, there's one here . . . here's another fellow . . .

They all look the same, but they're not—they're constructed different. Two are just lines—but one has Titanium in it!"

Jeremy stared. A car drove past. A bar of light flickered along the hedgerows. On a neighboring porch, there was a candlelit jack-o'-lantern. This was late October, and it would soon be the witching season.

"Titanium," said Jeremy.

"Yep. That's stronger than Kryptonite. You could shoot it with a bazooka, it would just get stronger on you. This line up here—I don't know what that's made of. I think it's just cotton. It's got some sort of paper in it."

Jeremy nodded. Well, this was fairly clear. The line between his parents was just a piece of old clothesline probably. You could cut that easy. You could run an eraser through it. But this line to his father—that had Titanium in it!

"And this?" said Jeremy. He pointed to the third line.

"Oh, that," said Pelligrew. "Well, that's just your mother connection. That's fairly strong. I think it's got nylon in it. It could hold up a horse, but you can't land a space craft on it."

Jeremy said nothing. He stared at the diagram. Right there, in that schematic, lay the whole of his heritage: three little figures with three ballpoint lines between them, only one of which counted, because it had Titanium in it.

Behind them, up on the porch, there was the sound of a door opening. A voice called out, "Jeremy? Jeremy, where are you?" Neither of them answered. Pelligrew folded the document packet. "Just remember what I told you—we're joined by Titanium, kiddo."

The other night, when he was listening to Gronsky, this strange revelation had suddenly dawned on him: that were he to meet Gronsky's wife in some bar, some supermarket, he might find her appealing, might even crave sex with her. That was not impossible. We all feed off rejects. One man's discard is another man's lagniappe. Like a circle of serpents, some lascivious daisy chain, all men and all women are joined bunghole-and-tongue together.

Only now, as he stood up and looked around toward Elizabeth, he realized, corollarily, that this was a two-way avenue: that what *he* had rejected, another might covet. The very idea made him bristle with jealousy.

Tall, slender, provocatively bowlegged, wearing a light cotton dress and a dark green cardigan, Elizabeth stood etched against the yellowing porch light like some pale blond beauty from the F. Scott Fitzgerald era. There was a breeze picking up. Her arms were folded. Against the light through her dress, her bare legs were visible. She shielded her eyes and looked out toward the streetlight. "Jeremy, come in! C'mon, I got supper waiting!"

Jeremy stood up.

"We're coming!" said Pelligrew.

They headed across the lawn. There was a soft crunch of oak leaves. It was *his* house, *his* woman, *his* son, and *his* supper waiting—only none of them were his, because he had no title to them.

"Who won?" said Elizabeth.

"*We* did!" said Jeremy.

Pelligrew said nothing. He retied his shoelaces.

"Would you like to come in?"

He still said nothing. He put down his foot and began retying his other laces.

"Listen, Don," said Elizabeth when she had called him three weeks ago (he was in bed at the time with a black girl from Greenpoint; she had a neck like a swan and blue-green fingernails; he had just met her that morning in the Times Square subway station)—"Listen, Don," said Elizabeth, "I know you hate when I call you, but I think there's something we have to talk about. I've been going with a doctor. His name is Ira. He's a good man, Donald. I'm terribly fond of him."

Pelligrew lay scowling. The black girl was fondling him.

"What kind of a doctor?"

"Just a doctor," said Elizabeth. "Well, okay, if you must know, he's only a chiropractor, but he's very successful, and he's wonderful with Jeremy—"

Pelligrew shot up. His temples grew scarlet. "Are you trying to tell me you've fallen in love with a *chiropractor?*"

"He's a fine man, Donald—"

"You whore!" cried Pelligrew. "I will not have my bloodline despoiled by a spine specialist!"

And he had meant it, too. That was in early October, and ever since then he had waged a one-man guerrilla war. Not only was he determined that he would never meet Klimefogler, he was doing everything he could to make domestic life miserable for him.

"I wish you'd come in. I'd like you to meet him."

Pelligrew didn't answer. He looked at the storm door. Through the glass-panel top he could see their well-lighted living room. A man with a beard sat in front of the television.

"Oh! That reminds me," said Pelligrew. He reached in his pants pocket. "You should tell your boy friend to be a little less careless, Elizabeth. A car registration is an important document. He shouldn't leave it around where a stranger can get to it."

Elizabeth scowled. "You don't want to meet him."

"I don't have time. I've got an important date tonight."

"You never have time."

"I've got an important date tonight! Maybe next week. Maybe next year sometime . . ."

"Donald!"

He paused.

She came down off the porch a step. She was still in her twenties. Her skin was like milk glass. He was sadly reminded of how delicate and pure she looked. It was all he could do not to reach out and pull her toward him.

"We're living together."

Pelligrew said nothing.

"It'd be a whole lot easier if you'd act more mature about it."

He still said nothing.

"After all, I was married to you. You're Jeremy's father. It'd be nice if we worked together."

Pelligrew just glowered. It would be nice if they worked together. As if Jeremy were a frog, and they had been assigned to be lab partners. He had no desire to work with anybody. It was a question of turf. It was a question of principle, damn it!

Perhaps here it should be noted that, in today's troubled atmosphere, wise are those women who do not marry lawyers. It's not that all lawyers are invariably bad husbands, it's just that it's rough when you go to divorce the buggers. Take Pelligrew, for instance. He had shown her no mercy. Why, he hadn't even allowed her the benefit of child support. Since the day he had left he had been paying her alimony, which was a tax break for him and kept her from remarrying anybody. That was one of many tricks. He had a veritable quiver full. He had written a clause that would restrict her mobility. If she ever tried to move beyond a fifty-mile radius from him, she would immediately surrender all rights to Jeremy. So he had her surrounded. She was like a thing on a tether. She could breathe, eat, and screw, but she could never be free of him. Freedom was a right that was reserved for superheroes. If Klimefogler were smart, he'd get the hell out of there.

"Jeremy seems to like him." This was Elizabeth talking. "Tell Daddy, Jeremy—you like Ira, don't you? You know what he did? He fixed Jeremy's bicycle for him. I asked you to do it, but you kept procrastinating."

Pelligrew looked at Jeremy. He was hanging on the porch rail. There was a dried harvest wreath strung up on the door knocker. Next week sometime—was it Monday or Tuesday maybe?—this street would be haunted by ghoulies and hobgoblins.

"Unh-unh!" said Jeremy.

"What do you mean?" said Elizabeth.

"He didn't fix it. The chain came back off again."

"Well, he *tried* to fix it—"

"He never fixed anything! He's not my father! I refuse to listen to him!"

Elizabeth looked flustered. Pelligrew just smiled.

"Well, be that as it may, you seem to have fun together . . ."

"No, we don't!" cried Jeremy. "He's too old! He's got whiskers on him! I don't like him! I'm not going to listen to him!"

"I gotta go."

"You just stay where you are, Donald!"

"I'm gonna be late . . ."

"You've been brainwashing Jeremy!"

"It's quarter after seven!"

"You've been poisoning his mind again! I'm not going to have it! I deserve to have happiness, Donald!"

Pelligrew just smiled. He trudged back across the oak leaves. It had been a glorious day. He had made everybody miserable. And now he was off to keep another appointment. He had some matters to clear up concerning two women and a codicil.

12

Halloween went. They were into November now. The streets became wet. It was the advent of flu season. Gronsky and Pelligrew took their boys to the park one Sunday. Shaughnessy went to Boston to visit an ailing relative. In between times, they talked. They ordered steak from Balducci's. They went up to Shaughnessy's and drank heavily till midnight. They went to movies together. They met at the Gingerman. They argued about politics, religion, the football season. These were the good times. They were like temporal oases. Years from now they would look back and wonder at them. They were rip-roaring, personal, and ultimately perishable. Had a woman been present, it would have all seemed quite stupid to her.

Late one Friday (counterclockwise, McBurney time), Shaughnessy had just completed his allotted ten miles, he was leaving the track, headed over toward the drinking fountain, when an exchange took place that would have historical significance for him. It had been a terrible week. He had contracted a virus. It was not exactly the flu, but it was enough to debilitate him. He had gotten a call from Sarah saying that Jaime had been truant again, and there was an appointment next week with the junior high's guidance counselor. That was on a Monday. On Tuesday, he was arrested. Well, not exactly arrested, just called in for questioning. It seems that somebody had been using his American Express Card and run up a bill totaling thousands in a Midtown massage parlor. Jesus Christ! On Wednesday, it rained. Thursday, at the office, he had spilled coffee on a drug layout and in a fit of pique had gone over to McBurney's, where the runner in mauve had tried to pour Pepsi on him. So now, exhausted, leg-cramped and sweat-beaded, walking toward the fountain to the left of the elevator, he was not in any mood to suffer further disruption or to encounter alien emotions among the trash of his life-style.

"Excuse me," he said.

The girl didn't answer. She was standing at the drinking fountain, putting on eye liner. She wore bright yellow tights and a flaming red warm-up jersey. Her ears were interred inside a stereo headphone set.

"Excuse me," said Shaughnessy. "You're blocking the drinking fountain."

The girl just stood there. She was looking in her compact mirror. One magnified eye seemed to hang in the atmosphere. There was a half-submerged sound of rock from her headphone set.

"Aw, fuck," muttered Shaughnessy. He just shoved on past her. He hated headphones. He hated wild warm-up outfits. He hated girl runners, and he hated neurotic types, and he hated bleached blondes, and this girl was all of these.

"Hey!" she shouted.

Shaughnessy ignored her. He closed his eyes and turned on the water spigot. The water flowed down over his hair, his cheekbones. He turned up his face and filled his mouth like a water bucket.

"What are you *doing?*"

He wasn't doing anything. He opened his eyes. He made like a drowning man. He sucked in, he spat out. He made strange strangled gurgling noises. When he finally stood up, he found she was glaring at him.

"The least you could do was warn me!" she shouted. "I mean, that's just decency. I would have made room for you. Now look what you've done. Those were my last good eyelashes. Look at this powder . . . Gawd! That's ten bucks worth of stuff you've ruined!"

Shaughnessy stood blinking. He didn't know what she was talking about. She pushed him aside and stuck her hand in the water basin. She pulled out a rouge brush, a lipstick, a powder container. They were all soaking wet. Her fingers were dye-coated.

"You idiot!" she muttered.

Shaughnessy just stood there.

"Now what am I gonna do? They got a lock on the ladies' room. I got a show at seven. They don't have a makeup man. I'm already late . . . Oh, God, my mascara's in there . . ."

She was about five-foot-one, one hundred pounds even. She had the kind of body one associates with gymnasts. Her canary-yellow hair was swept up like a pin-up model's. She had the nostalgic sexuality of a World War Two factory worker.

"I'm sorry . . ." he muttered.

"You're sorry . . . *He's sorry, ladies!* I've got my eyelashes down there. They'll have to take the whole drain apart. God, you stink. This place smells like a sewer system. At least at the Racquet Club the men wash their gym shorts sometimes."

And with that, she left. She stepped onto the elevator, the doors closed behind her, and she never even looked at him. Shaughnessy just stood there. He had a strange kind of tingling feeling. Subconsciously, inaudibly, he could still hear those headphones rattling.

That was on a Friday. He didn't see her on Saturday. The gym was closed Sunday, and he ran on Fifth Avenue. The following Monday she was back on the running track, and this time she was wearing a tiger-striped Danskin outfit.

"Hi," said Shaughnessy.

The girl stared sullenly at him.

"I'm sorry about Friday."

"You still have those gym shorts on."

"I was gonna have em cleaned. I didn't get to the laundry yet."

"Yeah, well, save yourself the schlepp. Use them to clean out your carburetor."

She was not all that fast. He found it hard to hold back with her. They rounded a curve and went into the straightaway. Finally, frustrated, he poured on the steam, completed a lap, and came up behind her again.

"I'm surprised you're here."
"My membership's paid."
"You said you preferred it at the Health & Racquet Club."
"I do. Who wouldn't? They don't put locks on their ladies' rooms. Look, do me a favor—don't rub your elbow on me."
Shaughnessy said nothing. He couldn't quite get the hang of this. Her wit was urban, but it was lacking the accent marks. Philadelphia? he wondered. Chicago? Los Angeles? Whatever it was, it was needling and frustrating.
"Which club do you go to?"
"Huh?" She looked at him.
"For God's sake," cried Shaughnessy, "why don't you take those damn earphones off!"
"Huh? Why should I?"
"Because I'm trying to talk to you! You look ridiculous! You look like a jigaboo in em!"
The girl said nothing.
"Jesus Christ," muttered Shaughnessy. Then: "Goddamn," he shouted, "I'm gonna blow up the Sony factory! You know what those are? Those are the Japs' revenge on us! The whole country's collapsing because no one can talk to each other! . . ."
And with that, he took off. He ran thirteen more laps. He did more than run them, he almost sprinted them. Finally, realizing that he was about to exhaust himself, he slowed down the pace and settled back in beside her again.
"My name's Ted."
"Good for you," said the woman.
"What's yours?" said Shaughnessy.
"You gonna send me a Christmas present?"
"No, I'm just curious. My name's Ted Shaughnessy. I'm trying to be civil. You're making it difficult."
The woman just smiled. She didn't have to be civil. She had small, firm breasts and the legs of an athlete. Her face was not classic—it had a broken-nosed punk quality—but in the great scheme of things, she had quite a bit going for her.
"You come here often?"

"No. Very seldom."

"Where do you go?"

"I already told you that."

"Those clubs are all over. They got one on Thirteenth Street. Is that where you go? They got one up off Lexington . . ."

The girl didn't answer.

"They've got one up by Saks."

Still didn't answer.

"They've got one up on York and something. I'd like to try one. I've never been there. I hear they've got Nautilus. I used a Nautilus in Boston one time . . ."

By now they had traveled some two or three miles together—a bit more for Shaughnessy, if you counted his show-off laps. He was beginning to feel tired. He had an ache in his chest muscle. His razor wound was healed, but it still caused him problems sometimes.

"Where are you from?"

"Who cares?" said the woman.

"I'm from Boston."

"Yeah. I think we've established that."

"And you?" said Shaughnessy.

"L.A. California. San Bernardino. I was born in a Jack In The Box."

Shaughnessy said nothing. This seemed totally alien to him. He had never met anyone from "L.A. California" before. As far as he was concerned, that was just a wasteland with freeways on it. The total sum of his knowledge consisted of two Ross MacDonald novels.

"You like New York?"

"I've been here eight years," she answered.

"Yeah, I like it too. It's one of the world's great metropolises. Of course it's not like Boston, but it's a city of significance. It's got flesh-and-blood people. You're probably not used to that."

The girl just kept running. He was really feeling tired now. Was it his imagination, or was she quickening the pace on him? She looked totally fresh. It was as if she had ice skates on. They rounded the loop at about a seven-minute-mile pace.

"You're good," said Shaughnessy.

"So-so," she answered.

"Which club do you go to?"

"Why are you so interested?"

"I just am. I just wondered."

"The one up near Saks. Wednesdays at five. Now, if you'll excuse me, I'm leaving now."

And with that, she took off. She didn't run off, she flew off. She circled the track about thirty more times, waved good-bye, ran out through the exit gate, ran down the steps, and that was the last he saw of her.

At least till Wednesday. Carrying a blue Nike gym bag, a clean pair of shorts, and a new athletic supporter, he sat in the lobby of the New York Health & Racquet Club and glowered disapprovingly at all the lithe young bodies present. He already disliked it. It had carpets on the floor. There was a palm tree in the corner that looked like styrofoam. A manager walked by wearing a blazer with a monogram on it. The place reeked of reverence, like a Beverly Hills funeral parlor.

"Oh, it's you," said the girl. "I figured you'd be here"—and suddenly she was in front of him wearing a felt hat with feathers on it. She wore baggy pink pants and spiked heels with glitz on them. She looked like a refugee from an A & S bargain counter.

"Hi," said Shaughnessy.

"Hope you brought decent gym shorts." She pointed to the locker room. "I'll meet you upstairs," she said. "We'll start on the Exercycle. We'll run, then I'll Nautilize with you. Maybe when we're through we can go for a swim or something."

Shaughnessy nodded. He went into the locker room. He could have told you from the beginning that this was a complete waste of resources. She was a kook. She was crass. She had the smell of the freeways on her. Even if he got her, what possible future was there?

Even if he got her . . . Well, yes, that was a conundrum, because in the year since his divorce he had yet to get anybody. He had undressed a few, he had climbed into bed with them, but that was about it—he had some kind of functioning problem. "What's the matter?" said the women. "Nothing," he'd answer them. "Try to relax." "I *am* relaxing"—and a cold paralysis would spread out from his pelvic area, and he could feel himself slipping into some clammy-palmed purgatory. It was a terrible feeling. It dogged him constantly. He tried to drown it, but it grew stronger on Cutty Sark. For the past twelve months, since he had been living in the Village, he had been walking the knife edge between yearning and celibacy.

"It's the disease of our times. It's like an epidemic." This is what a woman in the Lion's Head had said to him. She had a pock-marked face and wore glasses with a safety pin through them. She was holding forth to any man who would listen to her. "This whole city's impotent! They're either gay or malfunctioning! I've had four different boy friends, and none of them could do it with me! What's going on? You wonder we're frustrated? I'm gonna move back to Queens. At least out there they get hard-ons sometimes." And Shaughnessy had just sat there, ordering Cutty after Cutty, feeling inwardly revolted at the mere suggestion, and later that night he had trudged back to his apartment feeling angry, depressed, blind-alleyed by circumstances.

Now, as he sat there in that dun-colored locker room, thinking about the girl who was upstairs waiting for him, he had half a mind to turn around and walk out again. Firm thighs or no, he could see no percentage in it.

"Thanks," he said. He took a key from the locker attendant. He put on his shorts and went up to the warm-up area. She was already there, sitting on an Exercycle. She was wearing her headphones and reading *Variety*.

"You in theater?" said Shaughnessy.

"Kind of. Television."

Shaughnessy sat down. He put his feet on the tension pedals. Tonight she was wearing a pair of brief-cut running shorts. She was really quite sexy, although he tried not to think about it.

"Channel 0," said the woman.

"Oh?" said Shaughnessy.

"You know. Cable. We have an audience of dozens. I'm on

every week. I've got a talk show at seven. Maybe you've seen it. We talk about health-care issues."

Shaughnessy said nothing. He had never seen it. The warm-up room was filled with out-of-shape office workers. Through a glass partition there was a long row of running machines. People were lined up like hamsters in a treadmill showroom.

"What's your name?" said Shaughnessy.

"Sandra. Bolgner. Only I don't call myself Bolgner—that's one of those immigrant nonsense names. I got it legally changed. I changed it to Silk. Sandra Silk—that's a lot more mellifluous-sounding."

Shaughnessy sat pedaling. Jesus Christ, he ruminated. He had nothing against Jews—that was not one of his prejudices—but he did not like Jews who tried to pretend they were Wasps and dyed their hair gold and used ill-sounding pseudonyms.

They got off their bikes. They went into the running room. While they were waiting in line, Sandra worked on her muscle stretching. She bent down. She stood up. She did side bends and back bends. Shaughnessy ogled. Her ligaments rippled at him.

"What's the name of your show?"

"Huh?" She stared at him.

"I said what's your show called? What kind of health do you talk about?"

"How many kinds are there? It's called 'Smooth as Silk.' We talk about nutrition. Vitamins. Dieting mostly."

Shaughnessy scowled. He *hated* nutrition groupies. He did more than hate them, he considered them perpetrators. All those crazy neurotics guzzling rose hips and kelp tablets—they were effeminate at best, at worst they were evil possibly.

"Of course you know that's bullshit."

"Come again?" said Sandra.

"I said it's bullshit. It's a sign of narcissism. All you're doing is creating more anorexia victims. I suppose you believe we're being poisoned by fertilizers."

Sandra bent over. She touched her toes.

"That's bullshit!" cried Shaughnessy. "You know nothing about chemistry! All you're doing is throwing sops to the paranoids. You and Gloria Swanson. I suppose you think sugar's bad for you."

Sandra stood up.

"What are you, some bone doctor?"

"I have a technical background."

"Big deal." She sneered at him.

"I have a technical background. Part medical . . . . part graphics, actually. I draw pictures of organs. I work for an ad agency."

"Oh, Gwaawd." Sandra smirked. She shook her head helplessly. A machine had become vacant, and she walked up and stood on it. "You work for the hucksters—the legalized poisoners—and you're trying to tell me you're an expert on body chemistry!"

Shaughnessy stood scowling. He was really getting mad now. The next machine became empty, and he went up and stood on it. He was not accustomed to running on a treadmill, and he began fiddling with the knobs, trying to locate the start button.

"It's a legitimate business."

"So's oil. So's tobacco farming."

"I read medical reports. We have doctors advising us."

"Golly gee, how impressive! We know all about those guys. They all get paid off by the fat-cat pollution merchants."

Shaughnessy was seething. He had started off loping, but now he reached forward and turned up the speed control. There was a mirror in front of him, and he could see his reflection in it. He looked like some beast in the throes of a rabies trauma.

"How old are you?"

"Who cares?" said Sandra.

"I do," said Shaughnessy. "You talk like a two-year-old."

"I'm thirty-one. I'll be thirty-two February. Why don't you slow down? We already know you're a hotshot, Cholly."

Shaughnessy glowered. He pushed up the speed control. Now he was going like a runaway steam engine. The sidebars shook. The control panel vibrated. The miles spun past as if he had been shot from a rocket launcher.

"You're an idiot!" cried Sandra.

"Why don't you mind your own business?"

"I mean, here I am—I'm trying to be nice to you. I gotta pay for this visit! I was all out of guest passes! What do you do? You act like a *re*tard on me!"

Shaughnessy ignored her. He was really moving. The miles spun under him in a whirl of gear cogs. By the time he was through, he felt tired. He felt wonderful. He stopped the machine and stood admiring his calf muscles.

"You know, of the three of us," he had said to Gronsky one evening as they were sitting in a watering hole up on Third called Melon's, "—of the three of us, Alex, you have the least healthy life-style. I mean, I know I smoke, but at least I work out each day." The reason he had said this was that that afternoon he had happened to attend a seminar with a client of Caduceus, and they had used computerized dummies to show the symptoms of heart attack and the proper method of resuscitation. "You're a candidate, Alex. I mean, what the hell, look at you. You smoke, you drink, you don't get any exercise. You oughta come to the Y. I'd help get you started. Here, feel my gut. I'm as hard as a rock, goddamn it . . ."

"Come on, hot dog." Sandra took him by the arm. She led him across a hallway and into the weight room. The machines stood in rows, like so many torture racks. Tank-topped patrons lay wheezing and grunting in them.

"You know how these work?"

"They're Nautiluses," said Shaughnessy.

"A gold star for you. You have to be careful with them. Actually, you should begin with a step-by-step regimen. You should fill out a card. You should have an instructor with you."

Shaughnessy smirked. He didn't need an instructor with him. He went over to a machine and began fiddling with the weight controls. There was a handlebar on it and some sort of pulley system. No goddamn girl was going to tell him about bodybuilding.

Sandra came over.

"What do you think you're doing?"

"What does it look like?"

"Preparing to hang yourself."

"Mind your own business! I know all about weight-lifting. How much do *you* press? I pressed two hundred pounds last Tuesday."

Sandra just smiled. There was some sort of harness device, but for the life of him Shaughnessy couldn't figure out how to fit in it. He shoved it aside. Who needs support systems? He straddled the bench and began tugging the handlebars.

"Excuse me . . ." said a woman.

"Go away," said Shaughnessy.

"Excuse me," said the woman, "but if you'll allow me to help you with it . . ." She was a small elfin creature in a monogrammed dancing outfit. It had the club's initials and the word "Instructor" on it.

"Fuck off!" cried Shaughnessy. He was pulling on the handlebars. They were enormously heavy, but he was managing to move them somewhat. The weights rose up. They came down like a pile driver. There was a resounding crash. The ceilings and mirror tiles rattled.

Sandra smiled. "Adorable, ain't he?"

"I'm afraid," said the woman, "I'm going to have to insist, sir . . ."

"Go to hell!" cried Shaughnessy. He tugged on the weights again. Again there was a crash. He sat glowering sullenly at them.

Next came swimming. Well, that was no problem, because the pool was so shallow and about the size of a badminton court. Shaughnessy had brought no trunks, so he showed up in his running shorts. He stood menacingly on the edge and scowled down at the lane markers.

"You do swim, I hope."

"Like Mark Spitz," said Shaughnessy.

She was standing beside him wearing a skin-tight tank suit. Through the sheer nylon's weave he could see two small nipples outlined. She climbed down the ladder and adjusted her swim goggles.

"See ya," she said—and with that, she shoved off. Shaughnessy stood glowering as her buttocks winked saucily at him. She completed her turn and was on her way back again. She was an excellent swimmer—graceful, coordinated.

Shaughnessy just stood there. Since his debacle of a year ago, when he had been expelled from a natatorium for almost scuttling a Finnish woman, he had become fairly well convinced that all swimming was sissified and that the people who did it were on a level with fencing masters. He went up to the edge. He looked down at the water. He bent his knees, crouched down for a racing dive—

"Hey, wait . . . !" cried Sandra.

"CHARGE!" cried Shaughnessy—

And he flung himself out and came down like an alligator.

Of course, in fairness to Shaughnessy, he did not really want this woman. In fact, he had already decided that she was totally repugnant to him. Her breasts were too small. She had bony elbows. When she spoke, she whined. Her voice was metallic-sounding. As he flailed down the pool, his head above water, moving diagonally across everyone's lap path, his lungs became filled with chlorinated anger. He would not only shun her—he might consider drowning her.

He completed four laps.

"About through?" he shouted.

"No!" cried Sandra. She was on lap number ten now. Shaughnessy said nothing. He struck out for four more laps. She was indefatigable! She was like some sort of swimming machine!

"Stop!" gasped Shaughnessy.

"I'm going for a hundred!"

"No you're not!"

"Go to hell!" she taunted.

She completed her twentieth. She completed her thirtieth. Her breathing was flawless. Her legs moved powerfully.

Shaughnessy climbed out. His chest was heaving. His eyes were inflamed. He was half-asphyxiated. He watched as she approached . . . He hovered over her . . .

"CHARGE!" he shouted—

And with that, he cannonballed her.

Silence. Cold silence. It was about quarter after seven now. Through the Thermopane glass they could see the spires of St. Patrick's. Sandra was picking on a salad with bean curd in it. Shaughnessy stared glumly. He felt dumb. He felt nauseated.

"I guess you're mad."

No answer from Sandra.

Shaughnessy fidgeted. He looked at the diners present. They were in the health club's restaurant and most of the people wore warm-up outfits. At one end was a counter featuring yogurt and carrot products.

"I'm sorry," he muttered. "I didn't mean to land on you."

" 'sokay. Forget it." She reached for some wheat germ.

"I was trying to be funny. I guess I misgauged it somewhat."

"Don't worry about it." She took a sip of her citrus product.

Shaughnessy scrunched down. He felt completely humiliated. She was not that bad. In fact, she had good qualities. When they hauled her out of the pool, she hadn't even shouted at him. All she had said was "You fucker." She had refused first-aid offers.

"You know what I think?"

"No, what?" said Shaughnessy.

"I think you're scared."

"Aw, c'mon. That's ridiculous."

"You're scared of women. You're scared of yourself, maybe. That's all right. I have no designs on you."

Shaughnessy said nothing. He reached for a cigarette. This was the third time that day he had tried to ignore the "No Smoking" posters. The first was in the gym. The second was in the sauna. Each time he had been reprimanded by one of the staff members.

"Don't smoke," said Sandra.

"Why not? I want to."

"That's not the point. They don't allow smoking here. You're only doing this to try to alienate me. You don't have to try. You've already accomplished it."

Shaughnessy scowled. He put back the cigarette.

"Don't worry about me—you're the last thing I'm interested

in. I've had eight years of shit. I've been fucked by the best of em. The last thing I need is another asshole to hassle me."

She looked down at her plate. She was really rather vulnerable. Through her bluntness, her sarcasm, there was a soft, almost yearning quality. Shaughnessy glowered. There was a return of the tingling feeling. He scraped his feet. He shared part of a bean curd with her.

Perhaps his worst infraction—even worse than the smoking—was when he had come up here and tried to order a hamburger. "Well done. With fries." The waitress had stared at him. What was he, some looney? They didn't serve poison here.

Oh, my god, thought Shaughnessy. But he *detested* vegetables. Tried asparagus once, had almost choked on it. "Got any B&M baked beans? . . ." "Come on!" said Sandra, and she had pulled him away before he could do any more damage.

Now, empty-plated, sitting at that table, watching this aging ex-surfer chow down on tofu, all he could think of were triglycerides and nicotine. Nicotine and sex. Perhaps a bottle of Cutty Sark . . .

"So after I left L.A."—this was Sandra speaking—"I came to New York thinking I could make it as a singer maybe. I had done some acting—I was a Playhouse graduate—but I thought New York would be easier, there'd be less competition here." She nibbled a mung bean. "Well, of course that was crazy. Like it's still the Big Apple. It's just one big merry-go-round. I did some modeling. I almost starved to death. I couldn't go back. I had my mother, this stepfather . . ."

Shaughnessy just sat there. He had one cigarette left. He could feel it in his pocket, snuggled deep in the tinfoil. He loosened the seal. He pulled back the tinfoil. He could feel it in there, so lonely, so lethal-looking . . .

". . . So that's about it. I lived with this guy awhile. It didn't work out. I guess we had cultural differences. He kept beating me up. I had to go to the hospital. I got into Plath, I did the whole feminist bit . . ."

Shaughnessy felt strangled. He looked around at the diners. They were all so smug, so vain, so pampered-looking. What were they afraid of? Aging? Mortality? He would love to light up. He would love to blow smoke on them.

". . . So when I say I'm not interested, don't take that too personally. I think you're attractive. You've got a very nice body on you. But if we got involved—well, it wouldn't work out, would it? I've got my career . . . two cats . . . It's all coming together for me . . ."

Shaughnessy sighed. He reached in his pocket.

"What are you doing?"

He took out the cigarette.

"Please don't. Be sensible."

"I am being sensible. I'm tired of sitting here. I don't like this atmosphere."

Sandra didn't answer. She picked at a cucumber.

"I hate this place. I hate everything about it here. The men look like queers, the women look phony to me. You look phony. I don't like that hat you're wearing."

She put down her fork. "I ask you. Don't do it."

He patted his pockets. He pulled out a matchbook.

"If you light that up, you've had it. I mean it. I'm walking out. Don't make me do that to you."

He tore out a match.

"You don't believe me . . ."

He struck a flame.

"I'm not going to take this from you . . ."

He lit up. He inhaled.

She stood up.

She walked out on him.

Fuck it, he thought. He hadn't wanted her anyway.

13

According to Gronsky's pocket calculator, a trim-line Sharp that he kept in his briefcase, at his present rate of spending, counting garage fees and meal charges, he was about to owe the Plaza over four thousand dollars. He stared at the digits. He must have miscalculated. He tried it again. No, that's what it came out to. If he stayed there much longer, he would have to sell his Volvo. Obviously, in retrospect, he had not thought this through too clearly.

"Hello, Mandy?" he said.

"Hello, Alex? Is that you?"

His expenses were one thing—but they were not the worst thing. The worst thing was psychic. It was like an emotional corrosive—as witness this exchange during the week after the football game:

"How ya doin?" he said.

"I'm fine. How are *you* doing?"

"I'm fine," said Gronsky. "Listen, tomorrow's Halloween, Mandy. I thought maybe I could drive up there and take Bobby around with me. Those roads get dark. I'd like to see how he's dressed this year . . ."

Silence. Nothing. Then:

"I'd rather you wouldn't."

"Why not?" said Gronsky. "That's a family tradition, Mandy."

"That may be—but things have changed, Alex. Ingrid's taking him. It'll be a lot more comfortable for us."

Ingrid's taking him. Gronsky said nothing. There were so few family rituals in which a man could participate, and now, inexorably, the doors were closing on him. Soon even their house would become off limits to him.

This was one problem—loneliness another. For the past seventeen years he had become accustomed to family life, and now, cut off, thrown back on his resources, even the city seemed to be turning hostile toward him.

"So what's your story?" The redhead smiled warily.

"Story?" said Gronsky.

"All you men have got stories, don't you?"

"Oh." Gronsky nodded. "Well, I guess so. I'm separated . . ."

"Oh, Gwa-a-awd!" said the redhead—and she turned back to the bartender.

So it was not that easy. He stayed in, he watched television. He saw movies by himself. He went to bars and watched other people. His only transfusions came from Shaughnessy and Pelligrew, whose parallel needs seemed to fill some vacuum in him.

Then, early in November—it was the beginning of flu season—he was sitting in his office trying to ward off a throat tickle when there was a flurry of activity, a rustling down the hallway, and into his office burst Eastman, his father-in-law.

"*What's this?*" cried Eastman.

Gronsky looked at him.

"What the fuck *is* this?" He shoved some papers at him. Given their volume, they looked like a phone directory; in reality, however, they were Gronsky's expense account.

Darryl Eastman was a short, squat autocrat whose red pigmentation had spent years rearranging itself. It had begun in his hair, moved around to his earlobes, and now seemed to reside across the top of his frontal lobe. To say that Gronsky liked him would have been to exaggerate, but it's true that over the years he had managed to conform to him. When Eastman expanded, Gronsky grew smaller. It was a symbiotic bond. It worked well for both of them.

"What's the matter?" said Gronsky.

"What's the *matter?*" cried Eastman. He began riffling the papers. His hands were trembling. "Line twenty-four . . .

What the hell did I do with it . . . Ah, there! There it is! That's what's the matter, damn it!"

Line twenty-four: "Travel & Entertainment." In any salesman's budget, that's the handiest catchall, but in this case it seemed to have caught more than its share. The figure was higher than there were spaces to write it in.

Gronsky sniffled. "I've got receipts for it."

"You've *what?*" cried Eastman.

Gronsky reached for his handkerchief.

"Re-CHEEZH!" he sneezed.

"It's over four thousand dollars, Alex! You're going to sit there and tell me you've got receipts for it?"

That was on a Tuesday. The following Thursday, having finally been prevailed upon to vacate the Plaza, he checked himself into a more modest hotel whose commercials he had seen on late-night television. "When you've seen all there is to see in New York," they advertised, "and chased all the fun things there are to chase, relax and unwind at the charming Cotswold, conveniently located on historic West Thirtieth Street." Well, it was not quite that. It was cheap, it was garish. Their monthly rates started at four hundred dollars. But, living as he was on a day-to-day basis, it seemed preferable somehow to signing an apartment lease.

"Hello, Mandy? You called me?"

"Alex, where *are* you?"

"I'm fine," said Gronsky.

"That's not what I'm asking, Alex."

"Can I talk to Bobby?"

"I know all about it. You brought it on yourself. You have no one to blame for it."

The room from which he was calling was Room 604. It had a broken-down dresser, a bed, a night table. At the foot of the bed there was a hot-plate/refrigerator unit. Through the paper-thin walls he could hear Room 602's orgasms.

"Can I talk to my son?"

"He does not wish to speak to you. Four thousand dollars! What on earth were you thinking of? You just ought to be thankful he didn't fire you. He could have, you know. He was eminently fair about it."

Gronsky said nothing. There was nothing he could say. Eminently fair. The soul of magnanimity. And in a way that was true —Gronksy couldn't contradict it—although there's a kind of fairness a man finds eviscerating . . .

What had happened was this: That morning, at the office, there had been a message waiting with Marie, his secretary, saying that his father-in-law, Eastman, would like to talk to him— "right away," said Marie; "it sounded important, Alex." So Gronsky had nodded and trudged off down the hallway—it would not be the first time they had started the day this way— and when he got to Eastman's office, balancing his coffee, he had knocked on the door and walked in as he always had . . .

"Ah, Alex!" said Eastman. "Come in, come in." He was sitting at his desk, turned diagonally to the windows. It was a spacious office, professionally decorated. Snapshots of Mandy smiled down from the wall spaces. "You know Angie, I believe." He gestured toward a sofa. Gronsky said nothing. He did not like the feel of this. Because of all the people he had expected to see there, the last was that son of a bitch Angelo Karpeghian . . .

"Oh, Alex," said Mandy, and now her voice was conciliatory. He was sitting on the bed, staring at the television. It was a cable set, the volume turned down. There was some talk show on about nutrition and diet fetishes. "Oh, Alex," she was saying, "I know this is hard on you. It's hard on me. It's hard on everybody. But if you could only just once try to see it from *my* side. It's not like you think. I'm not the monster you say I am . . ."

The last time Gronsky had seen Angelo Karpeghian was that evening last October on the five thirty-seven. It was he who had made that remark about Revlon, grinning sardonically as he dealt out the poker hands. About two weeks ago there had been some scuttlebutt at the office that somebody new was coming on board, but no names had been mentioned, it was all very vague, and frankly Gronsky hadn't paid much attention to it.

"Now, as you know," said Eastman, putting his elbows on his desktop; his forehead was glowing with an air of effusiveness; it

was an attitude Gronsky had learned to distrust; Eastman was always effusive just before he clobbered you. ". . . as you know," he said, "I've been somewhat concerned, Alex. There was that Revlon problem. You've been missing appointments lately. I need not mention our little expense-account brouhaha. We all make mistakes. I wouldn't hold that against you . . ."

And Gronsky had nodded. No, there was no need to mention that. He was beginning to perspire. His trousers felt sticky. Eagerly, almost desperately, he clung to his coffee mug. The coffee, lukewarm, had an acrid, metallic quality . . .

"I'm worried," said Mandy.

"About what?" said Gronsky.

"About you. Your health. Your voice doesn't sound right to me."

"I'm all right, just a cold."

"I doubt that you're eating properly. What are you eating? You're not putting on weight, are you?"

"I think you know, too, that I'm fond of you, Alex. You're my daughter's husband. We've often played golf together. I was just saying to Angie, 'This is one loyal man, Angie. You may question his judgment, but not his integrity' " . . .

"Alex?" said Mandy. "Alex, are you there?"

"I'm here," said Gronsky. He opened his eyes again. All day long this same scene had replayed itself: Eastman, that office, Karpeghian just grinning at him . . .

The hotel room was cramped. That was one of its problems. The commercial had touted it as being "newly redecorated." And in a way, it was. It had repainted woodwork and a pastoral wallpaper with quaint scenes of Italy on it. But there was a decay, a decrepitude, that the paint couldn't cover. Gray crumblings of plaster lay on top of the baseboards. He had an uneasy feeling that if it weren't for the wallpaper, the joists, the rafters would come tumbling down on him . . .

"Then I'll quit!" he was shouting.

"Now, let's not be rash, Alex . . . ."

"You've been promising me that job for seventeen years, Darryl!"

"Well, I've changed my mind! I don't think you're qualified! I happen to think Angie'll be a better administrator!" . . .

"Alex, say something."

There was nothing he could say. He sat with his head against the wall behind the bedstead. On the other side of the wall, behind a mural of Castel Gandolfo, Room 602 was rising to ecstasy . . .

"I'm surprised at you, Alex! You of all people! You know what it's like to be a member of a team, don't you? You've got your line, your quarterback. We can't all be glory boys. Surely back in college Woody Hayes must have told that to you" . . .

"Would it help any, Alex, if I said I missed you? I do, you know. This has not been easy for me. Yesterday morning I was cleaning out the basement and I found that old kite that we took to Pound Ridge that Sunday" . . .

"But goddamn it," cried Gronsky, "I never knew Woody Hayes!"

"Don't be so negative! See, that's this guy's trouble, Angie. He denigrates himself. He doesn't think positively. That's one of the failures I want you to try to correct in him" . . .

"I don't know, Alex . . . maybe we should go to a therapist. I hear there's a good one at the Yorktown shopping center. Would you be willing to try? Would you at least try to talk to him? We're never going to make it if you're not willing to talk about it" . . .

Gronsky just sat there. Room 602 vibrated. On the TV some blonde was talking about lecithin.

"Alex, say something."

There was nothing he could say.

"Good-bye," he said—and he depressed the receiver button.

14

As he would later admit, he should have known better, although even in this he would be hedging the truth a bit. Because the truth of the matter was, he *did* know better—it was just that the knowledge didn't seem too important to him.

"Can we turn on a light?"

"What for?" said Emmy.

"I'd like to see you."

"It shines in my eyes, Donald."

"I'll tip the shade."

"It shines in my eyes, Donald! Don't be so rude! I have sensitive optic nerves!"

The events leading up to this piece of domesticity may require some explaining, since there has been no preparation for it; the last that was seen of Emmy Schoenstein, she was in P. J. Clarke's, and she was hollering and screaming at him. But appearances are deceptive. The day after the funeral, while he was still somewhat groggy from his all-night drinking session, Pelligrew had picked up the phone, called this very same Emmy, and, as if nothing had happened, said, "Now about that codicil . . ."

"Are you kidding?" said Emmy. "After the way you acted?"

"What do you mean?" said Pelligrew. "I didn't act any way. We had Lilah sitting there. She was trying to play games with me. I didn't like that. I had to do something, didn't I?"

One of the many remarkable traits for which The Phantom was notorious was that there was no such thing as having left a "burned bridge" behind him. Neither shame nor rejection seemed to have any meaning for him; on the contrary, if anything, they just piqued his enthusiasm. On more than one occasion, when he had felt bored or at odds with himself, he had called up all the women he had ever humiliated, invited them over for a white wine and cheese party, and they would sit there in his living room literally bristling with hostility. Didn't bother him. He seemed totally oblivious to it. He would talk about baseball, regale them with childhood stories. Even when it emerged that they were all his ex-conquests, he saw no reason at all why they should not get along together.

And this was his attitude toward Emmy Schoenstein. Why should she be angry just because he had humiliated her? He was a likable fellow. There was an eligible-man shortage. A woman her age just had to learn to be tolerant, damn it.

"Well, all right," agreed Emmy, although it took some cajoling, because Lilah, after all, was also her daughter, but Pelligrew had the advantage of two potent weapons: the authority of his profession and his unabashed cheekiness. So the following Thursday, at a restaurant called Neary's, at a table toward the back, far away from the bar crowd, he and Emmy had sat down and had a drink and a sandwich and talked coolly and rationally about the recourses open to her. He explained them all admirably. He talked about probate. He also happened to mention that he admired her breast structure. "I suppose it's not proper for me to bring this up," he said, "but I've never forgotten how terrific in bed you were . . ."

That was on a Thursday. They met again Sunday. He had driven back from Paterson following his encounter with Elizabeth, had gone straight to Emmy's over on East Fifty-seventh Street, had some wine, munched Triscuits, and amended the codicil. It was strictly platonic. It was the rekindling of a friendship. Around midnight, at the door, he had shown a slight bit of hesitancy. It was only when her kiss went a second beyond propriety that he had drawn back, sighed, and said, "Oh, God, here I go again . . ."

So it was a natural development, a kind of spiritual Hegelianism, this sensuous older woman and this man who had power over her. It was only inevitable that they'd squabble over bed lamps. How was she to know he wasn't the least bit interested in her?

"Hello, Lilah?" he said. (This was the following Tuesday. He had secured Lilah's phone number out of her mother's pocketbook. Lilah, a senior, was now living with a girl friend, a kind of first-step-to-freedom, as is so common among city kids.) "Listen, Lilah, this is Don. Now don't hang up on me. I know you're still angry, and I can't say I blame you for it, but something's been happening that's very distressing to me, and it would be a dereliction of duty if I didn't at least warn you about it." (Ah, Lilah, sweet Lilah, dark seed of my fantasies, embodiment of my dreams, driving force of all handjobs—please listen to reason; this is your lawyer speaking; this is the voice of wisdom; this is raw male maturity, baby.) "I've been having some talks with your mother lately. It's about that will. It's very disturbing to me. I'd be violating her confidence if I told you too much, but I think you should go home and take a look at that codicil."

"How come?" said Lilah.

"She's made me change it."

"What do you mean, 'made you'?"

"Try not to be angry, Lilah. I got you back your ten thousand dollars, but your mother's insisting on having power of attorney over you."

He he he! He hung up the phone, and the following Friday, when he returned to Emmy's, it was with no great surprise that he crossed the threshold and found Jewish Princess II curled up in an easy chair.

"She's moved back," whispered Emmy.

"Oh?" said Pelligrew.

"She says she has the feeling she should keep an eye on things. I told her that's silly, but she won't listen to me. I get the distinct impression she thinks we're plotting something."

And so this was how, having started at zero, or perhaps less than zero—at zero minus enmity—the indomitable Phantom, never lacking audacity, soon found himself confronting:

The Mom-Daughter Rivalry Syndrome

"Please, Lilah, go easy. Lay off the potato chips."

"Why? Why should I? I like potato chips."

"We must remember our thighs, dear . . ."

"Ha! It's *you* with the thigh problem. Don, you should see it—all that flesh, that cellulite . . ."

Or:

"Mother, tell Donald about that time you had breast surgery."

"*I beg your pardon!*"

"It was really disgusting, Donald. They slit her boobs. They put in this silicone gunk. She was sick for a month. She's still got the scar tissue . . ."

Of course Pelligrew enjoyed it. It was like an experiment in fission. It was like the creation of a schism through the center of the universe. And he would sit there passively, radiating innocence, seemingly unaware of all the lightning surrounding him.

"Turn on the light."

"I don't want it," said Emmy.

"What are you afraid of? I've seen women's bodies before."

"Good. Use your memory. I don't like it shining on me. Honestly, Donald, you can be so impossible!"

Pelligrew lay back. It was about quarter after one now. There was a fluorescent dial on the G.E. clock-radio. When they had last made love, it was about quarter after twelve. He had had an hour to recuperate, which would normally be plenty for him.

Earlier that evening, while they were sitting at the dining table—just Emmy, himself, two lamb chops with mint sauce on them—Lilah had strolled in wearing panties and a T-shirt. "Hi!" she said, and she sat down at the table with them.

"Lilah," said her mother, "go put on something decent."

"This is decent. You can't see anything."

"That is *not* the point! We are trying to have dinner, darling!"

"Donald doesn't mind. Could you please pass the salad, Mother?"

And, indeed, Donald didn't. He felt a surge through his carotids. His heart was thumping like a phobic jackrabbit. Below the lace of her pants he could see those long olive cheetah legs—so smooth, so fluid, so conducive to appetite.

Oh, Lilah Lilah Lilah . . . See, this wasn't mere lechery. Lechery's cheap, it's just a matter of gland function. But this, this was *real,* it was on a level with poetry; why, if he didn't watch out, it could become almost emotional for him. Consider the meaning: He had been giving this some thought, and the way he saw it, there was a kind of a bond here. It was a mystical tie, a sort of—Jungian archetype! Why, it might even shed light on the very essence of humankind! For if his hunch was correct, and he was quite good at hunches—when you're a man of his cunning, you live by your instincts—his sperm and Lilah's ovum had already osculated, only the fruit of their union had been plucked before harvesttime. That being the case, and he suspected it was, then it was perfectly clear that they were into primordials here. A seal had been struck—a kind of spiritual compact—and to reheal the breach was nothing short of inevitable.

The only problem now was what to do about Mother. And the answer, of course, was that he had to accommodate her. Which wasn't that easy because (a) she was voracious and (b) she was refusing to turn the damn light on for him!

"I have to have light!"

"What is this thing about light, Donald?"

"I'm not that young. I need visual stimuli."

"For God's sake!" cried Emmy. She fumbled with the lamp switch. An intense white funnel poured out on her nakedness. . . .

"What are you trying to do, make me hate my own daughter, Donald?" This from Emmy after they had finished their dinner earlier. She had finally convinced Lilah that it was time to do homework, and Lilah, smiling, said, "Have a real super time, you two!"

"Why do you say that?"

"Oh, come on, I'm no fool, Donald. I've seen how you look. I've seen how you ogle her. You had your chance. She's no longer interested. It's you and me now. Let's not be greedy, shall we? . . ."

He was beginning to get hard. It required some assistance. For one thing, an hour wasn't as long as it used to be, and for another there was the problem of his own inertia, created both by Emmy's age and those bothersome scar tissues. Once, last year, when he was roaming D'Agostino's, patrolling the waters like an enemy submarine, he had happened to connect with a young woman named Moira, who, as he later found out, had been a recipient of heart surgery. The scar was enormous. It ran the length of her esophagus. Worse than that, her heart made a ticking sound. It had a plastic valve, and it sounded like a Timex. Neither sleep nor orgasm could disrupt the cadence of it. Now, months later, lying there with Emmy, seeing those two fine lines beneath the folds of her mammaries, he couldn't help wondering how much of this was real and how many of man's pleasures were really owed to the plastics industry.

"Let me get on top."

"Why should you get on top?"

"Because. I want to. It makes me feel dominant."

"You idiot," laughed Emmy, and she rolled over on her back. He mounted her midsection and began caressing the scar tissue. . . .

"What's it like?" said Lilah.

"What's what like?" said Pelligrew.

He had happened to run into her while cruising the park one evening. Lilah, in shorts, had been circling the reservoir. There was a thin line of sweat across the mounds in her T-shirt.

"You know," she said. "Going to bed with my mother."

Pelligrew said nothing. He picked up a pebble.

"She's older than you. She'll be forty-five Saturday. I always assumed you had a thing about younger girls."

Pelligrew smiled. "Like you?" he said, eying her.

Lilah scoffed. "Ha! Not on your life, mister! You had me once.

You fucked me up royally. It'll be a cold day in hell before I let you do that again! . . ."

"Roll over," he muttered.

"*Now* what's the matter?"

"I've changed my mind. I want to try something else with you."

Emmy rolled over. She was lying on her stomach now. "Just watch what you're doing. I don't like that anal business . . ."

None of these positions seemed right to him somehow. When he had her on her back, her face was too visible, but when he was on *his* back he couldn't see the night table, and not seeing the night table meant he couldn't do anything with her.

The bedroom in which they toiled was spacious, well-decorated. It was one of those luxury buildings overlooking the Queensborough. Through the half-opened blinds he could see the late-night traffic moving. Cars were exchanged like so many tracer bullets.

"Okay, now move back . . ."

Emmy obliged him.

"There, that's better . . ." He had managed to penetrate. He was kneeling behind; she was hunched over doggie-style; by moving his head, he could just see the night table. . . .

"When was this taken?"

"What do you mean?" said Emmy.

This was two weeks earlier, and they were preparing to make love together. Pelligrew, naked, was staring at a photograph. It was the very same photo he had spotted that first evening.

"This photo of Lilah."

"I don't know—several years ago."

Pelligrew said nothing. It was a casual reference. But later, surreptitiously, while Emmy was in the bathroom, he had removed it from the mantel and put it on the night table. . . .

"Oh, *yes!*" murmured Emmy.

Pelligrew grunted. Could Lilah hear this? There was not that much soundproofing. She'd be lying in her bed, curled up in the womb position, the wallboards reverberating with bed squeaks and mommy sounds . . .

"OH, YES! OH, MY GOD! . . ."

Pelligrew was thrusting. The object of his desire was in full line of view now. She couldn't have been more than fourteen years old. She was dressed in a bikini; she was smiling voluptuously at him . . .

"OH, JESUS! . . . OH, GOD!! . . ."

Yes, Lilah . . . I'm coming, baby . . .

They were beginning to climax, they were rising to ecstasy . . .

And thus, craving the daughter, he satisfied the mother—which, as he would later admit, he should have known better than.

15

While on that very same night, about forty blocks south, having run his ten miles and showered at McBurney's, Shaughnessy, in jeans, carrying his blue Nike gym bag, was about to encounter his own kind of destiny. He was teetering on depression. That was a recurrent malady. It had, he had read, something to do with brain chemistry; either too much or too little or too thin or too viscous—he wasn't quite sure, but it was the curse of all Irishmen. He crossed Fourteenth Street. He skirted the meat market. He crossed Horatio and headed toward Jane Street. In another few blocks he'd be home in his apartment. If all went well, in an hour he'd be drunk again.

Shaughnessy's national heritage and his brain notwithstanding, there were less recondite reasons why he might feel preoccupied. His existence was hopeless. Everything was closing on him. Even these workouts were becoming a drag for him. He had not seen Sandra since that night at the Racquet Club. He kept looking at McBurney's, but she never materialized. And, indeed, why should she? He had acted like an idiot. Besides (as he put it) he wouldn't have wanted her anyway.

So he was at odds, he was frustrated. He was also guilt-ridden. Last week, over in Brooklyn, he had seen Jaime's guidance counselor, and he had learned, to his surprise, that instead of going to school all day, Jaime had been spending her time on the New York City subway system. "Are you crazy?" he had said, looking past Sarah toward their daughter, who was sitting, slouched, near the counselor's elbow, and Jaime had just smirked and rolled her eyes wearily. "Go to hell," she mouthed, and she stuck her tongue out at him.

"That's all Sarah's fault," was how he had put it to Gronsky as they were sitting one night in the Buffalo Roadhouse. They had been waiting an hour for Pelligrew to show up, but he seemed to be preoccupied up on East Fifty-seventh Street. "Sarah's the mother. She should act more responsibly. You know what she's doing? She's spending half her nights barhopping. She picks up strangers—I mean losers, real sleazes, Alex. I don't get it. She must be having an identity crisis."

"And what about you?"

"What do you mean?" said Shaughnessy.

"You're her father. Aren't you responsible?"

Shaughnessy scowled. He toyed with an ice cube. It was the one area to which he just couldn't seem to address himself.

"Hi," said Mr. Poukos, standing by his glass shop.

Shaughnessy just nodded. He did not feel like socializing.

"You shouldn't oughta keep your young lady friends waiting," said Poukos. "Someday they leave, they may not come back again."

Shaughnessy said nothing. That made no sense to him. He started up the steps toward the door of his apartment building. Suddenly he was aware that there was an object on the doorstep. Something in a blanket was lifting its head toward him.

"You're late," said the something.

Shaughnessy just stared at it. It grew feet, then arms. A face looked out at him.

"Mr. Poukos here told me you're usually back by seven. I've been waiting since six. I'm practically freezing my buns off."

It was an old gray blanket, such as the kind used for bedrolls. For a moment he wondered whether she had anything on under it. When she took it off, she revealed knickers and a waist jacket. The jacket was yellow and had a brocaded red dragon on it.

Shaughnessy just stood there.

Mr. Poukos beamed.

"Come on," said Sandra, and she led him to the doorway. "I do hope you haven't forgotten your key again. I'm not dressed for climbing, and that doesn't look safe up there."

There had been several recent changes in Shaughnessy's apartment, although none of them, unfortunately, could be called an improvement. His door had been jimmied, and now there was no lock on it, and it was perpetually ajar so that anyone could enter it. That was all right. There was nothing worth taking. Two nights ago somebody had walked off with his percolator. That was the last salable thing he had left in the apartment. Even the sofa had a new cigarette hole in it.

"Nice place," said Sandra.

Shaughnessy didn't answer. He headed toward the kitchen and his stowaway Cutty Sark bottle. "Want a drink?" he said.

"I don't drink," said Sandra.

Shaughnessy said nothing. He went rummaging through the glassware cabinet.

During these intervening days, since that fiasco at the Racquet Club, he had spent a great deal of time trying to "rearrange" this woman. He had tried to make her uglier, more misshapen, less provocative, like some Catalina Venus who had been despoiled by vandalism. It hadn't worked. Her nose kept returning. He'd take away her bust, but it would find its way back again. Now, as he emerged, carrying his bottle of Cutty Sark, he had to admit that there was not that much wrong with her.

"Do you always do that?" She had taken off her jacket now. She was wearing a vivid red camisole with crisscrossing laces down it. Through the openings of the laces he could see her bare abdomen. It looked cheap. It looked tawdry. It was also exciting to him.

"Do what?" said Shaughnessy.

"Come home and get blotto."

Shaughnessy said nothing. He took a seat on a Bauhaus chair.

"Just asking," said Sandra. She went over to the sofa. She shoved aside some garbage and plopped herself down on it.

When he had first moved in here, infused with optimism, inviting young ladies to come home and have dinner with him, he had often become irritable over their inherent nesting instincts and their insidious attempts to make the environment more pleasant for him. "Now if we'd put the fern over there," they'd tell him—or "Let's move the couch back here by the radiator . . ." and Shaughnessy, scowling, would retreat into sullenness, saying, "It's my apartment. Just keep your mitts off of it."

Sandra, on the other hand, seemed completely oblivious. By her elbow was a paperweight that had been cracked during the razor brawl. She made no attempt to join the two jagged ends together, or scrape off the dust, or even arrange it on the table properly. "I think the designer look is so tacky," she said seriously. "It's nice that a man can have a place to call his own." She unwrapped some Trident, offered some to Shaughnessy. She balled up the paper, tossed it at the radiator.

Jesus Christ, thought Shaughnessy. He didn't know what she was doing here. Or, rather, he *did* know, and the idea terrified him. She had come to make love. She had come to have sex with him! Of course! That was it! There could be no other reason for it.

"I got tired of waiting. I thought maybe you'd call," said Sandra. "I'm in the book. It wouldn't have been hard for you. But after a couple of days, I thought, Okay, I'll call him. They gave me your address at the McBurney's records office."

Shaughnessy scowled. He took a swig of Cutty.

"You got any fruit juice?"

He shook his head negatively.

"I like fruit juice," said Sandra. "I like guava and kumquat juice. You mix em up, you stir in some honey with it . . ."

Shaughnessy stood up. "I don't find them, they find me," he had said in response to a question that Pelligrew had asked him. They had been sitting in the White Horse, and they had been talking about women. It was a subject on which Pelligrew was particularly inscrutable.

"What do you mean, they find you?"

"I don't know, they just do," said Shaughnessy. "Sarah came to me. I never went looking for it. When they want you, they come. It's not the man's choice, really. We delude ourselves into thinking we're chasing them."

And Pelligrew had said nothing, because that was not his assessment, or it might have been partially, but there was a good bit more to it obviously, and at midnight he had left to meet a woman uptown somewhere, and Shaughnessy had just sat there waiting to be "found" before he went home that night.

"We got some water if you want."

"What kind?" said Sandra.

"I don't know—*water.*"

"I don't drink tap water."

"Jesus Christ!"

"I only drink bottled water. You should too. City water's got poisons in it."

Shaughnessy poured another scotch.

"You look nervous," said Sandra.

Shaughnessy said nothing.

"You don't need to be nervous. You know, for a guy who's obviously so physically attracted to me, you certainly do have a put-offish way about you."

Shaughnessy scowled. "What's that suppose to mean?"

"What's that supposed to mean. Well, it means what I'm saying, actually. You want me so badly it's almost ludicrous. I'd like you, too, only it's not the right timing for it."

"I don't want you."

"I don't want you either. That's what I'm saying—it would be a ridiculous karma for us. Only it's disconcerting when a man keeps looking at you and making a fool of himself by acting so hostile toward you."

Shaughnessy glowered. "I don't even like you."

"I don't like you either."

"I think you're a space cadet."

"I think you're a chauvinist. You obviously drink too much . . ."

"I think you look cheap! I'd be ashamed to be seen with you!"

Good. That was over. Now they could relate more meaningfully.

"I hate California. I'm sorry we annexed it."

"You've never even been there."

"That's right, and I'm proud of it. There's nothing to see. It's just an addlebrained fairyland."

"Whereas *Bwawwston* . . ." sighed Sandra.

"Boston's got history."

"Boston's got shit. A bunch of closed-minded cod snappers . . ."

"You've been to Faneuil Hall?"

"I have. I hated it! They should have let the whole slum sink back into the ocean somewhere!"

Oh boy oh boy oh boy. There was a lot Shaughnessy could tolerate. He could tolerate headphones. He could tolerate dragon jackets. But he did not have the wherewithal to tolerate stupidity. He poured another drink. He propped his feet on the coffee table.

"And Harvard," he said. "I suppose that's nothing."

"It's a very good school. Did you go to Harvard?"

"I used to walk through it."

"That's very heady."

"It's better than Berkeley—all those state-run diploma factories . . ."

He went out into the kitchen. He got another ice cube. His mouth felt dry, his hands were trembling. Never had he met such a combative personality. He came back into the living room, the bellicosity oozing from him.

Sandra smiled. "You're so obvious, Shaughnessy."

"I suppose Steve Garvey's your idea of a baseball player."

"So very, very obvious . . ."

"He's just a cardboard stage prop. Jim Rice and the Yaz—now those guys are Baseball Players!"

Sandra yawned.

"Let's talk about cuisine."

"Yes, let's. You're so knowledgeable."

"Let me tell you about cuisine," said Shaughnessy. "California's sucks! You keep your forks in the refrigerator. That's the sum of California's contribution to kitchen art."

"I like cold forks."

"It's an L.A. pomposity!"

"They're a nice touch with salad."

"A Parisian would vomit on it!"

"What's Boston got? A bunch of baked beans with ketchup on them? That's a wonderful staple, if you're into loud-farting contests."

Shaughnessy was seething. He hated this woman! He hated her crudeness, her brashness, her cynicism. He took his feet off the table and poured another scotch. He was beginning to wish he had a quart or half liter with him.

"If California's so great, what did you come to New York for?"

"I like New York. It's a lot like Los Angeles."

"It is *not* like Los Angeles! Queens is Los Angeles! Manhattan's like Boston. It's got an urban reality to it."

"You know, I really don't know why we even bother to talk," said Sandra. "We obviously can't agree, your views are so antiquated."

"My views are objective."

"You represent the past. I represent the future. That's obvious to anybody."

Shaughnessy scoffed. "I suppose you like fairies."

"If you're referring to gays, I see nothing wrong with them."

"You're one of those dizzyheaded groupies who hangs around CBGB's and discusses Art Deco with hair stylists and decorators!"

Sandra leaned back. "Whaddaya say we just fuck."

"That is typical of your approach!"

"Well, you obviously want to."

"I do not."

"You do too."

"I do not! I'm appalled by you! You have no class. You seem to have been raised on a freeway somewhere."

Sandra smiled. "You can't get it up."

"Aw, Jesus!" cried Shaughnessy. "See, that's what I'm talking about . . ."

"You're a typical drunk Irishman who likes to strut and sound off, but when the chips are down, your little dickie just wilts on you."

Shaughnessy stood up. "I resent that remark!"

"Big deal," said Sandra.
"I didn't invite you here!"
"You did."
"No, I didn't!"
"Yes, you did."
"No, I didn't, damn it! You're pushy and you're rude and—and your hair isn't natural-colored!"
He was pacing the floor. He was furious. He was beside himself. A surge of adrenaline seemed to race through his capillaries. An urge to destroy joined an urge to procreate. Suddenly, and without warning, he lunged at her camisole.
"Okay, cool it, you bastard . . ."
He was tugging at the lace ends.
"Whaddaya think you're doing? You didn't ask my permission first."
He was holding her against the couch while he pulled at the crisscrosses. She was resisting, but not much. She smiled at him tauntingly.
"You're an idiot," she said.
"I never invited you."
"Aw, come on, come o-o-on! All that little boy show-off stuff . . ."
"I never said anything."
"Your actions said everything. When a grown man does cannonballs, I'd say that speaks rather eloquently actually."
Shaughnessy growled. He yanked off the camisole. She had no bra on. Her body was lean-looking. Her breasts were firm, but tiny and cone-shaped. When she leaned back, like now, they seemed to recede into fleshy places.
"You don't even have tits."
"Oooooh! Picky! Picky! Picky!"
"I hate titless women. That's just another androgynism."
"I'm a human, not a sow—and the word is androgyny, *Dummkopf* . . ." She was arching her back. He was fumbling with her knickers zipper.
"You got any coke?"
"I'm not one of your junky friends."

"Oh, that's right, I forgot. The guardian of morality. True to his heritage, he avoids modern decadence. He's pickling his liver and saving his nose for posterity, gentlemen . . ."

Her knickers came off. She was tugging at his belt buckle. "You know, I've been meaning to tell you—you're a lousy runner."

"I'm better than you."

"You're uncoordinated. You run like a crab. Everyone laughs at you."

He tugged at her pants. She was lying there sniggering at him. "What's this?" she said—and she pulled on his genital. To Shaughnessy's surprise, it was as hard as a broom handle. In another few seconds, he was thrust deep inside of her.

"You were saying . . . ?" he muttered.

"Okay. I was wrong maybe."

"You bet you were wrong! You've been wrong about everything!"

"Maybe so, maybe not. It's a bit early to tell. It remains to be seen, if all you know is the missionary . . ."

And so on and so forth. They sniped, they backbit. They clawed and bad-mouthed toward the acme of animalism. The east met the west. The past met the future. The Dodgers beat the Red Sox. And nobody had wanted it.

16

Room 602 was five-foot-eleven. She had orange corn-rowed hair and skin like coal tar. When she whispered, she keened; when she spoke, she bellowed; when she bellowed, like now, it was with the wail of an air-raid siren.

"You mofuggin sheeit, don' you han' me no jive, man! Ya lil mofuggin Hindi, I shoot your goddamn ass off! I pays my beels, don' you han' me no 'loud' sheeit! I got my rights in dis place! I'll git my man hea, he'll off you, mofug!"

Gronsky said nothing. The desk clerk scowled stoically. He was an ill-tempered Indian named Jawaharial Padjwani. Frankly, it was doubtful if he knew what she was saying, which was probably to his advantage, since she was not speaking kindly of him.

"You git the mofuggin cops, we'll see what's what!" she was shouting. "I pays off dis place. I pays off everybody! I git my man in hea, he's got a .357! He's gonna shoot your ass! He's gonna blow a hole in you!"

According to the clock on the wall over the manager's office, it was 8:05, which, at the Cotswold, was Bitching Hour. Every morning, between seven and nine, there was a convergence toward mayhem between the guests and the hotel management. The rent was too high. The rooms had cockroaches. Somebody on Five had set a fire in the ladies' room. To which Jawaharial Padjwani would respond by sneering, turning his back, and mumbling something in Urdu at them.

Gronsky's complaint was that he had a rat in his room. It was not a big rat—it was about the size of a chipmunk—but it was disconcerting, when he was trying to watch television, to see this black furry Thing peering out of the radiator at him. He had complained twice last week. Padjwani just ignored him. "Well, I thought you'd want to know, because it could cause a health problem." "Abbla dak!" said Padjwani, returning to his mail-sorting. He had better things to do than to listen to rat complaints.

So there was a problem with this rat, and he had a problem with his shower head, and he had a problem with the television, which kept coming and going on him, and he had a problem *(big* problem) with Room 602, who kept screaming and cursing and banging the walls during orgasm. Other than that, he was in pretty good shape. He'd go out every evening, grab a dinner at Nedick's. He'd roam Herald Square. He'd stare at the dope pushers. He'd walk up to Macy's and make eyes at the window mannequins. It was not all that bad. In fact, he found pleasure in it. One of the great revelations for the suddenly separated: The sun comes up, and the sun goes back down again. Life goes on, whether or not we're in favor of it.

No, Gronsky's greater agony lay at work, during weekdays. Every morning he'd report to the publisher's office, and there, with Karpeghian, in a spirit of teamwork, he'd watch everything he cherished become warped and obliterated.

"I think our first priority should be to cut editorial."

"I don't," said Gronsky. "Our clients won't stand for it."

"Why not?" said Eastman.

"It'd ruin the environment. I can't go to Revlon if all we're running is coupon ads."

And Eastman would lean back. "What do you say, Angie?"

"Well, I hate to say it, but I think Alex is exaggerating."

"I am *not* exaggerating!"

"He'll just have to work harder. We're not running this business to make our salesmen's lives easier for them."

It was trying, it was humiliating, and it was also ironic, because they were not always wrong—in fact, in most cases Gronsky was. They squeezed editorial, they boosted their ad rates, they did everything cockeyed, and their revenues multiplied. The result for Gronsky was a diminution of stature. He'd sit in those meetings, watching his ego evaporate, while Karpeghian, smiling, kept whittling away at him, until finally, as of yesterday, they had ceased inviting him.

"Ask heeim!" said the black woman, suddenly pointing at Gronsky. "He live next doah! You never hear him complain!"

The desk clerk smirked.

"You jis pickin on black girls! You got white whores in hea, you ain't hasslin dem, is ya?"

Gronsky said nothing. He didn't want to get involved in this, although maybe he should have, since the woman was a lunatic. Last night, at around midnight, she had thrown a knife at her television set. It had gone clear through the wall and pierced his Castel Gandolfo mural.

"Fuckin Hindi!" she was crying. "Dis man hea, he's a gentle man! You's a gentle man, honey. You knows class when you sees it. You knock on my doah. I takes good care of you. I got ways and I got ways. WHOOEEY! We have a good time, honey!"

Gronsky nodded.

He turned to Padjwani.

"Look, it's about that rat . . ."

"Abbla dak!" cried Padjwani.

"I asked you last week—"

"Abbla dak! Abbla dak!"

"Well, I'm not paying my rent until you've called in a fumigator!"

And with that he left—he just walked out on them, descending the steps toward the smoked-glass entranceway, pulling up his coat against the wind on West Thirtieth Street, and trudging north toward the Herald Square subway station.

That was in the morning. That same afternoon, when he came home from work and stepped off the elevator, his nostrils were greeted by an odor so noxious that it pierced his sinuses and stabbed clear to the mid-brain area. "Jesus Christ!" He stared down the corridor. A bluish gray cloud hung from all the ceiling fixtures. You could actually see it encircling the light bulbs, swirling in eddies like the fog in a werewolf movie.

"Well, I hopes you's satisfied!" said 602, glowering at him as he stood in front of his door trying to locate his room key. She was standing in her own door, nothing on but a garter belt. Her eyes were red. Her voice made a rasping sound.

Gronsky didn't answer. He was patting his coat pockets.

"Blame heeim!" she was shouting to a man standing behind her. He was a potbellied white man wearing pants with no zipper in them. His eyes were swollen. His fat cheeks had tear stains on them.

Gronsky found his key. He inserted it in the door lock. He opened the door and was about to enter when a dark gray cloud rolled out of the room, attacked his scleras, and drove him back in the corridor.

"What the hell? . . ."

"Iz tole you!" said the prostitute. "We alls tried to tell you, but you wouldn' listen to us! What did you expect? Yous think they use D-Con hea? You's livin in de Cotswold, not de Waldorf-Astoria, mofug!"

Gronsky said nothing. The stench was unbearable. His eyes were on fire, his lungs were asphyxiating. He went back down the hall and began punching the elevator. When it refused to come, he looked around for a fire exit.

"Goddamn it," he cried when he was back in the lobby, pounding on the desk and screaming at Padjwani, "there's enough gas up there to kill off half of Manhattan! I was trying to kill a rat, not the whole Russian army, idiot!"

"Abbla dak!" cried Padjwani.

"Yeah, yeah, yeah—abbla dak! Well, I'm not going to pay! You can abbla dak *that*, asshole! I demand another room! I demand to see the manager! I demand to see anybody, just as long as he can communicate with me!"

"Oh me oh my!" was 602's opinion when he was back upstairs, having gotten nowhere with the Indian. She and her customer were still standing in the hallway. Now there were other guests there, and they all seemed angry with him.

"Go away," said Gronsky.

"That po little critter . . ."

"Just leave me alone! This is none of your business, damn it!"

"He ain't never harmed no one. All he wanted was bread crumbs. I hopes you's satisfied. You's a fuckin assassinator!"

Gronsky went in. The room was half-shadowed. There was gas in the draperies, the bedspread, the pillow cases. He went over to the window. He tried to open it. The muscles in his throat made involuntary retching movements.

"Aw, shee-it!" said the prostitute, who had followed him inside. She was standing by the dresser looking down toward the radiator. There, on the floor, its feet up in the air, lay a three-inch-long rodent. It was staring at them dead-eyed.

"That po lil thing . . ."

"Just get out of my room, damn it . . ."

"That ain't even no rat. Thass jis a po lil house mouse, mofug . . ."

"GET OUT OF MY ROOM!" Gronsky grabbed her by the elbow. He pushed her outside—and slung the "house mouse" out after her.

Later it was conjectured that it might have been the rat toxin. There was a distinct possibility that he was suffering from brain damage. Such things do happen. Shaughnessy explained it to him. It had something to do with the central nervous system. Whatever it was, as he sat there in that room, staring through the mist at the spot where the mouse had lain, he was suddenly overwhelmed with a sense of injustice. And he decided, right then, what it was he should do about it.

"Where is she?" he cried.

"Where's who?" said Mandy. She had just stepped out of the shower and was putting on her bathrobe. She had heard the car enter, then the slamming of the car door, then a ferocious banging that made the shower stall's glass rattle.

"Don't give me that! You know!" cried Gronsky. He pushed open the door and barged into the foyer. Later she would remark that there was an unusual smell about him. It smelled like gas. It was intoxicating, nauseating.

"How dare you!" cried Mandy.

Gronsky didn't answer. He went into the living room. His

voice had a bullhorn quality. "I KNOW YOU'RE IN HERE! THERE'S NO USE HIDING FROM ME! THIS IS ALL YOUR FAULT, AND I'VE COME HERE TO PAY YOU FOR IT!"

From New York to Mount Kisco takes some forty-five minutes—somewhat less if you're traveling at seventy. Gronsky had made it in about twenty-eight minutes. He hadn't even slowed down at the Yonkers toll collector's. And as he drove he kept seeing the expression on that mouse face—those two gas-filled eyes with the accusatory sparks inside them. "Murderer!" they cried. "Madman! Exterminator! Even your wife would rather be screwed by a Swedish woman!"

"I KNOW YOU'RE IN HERE!"

"If you're talking about Ingrid—"

"I AM TALKING ABOUT MORALITY! I AM TALKING ABOUT JUSTICE, DAMN IT!" He headed toward the kitchen. He banged through the dining room. A piece of rare Waterford crashed into a radiator.

(Later it would be remarked that he seemed to be breathing heavily. "And when he did this," they'd ask her, "what was his breathing like?" and Mandy would recall how he had thrown a mop at her and his eyes had bugged out and his snorts seemed irregular to her.)

"I am trying to tell you that Ingrid's not here!" she shouted.

"DON'T HAND ME THAT! DON'T TRY TO LIE TO ME!"

"I'm not lying, damn it! She took Bobby to Cub Scouts! They have a meeting tonight! It's their big pinewood derby contest!"

Gronsky said nothing. He headed toward the stairwell. Again he went reeling through the ill-fated dining area. He picked up a chair and threw it at the dining table. A piece of Baccarat joined the fallen Waterford.

("Did he smoke?" they'd ask. "About two packs a day, maybe." "I suppose he drank . . ." "Yes, heavier than most people." And they'd stroke their chins and nod professionally and the points of their pencils would make minuscule scratching noises.)

The room they had given Ingrid was a disused guest room that had a bed, a dresser, a desk, and a dormer window. There was a time, back when, when Gronsky had coveted it. He had talked about making it into an "office"—a "study" possibly.

"I KNOW YOU'RE IN HERE!"

"For God's sake!" cried Mandy.

He went into the room and began rummaging through the clothes closet. Sweaters, blouses, blue jeans, bikini briefs—he threw them on the floor and ground the heels of his shoes in them.

("Did he complain of numbness? Tingling? Headaches?" "No, I don't think so. He didn't complain about anything. He just ranted and raved and carried on like a crazy person. He had this light in his eye. He kept talking about Hasselblads.")

"YOU IDIOT!" cried Mandy. She had him by the necktie. They were rolling on the bed amid a residue of camera parts. Springs and grommets and shutters and drive-shaft couplers kept flying out of the case in a mass disassembly process.

("I see. So he attacked you . . ." "No, he attacked our maid's camera, actually. He found it in a drawer, and he began screaming and yelling at it. It was a very expensive camera. She had brought it from Stockholm with her. It was her prize possession. It cost about five thousand dollars, probably.")

"ALEX! STOP IT!"

"THOSE GODDAMN PINKOS! . . ."

"LOOK WHAT YOU'RE DOING! MY GOD, YOU'RE BREAKING IT!"

"THIS'LL TEACH EM! TRY TO OVERTHROW ME, WILL THEY? THOSE LITTLE FISH-EATING PERVERTS—THEY'RE WORSE THAN THE COMMUNISTS!" . . .

("Hmmm. I see," said the experts. "Well, that's a classic pattern, really. Type A personality—hard-driving, frustrated . . . Probably had a history of nerves and high blood pressure. It's just too bad you didn't come to us earlier with it.")

The Zeiss Planar lens got ground into table salt. The precision-ground viewfinder was cracked like a spider web. The bellows, the extension tubes, the shutters, the tripod couplings—they all became twisted as if they had been caught in an airplane engine.

"ALEX! STOP IT!"

"LIBERTINE! . . . PERVERT! . . ."

They were groveling on the bed. The camera disintegrated. Which might have been worth it if it had led them toward intercourse. Unfortunately, it didn't. It just led them toward legal action.

Part Three

17

What he needed was chairs. He had crackers, he had onion dip. He had kosher beef canapés that he had picked up at Zabar's. He had wine, he had scotch, he had vodka, he had cocktail olives. About the only thing missing was enough surfaces to put people.

Pelligrew had been planning this party since early December. He had originally proposed it for the week following Christmas, but that had turned out to be hectic for everybody, so he had postponed it till January, when the city had recovered somewhat. And now January had gone. He wasn't sure where it had gone to. He had reached that age when all time accelerates. They were into February, knee-deep in blizzard weather, and if he didn't have it now, there was no telling when he'd have it.

"A *party?*" said Shaughnessy. The idea seemed to floor him. Parties were for girls. They required planning and ordering things. He thought it unseemly for a man to have a party, but if Pelligrew was serious, he'd be willing to go to it.

"It'll be good," said Pelligrew. "There'll be all sorts of women there. In fact, that's the problem—there may be too many, really. Lilah's coming. There'll be this girl from the Fashion Institute. Who knows, Alex, even *you* might latch onto somebody."

And Gronsky had laughed. Fat chance of that. Last month he and Mandy had gone to an attorney's office, and they had hammered out an agreement on the order of the Marshall Plan wherein Mandy and Bobby got the majority of everything. He had also agreed to pay Ingrid for property damage. They had settled out of court for three thousand dollars. It would not be enough to replace her Hasselblad, but it was a good bit of money, and she could at least get a Leica out of it. So he was not in great shape for meeting new women. He was miserable at work. His car was deteriorating. Nevertheless, it would be something to do. Sure, he'd go; he had nothing much better planned.

Pelligrew was hyper. He had been up since six-thirty. He had been out in the kitchen making compotes and salad molds. He had consulted James Beard. He had stocked up on Mondavi. Now if only he could get hold of a few chairs to put women on . . .

"Hello, Linda? This is Don."

He was calling Linda Cauthen.

"Hi, Don. How are you?"

"You wouldn't have any chairs, would you?"

Linda was a blonde who lived three doors down from him. She was attractive enough, but a bit staid, a bit Waspy for him.

"Chairs?" said Linda.

"Folding chairs . . . kitchen chairs . . ."

"I have some card-table chairs . . ."

"Great. Just hold on," he told her. He tucked in his shirt, ran his hands through his hair, and in another ten seconds he was pushing her door buzzer.

These parties of Pelligrew's had a way of mushrooming. He'd start off by calling maybe nine or ten girls he knew, but then he'd start thinking about the others he had slept with, and he'd call them up, then he'd start on the new prospects. In the table by his bed, second drawer from the bottom, scribbled on matchbooks, old laundry lists, cocktail napkins, was a six-inch-deep rat's nest full of first names and phone numbers, the majority of which were by now unfamiliar to him. That made no difference. He'd call them up anyway. He'd ask how they were. He'd cajole them, he'd sweet-talk them. "Listen," he'd say, "I've been wanting to see you again. I've been so damn busy . . . Could I see you on Saturday maybe?"

And the thing is, they'd come! They'd drive clear in from Hempstead for him. They'd arrive by car, by taxi, by subway transfer, and they'd show up at his door wearing lipstick, tight Jordaches, only to find, to their surprise, that so had three dozen other women. Which was okay by him. "Jeannie, I'd like you to meet Katherine . . . Carlotta, this is Beth . . . You've all met Yolanda, haven't you?"—and so on, ad nauseum, the girls squirming and fidgeting, wanting to flee but having nowhere to go that evening.

On this particular occasion, with the usual finagling, he had managed to arrange it so that Lilah would be there: Lilah sans Emmy, a kind of dark nubile centerpiece, a tender young morsel for all the others to sniff around. He did not want Emmy, because Emmy was possessive. Emmy was older, and she could not be intimidated. Lilah, on the other hand, was still impressionable, and he wanted her around when all the female hostility started.

"Hello, Emmy?" he said. (Here's how he handled it.) "Listen, Emmy, this is Don. I've been planning to have a party. You've had me over to your place so often—I was sort of hoping I'd have a chance to reciprocate."

"Sounds super," said Emmy. "Only I can't make it Friday."

"Oh?" said Pelligrew.

"Friday's my theater night."

"Aw, shucks, that's a shame. That's when I'm having it. Well, look, I promise, we'll make it some other weekend."

He he he! And now back to the other women: "Did I say *Saturday?* I don't know what I was thinking of. I meant to say Friday. I'm going to be out of town on Saturday. Can we make it Friday? I'm so looking forward to it . . ." And some would say no, they were engaged on Friday, and others would say fine, that actually Friday would be better for them, and there was a third group (inevitably) who had been busy on Saturday, but now that it was Friday, that put a whole different light on matters. It all worked out. These things always worked out for him. The New York female can be extremely accommodating. And then he called Lilah and said, "I'm having a party Friday. Your mother can't come, but you won't disappoint me, will you?"

So now he was hyper. The way he envisioned it, there would be all these lithe hopefuls coming to hop into bed with him, and when it finally seeped through that it was Lilah he wanted, the sexual anxiety would be almost unbearable.

"Hi. How ya been?"

"Pretty good," said Linda. She was a tall, slender woman in her mid- to late thirties. Judging from her appearance, she was not unsuccessful. She wore an expensive white cashmere with a monogrammed L on it.

"How many do you need?"

"I'm not sure," said Pelligrew.

She smiled appraisingly, adjusted her eyeglasses. She reminded him somehow of a faded white flower, which, for some reason or other, had survived past the picking season.

On Pelligrew's better days, during the spring, the autumn, patrolling the streets or cruising the subway platforms, he would suddenly have this sense of how wonderful all women are and what foresight it had taken for God to have made them such. After all, what were they? They were lop-fronted bipeds, their bone structures hinged at irregular intervals, protuberances on top, an auricular sex channel, bucket-shaped hips, and devoid of all muscle sculpture. But wasn't it amazing? It all seemed to work somehow. They all had these tits that seemed to cry out for fondling; they all had these legs that seemed to beg one to burrow through them—not repeatedly, perhaps, but just to say you had been there once. So that now, as he stood there, examining this neighbor lady, surrounded by her taste and her feminine bric-a-brac, he suddenly wondered if he had become too prejudiced. He supposed even Wasps must be good lays for somebody.

"I've found three," said Linda. She was rooting through a storage closet. She was bent over doggie-style, her rear end turned upward toward him. Every so often, she would hand back a chair to him. Through her white linen slacks he could see her lace panties outlined.

"I'm having a party. You want to stop over?"

"I can't." She stood up. "I have an important client meeting."

"Oh." He nodded. He stared at his feet. He hated Wasp blondes who had important client meetings.

"Well, if you change your mind . . ."

"Thanks." She smiled at him.

"I'll bring these back . . ."

"Anytime—don't worry about it."

He nodded, went out. He went back to his apartment. If she did come over, he'd let Gronsky deal with her.

Ten minutes to seven. Goddamn! thought Gronsky. He looked at his watch as he stepped out of the subway entrance. The party was at seven, and it was just two blocks away from here. If only, just once, he could arrive fashionably late somewhere.

After seventeen years of living in New York—if not in the city, at least in the suburbs—he had become pretty well assimilated to New York's way of doing things, including most of the mores so astounding to hinterlanders. He ignored all the wait lights. He was surly to strangers. He rarely, if ever, gave his seat up to anybody. About the only vestige of his uncivilized upbringing was that he could never manage to be late to a cocktail party.

Now, as he stood there at Ninety-sixth and Broadway, wondering what to do (grab a quick cup of coffee, maybe?), yet another concern began to intrude itself, provoked by the snow that swirled past the store windows. The forecast, he remembered, had talked about snow flurries, and he had briefly debated whether he should bring his Totes with him. He had decided against it, because, although he might need them, Shaughnessy and Pelligrew always scoffed at such pragmatism.

An observation: In any trio of comrades, in any swarm that joins to act as an organism, there are specialized roles for each individual; the functions may vary, but they lock like a jigsaw puzzle. Shaughnessy, for example, seemed to represent boyhood. He had a misspent vitality that took them back to their teen-age days. Even when drunk, he always amused them. It was like turning back the clock to a more primitive social level. Pelligrew, quite obviously, had a different specialty. His ways with women were by now not unknown to them. As Shaughnessy had once noted, "You know, I suspect he's a bastard, Alex, but I can't seem to care. I'm envious as hell of him."

Gronsky, unfortunately, was the bulwark, the father figure. Whenever he was with them, he felt wiser, more level-headed. It was not that much fun, but one does what one has to, whether it's being on time or worrying about snow warnings.

Now, as he ascended the steps up to Pelligrew's, noting with displeasure that the snow had begun sticking, he began to regret that he had his brand-new black loafers on. Ninety-five bucks. He should have brought his galoshes, damn it.

"Can I help you?" he said.

There was a girl in the foyer. She was dark-haired, short, wore a man-tailored overcoat. She was bent over sideways trying to look at the mailboxes. The snow in her hair seemed to glisten like rock crystals.

She looked up, startled.

"Try Spahn," said Gronsky.

She smiled at him quizzically. Her face was Sicilian. She had heavy black brows and an aquiline nose structure. The tuck in her chin contained a small roll of baby fat.

"I beg your pardon?"

"You're looking for Don, right?"

She nodded uncertainly. "If that's what he's called nowadays."

"You'll find him listed under Spahn—for Warren. Don't ask me. Just a second—I'll push it for you."

The girl stepped aside while Gronsky pushed the button. She was not really beautiful—that would have been flattering to her—but she was . . . well, what was she? She was young. She was sensuous-looking. It took him a minute to find just the right word for her.

"Fresh" was the word that finally occurred to him after the buzzer had sounded and they were climbing the stairs together. Her Cossack-style boots made clicks on the stair risers. Gronsky, following, took notes on her hip structure.

"You known Don long?"

The girl didn't answer. Was it Gronsky's imagination, or did he detect a slight hesitancy? Perhaps, like him, she had meant to be tardier. He wondered if that gave them a little something in common maybe.

"Hey! Alex . . . Mary Anne! . . . Come in, come in!" The door was open, and there stood Pelligrew. He was wearing no shirt. His hair was matted. A dollop of lather ran the length of one sideburn.

"I knew it," he said. "It had to be you." He kissed the girl, shook hands with Gronsky. "I presume you've met? This is Mary Anne Delucci. Mary Anne, this is Alex. Here, you can give me your coats, why don't you?"

Gronsky just stood there. As she was taking her coat off, he got a better idea of Mary Anne's true proportions. She was not all that thin—in fact, she was curvy. Her ample young breasts put a strain on her shirt bodice.

"I guess we're early . . ."

"That's okay," said Pelligrew. "I don't mind you—I just hate it when *he's* early. Here, pour yourself a drink. There's ice in the freezer bucket. Goddamn it, Gronsky, do something useful, will you?" . . .

There were the usual amenities:

"What do you do?"

Mary Anne smiled. "I design. I design things."

"I see," said Gronsky.

"Silk screens . . . textiles . . . I'm a dress designer. At least that's what I want to be."

"Oh." Gronsky nodded. He poured a Mondavi for her.

"And you?"

"I'm in sales. I sell ad space to advertisers."

The girl didn't comment.

"All those ads in those magazines—they all have to be sold. I work for a supplement."

How old was she? Twenty-four, twenty-five, maybe. Far too young for an old duffer of his status—but still, she was sweet. She had a genuine air about her. He gave her a drink, tried to pull in his stomach muscles.

"Have you known Don long?"

"A few months," said Gronsky. "And you?"

"A few years. I met him four years ago. To tell you the truth, I was surprised when he called me. It's been so long, I thought he'd forgotten me."

Gronsky said nothing.

"Is it snowing?" said Pelligrew. He was calling from the bedroom, where he was putting his jacket on.

"It's just started," said Gronsky.

"Mary Anne goes to F.I.T. Do you know about F.I.T.? You can talk about F.I.T., why don't you?"

Okay, good idea.

"What's F.I.T.?" said Gronsky.

"That's where I go. It's the Fashion Institute."

"The In—"

"Of Technology. On West Twenty-seventh Street. I've got three more months. It's not really that interesting."

Pelligrew came out. By now he was dressed. He had on pleated gray slacks and a coat with the collar up. It was a Pelligrewvian habit never to look too assembled—a holdover, perhaps, from his Georgetown postgraduate days.

"Hey, do me a favor . . ." He turned to Mary Anne. "Go out in the kitchen and look in the ice box. You'll see a red and white bowl, it's got Saran Wrap on top of it. Bring it in here, and bring in some crackers with you."

Mary Anne obeyed. The two men looked after her.

"Well?" said Pelligrew.

"I like her," said Gronsky.

"I do too. She's my social safety net. If Lilah falls through, I've got her as a substitute."

Gronsky said nothing. He felt a slight twinge of envy.

"She's terrific in bed, but she's a little too eager for me. You know what she did? She canceled a date for me. I don't like that. I find it unchallenging."

Gronsky laughed. "You're a bastard, you know that?"

"Look, do me a favor—sort of help keep an eye on her. Say things. Amuse her. Keep her preoccupied. You can do that. You can talk about football with her."

"You are really something else."

"I've got my hands full this evening!"

"For the life of me, Don, I don't know why they put up with it."

"Neither do I. It's been keeping me up nights."

Gronsky laughed. He was still holding his stomach muscles.

"Where are we?" said Shaughnessy.

The bartender stared at him.

Shaughnessy glowered back. One eyelid was drooping. He reached in his pocket, pulled out a fistful of subway tokens. He stacked them on the bar like chips in a poker ante.

It was a quarter after seven, and Shaughnessy was plastered. He hadn't even made it as far as Pelligrew's. He had stopped for a drink at this place up on Columbus, and now, for the life of him, he didn't know what he was doing there. He stared at the tokens. Was he celebrating something? If so, what? He had nothing to celebrate. The present looked bleak, the future looked miserable. He felt like a rat being pulled through a manhole cover.

This party of Pelligrew's had roused ambivalent feelings in him. He had wanted to go, but he had Sandra to deal with. They had been seeing each other about three nights a week now, and on the other four nights he had been running and hiding from her. He still didn't want her. In fact, he resented her. Why, of all women, did *she* have to cling to him? At least, before, he had still had his fantasies. Now, with her, the world was so *real*-looking.

"Why not?" said Sandra.

"Because," said Shaughnessy.

"I want to be with you."

"I don't care—it's a bachelor party. I have no commitment. I've already explained that to you. I'm going alone. I don't want to argue with you."

Sandra said nothing. They had been sitting in her apartment, a second-story loft on the corner of Christopher Street. Like the woman who live there, it had an unkempt air about it. The walls were adorned with old Che Guevara posters.

"You're going to pick up a woman."

"I might," said Shaughnessy.

"You're going to sit and get drunk and end up putting the make on someone."

"So what if I do? Hey, look, I'm a man, goddamn it. Leave me alone. I never made any promises to you."

Sandra said nothing. Her face looked wistful. She was sitting on the sofa wearing a faded pink bathrobe. Her eyes were unmade up, she had her hair up in curlers. She had forsaken Betty Grable for the new "wet-and-kinky" look.

"I'm not trying to nag."

"Well, then don't!" cried Shaughnessy.

"It's just that I'd like to be able to share things with you."

"There's nothing to share. I'm going to Pelligrew's. As far as I know, there won't even be any women there."

Well, that wasn't true, and he felt foolish for saying it. Of course there'd be women. There'd be a veritable harem of them. It was just that, by God, he was still his own person, and no canary-haired kook was going to mother or castrate him.

"Then *I'll* go out, too."

"Go ahead," said Shaughnessy.

"I'll go out with men."

"You can do what you want to, damn it. I'm not your husband. I have no commitment to you. I had ten years of marriage, and that's plenty for anybody."

Sandra got up, walked over to the bathroom. She slammed the door shut, then there was the sound of the tap running. Shaughnessy just sat there. "Jesus Christ," he muttered. He snatched up his parka vest and took off toward the subway station.

This little contretemps had taken place about six, and, as he sat on the D train heading out of West Fourth Street, he suddenly realized that he had been precipitous; he was going to be early, which was an unpardonable gaucherie. So, revising his game plan, he got off at Eighty-sixth Street. He wound his way north, headed over toward Columbus. He'd stop in a bar, have a couple of calm-me-downs. He'd show up about eight, when he was more in control of himself.

The reason he did not want Sandra to go was that, for one thing, he wanted to be alone with his men friends. When Sandra was around, she ruined everything. She was so dour, so *female.* She just scowled disapprovingly at them. A second, better reason was that he wanted to meet women. Restored to his manhood, he yearned for variety. Never does the world seem so rife with potential as for the man who has just discovered that he can still get a hard on.

The bar Shaughnessy had picked was up on Columbus in the Nineties. It had an awning out front with the name "Bocusse" on it. He had no idea how this word was pronounced, but it looked relatively chic, and he'd make a valuable addition to it.

"What'll you have?" said the bartender.

"Double Cutty, no water." He plopped himself down on one of the blond hardwood barstools. Yeah, Bocusse's was nice. It had ferns. It had cocktail waitresses. He guzzled one scotch, promptly ordered a second one.

Here's how he saw it: He'd arrive about eight. There'd be two dozen women, their spines curved like reptiles', their eyes peering out over the rims of their wineglasses, all trying to look gay while their pores oozed loneliness. And into this mélange, this predatory jungle, strolling casually (having just been with a woman, maybe?), he, Ted Shaughnessy, would suddenly appear, looking disarmingly virile in his blue jeans and running shoes. That's how he saw it. The only problem was, as he finished his second and began downing his third, instead of disarming, he was becoming disjointed. His eyes were fogged over. He was listing to starboard.

"Another," he said.

The bartender nodded.

He leaned back in his chair, put his knee on the bar rail. On the coaster in front of him lay the neat stacks of subway tokens. Good as cash. So a cabbie had once said to him.

Midway down, as his teeth hit the ice cubes and his mind flitted feverishly among brunettes and redheads, his fantasies were enjoined by yet another chimera who had long auburn hair and a face like Faye Dunaway's. "Excuse me," she was saying (although this was really his mind talking)—"Excuse me," she was saying, "but I understand you're an illustrator"—and Shaughnessy would scowl, look masculinely indifferent, say, "Well, yes, in a way . . . in a medical capacity . . ." She'd be standing in a corner. Her name was—Samantha! She had white, even teeth, and she was a graduate of Wellesley. Dressed in beige tweed, she had a small flat in Riverview, and she had just blown in from some posh East Side art gallery. "Could you teach me?" she'd say. "I find medicine so interesting!" And Shaughnessy would smile, and he'd light up two cigarettes, and the only hint of her unbridled passion would be the oh-so-slight way that her body leaned into him . . . .

What time was it? He stared at the clock. It was quarter to eight. Where the hell was he? He seemed to recall that it was about seven blocks north of here. Plenty of time. Plenty of time for another one . . . .

And now it was eight. Samantha was giggling. She had taken him home to her twentieth-floor penthouse, and there, by the light of her wood-burning fireplace, she was coming to climax, while maintaining gentility . . . .

Oh, God . . . He nodded. He was completely noncompos. He called over the bartender, ordered a cup of black coffee. He drank that down, then ordered another one. It was twenty to nine. He'd better get the hell out of here . . . .

And the thing about it was—the thing that appealed to him—was that everything about her was so opposite of Sandra. She had class. She was gentile. She had been brought up in Boston. When they ate, at "21," she never dropped her alfalfa sprouts . . . .

"How mush?" he muttered.

"That'll be twelve sixty-five."

He dug in his pocket. He pulled out more subway tokens.

The bartender stared.

"Keep the shanje," said Shaughnessy.

He lurched toward the snow, where Samantha lay beckoning.

18

Gronsky was rolling. That didn't happen very often. Usually, at parties, he just sat and looked overweight, but tonight, for some reason (perhaps from holding his stomach muscles), his brain had risen to an unusually high humor level.

"What I'm trying to say—"

"Who cares?" cried Shaughnessy.

"Goddamn it—" laughed Gronsky.

"Alex, nobody gives a shit! Thad is one of the things you're gonna have to recognize! You are basically irrelevant! Nobody's interested in you!"

Gronsky laughed. Oh, God, this was great. He was standing by the sofa, his arms gesticulating, trying, as he had for the past fifteen minutes, to drive home a point that would leave the company in awe of him.

"Excuse me—" said Pelligrew.

"Bullshit!" cried Gronsky. "No, listen, I'm serious . . . I want your opinion, ladies . . . When you're a girl you're a woman, and when you're a woman, you're not. Thass the law of the land! Thass whad Betty Friedan tole me!"

The "ladies" said nothing. There were about twenty of them present, festooned about the room in little clusters of awkwardness, their bright, rouge-brushed faces all pressed in anxiety, their snug-fitting denims showing strains at the razor creases. Pelligrew was happy. He was at the height of mysteriousness. His black smoldering eyes seemed to sear into all of them. When they tried to smile back, he'd just scowl and look offish. He'd lean over toward Lilah, whisper something inaudible to her.

"No, listen—" said Gronsky.

"I will not!" cried Shaughnessy, who, having arrived about nine, was unusually obstreperous. He had already tried to feel three women's bosoms. He was now stretched out flat across the top of a butcher block. "I have been listening to your opinions for the past hundred years, Alex, and—forgive me—I'm sorry, I know this is hard on you—but after careful what-have-you—not to mention analysis—I have come to the conclusion that you have nothing to say to people!"

"Excuse me—" said Pelligrew.

"Go to hell!" laughed Gronsky.

"No, I mean it. Forgive me, I don't mean to embarrass you. It is a well-established fact that all Ohioans are tedious. Iss something in the soil. It has t'do with the hog manure."

Pelligrew, still sober, was standing next to Gronsky, while beside him stood Linda, who had dropped over after all. He had been trying, futilely, to introduce her to Gronsky, but Gronsky, transported, was having nothing to do with it.

"When I was a kid—"

"You were already boring!"

"—my mother played bridge with a bunch of ole ladies, damn it! And she'd say, 'Now, Alex, today the *girls* are coming over.' Thass wha she'd call em. Her friends were all 'girls' to her—"

"Listen, Alex—" said Pelligrew.

"So what?" cried Shaughnessy.

"I am tryin to esplain—"

"This is a major embarrassment, Alex! You are addressing an audience of sophisticated women, and you are boring them to tears with what your midwestern mother tole you!"

All in all, there were some thirty-odd people present. They had been arriving in dribbles since about a quarter after seven, knocking off snow, folding their umbrellas, trying to look at ease among the pierced ears and eyelashes. They were not all women. There was a sprinkling of men there, although Pelligrew had made sure that they would all be nonthreatening. There was a professor from Hunter, a couple of law clerks, an anonymous bureaucrat, a Community Board Seven member . . .

Gronsky laughed. This was really terrific. He raised his glass, went to take a swallow. On the way to his mouth, he got snagged on a table lamp. The vodka spilled out and onto Mary Anne's blouse front.

"I'd like—" said Pelligrew.

"You're a bastard!" laughed Gronsky. He was patting his pockets, trying to locate a handkerchief. "I am trying to mag an astude observation here! There are no more 'girls'! We got nothin but 'women' nowdays!"

"If you would—" said Pelligrew.

"So what?" said Shaughnessy.

"I think iss important! No, iss not, iss absurd, goddamn it! Iss just one more symptom of all this damn women's lib bullshit! Some hippie in jeans, I'm s'posed to think she's a 'woman' suddenly!"

Poor Linda Cauthen. She had arrived behind Shaughnessy, impeccably dressed, carrying a red leather briefcase, explaining to Pelligrew that her meeting was canceled and she was just dropping by to see how they were doing here. "Oh, great," said Pelligrew, and he had nodded, "come in," and then he had stood there awkwardly, at a loss what to do with her, until finally, desperate: "Have you met my friend Alex yet? I think you'll enjoy him. You'll have so much in common with him." That had taken place about ten minutes earlier. Since then, smiling wanly, at sea with the subject matter, she had been standing there clutching at a half glass of spritzer, while Gronsky, that dreamboat, completely neglected her.

"Not true!" cried Shaughnessy.

"Iss too!" cried Gronsky.

"Iss not! I'll prove it!" He swung his feet off the butcher block. "If she comes from Texas, she's a 'girl'—she's stuck with it. She's only a 'woman' when she buys things in Bloomingdale's!"

"Listen, Alex—" said Pelligrew.

"Pleased to meetcha," said Gronsky. "No, wait a minute, damn it—here's how we'll settle it. If she's younger than you, you have to call her a 'woman,' but if she's older than you, you have to call her a 'girl' again."

Shaughnessy, pie-eyed, unconstrained by formalities, had by now decided to vacate the butcher block. He stood unsteadily, took a few faltering steps, then sat down abruptly by the leg of the coffee table.

"Do you always do this?" This was Mary Anne speaking.

"Whassat?" said Gronsky.

She pulled out her blouse front. "I *mean,*" she said. "It's the third time this evening. I keep trying to move, but you always keep finding me."

Gronsky blinked. "Oh, Jesus," he muttered.

"It's all right, it's not new . . ."

He pulled out his handkerchief.

"Aw, shit . . . oh, Jesus . . ."

"If you can get me some water, maybe . . ."

He was dabbing at her breasts. "Look, I'll pay for the dry cleaning . . ."

"Listen, Don—" said Linda.

"Just a minute," said Pelligrew. "Goddamn it, Gronsky—"

"I'll pay for everything . . ."

"Gronsky, goddamn it, that's my social safety net . . ."

"Thanks for the drink. Say good-bye to your men friends for me."

Meanwhile, Shaughnessy, completely ungovernable, was groveling about the floor, trying to look at girls' underwear, haranguing the Pope, reciting the catechism, billing and cooing to some young brunette's calf muscles. This party hadn't gone quite the way he had hoped it would. In the first place, there was no sign of Samantha anywhere, and in the second place, they were beginning to run low on Cutty Sark, the realization of which instilled a sharp pang of terror in him. "I love you," he was saying. The calf muscles twinkled. "I wanna take you home . . ." They rippled provocatively. He lay there blinking. He hunched up on his knees. He coiled back like a cobra. He lunged out awkwardly—

And that's when Lilah, who was the first to notice, came over to Pelligrew, who was standing next to Gronsky, leaned over slightly, showing a brief glimpse of cleavage, and whispered something while nodding toward the doorway.

At the time this happened it was twenty-five of ten. Outside, on the ledges, the snow was accumulating. Inside, the temperature was reaching the boiling point. All it would take was one spark, one catalyst . . .

Lilah pointed. Pelligrew squinted. It was standing in the doorway carrying a white overnight case. It had on a black satin jumpsuit and a pair of green cowboy boots. Slung over one shoulder was a portable makeup mirror.

Pelligrew had been managing to avoid this since that day last October when, having borrowed his toothbrush and violated his privacy, the girl named Ruthie, fearing for her life, had fled out the door wearing his best purple necktie. She had called him four times, but he was never available. Finally she had resorted to sending him postcards. "Are you angry?" they asked. He never responded. He hadn't even called her until the day before yesterday.

"Yoo-hoo! Dwonnie?" she said.

Pelligrew just stared.

"Dwonnie?" she said. "Do I got de wrong night mebbe?" He watched as she advanced, making her way through the maelstrom. The ankles of her boots were all baggy, like pachyderms'.

Picture a gulch in the Arizona desert—some dry, horrible place filled with vultures, tarantulas, a place where only the rattler survives, slithering among rocks with the scorpions and Gila monsters. And now imagine this same place internalized—a bleak, psychic landscape up on West Ninety-seventh Street—just as hostile, just as formidable, with predators lurking near every end table. That's how this was. And here came the victim. She looked like a rabbit that had strayed from its munching ground. She had snow in her hair, her mascara was running. "Sowry I'm late. I got stuck in de subway tunnel . . ."

Later they would all have a hard time remembering. Was it Ruthie who screamed, or was it the girl by the stereo? Was it Lilah who cursed, or was it the one named Carlotta, who had suddenly become aware that there was a man on her calf muscle?

Whoever it was, it was definitely unpleasant. There was also confusion as to the mystery of the suitcase. Some would state flatly that that was Pelligrew's doing, and others would say, no, that it just happened spontaneously.

Be that as it may, the important thing is, it took a couple of seconds for the whispering to stop, and there was another few seconds of strained introductions, in which Ruthie, curtsying, grew increasingly red-faced.

"I'd like you to meet Betsy . . ."

"Pleezed t'meetcha," said Ruthie.

"And this is Mary Anne . . . I believe you've met Lilah . . ."

"How do. Pleezed t'meetcha. Dis is very embarrassin. He shoulda oughta twold me he was havin a pwotty heah . . ."

The makeup mirror had a white plastic frame and an electrical cord that hung down like a monkey's tail. Every time she moved, it seemed to snag on the furniture. Its round cyclops eye spun lights off the wall moldings.

"You planning to stay?" This was from Lilah.

"Huh?" Ruthie gaped.

Lilah just smiled at her.

"He shoulda oughta twold me. Dis is very embarrassin. You shoulda oughta twold me you was havin a pwotty, Dwonnie . . ."

And that's when it happened. Maybe it was Lilah. When you're eighteen and gorgeous, you do dastardly things sometimes, and it would not have been hard, when no one was looking, to open that latch with a finely honed fore talon. Or maybe it was elves. That is not beyond reason. There are sylphs in this world who are sensitive to status, and they are particularly disapproving of young Polish secretaries who travel from Brooklyn carrying tomorrow morning's clothing with them. Whatever the cause, the suitcase fell open, the bottom dropped down, spilling nightgown and lingerie, a pair of Bon Jours, a blouse, some pantyhose, a tube of depilatory, and an Oral-B toothbrush holder.

The women just stood there. There was silence all around.

"My, my . . ." Lilah smiled.

There was a muffled snicker.

For a moment even Ruthie seemed incapable of movement.

"When we come to Donald's, we're prepared for anything . . ."

And that's when Pelligrew made his first major *faux pas.* Thirty-nine years of living on the precipice; two fifths of a century of flawless tightrope walking, and he finally does something that's admittedly asinine. Because buried in that clothing, surrounded by underwear, nestled in bra cups and hankies and tissue paper, lay a small plastic case about the size of a clam shell and covered all over with daisies and daffodils. If he had been his usual astute self, if his wits had been about him, he would have realized immediately that this object was dangerous, but all he could think of, since it was lying by his foot, was that the gentlemanly thing would be to pick it up for her.

"Here, you dropped this . . ."

That's how he put it. He was completely innocent. He was just being polite to her. He picked it up, he extended it openly—and that's when Ruthie began screaming and shouting at him.

Well, how was he to know? He didn't know about diaphragms. Rather, he knew about diaphragms, but their containers weren't familiar to him. We all have our specialties. His happened to be fucking. You wouldn't ask Van Cliburn if he could come tune your piano, would you?

"YOU BEYASTAHD!" screamed Ruthie, and first she began blubbering, and then she began crying, and then she began bellowing at him, and Pelligrew just stood there, staring at that diaphragm case, totally confused as to what the commotion was.

And that's when Ruthie, snatching the case away, clutching at her suitcase and her Miss Clairol makeup mirror, shouldered past Lilah, ran into the kitchen, and, screaming hysterically, began breaking his wineglasses.

All of this happened within the space of three seconds. That's important to know, because it explains his reaction lag. Normally The Phantom had very fast reflexes, and was more than a match for any woman in cowboy boots. But this time was different. He had been caught by surprise. She was there one second, the next she was gone, and the next he could hear his cabinet doors opening, followed by curses and the splintering of stemware.

"I HATECHUZ, DWONNIE!"

CRASH!

There went one . . .

Pelligrew was stunned. He didn't have many wineglasses.

"I HATECHUZ! HATECHUZ!"

CR-R-RASH!

There went two . . . .

He had been meaning to buy some, but he hadn't gotten to the Pottery Barn.

But now he was moving, he was his old lightning self again, weaving, dodging, trying to get to the kitchen, trying to stop this latest in a string of neurotics before she could sack the premises and sabotage everything.

Only he was a little too late. There was glass lying everywhere. There was glass on the floor, on the counters, the windowsill. The window was open, and there stood Ruthie. She was about to eject his Cuisinart food processor.

"Okay, goddamn it—"

"You had no right t'do dis!"

"Put it down . . . Let's try to be reasonable . . ."

"You had no right t'do dis! I am a sensitive human! I nevuh hoit chuz . . . I nevuh hoit nobody . . ."

The Phantom smiled.

"You keep yoah distance! . . ."

He held out his hand.

"I wahn you, Dwonnie! . . ."

He reached out slowly—and then he lunged . . .

There was a scream—a crash—a breathtaking freefall . . .

19

"So anyway—" said Gronsky as they were crossing Sixth Avenue; by now his loafers were snow-stained and waterlogged; ninety-five bucks—that's how much he had paid for them, and even that was a bargain, because they were Italian-made loafers, damn it—"so anyway," he said, "I'm sitting in this bar, see, and this woman comes in—she's in her fifties, she's sixty, maybe—says, 'Is this seat taken?' I say, 'Not that I know of,' so she plops herself down, she starts smiling and winking at me . . ."

Mary Anne said nothing. It was about twenty after twelve now. The Village was wearing one of its nostalgic Old London looks. Snow hung softly from the ledges, the cornices. The dim-lit streetlamps had halos of white around them.

"So then—" said Gronsky.

"Turn left," said Mary Anne.

"So then," he said, "she pulls out this pocketbook. She's got pennies in there—she's got nickels, some subway tokens . . . and she turns it upside down and just dumps them all over the place!"

Mary Anne's apartment was on Morton near Hudson Street. They had taken the local to the West Fourth Street subway station, and from there they had walked, cutting through side streets, their shadows pursuing across snow-studded window grates.

The party had ended on a discordant note. Pelligrew had tripped, hit his head on a counter top, Ruthie had screamed, there had been a gasp from the onlookers, and the Cuisinart food processor had ended up on the sidewalk. After the police had dispersed, and the neighbors had stopped gawking, and

Ruthie had come out from where she was locked in the bathroom, Gronsky had turned, said, "Come on—let's get out of here," and Mary Anne had agreed to go out and have coffee with him.

At the beginning of the evening, when they had first introduced themselves, he had been somewhat attracted but not that impressed by her. She was a little too short, a little too chunky; her eyes were too black, she was a little too ethnic for him. But as the evening wore on, her charms seemed augmented. He liked her laugh. He approved her ingenuousness. The least he could do, after the problems he had caused her, was to see that she got home, didn't get raped on some street corner.

"So anyway—" he said. They had finally reached Morton Street. Near mid-block she stopped. They were in front of a graystone. A streetlight illuminated the side of her cheekbone. Snowflakes glistened on the tips of her eyelashes.

"This woman—" he said.

"Would you like to come up?"

"Yeah, all right—for a minute. I really can't stay, though . . . She drops all these coins, I'm picking them up for her, and she hops off the stool and throws her goddamn skirt over me!"

Mary Anne's apartment, like so many young women's, was on the topmost floor of a heartbreaking walk-up. It was tiny, spartan, furnished with hand-me-downs. The sofa consisted of a couple of mattresses.

"Should I make us some coffee?"

"Yeah, all right—if it's instant . . . So anyway," he said, "she throws her goddamn skirt over me! I'm down on the floor, she's got me trapped in her petticoat, and she's laughing and screaming—and she's wearing no underpants!"

He had been babbling on this way for about the past half hour. It had started on the subway, where he had tried to explain football to her, then he had told her about his father, about his childhood in Steubenville, how he had injured his knee, his experiences at Quantico. Mary Anne, smiling, had just sat there and listened. Every so often she had her own points of reference. There was a therapist she had gone to who was a moonlighting cab driver; she had once had a roommate who tried to burn their apartment down. And Gronsky had laughed. He loved crazy stories. They seemed to confirm what he had always suspected: that New Yorkers were sick, only Ohioans were normal, and that the center of sanity seemed to reside out near Dayton somewhere.

"Take milk?" said Mary Anne.

"Huh? Oh, no. No, just black . . ." He had taken off his coat and was sitting on the mattresses. He felt warm. He felt good. He felt—well, he felt comfortable somehow. He might even go so far as to try relaxing his stomach muscles.

Earlier, in the diner where they had stopped and had coffee, they had seen that girl Ruthie sitting alone in a corner, and she had looked so pathetic with her suitcase and makeup mirror that Mary Anne, stricken, had gone over and talked to her. "He shoulda oughta twold me," was what Ruthie kept saying—to which Mary Anne would smile and put her hand on her elbow and say, "Listen, Ruthie, the guy isn't worth it. Take it from me. I know just what you're going through." To which Gronsky, of course, had little rejoinder, since the "guy" in question was his bosom pal Pelligrew, but he couldn't help wondering at the naïveté of women and why they were always being fooled by the charms of some ass bandit.

Four months, thirteen days, and one and a half hours: that's how long it had been since he had last had intercourse. Not that he was expecting to have intercourse now, but that's what it had been, and it had taken its toll on him. Sometimes he wondered if he would ever know love again. Maybe society had advanced too much for him. Maybe all women, enflamed by new freedoms, had become too voracious—just a little too cynical for him. It occurred to him sometimes, lying in his hotel room, staring at the ceiling or looking at television, that, whatever he had, it was no longer marketable. The women he wanted were all too young, too preoccupied.

Mary Anne came back in and took a chair, sitting opposite. Her face was flushed from the steam of the coffeepot. She leaned forward slightly and poured out two mugfuls. He was reminded again of how enticing her breasts looked.

"I'm all out of sugar."

"That's all right." He nodded.

She leaned back again and took a sip from her coffee mug. For a moment he detected a flicker of nervousness. He had seen that before. He had seen it at Pelligrew's.

"Well . . ." She smiled.

Gronsky said nothing. A moment ago, he had been bubbling with anecdotes. He had been talking about his job, about the desk clerk, Padjwani, about Room 602, whom they had hauled away yesterday . . .

"I'm married," he blurted.

Mary Anne said nothing.

"I'm technically married, but I'm legally separated."

"I know. You've said."

"I have a nine-year-old son. Wait—just a minute—I have his latest school picture here."

He was fumbling in his billfold. Mary Anne said nothing. An unanswered question seemed to hang in the atmosphere. They were trying to avoid it, but it couldn't be avoided. It was just too big. It was just too inevitable.

He took out the photo.

Mary Anne looked.

"He looks like you."

"You think so?" said Gronsky.

"I think so. The mouth."

"His eyes are his mother's."

"I wouldn't know that—but there's a definite resemblance there."

Gronsky nodded. He put back the photo. Silence again. The question grew larger. She sipped at her coffee. He sat there and fidgeted. Finally, with a sigh, he looked at his wristwatch.

"Well, look . . ."

"I know."

"It's quarter after one."

"I know. It's late."

"I've got to be going."

He stood up. She followed. They walked over to the door. The question grew larger. It hung like a scimitar.

Oh, how long had it been since he had gone through this foolishness? His college days, maybe, when he was first dating Mandy, standing at the door of the Kappa Alpha Theta house, hands crammed in chinos, smiling inanely at her? Do you never outgrow it? Does it follow you to the grave? When you're seventy years old, hobbling around on a walker, do you still stand there awkwardly at the door of some widow, saying, "Well, it's been nice . . ." and feeling your heart pounding?

"Well . . ."

"It's been nice."

He was fumbling with his muffler. Mary Anne, in bare feet, was holding the door for him. He buttoned his coat. He pulled up his coat collar. He put on his gloves. He looked around at the room again.

"I was wondering . . ." he said.

Mary Anne smiled.

"Well, I know this sounds silly, and you probably aren't interested . . ."

Her head cocked slightly.

". . . but I enjoyed this tonight. I mean, talking and all. I really liked talking to you."

She smiled again. "Yeah, I liked it, too."

"I mean, it's my fault, I guess—it's like I was trying to say earlier—but there are so damn few women I feel comfortable talking to. I really enjoyed it. It meant a great deal to me."

She nodded, said nothing.

"So what I was going to propose . . . Well, now don't take this wrong—I know you don't know me well. You're probably busy—you've got a million and one boy friends—but I was wondering if maybe we could do this again sometime."

"I'd like that," she said.

"I mean, it's not like I'm pushing. I mean, I'd just like to talk. We could go to a movie maybe. We could go out to dinner. We could go for a hamburger. It's not like a date—there'd be nothing expected of you . . ."

"I'd like that, Alex."

"I mean . . . hell, I don't know . . . It's a crazy idea—I don't know why it occurred to me. I was sitting there thinking, I thought, Damn it, just ask her, Gronsky. What's she gonna say? It's not like I'm after something."

Mary Anne laughed. She leaned her head against the door panel. Her hair was pressed against the side of her temple. Gronsky scowled. He looked up at the ceiling. He shuffled his feet. He readjusted his coat collar.

"Alex?"

"What?"

"Do me a favor."

He shifted his weight. There was a change in the atmosphere.

"I'd rather for now we just keep it a friendship. I've got some things to work out. It's kind of hard to explain to you."

"Oh, sure." He nodded.

"Now don't take that wrong . . ."

"Oh, no . . . Hey, look . . ." He held out his palms toward her. "It was a crazy idea. I don't know why it occurred to me. I understand. You don't have to apologize . . ."

He was backing out the door.

"Wait a minute, don't go yet . . ."

"No need . . . don't worry . . . I don't know what the hell's wrong with me. I'm a middle-aged man. I've got a kid, I've got child support . . . You're absolutely right. Just forget that I mentioned it."

He was backing through the hall. He was heading toward the stairwell.

"Alex?"

No answer.

She came out into the hallway.

"Alex, come back!"

She leaned over the bannister.

He was muttering as he went, "I don't know why it occurred to me . . ."

20

"ACHHH!" cried Lilah.

"Now what?" said Pelligrew.

"You kicked my ankle! You keep kicking my ankle, Donald!"

"I didn't mean—"

"I keep trying to tell you! It's very tender! You keep scratching your toenails on it!"

Say this for Pelligrew—he was not without resources. He could always snatch victory from the jaws of fiasco. He may have lost all his wineglasses and totaled his food processor, but by the end of the night he had the prize he had hungered after.

Of course Lilah Schoenstein was her mother's daughter. She had been born to lure men like a horse to run furlongs. It was a genetic inheritance, a kind of sexual Tay-Sachs disease; one could almost expect it to show up in a blood sample. And along with these traits came a certain mentality, a carefully formed bias, almost as if she had been trained for it—which indeed she had. Emmy had seen to it. It was a code of behavior that had been passed from antiquity.

Rule number one was that every man has his purpose, and it is the woman's duty to find it and utilize it. Some men are rich, some men are lovers, some men are neither, but make excellent tennis partners. Emmy herself was the first to admit this: "I've always told Lilah that every man has his use, Donald. You, for example. You're terrific in bed, but I'd hate the idea of being fully dependent on you."

Rule number two was that, no matter how much men suffer, you must always realize that it's the woman who's victim. And the more beautiful the woman, the greater her affliction, until, if she looks like Lilah, she's almost reached leper status. It was an illogical view, a tough line to argue—sort of like being made President, then complaining about loneliness—but argue it she did, and if any man disobeyed her, she'd be the first to complain that his sex was mistreating her.

None of which, of course, was all that novel to Pelligrew, since he had a pretty clear insight into young Jewish Princesses. It's just that, on occasion, it could become a bit frustrating—like now, for instance, with the bedsprings vibrating.

"For Christ's sake, Donald . . ."

"Would you please just relax?"

"How can I relax? I'm in mortal agony!"

"I'm not even touching—"

"Your toenails are touching! They feel like sabers! They're gouging my capillaries!"

Pelligrew sighed. Wasn't this wonderful? It was just what he had wanted, and now he was getting it. And the strange part was, it only heightened his passion. The more she kvetched, the faster his pulse raced.

"Of course you know," she had said when they had retired to the bedroom and she had unhooked her bra, begun unfastening her dirndl skirt—"you know this won't work. I've been trying to tell you. I just hope when it's over you aren't too disappointed in me." And Pelligrew had smiled. Disappointed! he thought. Oh, boy, oh, Lilah, you don't know what you're talking about! And he had begun nuzzling her neck, fondling her nipples, his arteries throbbing as she began finding flaws in him.

"You know, sometimes," said Emmy a couple of months ago—it was on that same night that Lilah had shown up in her underwear; Emmy had finally insisted that she put on a bathrobe, and as soon as she was gone, Emmy had whispered to Pelligrew—"you know, sometimes," she said, "I think maybe I've spoiled her, Donald. She's really quite bitchy. She's almost intolerable. But when I get to thinking of how you men all keep drooling over her, I think, Good, serves you right. That's the price you can pay, goddamn it." To which Pelligrew had said nothing, because there was nothing he could say, because he had no idea what "price" she was talking about, but now as he lay there listening to her carping, he was beginning to find out, he was tasting that princesshood . . .

"OUCH!" she shouted.

"JEEZUS!" cried Pelligrew.

"What are you wearing? Are you wearing a wristwatch?"

"A wristwatch? No—"

"My God, it's a manacle! Please! Have some mercy! You keep raking my skin with it!"

The object in question was a silver ID bracelet. It had been given to Pelligrew by his first steady girl friend. That was at Hagerstown High back in 1958, and her name was Francie, and it had special significance to him.

"I don't see how—"

"Would you just take it off please?"

"I don't see how it could be causing such pain, Lilah—"

"Well, it is! It scratches! I'm not up to arguing with you! If we're going to make love, you can just take your damn shackles off!"

Actually, this bracelet had a bit of past history. He had taken it off when he had graduated from high school, and it had languished for years in the bottom of a jewelry box, until eventually it had looked like a barnacled anchor chain. But about four years ago, when he was still married to Elizabeth, seized by boredom, storm-tossed by restlessness, he had taken it to a jeweler, and the jeweler had cleaned it, and he had begun wearing it again—a sort of fifties anachronism. In some semiconscious way, it seemed almost symbolic to him. It was the mid-life equivalent of the black mask and Phantom cape. It protected him from age. It fended off impotence. It was a reminder of his youth, when the world seemed less complicated. Of course Elizabeth had balked. "What is *that?*" she had asked him, and Pelligrew had scowled, because it was none of her business, damn it, because what it was, obviously, was the beginning of the end, and, although he had never quite said that, he had expected her to realize it. Then, a few months later, when he had begun his promiscuousness, one of the first things he had done was to look up his high school flame. He had some half-cocked notion that he could renew former ties with her—seduce her, perhaps, even break up her family life. "Are you crazy?" she had said. (He had called her in Hagerstown.) "I've been happily married for the past fifteen years, Donald! I've got three lovely children, my husband's successful, and I should fly up there and spend the night in New York with you?" And Pelligrew had scowled. "Do you remember the bracelet, Francie?" "Not exactly," she had said—"that was an awfully long time ago . . ." "Well, you gave me a bracelet, and it had your name on the back of it, and it cost twenty-five dollars. I remember we talked about it." "Really, Donald . . ." "WELL, I STILL HAVE THAT BRACELET, FRANCIE! I HAD IT APPRAISED! IT'S WORTH TWO HUNDRED DOLLARS NOW! ONLY I TOOK OFF YOUR NAME! IT'S COMPLETELY ERADICATED! SO YOU CAN JUST SIT THERE AND ROT! OUR RELATIONSHIP'S OVER WITH!" And with that, he had hung up. He had felt angry, humiliated. That she could be happy while he was so miserable. Nevertheless, he still wore the bracelet. It reminded him of something. It was like some kind of "Rosebud" to him . . .

"There!" He harrumphed. He had taken off the bracelet. It made him feel nude. It made him feel violated. Lilah just smiled. She seemed to enjoy it. Her eyes were aglow with the delight of her power over him.

"I have one more small favor—"

"Forget it," said Pelligrew.

"I have one more small favor, and it has to do with your toenails—"

"My toenails are fine!"

"They are not, they're like bear claws, and I refuse to make love to a man who's got bear claws on him!"

Oh, my God . . . Jesus Christ! He rolled over on his stomach. It was as if all his worst nightmares were flying in through the window at him. He was trying to give his seed to this diasporic Fury, and she was mauling him to death and seeming to enjoy every minute of it!

"OKAY!" He was screaming. He was also getting up. "I'M GONNA GO INTO THE BATHROOM AND I'M GONNA CUT MY DAMN TOES OFF! I'M GONNA TAKE EACH TOE, AND I'M GONNA CUT IT WITH A RAZOR, AND I'M GONNA COME BACK IN HERE AND I'M GONNA LIE HERE AND BLEED TO DEATH!"

And that's what he did. Or at least he went into the bathroom. He got out some clippers, and he lifted the toilet seat, and he began clipping his toenails—clippy, clippy, clippy—muttering, "Jesus, you cunt—you just wait, I'll get even with you . . ."

"You know the trouble with you"—this was Elizabeth talking; it was their final conversation under the aegis of marriage vows; he was packing his clothes, and she was standing in the doorway, her young model's body looking haggard and argument-worn—"the trouble with you, you think only of yourself, Don. You can only respond to the things that exhilarate you. Sex, hostility, flirtation, and punishment . . . When are you going to learn that there's more to a relationship?" "Oh? Like what?" he had snarled. "Like friendship . . . like giving something . . ." "I gave you something! I gave you my son, damn it!" "You gave me nothing! You're like some sort of sex junky! All you ever wanted was to keep getting highs off me!" And Pelligrew had smirked. This was totally irrelevant. He was nearing middle age—he had twenty good years left—and he was not going to spend them with some cloying ex-hillbilly whose flat rural drawl had ceased to be titillating . . .

There! . . . He was done! His toenails were trimmed now. He went back into the bedroom, where Lilah was lying. She had the sheet pulled up, and she was examining her cuticles. Her eyebrows were knit. She was wearing her pouty look.

"Donald?"

"What?"

"Can I ask you something?"

He was pulling down the blanket and getting back into bed with her. He was absolutely "clean." There were no more sharp edges on him. He was as kosher as he could get without having a rabbi bless him.

Lilah looked thoughtful. He had returned to his foreplay. He was suckling her nipples. He was massaging her private area. She was still unresponsive. Her eyes looked distant. It was as if nothing he was doing was having any effect on her.

"Do you like me?" she said.

"Ungh." (He was gurgling.)

"Seriously, Donald—this is very important to me. I know you *want* me. Every man *wants* me. But that's not the point. I'm not sure if you *like* me really."

"I like you," he said. He was fingering her clitoris.

"I'm a very nice person. You may not believe that. You think I'm a bitch, but I'm not—I'm just principled. I have a lot of fine qualities. You could have a really great friendship with me."

Pelligrew said nothing. That detested word "friendship." What was it with these women that they all pulled the "friendship" gambit? They wrote essays about it. They wrote long-winded journal articles. They fretted it to death like a dog with a bedroom slipper.

"Well?" said Lilah.

"Well, what?" said Pelligrew.

"You have Alex and Ted. You have plenty of men friends. What about me? I have a lot of nice qualities. We could sit and get drunk. You could tell funny stories to me."

"Move your leg," said Pelligrew.

"I WILL NOT MOVE MY LEG, DAMN IT! LISTEN TO ME, DONALD! THIS IS VERY IMPORTANT TO ME! I THINK FRIENDSHIP'S IMPORTANT! IT'S THE HIGHEST RELATIONSHIP! I WANT TO BE FRIENDS! I'D BE VERY SUPPORTIVE OF YOU!"

Oh, dear God . . . heaven help him . . . She was shattering his eardrum. The sound of her voice seemed to bisect his nasal septum. He thought of Mary Anne. She would have been so much more reasonable. He remembered one night, when there was a fire, it was raining out . . .

"Well?" said Lilah.

Pelligrew said nothing. How long had he been hearing this? Since his first date in high school maybe?—Francie, his girl friend, when he was fumbling with her bra hooks, saying, "Donald, please don't! Why can't I be friends with you?"

He withdrew his hand. He rolled over on his back. Lilah, still scowling, was awaiting an answer from him. So all right, let her wait. He'd give her an answer. He'd teach her some things about the value of friendship, damn it.

"Because," he said finally.

"Because why?" said Lilah.

"Because. Just *because!* It's not something you ask somebody. Did you ever hear a man say, 'I want to be friends with you?' Of course you didn't. It'd be too damn humiliating."

Lilah looked thoughtful. "I don't understand—"

"You don't understand. That's because you're stupid. You know, I used to think females were extremely intelligent, but I'm beginning to realize you don't really know anything!"

His voice grew louder. His eyes were flashing. Suddenly he was seized with a strange hostility. It was as if some alien being, some wrathful ventriloquist, had crawled down his throat and was pulling his jaw muscles.

"I get so sick and tired of being asked to *confer* things, damn it! 'Gimme my rights!' 'Gimme the child I want!' 'Gimme a job!' 'Gimme equality!' 'Gimme fulfillment!' 'Gimme my happiness, Donald!' " His voice was shrill. He was choked with anger. He felt like a rapist who had at last found his quarry. If he could not have her body, he could at least steal her dignity. He would lay bare her soul. He would establish his primacy. "I mean, what the hell am I? What have I got, Lilah? Look around this room. What do you want from me? I've got a job I can't stand, no money in my bank account, I got a son in New Jersey that they're trying to steal from me!" By now he was up. He was fumbling with his trousers. " 'Friendship' you want! You want me to *like* you even! Why the hell should I? What'll you give me for it? The only thing I want is what you think is too precious for me!"

"I didn't mean that—"

"She wants *friendship . . . my God!*" He wheeled around angrily. He stuck out his finger at her. "You know the trouble with you? You think like the bolsheviks! You see yourself as deprived, and all us 'fat cats' should *give* things to you!"

He had ceased to make sense, and somehow he knew that, but the realization only made him feel angrier toward her. He was hobbling around the floor, trying to put on his loafers. Goddamn that guy Gronsky, walking off with his safety net . . .

"Donald, come back here!"

"Go to hell!" he shouted.

"Don't you dare walk away! Don't you dare try rejecting me!"

"FUCK OFF!" he replied—and with that, he stormed out.

Only of course he didn't stay out. After all, he was human, wasn't he?

"Doggone you, Alex!"

He was still descending. She didn't catch up until the second-floor landing. She grabbed at his sleeve. She spun him around. Her eyes were moist. She was smiling, but tremulously.

Had she been anybody else—had she been older, more worldly—had she been prettier, craftier, less compelled to explain herself—would she have let him keep going, this man who had nothing, this aging ex-jock who kept holding his stomach muscles?

"Would you *listen?*" she pleaded.

"No need to apologize . . ."

"Alex, doggone it—I *do* want to see you! It's just that there's someone . . . Well, there's not really someone. It's just that—oh, God—I need time to get stabilized."

Four months, thirteen days, and one and a half hours. No, *two* and a half hours—he had spent an hour in her apartment—and it had been so long, he couldn't remember. He had no idea how the other sex operated.

Back when he was living in Mount Kisco, taking the train with Bob Martin, sitting in that smoker working the New York *Times* crossword puzzle, sometimes they would fantasize what it would be like to be single—to have no responsibilities, not to be tied to a time schedule. "I'm afraid," said Martin, "we were both born too early, Alex. These women nowadays—they just put out for everybody. Why, there are these bars in New York—you know what they call them? They call them 'The Meat Racks.' It's like a goddamn white-slave auction." And Gronsky had nodded. Yeah, that's right, to be single . . . Only somehow reality didn't quite match the fantasy for him. Like Mary Anne Delucci, who had started off friendly, but as soon as he had asked had demurred, begun backpedaling . . .

"Please don't be angry."

Gronsky said nothing.

"I've just got this problem . . . Well, I guess it's a hang-up, really. You remember how I told you I had gone to a therapist? Well, I *had* to go, Alex. There was this guy, I was miserable . . ."

It was a narrow, cramped landing with one dimly lit light bulb. The walls were tile. It looked like a lavatory. As she talked, she was twisting a ring on her ring finger. Her lips were smiling, but her eyes had a frightened quality.

"I know it sounds silly. It's been over three years now. What can I say? I was young, I was stupid. You know what that's like? To be so much in love, and you're not thinking straight, and they pull out the rug on you?"

Gronsky nodded. He had a reasonable idea.

"So all I'm saying is that I need to go slowly, Alex. I do want to see you. I'd like to go out with you. But that's all, no more. Please don't be angry with me."

Gronsky said nothing. Her eyes were cast downward. She was looking at the floor, as if some answer were written there. So young. So fragile. It reminded him of something. It reminded him of Mandy on a night twenty years ago . . .

And that's when he did it. He didn't know why, really. He was just standing there nodding, and she was trying to explain to him, and then suddenly he was compelled by this reflex, this *impulse*, and the next thing he knew, he was grabbing her, kissing her . . .

Mary Anne drew back. "I'm sorry—please don't . . ."

He kissed her again.

"This is all so confusing . . ."

And with that, she turned. She ran back up the stairs again.

Gronsky stood looking. His heart was palpitating.

Oh, God! *Mary Anne!* He went reeling through the Village. He giggled up Seventh. He whistled through Jones Street. At Washington Place, he picked up a snowball. A taxi drove by. He jumped, threw a bullet pass . . .

On the northbound F up to West Thirty-fourth Street, in the back of the car, there was a boy and girl necking. The boy had his hand between her blue-jeaned thighs, and when he pulled it away, she looked cross, put it back again. Gronsky sat smiling. He knew just how they felt, by golly! He wanted to go up to them, say, "Hey, I'm just like you are! I'm forty-three years old, but I can still get a hard on, and there are girls half my age, and they've agreed to go out with me . . ."

And it was only later, when he was back in his hotel room, that grim little chamber with its hot plate, its rat odors, pulling off his shoes and hanging up his coat, that the fears, the self-doubts, began to come back again. He went into the bathroom. He took out his toothbrush. He stared at the mirror. "Impossible," he muttered. He went back to the bedroom. He turned on the television. *Sands of Iwo Jima.* He turned it back off again.

And it was only much later, when the lights were all out, and he was lying there remembering her laughter, her nervousness, that he suddenly realized. It struck like a thunderbolt. Of course. What a fool. Now it all seemed so obvious to him.

21

Shaughnessy's transgressions were a matter of record. He had spilled two scotches. He had peed on a toilet seat. He had gotten himself involved in that tirade with Gronsky in which, between them, they had managed to alienate everybody. But that wasn't the worst part. Oh, no, far from it. The worst part came later when he had spotted this calf muscle, and it had looked so inviting, so delicately feminine, that he had lunged across the floor, begun caressing and licking at it . . .

He remembered that now as he was lying on the sofa, his dignity shattered, his daydreams a memory, a deep laceration across the top of his forehead, his nostrils alive with the smell of Mercurochrome. Yes, that was the worst part. It was a sin and a sacrilege. Because later he had learned who the owner of the calf was, and he had found, to his chagrin, that she was an ex-nun from Maryknoll who now worked as a counselor at the Seventy-eighth Street Rehab Center.

Oh, God, that was terrible. It was worse than just terrible. He had offended the Pope. He'd have the Vatican down on him. He'd spend the next twenty years saying contritions, novenas, but it would do him no good, he'd be headed for purgatory . . .

"Do you really want to know?" The question was Sandra's. She was leaning over him, applying a cotton swab. It was apparently in response to some earlier question, only for the life of him he didn't know what it related to.

Somehow he had managed to stagger out of Pelligrew's (it came back swimmingly, as from the bottom of a scotch bottle), and the next thing he knew he was in front of his apartment arguing with a cabbie over the fare on the taxi meter. A solution was struck. They would make a small wager. Ten dollars said Shaughnessy could fly up yon fire escape. The cabbie had agreed, and Shaughnessy had tried—and he had ended up landing on Mr. Poukos's wine decanters.

That was at one. There was a gap in his memory. The next thing he knew he was down here at Sandra's, he was lying on this sofa, she was treating his injuries, and she was responding to questions he had no memory of asking her.

"Do you really want to know why I'm bothering to do this? I'll tell you if you want, although I don't think you'll like it much. I'm obviously not happy. You act like an imbecile. I may not be much, but I deserve better than you give."

Oh, God, he felt awful . . . Wait! Now he remembered! He had been recalling that famous old Groucho Marx chestnut—something about "any club that would have me for a member is not a club I would want to be a member of"—and he had said that to Sandra, only he had changed "club" to "woman," and Sandra had scowled, she didn't think it was funny, then he had hiccupped, rolled over, said, "Why do you bother with me?" and had lain there dreaming about burning in purgatory.

"Do you remember," said Sandra, "that first night we talked, Ted? I told you I used to do some modeling and acting jobs? Well, you might as well know, because you'd find it out anyway. That wasn't quite true. Those were very bad times for me . . ."

Shaughnessy just lay there. He felt like a mannequin. He had once know a mannequin—it was at the Waldorf-Astoria—and there were electrodes attached, and they ran to a computer, and you had to resuscitate the heart or the computer got mad at you . . .

"I never did hooking. At least I never sank that low. There was a black guy I lived with—he did the hooking. He'd go out every night, work the gay bars on West Street. He'd come back in the morning, start screaming and beating on me . . ."

Shaughnessy said nothing. She had handed him a magazine. It was a cheap, pulpy tabloid with a two-color cover on it. The cover showed a couple in the process of copulating. Inside were pictures of violence, pornography.

"I made a coupla skin flicks—you'd find out about those, too. I changed my name, I changed the color of my hair. I have no idea what's become of those loops, but I'm sure they're around, they're gonna pop up somewhere . . ."

Oh, God . . . He lay blinking. This was more than he could stomach. He had the unusual sensation that his insides were freezing. As if, returning to life, he had found a new death, some nightmarish hell full of sin and depravity.

"But I was determined to make it. See, I *knew* I could make it, Ted. I said, 'Someday, Sandra, this'll seem like a nightmare to you. You just stay off the junk. Keep going to auditions. You're gonna be big. This whole world'll look up to you.' "

Shaughnessy felt nauseous. There was nothing he could say to her. He lay staring at those photos, all those breasts, those perinea, and among them, *in coitu,* that frail, wasted Sandra, her legs spread apart, her eyes rolled ecstatically . . .

Sandra nodded. "And I *am* gonna make it, Ted. I got a letter today—just a minute, I'll show it to you. I feel it in my bones. It's all coming together for me. They want to start a new show—they want a whole different format for me."

She got up and went out. Shaughnessy just lay there. Oh, God . . . Oh, poor Sandra . . . All these poor desperate egotists . . . How often had he seen them waiting on tables in the Village, one foot dreamily planted on some rocket to star status? He closed his eyes. He could still see that tabloid. That she could have sunk so low. That she could have had so little dignity. Although in a way, he supposed, that had always been obvious—her hardness, her crassness, that smoke screen of "kookiness" . . .

She came back from the bedroom carrying a white piece of letterhead. She sat down and unfolded it, kneeling by the coffee table. Shaughnessy said nothing. He didn't want to hear it. She was beginning to read, but his mind started wandering.

" 'Dear Miss Silk . . .' "

It's all coming together for me. Isn't that what she had said? The Big Enchilada. It was everything he had always detested and ridiculed—coke and white wine and some hot tub in

Malibu. And yet, in a way was it really any different from *his* dream?—artistic celebrity—a house in the Hamptons—vacationing on Nantucket with the Lubalins, the Glaziers, having people nod knowingly and say, "Isn't that that great art director?" He supposed it wasn't. It was just a different perspective. It was the same bright sun shining down on Missouri, and in the west it was morning, and in the east it was noon, but it was still the same light, it was still the same fantasy . . .

"'So in conclusion . . .'" said Sandra.

Shaughnessy just lay there.

"And it's signed, 'Yours truly.'" She put down the letter. "Isn't that great? Oh, Ted, I'm so happy. We can get married, have a baby, we can move to the Coast someplace . . ."

Shaughnessy blinked. She was folding the letter. Her lips were drawn up like the mouth on a Kewpie doll. "I mean, not right away. I'm not talking right now, mind you. But maybe next year—or the year after that maybe . . ."

With pain, he sat up. His head was reeling. It was like swimming through a fantasy with endless striations—and in this one was marriage and babies and diapers and getting your brains baked white in the land of the Philistines.

"I'm not getting married."

"All right, we'll just live together . . ."

"I'm not getting married, and I'm not having children, damn it! What are you saying? Where's all this coming from? I had ten years of that. I'll never go back to it."

"All right, take it easy . . ."

"You don't know what you're talking about. You've never been through it. You have no real conception of it. It's like hell. It's oppressive—all those nights in that bedroom . . . Unh-unh! No way! That's one thing I'll *never* do!"

He had managed to get up and had begun pacing back and forth. His body ached. His mind was delirious. It was as if, instead of an apartment, he was trapped in a prison; he was like some beast in a cage, and he had to find his way out of it.

"Listen to me, Ted." Sandra was scowling at him. He kept heading toward the door, but then he'd come back again. His head was bandaged, he was stained with Mercurochrome. He was breathing heavily, like a dog who feels death pending. "Listen to me, Ted. I'm not getting any younger. I am thirty-two years old. You know your biology. I've got three more good years. I don't plan to have mongoloids. Now maybe it's silly, maybe it's selfish of me—"

"I refuse to discuss it."

"We don't have to discuss it."

"I know what it's like. I know how I'd suffocate."

"We don't have to discuss it. It's simply what *is*, Ted. I'm stronger than you. I'll always take care of you."

He stopped. He stood swaying. His cheeks were tear-streaked. The corners of his mouth were drawn down in a rictus caw. And suddenly, to his surprise, he heard himself whining—only it was not his voice, it was the voice of some helpless thing.

"Whatever you do—"

"I'm not going to leave you."

"I can't get married, but I need to have someone . . ."

"Don't worry, I'm here . . ."

"I'll do anything you ask. I'll give up drinking. I'll go to AA meetings . . ."

Sandra got up. She went over and held him.

"You were right all along. I've only been kidding myself. Before I met you, I couldn't have anyone. I'd try. I'd fail. They all seemed to scare me somehow . . ."

She took him by the hand. She led him back toward the bedroom. It was not really a bedroom, it was just a space made by room dividers. Like everything else, it had the last decade's look about it: folk art and candles and old antiwar posters.

"You know what I am? I'm a goddamn crustacean. That's what he called me. That's what Lee Schoenstein called me. I have no supports. I'm a spiritual coward. I can't retreat, and I'm afraid to go forward . . ."

Sandra just smiled. She leaned him back against a bedpost. She took off his shirt and began unbuckling his blue jeans. Shaughnessy, helpless, just stood there, arms dangling. He was like something bereft. There was no more resistance in him.

"I love you, Sandra. I've loved you from the beginning. It's just . . . I don't know, but you never seemed right for me. I wanted something . . . there were these things I was craving. . . . Well, of course it was stupid . . . It was unrealistic of me . . ."

She had unhooked his belt and was pulling off his Levi's. His torso was naked. He wore bikini-brief underpants. And now those were off, and he was alone, he was vulnerable. She slipped off her bathrobe. She came over and leaned against him.

"When I was a kid"—he was talking to the ceiling now; her muscular body felt soft and refreshing to him; her hands moved gently from his chest to his abdomen; she, too, was nude, and her pubes rubbed moistly on him—"when I was a kid, I wanted to play football. My mother wouldn't let me. She was afraid I'd get hurt or something. I pleaded and begged. She'd just sit there and scoff at me. She didn't understand. She never understood anything . . ."

Sandra said nothing. Her tongue felt his nipples. Slowly, methodically, she worked her way downward. He had begun to grow hard. She knelt, as if praying. He stood like a statue. His eyelids were fluttering.

"So one afternoon I went over to the coach, see. I said, 'Gimme a chance. Lemme put on a uniform.' So he did, and I went down and I stood around on the playing field, and they gave me the ball, and the linemen were grinning at me . . ."

And now, at last, her lips found his penis. Her tongue rolled clockwise; she went around it in swirling motions. She flicked at its head—then enveloped it inward. His eyes rolled back as he sought absolution from her.

". . . I'd try to get up, and they'd just knock me down, Sandra. I got so damn scared—I got scared what my mother'd say. I've always blamed her, but of course it was me. It was me who got scared. And the coach, he was laughing at me . . ."

And now, inside her, the channel seemed endless. It was like the forgiveness of God, or the grief of the Virgin, and as his weakness grew harder, her yielding grew stronger, until, finally, in dominance, he was completely submissive to her.

22

"Listen, about Mary Anne . . ."

Pelligrew said nothing.

"I mean, it just sort of happened. She was obviously uncomfortable, Don. I thought the least I could do was to see she got home okay. You understand. I wasn't trying to buddy-fuck you."

Pelligrew said nothing. His eyes were receded. They were sitting in a bar up on Third called Churchill's. It was the following Tuesday, and they were waiting for Shaughnessy. They were planning to have a drink, then take in a movie together.

Gronsky continued, "Of course, if you think you're still interested in her . . . I mean, I won't ask her out if you say you don't want me to. It's just that—I don't know, I suppose I felt comfortable with her. I'm obviously too old. I doubt if *she's* interested . . ."

When the light had finally dawned—when he was lying in his hotel room, and the events of that Friday had swum back through the darkness to him—it had struck him as obvious that what Mary Anne was saying was that, while she'd be glad to go out with him, she was in love with Don Pelligrew. Which, indeed, was quite natural. Pelligrew was handsome. He was slim, he was mysterious, he had those inscrutable black eye sockets. Why should she be eager to get involved with a Gronsky, when it would only remind her of the man who had rejected her?

Be that as it may—and he was not above jealousy—he would go to Pelligrew, he would lay it all out for him, he would explain in all candor that it was strictly platonic, and Pelligrew, of course, would react magnanimously.

"So anyway . . ." said Gronsky.

Pelligrew scowled.

"I mean, it's not like it's serious. It's not like I'm after anything. We'd just go to a movie . . . I'd take her out for a hamburger . . . It's no big deal. I've already discussed this with her . . ."

Pelligrew just sat there. He had been sipping Glenlivet, but now, abruptly, he changed to old fashioneds. He sat glowering into space. There was an uneasy silence. Gronsky wasn't sure whether he had even been listening to him.

Shaughnessy, as usual, was about a half hour late. By the time he showed up, it was a quarter after seven. He was showered, clean-shaven, and he had a bandage on his forehead. Much to their surprise, he ordered a glass of Perrier.

Pelligrew sat glowering. He was obviously upset at something. At one point he got up and went over to a phone booth. He dropped in a dime, uttered a few brief sentences, slammed down the phone, and came back and sat down again.

"So anyway . . ." said Gronsky.

"Jesus Christ!" cried Pelligrew. His brows were knit. His jaw was clenched menacingly. "Why should I care who the hell you go out with? What do you think, I'm like some sort of harem keeper?"

Gronsky smiled. "I didn't mean *that*, Don—"

"You know, I really don't get it. I really don't get you, Alex. I had this very nice woman—I had this *great-looking* woman for you—and what do you do? You act like an asshole toward her."

Gronsky looked puzzled. The memory was hazy.

"I mean, what do you think, you think I cast voodoo spells? You think because my son doesn't happen to like chiropractors, you think it's my fault? You think I've got radar power?"

Gronsky said nothing. This was totally befuddling. He had assumed they were talking about Mary Anne Delucci. Now it turned out they were talking about Elizabeth. Or perhaps it was Jeremy. Or perhaps it was chiropractic.

"Don't get upset—"

"Who's upset?" cried Pelligrew. "I'm not upset! Why should

I give a shit? You don't like Linda, that's your shortsightedness. I don't care. I'm not running a dating service."

"Who's Linda?" said Shaughnessy.

"I'm not sure," said Gronsky.

"*Great-looking* female! Great-looking *ass,* goddamn it! She's mature, she's successful—she's like you, she's traditionalist . . . but if you don't want her, I've got nothing to say about it!"

Gronsky just sat there. Where on earth was this coming from? He tried to retrace the thread of their dialogue. They had started off talking about Mary Anne Delucci, and they had ended up swimming in a cesspool of grievances.

"Look, I'm sure Linda's nice—"

"*Who cares?*" cried Pelligrew. "You don't care! You were too busy tit-gazing! Go ahead! Fuck it! Take Mary Anne Delucci! She's nice too! I'm sure you'll be happy with her!"

And with that, he stood up. His black eyes were smoldering. He downed one old-fashioned, quickly ordered another one. He went over to the bar, got change for a dollar, went over to the phone booth, began punching out Touch-Tones.

"What was that all about?" The question was Shaughnessy's. Pelligrew by then was well out of earshot. They could see him in the phone booth, his shoulders hunched over, dialing, shouting, hanging up, and then redialing.

"Who knows?" said Gronsky.

Shaughnessy smiled. "If I didn't know better, I'd say he was jealous, Alex."

Gronsky laughed. If they didn't know better . . .

He stared at his glass.

But of course they knew better, didn't they?

"Hi."

"What, *again?*"

Pelligrew squirmed. He pulled the door closed and nuzzled the receiver. Through the finger-smudged glass he could see the back of Gronsky's head. Shaughnessy, still sober, was nursing a grapefruit juice.

"Look, I'm sorry I shouted."

"Darn it, what's going on there, Donald?"

"Just accept my apologies. I'm sorry I yelled at you. You have a perfect right to see anyone you want. That's one thing about me—I never hold on to people."

There was a silence on the line. That was one thing about him. Never mind the fact that he was jealous of Klimefogler; never mind the fact that he had called his old high school girl, and when she wouldn't leave her husband, he had accused her of perfidy. That was one thing about him—he never held on to people: just his son, just his wife, just the women he'd slept with. He was like a nervous old lion whose pride was deserting him. He had to cuff them into line. He had to reassert patriarchy.

"See, it's just that I was thinking . . . well, I got to thinking about *us*, goddamn it. When I saw you last Friday—God, you really looked great to me, and I got to thinking about us and all those times in that hotel room, and then when we were down at your place, when you were living on Sullivan Street . . ."

Mary Anne chuckled. It was a clear, bell-like chuckle, and for a moment he actually did feel transported: how young she had been, how pathetically innocent, how bashful she was that first time they'd slept together . . .

"You are something else, Don. You are really a bullshitter."

"No, I'm not! Cross my heart! That was an incredibly bad period for me! I mean, there I was—I felt emotionally threatened. I still had Elizabeth . . . I had a kid, I had money problems . . ."

Oh, God, all these lies! That was the trouble with women. They never succumbed unless you sacrificed honesty. Which he was willing to do, but it really did bother him. He wished they'd just screw and not care how he felt about them.

Again there was silence. He could hear her wheels turning. That was one of his tricks: He could hear women's brains function. He didn't know why, it must have been something he was born with. They made little squeaks. They sounded like starlings chirping.

"I'll tell you what *I* think." Her inflection was measured. Overcoming her feelings, she was summoning up counterforces.

She was about to deliver some intuitive *bon mot*, which, to a man like The Phantom, was like a wood cross to Dracula. "I'll tell you what *I* think. You've been talking to Alex. You've been sitting in some bar, and he's been telling you about Friday, and even though in reality you aren't the least bit interested in me, you decided you'd call and try to reassert power over me."

Pelligrew scowled. "What makes you say that?"

"Because I know how you are. I know how you operate. You've got to be the world's most insecure man, Don. Why else would you suddenly be making these phone calls to me?"

Hmmmm. He switched ears. She was smarter than he had realized. Women of twenty-four aren't the same as when they're twenty. When they're twenty, they're nice. They're even nicer in their teens. Intelligence expands in proportion to waist sizes.

"That's not true," he said finally. "I haven't seen Alex."

"Then why did you just call me and accuse me of seducing him?"

"I don't know, I just did. It was an idea that flashed over me. After I came to last Friday, I looked around, you had left with him . . ."

Again, she chuckled. Damn, that laugh was unsettling! He was beginning to realize why Gronsky was interested in her. From his own point of view, she was just a good bed partner—but he had to admit, there was a flair, an ingenuousness . . .

"Look, Don, let's be honest. I was twenty years old then. I had just made the break from a strict Catholic upbringing. I had moved in from the Bronx, I was practically a virgin, and the first man I meet is this tall, dark-haired married man . . ."

Pelligrew said nothing. This was all so beside-the-point. The point, as he saw it, was that she had once been in love with him; and if she had felt that way once, she could feel it again, goddamn it. He didn't care about hearing what a cad and a heel he was.

"Look, I'll admit I was wrong . . ."

"I mean, damn it, you *hurt* me, Donald! I loved you so much. You were all I could think about. For the past three years I haven't gone out with anybody. I swore never again would I let a man do that to me."

Oh, hell. Jesus Christ. What was it with these women? Why did they insist on unburdening their souls to him? All he really wanted was to establish his domain—to stake out his turf, like a dog stakes out fire hydrants.

"Do you like him?" he asked.

"You mean Alex? I like him."

"Yeah, but I mean do you *like* him? Are you going to go out with him?"

"Honestly, Donald, this is totally absurd. If he asks me, I'll go. It's none of your business, is it?"

Pelligrew grimaced. It was too his business! It was very much his business, because it was bordering on—on *incest!* Once he had screwed them, they were forever his property, and if they didn't know that, they were no better than Elizabeth!

"If we could just have one drink . . ."

"I don't see the purpose, Donald."

"I just want to see you. Is that such a crime, damn it? I like you. I miss you. I didn't realize I missed you, but now I do. I just want to be friends with you."

More wheels turning. He tried to decipher them. He thought he could hear caution, the stirrings of maturity—but he also heard youth, and desire, and loneliness—that indomitable urge to believe the impossible . . .

"I don't think I should."

"Why not? You're afraid of me."

"I'm not afraid. It's just that I know better . . ."

"I'll call you tomorrow."

"Donald, please—have some mercy, will you?"

He smiled.

He hung up.

He'd teach that Gronsky a thing or two.

23

February ebbed and spring approached fitfully. True to his intentions, Gronsky did see Mary Anne. He took her to movies, they went out for hamburgers; one rainy Saturday she even looked for apartments with him. As April approached, there was a flurry of excitement. Sandra was appearing in her first big "showcase." It was a regional hookup, carried by satellite, featuring nutrition, diet, and fad female health issues. Shaughnessy, of course, was confident of failure. The format was wrong, the subjects were ludicrous, nobody would want to watch a show about health care, and particularly not at night opposite a "Dallas" or "Love Boat" episode. Nevertheless, he was ambivalently supportive of her. "It's important that she do it to get it out of her system," he told people. "Besides, there's the money. I have to admit, they've been generous with her. She's making more on this show than she's ever made in her lifetime."

Pelligrew during this period was in one of his "lying low" stages. He did that sometimes—he became invisible. He'd sit in his apartment, he wouldn't answer the telephone, he'd vent his wrath on the world by withdrawing his presence from it. Shaughnessy and Gronsky were genuinely baffled. "You don't suppose," said Shaughnessy, "he's mad at us, do you?" "No, I don't think so," said Gronsky. "I think he's just moody. He's probably trying to give the slip to some woman who's after him."

The premier of Sandra's show was on April the thirteenth. The problem was to find a set they could watch it on. Gronsky had cable, but his room was too cramped, and Pelligrew had it, but he wasn't answering his telephone. So they decided to watch it from a bar on East Fiftieth Street. It was a place called Runyon's between First and Second, and it had two large TVs—one in front, one in back—and they could commandeer whichever the other customers weren't interested in.

"Jesus," said Shaughnessy. They were standing out front. The place was so packed, they couldn't get through the doorway. Men carrying Millers were crowding the sidewalk. There were Islanders T-shirts, inclinations toward drunkenness.

"You're right," said Gronsky. "We can't watch it here."

"Where can we go?"

"I dunno, we'll find someplace"—and they headed up Second under the darkening twilight, mingling with the throngs that seemed to appear every springtime.

There had been several recent changes in Shaughnessy's lifestyle, perhaps the most notable of which was that he seemed to be drinking less. An understatement. He was totally abstaining; he would sit all night nursing fruit juice and mineral water. "What's the matter," laughed Gronsky, "you going cold turkey on me?"—to which Shaughnessy would shrug and mutter something nonsensical, because there are Faustian pacts that are better left private, and particularly those made during acts of fellatio.

Another notable change was that he had moved in with Sandra. He was refusing to admit this—he still kept his apartment—but the majority of his clothes were now hanging at her place, and it was fairly obvious that he was becoming domesticated. "Well, I can tell you about that," he said one night to Gronsky. "I had a friend of mine once who had a 'warm log' hypothesis. He said all a man needs is a warm log to sleep with. And that's what she is. She's my replacement for Cutty Sark." But Gronsky was dubious: "We aren't losing you, are we?" "Hell!" laughed Shaughnessy, and he stared at his Perrier. "The one thing she knows is that a man needs his freedom. I told her that, Alex—I've made no commitment to her."

A block or so north, up on East Fifty-first Street, there was an Italian restaurant called Paparazzi's. It had a dim-lit bar, a suspended TV set, and, perhaps because it was Monday, it seemed more reasonably occupied.

"Wanna try it?" said Shaughnessy.

"Might as well," said Gronsky.

They went in and sat down. It was unpretentiously comfortable. There were about a half-dozen men strung out along the bar. They were of no particular stripe—some were laborers, some business people.

"You got cable?" said Gronsky.

The bartender nodded.

"Could you do us a favor and put it on '0' please?"

The bartender obeyed. Gronsky ordered a vodka. Shaughnessy, God bless him, made do with a Perrier.

"What are you gonna use to lead off?" said Shaughnessy when he was talking to Sandra the other night after dinner. Sandra, as usual, was surviving on salads. Shaughnessy had sent out for a pizza with anchovies. And Sandra had just smiled. "You'll have to wait and find out, Ted." "If you're smart," said Shaughnessy, "you'll do something with sex in it." "Why's that?" said Sandra. And Shaughnessy just smirked. These goddamn women—they had no handle on anything.

Of course Shaughnessy had his theories about the breadwinning female: He likened them to children using Tinkertoy lawn mowers. "About the only thing that matters is that they *feel* like they're working. They're just imitating Daddy. You can't take them too seriously." To which Gronsky had demurred: "I know some pretty sharp girls, Ted . . ." "Yeah, sure," said Shaughnessy, "if they've got their husbands behind them. You mark my words; she doesn't know what she's doing, she's gonna fall on her face, and she's gonna come crying to *me* about it."

The television flickered. There were some headlines from Reuters, there were a couple of minutes of Dow Jones averages, then finally a logo, some computerized visuals, and an enthusiastic voice exhorting, *"Let's Get Physical!"*

Gronsky nodded. "Good title," he muttered.

Shaughnessy said nothing. He had not been consulted on it. As a matter of fact, he had not been consulted on anything. Which in the past few weeks had become a bone of contention with him.

"And now, here's your host—Miss Sandra Silk!" The logo faded to a red velvet backdrop. There was the sound of applause, a recorded theme song, then on walked Sandra holding a thin, phallic microphone . . .

("But why not?" said Shaughnessy. "Because!" said Sandra. "Think about it, Ted! I'd rather not have you there. It's bad enough having to do the show live. If my crew sees you, it'll be a total fiasco." And Shaughnessy had snarled. If her crew saw him. Just because he had happened to have a fight with her cameraman. Just because he had happened to call her producer a fag, her director a pervert, accused her script boy of sodomy . . .)

Camera One: Close-up. Sandra bowing. Gronsky, in mid-drink, readjusted his tortoise shells. Was he really seeing what he thought he was seeing? The picture was grainy, there was a bit too much color in it . . .

"Hi! My name's Sandra, and this is 'Let's Get Physical!' Before we get started, are there any men in this audience?" She shielded her eyes, squinted out toward the studio. "I see one . . . There's another. . . . It's gonna be a rough night, fellas . . ."

Gronsky sat blinking. It had taken him by surprise, because this wasn't the Sandra he was accustomed to seeing. The Sandra he knew was petite, rather common, whereas the girl on the tube looked feline, provocative . . .

" 'cause tonight," she was saying, "is the night you get yours, guys. My guest is gynecologist Dr. Sidney Lubkin, and the subject we're discussin's gonna knock your socks off. I mean, it's gonna blow your mind. I mean, you're gonna run out the back, Jack! . . ."

There was a swell of applause. Shaughnessy sat frozen. And now, for the first time, there was a shot of the audience. It was one of the more bizarre-looking crowds ever to appear on a picture tube—an amalgam of street people, punk-rockers, lesbians . . .

("Whaddaya mean, you want me to put up handbills?" "Oh, come on, Ted—this is no big deal, is it? It's a crummy old studio down in Tribeca on Duane Street. I can't walk in there and find the audience empty, can I?" And Shaughnessy had grumbled.

He didn't want to post handbills. He didn't believe in such graffiti—it was just another damn eyesore—but she had stared at him coldly, and he had finally relented, posting three at McBurney's, six more along Christopher Street . . .)

There was a commercial for vitamins, two motion-picture trailers, another commercial for a mail-order Exercizer, twelve seconds of static, a station identification—then finally back to Sandra holding a blue and white book jacket . . .

"You know, you gotta admit"—this was the bartender speaking; he was leaning toward Shaughnessy, his mouth twisted sideways; in his left hand he was holding a half-peeled lemon; in his right was a knife that had been honed to a sliver—"you gotta admit, that is one sexy cunt, ain't she?"

Shaughnessy squinted. His pupils contracted.

The bartender shrugged. "I'm just givin you my opinion." He furrowed his brows and went back to his lemon slicing.

"Now Dr. Lubkin"—there had been a switch in the backdrops; she was sitting on a stool in front of an industrial-type window; a backlighted scrim looked out on a cityscape: tar roofs and smoke stacks, a zigzagging fire escape—*"according to your book, there's a specialized area—"*

"It's a collection of tissues—"

"—in the female vagina—"

"It's a whole separate organ—"

"—which, when properly stimulated, causes a woman to climax in the same way a man does."

The doctor being questioned was a small, owlish figure with horn-rimmed glasses and a befuddled expression. Through some trick of the camera, he appeared lilliputian; Sandra, on the other hand, looked like an Amazon.

"Now what I'd like to know"—she was sitting with her legs crossed; she leaned forward slightly, tapping the doctor on the knee; her gown, which was white, was slit up to the waistband; the doctor, embarrassed, was having a hard time looking at her—*"what I'd like to know is how you found this contraption when the man I've been living with has spent the past six months look-*

ing for it. I mean, he's pretty good—I'd rate him a six—but if you'd tell him where it is, we'd both be appreciative."

There was a hoot from the women.

Shaughnessy just sat there.

Dr. Lubkin, squirming, tried to smile toward the camera. *"Well, I can hardly speak—"*

"I mean, am I right, or am I right, girls? What is it with these guys they try to tell us what we're *feeling?"*

"Hey, turn up the sound!" It was a command from the back. A small cluster of hard-hats had been sitting by the men's room. Now they came forward, took positions on barstools. They stared at the set. Their faces hung slack-jawed.

"Now what I'd like to know, Doc, is where this magic spot's located. I mean, the world's been goin at it for about ten zillion years, right, and here you come along—where's your office, in Teaneck?—and you claim you've found something that no other man's found before."

The doctor grew red. *"It's in the anterior wall—"*

"Try not to point."

"I don't believe I was pointing . . ."

"I believe you were pointing. Try to remember your manners. This is a television show. We're not back in the radio era . . ."

By now the uproar had grown in volume. The women in the studio had begun stomping their feet. A foreign object was hurled toward the doctor. There was laughter, derision. There was an occasional cat whistle.

"Gimme a drink," said Shaughnessy.

The bartender looked at him.

"You heard me, goddamn it! Double Cutty, no water!" He put down his Perrier and shoved it toward the bartender. His face was pale. His hands were trembling.

("What makes you think I should do something with 'sex'?" said Sandra. "Aw, come on," said Shaughnessy, "I'm in advertising, Sandra. You wanna do something that'll get you noticed? Appeal to their glands. That's rule number one, damn it." And Sandra had smiled. "I'm surprised you'd say that." "Well, it's cable, right? I mean, it's not like the networks. Talk about impotence. Talk about herpes. How else you gonna compete against the tits on 'Three's Company'?" . . .)

"Ain't this about the goldangedest show you ever saw in your life?" It was from a slim blond man sitting on Shaughnessy's left. Judging from his twang, he was an out-of-towner—some conventioneer, maybe, from Texas or Arkansas. His face beamed broadly. "Where I come from they'd have the goddamn Klan and the PTA down on em. Although I gotta admit"—he winked at Shaughnessy—"I wouldn't mind suckin a little bit on that pussywillow . . ."

Shaughnessy glowered.

"Take it easy," said Gronsky.

The Texan drew back. "Hey, I meant no offense, mister . . ."

Shaughnessy was seething. His chest was heaving. "You better shut the fuck up . . ." His right fist grew white-knuckled.

"You were saying, Doctor . . ."

"In my preliminary studies—"

"Excuse me, but can I tell you about my gynecologist? I've got a Jewish gynecologist, he carries a gun in a shoulder holster. What do you think of that? Do you think that's a good bedside manner, Doctor? . . ."

"Take it easy!" cried Gronsky.

Shaughnessy was bucking. Gronsky had him around the middle in a soft-shouldered bear hug. "He's crazy!" cried the Texan. He was trying to get away. Two barstools fell over. There was glass on the counter top . . .

"I mean, is that what you'd call standard medical procedure, Doctor? To get a woman in the stirrups, then walk in with a shoulder holster? He says he's afraid of getting mugged by drug addicts. To me it sounds Freudian. Course I'm just the patient, aren't I? . . ."

"Look, I'm sorry," said the bartender.

"It's all right," said Gronsky.

"It is not all right. He assaulted a customer . . ."

"You don't understand. It was the other guy's fault. No harm done. Look, I'll pay for the damage, right? . . ."

"Well, I'd like to say this—"

"Sorry, we're all out of time, Doctor. I think the audience'll agree, you've been a good sport for coming here. You women out there, you go buy this man's book, hear? Till next week, good night—and 'Let's Get Physical!'"

"Well, I'll say this," said Gronsky when they were back on the sidewalk; they were heading west on East Fifty-third Street; the night was oily; the streetlights looked aqueous; the boutiques seemed to shimmer, as if enveloped in cellophane—"I'll say this for her, Ted—she didn't seem nervous." He nodded solemnly, adjusted his eyeglasses. Shaughnessy said nothing. His gait was uncertain. After four or five doubles, he was his old drunken self again.

Oh, the shame! The embarrassment! He had felt absolutely mortified. It was about the most tasteless performance he had ever seen on television. That dress she had on! And those references to *him!* What the hell did she mean she'd rate him a *six*, damn it?

It had been almost six weeks since he had taken a drink—one and a half months of Cuttyless purgatory. "See, I knew it," said Sandra. "I mean, it's not like you *needed* it. All you really needed was just someone to care for you." Yeah, that's all he needed. All he needed was Sandra. All a man really needs is just a good, loving woman, right? What a delusion! He was an *alcoholic!* Why in God's name couldn't she at least admit that much?

They entered the subway at the corner of Third. There was an F train just pulling into the Jamaica-bound platform. The air pumped forward like gas through a camshaft. Shaughnessy staggered, propped himself on an I beam.

"I'm gonna leave her," he mumbled.

Gronsky said nothing.

"I mean it, Alex. She's never been right for me. You know wasshe wants? She wants a hot tub in Malibu. She wants a fuckin Mercedes and all that Rodeo Drive bullshit."

He stared at the track. His eyes were bleary. By now the F train had pulled out for Queens. At the other end of the station there was a violinist playing Haydn. The strings seemed to scrape along the paint-chipped corridor.

Shaughnessy's mind skipped a beat. He thought of Jaime, his daughter—Jaime, who had traveled every mile of these tunnels, sitting among the winos, the hopheads, the Jesus freaks, her taut-bosomed body growing daily more tantalizing. Had she seen the show? Had she watched it with Sarah? Had the two of them sat there in that darkened apartment, transfixed by the wonders of "Daddy's new plaything" as she blithely described Daddy's place in the Fucking Order? Oh, God, this was awful! It was all so grotesque, being in love with a woman he could never approve of, while approving of a woman he had never felt love for, as if love and approval weren't even on speaking terms.

Of course, Gronsky had it wrong. That was so typical of Gronsky. Gronsky had assumed that the show was a failure. It wasn't a failure. It was the opposite of failure. That fact had been apparent from the opening monologue.

"You know who she's like? She's sort of a young Goldie Hawn type." That was what a man sitting four barstools down had said, and the bartender had said no, she was more like Deborah Harry, or a peroxided Cher, or that dancer, that Heatherton woman. Well, whatever it was, they all seemed to like it. Their eyes had never left that goddamn television. They disrobed her. They pawed her. They mentally ravished her. And everything she did said, "That's all right—you can do that to me."

See, that was the problem—that had always been the problem. There was something about her that was so damn *attainable.* It said, "Look at me, fellas, I'm *everybody's* woman. I'm easy as pie. You can do anything you want with me." Which in life is revolting but onstage is a virtue. No, it wasn't Sandra's failure that was eating his guts out—it was the frightening specter of her unqualified success. She was going to be a star! He was being psychically castrated!

As luck would have it, the E train came first. There was a stir in the air—then a groundswell of wheel noise. He stood with both feet on the edge of the warning line. The train rocked slightly as it bulleted forward.

"Ted, you all right?"
"I'll call ya," said Shaughnessy.
The doors slid open. Shaughnessy stepped in.
"I'll see ya tomorrow."
The doors closed behind him.
The train pulled out as the violinist played "*Liebestraum.*"

24

It was a delight and a surprise one warm afternoon when Gronsky, in his office, saw the button light up, then heard the intercom buzz and Marie, his secretary, saying, "Excuse me, Alex—it's Mr. Pelligrew on two calling."

Mr. Pelligrew on two . . .

"Jesus Christ!" bellowed Gronsky.

"Hi, Alex, how are you?"

"Where the hell have you been, damn it?"

"Whaddaya mean, where've I been? I haven't been anywhere. I was just calling to ask if you'd like to come up this evening."

Gronsky laughed. This was so like Pelligrew. He had all but disappeared off the face of the earth, and when he finally turns up, it's as if nothing had happened, all he wants to know is if you'd like to come up that evening.

"Your place?" said Gronsky.

"Yeah, why not? About seven."

"Well, it's all right with me, but I'd rather ask *you*—"

"See you then," said Pelligrew, and with that, he hung up. Gronsky, perplexed, sat staring at the telephone.

What he had wanted to say, only he hadn't had a chance to, because Pelligrew, still quirky, wasn't in the mood for conversing, was that after seven long months of living at the Cotswold, he had finally found an apartment up on East Eighty-seventh Street. It was not all that much, just a small, sterile cubicle, one window looking out over Carl Shurz Park, but it was bright, it was his, there was no smell of rat poison, and he would have liked to have had his friend come over and look at it.

Oh, well, what the hell . . . It was already after five. He put away his papers, he closed up his briefcase, he said good night to Marie, avoided Karpeghian, and in another few minutes he was safe in the elevator.

Gronsky's workdays of late had become increasingly intolerable. He was finding it harder and harder just to get up in the morning. He had Karpeghian to deal with, he had Eastman cold-shouldering him—every minute in that office seemed to last an eternity. "You know, the trouble with you," Karpeghian had told him once (it was one of Karpeghian's variations on the Eastman "Dutch uncle" chats), "you've never put yourself in the old man's position, Alex. Consider how *he* feels. The hurt. The indignity." And Gronsky had just stood there. What hurt? What indignity? What had he ever done to make Eastman uncomfortable? "Well, you know"—Karpeghian smiled—"of course, it's none of my business, really, but she's all he has left. She's his flesh-and-blood daughter, Alex."

And suddenly it had dawned. It was those words "flesh-and-blood." He had married Eastman's daughter, he had been foresworn to take care of her, and after seventeen years of mortgages and car payments, she had handed down her verdict by renouncing her womanhood! Of course, he had no illusions that Eastman must have known this. They had never discussed it, it was not something one talked about, but he would have to have been blind not to recognize the oddity of a woman keeping house with a twenty-year-old Swedish girl. What Gronsky hadn't realized was how Eastman might interpret it. What kind of an incompetent would lose his wife to an *au pair* girl? It was a family disgrace, it was a stain on their bloodline, and Eastman, quite naturally, held Gronsky accountable for it.

Gronsky looked at his watch. It was twenty after five. His original intention had been to go to his apartment, clean up, change his clothes, watch the six o'clock news, then hop in a cab over to West Ninety-seventh Street. But the night was so warm, the twilight so halcyon, the girls looked so nice in their light sleeveless camisoles, that he decided not to stop at his apartment at all. He'd go straight up to Pelligrew's—on foot, if his knee was willing.

As he headed up Lex toward East Fifty-ninth Street he felt unusually happy; he was reminded of summer. This summer he was hoping to take Bobby to Long Island. They'd swim, they'd fish, they'd take a boat ride off Montauk. Poor Bobby, thought Gronsky. That was his biggest impediment. He got to see him only about every other weekend, and every time he did there'd be this lump in his throat, and he'd have to cough, turn away, trying to conceal all the hurt he felt. Ah, the American salesman! The inveterate sentimentalist! How often had he seen it at conventions, on business trips, some florid-faced clown, his eyes puffed with liquor, showing pictures of his kids to all the B girls and prostitutes. There's no gentler father than the absentee father. He weeps, he boasts, his heart flows with tenderness, and it's only when he's home that the drudgery sets in, and he becomes the same remote fixture that fathers have always been.

He cut into the park behind Grand Army Plaza, curved his way west around the Pond, Wollman skating rink, stopped for a moment to light up a cigarette, scowled at two blacks dealing grass by a trash barrel. The joggers were out. They descended in waves on him, their sweat-smeared bodies looking hard, athletic, trim accountants, trim lawyers, trim realtors and bureaucrats who only an hour ago had been smothering in skyscrapers. And there were men riding bikes. They had their hats turned backward. Their rear ends sat high over the backs of their pommels, their shoulders slouched forward, their necks crooked like ducks' necks, their lips puckered out over the tongues of their police whistles.

Last week he had seen Bobby. They had had a wonderful Sunday. They had taken a subway down to the South Street Seaport, and they had climbed around the ships, played tag among the rigging, watched a narrated film about the adventures of whaling life. He had enjoyed doing that. They did all the cliché things. They rode to the top of the Empire State Building. They took a Circle Line cruise. They did the Museum of Natural History. And everywhere they went, Gronsky would cling for dear life to him.

There had been an article once—where on earth had he seen

it?—about fathers and their children in New York on a Sunday, and how you could always spot the ones who weren't living together because the fathers held those hands just a little too desperately. In the seven or eight months since his own separation, Gronsky had become very astute at observing such nuances. He could see it in their eyes, in their solicitous mannerisms, in their obvious confusion as to what role was expected of them. Such sad little cameos. He could hardly bear looking at them. He wished he could approach them, say, "Excuse me, you don't know me, but I know just how you feel, and after you've dropped off the kid, if you're not busy tonight I know a bar on Third Avenue . . ."

There was a girl on a skateboard. It was a strange-looking contraption. It had a motor on the back and a remote control clutch cable. As she putt-putted past, Gronsky watched her admiringly. She was statuesque, gorgeous—one of those porcelain-skinned model types.

He thought of Mary Anne. Of course she was no model type. She was just a pleasant-looking woman with unusually soft irises, and when she wore her hair back, there were these wisps from her sideburns, little charcoal reminders of how tender and real she was. "Well, whaddaya think?" They were standing in his living room. The room was bare, the walls had fresh paint on them. When they talked, there was nothing to soften the echo. He looked around proudly, as if it were something he'd built for her. And Mary Anne smiled. "I think it looks nice, Alex." "I'll put the couch over there. I've already ordered a television. If I can find one on sale, I think I'll pick up a stereo. I'll put the speakers in here, I'll build a shelf for the turntable . . ." Mary Anne said nothing. She was wearing Calvin Klein jeans, a flounce-front blouse, and an old pair of Mushrooms. She had that tentative expression, as if to say, "What am I doing here? Why should I care where this man puts his stereo speakers?"

When he got to Sheep Meadow, his knee began throbbing. He sat down on a rock, watched some kids playing Frisbee. The lozenge sailed out, seemed to hover, cut back again. He put out his cigarette, promptly lit up another one.

Last week she had come over and helped him set up for housekeeping. They were standing in the kitchen, and she was up on a step stool, her blouse stretched tight, her heels uplifted, her dark midriff bare as he handed her shelf paper.

"Would you go back if she asked?"

"Beg pardon?" said Gronsky.

Mary Anne smiled. "Never mind. Just wondering." And she had climbed down off the stool, placing her hand in his large hand, her head tilted sideways, admiring her handiwork.

He thought about that now as he skirted the baseball diamond. There were some lovers by the backstop, and he tried to keep clear of them. He couldn't help wondering if what she had said had been valid. If Mandy were to ask, would he indeed have gone back to her?

At the transverse road running by Tavern on the Green, the throbbing came back, only this time more powerfully. He climbed over a railing, hobbled into the parking lot. He flagged down a cab that had just dropped off dinner guests.

A few years ago, when he was still very married, he had had a passionate affair with one of his co-workers' secretaries. Her name was Maureen; she was absolutely beautiful, and they used to meet every noon at a hotel down on Madison. It was his one brief flirtation with the art of unfaithfulness. They made quick, breathless love. They took long, soapy baths together. And afterward they'd lie there, and she'd tease him and giggle at him, and he'd roll over on his back, and she'd climb up on top of him . . . He thought of that now. Of course, it had ended predictably. He had walked in one morning, and she was sitting there crying, and on the blotter by the phone was a terse note from Eastman—no warning, no scolding, just a slip and a severance check. It was a devastating moment—and it had been so damn unfair to her. He was as guilty as she was, but it was she who was punished for it. Odd how that works. It's always the woman. And that night, over dinner, Mandy had glowered at him . . .

The cab crossed Columbus. Gronsky looked at his watch. Twenty to seven. Jesus Christ, he was early, damn it! And Pelligrew would be there, half-dressed, with his hair still wet, saying, "For God's sake, Gronsky, can't you ever be late for once?"

He got out of the cab, handed the driver five dollars. Down the street and to the right there was a new co-op housing project. It had oddly shaped balconies and a powdery white brickface and looked totally out of keeping with the rest of the neighborhood. "It's the Arabs, goddamn 'em!"—that's what a cabbie had once told him. "It's all those goddamn Arabs—now there's no place for poor people!"—and he had gone on and on about how the city was being ruined, and the destruction of its character, and the abominable new architecture. And Gronsky had just smiled. It was so totally nonsensical. Why should you complain about what was clearly an improvement? Would he have preferred to go back to the decay and the bankruptcy? What was it with some people that they clung to the past so much?

He gave the driver his tip, crossed the street toward the sidewalk. It had been almost three months since he had stepped on that sidewalk—almost three months since he had walked up those porch steps, opened the door to the foyer, seen a girl at the mailboxes . . .

"Listen, about tonight, Alex . . ." She had called him that morning. He had been sitting in his office going over a marketing strategy, and Marie, over the intercom, had said, "It's a Miss Mary Anne Delucci, Alex," and he had been pleasantly surprised at the warmth that crept over him. "It's about tonight, Alex—I'm afraid I can't make it. I have to go to the Bronx and make dinner for my brother. His wife's got bronchitis, and he's helpless without her. I'm awfully sorry. Could we make it tomorrow maybe?" "Oh, sure," said Gronsky, and he had glanced at his desk calendar, tomorrow would be fine, all his evenings were free that week, and he had erased her name one place, written it in in the next place, he'd see her tomorrow, they'd go out for a pizza maybe. Only when he had hung up the phone and leaned back in his desk chair, he had felt a sense of loneliness, as if a void had descended. These occasional outings had come to mean so much to him. Just her smile, her presence, the goodness she radiated . . .

Was it possible, he wondered as he ascended the porch steps, those same marble steps with the ornate concrete balustrade—was it remotely possible that he was falling in love with her? That what had started as a friendship was now somewhat more complicated? He stood in the foyer. He looked down at the door buzzers. Pelligrew, as usual, was using a new *nom de guerre.* "Warren Spahn" was crossed out and in its place was "Ewell Blackwell." Gronsky smiled to himself. The guy did know his baseball pitchers.

"Can I help you?" said the voice.

He turned, looked up, startled. It was a midwestern voice, the kind he had known since childhood. She was standing in the door carrying a Daitch-Shopwell shopping bag. She looked vaguely familiar, but he was a long way from recognizing her.

"Huh? Oh, no, I'm just looking . . ."

"Try 'Blackwell,' " she offered.

Gronsky nodded, pushed 'Blackwell.' There was no response from the door buzzer. The woman, who wore glasses, had taken out her house keys. He helped her with her groceries while she unlocked the door for him.

"Alex, I'd like you to meet someone . . ." The sound of hoarse laughter, Shaughnessy lying on his back, his feet on the butcher block, saying, "Forgive me, Alex, but you are totally irrelevant!" and Gronsky guffawing, trying to locate his handkerchief . . .

She was a tall, slender woman in her mid- to late thirties. She had a milk-white complexion and silvering blond hair. When she smiled, there was a quality of lonely acceptance, as if to say, "I know who I am—why haven't you others caught up with me?"

"You don't recognize me, do you?"

"I'm afraid . . . not entirely . . ."

"I'm Linda Cauthen. I met you last February."

"Oh." Gronsky nodded.

"Of course there were so many people there. And I didn't stay long. You seemed fairly well occupied."

"Who's Linda?" said Shaughnessy.

"I'm not sure," said Gronsky.

"Great-looking female! Great-looking ass, goddamn it! She's mature, she's successful—she's like you, she's traditionalist . . . but if you don't want her, I've got nothing to say about it!"

They mounted the staircase, Gronsky with shopping bag. She wore sheer seamless stockings and a form-fitting business suit. As he ascended behind her, he studied her backside. *Great-looking female! Great-looking ass, goddamn it!*

"My name's Alex," said Gronsky.

"Yes, I know. You're the football player."

Gronsky said nothing. He looked in her shopping bag. Some Weaver's fried chicken, four Stouffer's, two Swanson products—the sad little items of the single career woman.

At the landing, she turned.

"I go this way," she said.

Gronsky handed her the bag. Their fingers touched briefly.

"Thank you."

She smiled.

She walked off down the hallway.

Gronsky just stood there. There was something remarkable . . .

"I knew it! You're *early!*"

"I rang you downstairs."

"Jesus Christ, Gronsky, you are an inveterate midwesterner!" —and there stood Pelligrew, the same old Don Pelligrew, fresh from the shower, his hair with water still on it.

Gronsky nodded, stepped in. It was just as it had always been. The same old tired jokes, the same old coarse insults, the same L-shaped room with the same disused lawbooks, the same corner chair where he invariably plopped himself.

"Where the hell have you been hiding?"

"I haven't been hiding. Here, pour yourself a drink. I'll be back in a minute"—and, buttoning his shirt, he disappeared down the hallway toward the bedroom and the bath. There was a sound like a toilet running.

Gronsky sat down. He felt tired, he felt radiant. He picked up an ashtray. It contained a barrette and a bobby pin. He smiled to himself. He pulled out a Viceroy. His mind was still puzzling over his encounter in the hallway.

"You know the trouble with us?" (This was Shaughnessy speaking. They had been sitting in a bar called Cincinnati. It was a quasi-chic eatery down on Third, just off Gramercy, and it had been Gronsky's idea because the name held fond memories for him.) "You know the trouble with us men? We overlook temperament. Think about it, Alex—it's the most obvious element. Have you ever heard a man say, 'I'm in love with her temperament'? And yet, if you don't have that going, you don't have a thing, damn it." This was Shaughnessy's big virtue—he could be astonishingly clearheaded. Particularly when he was talking about relations in abstract. It was only the specifics that seemed to confuse him. He was by nature a generalist. He should have been a philosopher. "There's a woman over there. What am I attracted to? I'm attracted to her tits, her big eyes, her long legs, maybe. If I really get to know her, I might find I like talking to her, I like the way she laughs, I like her cooking, her orgasms. But what does that mean? It doesn't mean shit, Alex. We're completely ignoring the most obvious element. And so do the women. A man's looks, a man's bank account . . . They never seem to focus on what'll really do right by them." He belched. He leaned back. He took a deep draft of Cutty Sark. "It's the temperament, Alex—it's the basal metabolism. You either share it or you don't, and if you don't, you're in trouble. Sooner or later, it's gonna come tumbling down on you."

Gronsky thought about that now as he sat smoking his cigarette, tapping the barrette against the edge of the ashtray, trying to figure out what Shaughnessy had meant and what it might have to do with that woman and her shopping bag.

"Did you see Sandra's show?"

Pelligrew was back in the living room. He had his socks in one hand, a pair of shoes in the other. He sat down on the couch, began untangling his shoelaces. There was an excitement about him, some edge of anxiety.

"Oh, yeah, she was good."

"I tried to call you that night."

"She was really terrific. I thought she looked wonderful. Hey, pour yourself a drink. There's some ice in the ice tray. I forgot to buy vodka, but I think there's a little there."

There was something not right, but Gronsky couldn't quite place it. It was not only psychic, it was real, it was tangible. Some sight, some sound, some out-of-place puzzle piece . . . He went out into the kitchen, began fumbling with ice cubes.

"And you know Shaughnessy," he was saying—he was talking over his shoulder now; the ice cubes were stuck, and he gave them a rap on the counter; through the door, in the living room, Pelligrew sat staring at him; his eyes were opaque; there was an unspoken question in them—"and you know Shaughnessy," he was saying, "he's having a hard time accepting it. Apparently the show's gotten a lot of publicity. I hate to say it, but I think he feels jealous of her. He's got a tiger by the tail, and he doesn't know how to handle it."

Pelligrew said nothing. He seemed suddenly uninterested. Gronsky had located the vodka, drained the last of the bottle. He came back into the living room feeling somewhat dislocated. Some object, some knickknack, some absence of furniture . . .

"Oh, and I got a new apartment."

"So I heard," said Pelligrew.

"It's on East Eighty-seventh."

"Near East End Avenue."

"Well, yeah, that's right. It's near East End Avenue. It's just a small one-bedroom, but it's got a pretty good view from it . . ."

And now suddenly he got it. It wasn't the absence of something—it was the opposite of absence, it was an unwonted presence. It was the sound of that toilet. It wasn't a toilet. It was the shower that was running, only now it had stopped running.

Gronsky scowled. He looked quizzically at Pelligrew.

"You got somebody in here?"

Pelligrew said nothing.

"I mean, Jesus"—Gronsky laughed—"it's not even seven yet. I haven't even eaten, and you've been fucking some broad already?"

Pelligrew frowned. "You shouldn't have come early." He got up from the sofa and went out into the kitchen. He opened the refrigerator, pulled out some soave. He poured himself a glass and came back and sat down again.

The seconds ticked by. There was the sound of a door latch. Footsteps in the hall. A squeak from the bedroom.

"Who is it?" said Gronsky. "You got Lilah in there?" He was grinning lasciviously. "Hey, it's not that ex-nun, is it?"

"Have you seen my barrette? I left it here somewh—" and suddenly she was there, she was at the entrance to the living room, her hair was still wet, her blouse was unbuttoned, her skirt was half-zipped and pulled askew on her abdomen.

It was his body that caught it. Gronsky's mind was incapable.

Pelligrew scowled. "I can explain all this, Alex . . ."

Neither said a word. Mary Anne just stood there. Her mouth hung agape, her eyelids blinked rapidly.

"I can explain all this, Alex. See, it just sorta happened. Well, I had this idea . . . I thought we could all get together maybe . . . I called Mary Anne, she agreed to come over . . . You know how it is. Well, hell, we *did* go together . . ."

Gronsky said nothing. He was incapable of speaking. Mary Anne, hangdog, stood staring at the stereo. When she finally turned around, there were tears in her eyes. Her fingers, trembling, held the front of her blouse shut.

"You're a liar," she muttered.

Pelligrew said nothing.

"That's not true, and you know it. You did this on purpose."

"Hey, whaddaya mean? I didn't do anything! You agreed to come over, we had a few drinks together . . ."

Gronsky just sat there. He couldn't feel anything. He had vodka in his mouth, but he couldn't even taste it. It was as if every pore, every gland had stopped functioning, and all he could feel was this coldness, this numb feeling.

"I gotta be going."

"Oh, Alex, please listen . . ."

"Hey, don't go," said Pelligrew. "Look, I'll make it all up to you . . ."

"I'm sorry . . . I'm going . . ." He was up. He was walking. It was as if the world, his whole life, had suddenly reversed itself.

Part Four

25

"Dear Don," said the letter (yes, he had actually *written* this; when Shaughnessy heard that, he couldn't believe it; only women wrote letters; letters took *effort*; men who wrote letters were either queer or neurotic somehow)—"Dear Don," said the letter, "In my haste last evening, I seem to have forgotten my elephant-skin briefcase. Please be so kind as to give it to this messenger. Thank you. Yours truly, Alexander A. Gronsky."

"Jesus," said Shaughnessy.

"Yeah, I know," said Pelligrew. It had arrived the next morning at about eleven o'clock. Pelligrew had called Shaughnessy and read him the letter, and Shaughnessy, stunned, had taken a while to react to it.

"What the hell did you do?"

"I didn't do anything!"

"Aw, c'mon," said Shaughnessy. "You must have done *something* to him."

"No, I didn't! I swear! I didn't do anything! . . . Well, maybe I did . . . but it was all his own fault, goddamn it!"

And now it came out, in somewhat elliptical fashion, that he had just happened to be talking to Mary Anne yesterday, and she had just happened to come over, and he had just happened to make love to her, and Gronsky, that idiot, had just happened to come early, damn it.

"Oh, my God," said Shaughnessy.

"Well, it wasn't *my* fault!"

"Yeah, but Jesus," said Shaughnessy, "you knew how he felt about her . . ."

"He had no right! He had no right to feel that toward her!

She was *mine!* She loved me! She's always been vulnerable to me!"

And so it came about that a breach was created, a festering canker that threatened their triad, whereby Gronsky saw Shaughnessy, and Shaughnessy saw Pelligrew, but between Gronsky and Pelligrew there was a cessation of dialogue.

"Listen, Alex—" said Shaughnessy.

"I don't want to talk about it."

"Look, I know how you feel, and I can't say I blame you much, but for Christ's sake, Alex, that's the woman's prerogative. You know what I mean. You can't just blame Don for it."

Oh, can't I? thought Gronsky. Oh, couldn't he blame Pelligrew? We'll see about that. He could blame whoever he wanted for it. He could blame Mary Anne Delucci, he could blame Pelligrew, Mandy . . . if Shaughnessy wasn't careful, he might even blame *him* for it.

It has been insightfully observed that in any male bonding there is an element akin to sexuality; there is a potential for hurt, for envy, for jealousy—all the same peevish wounds that exist between married people. And that's how *they* were. They were like two quarreling lovers. Neither of them was willing to speak to the other one, and with each passing week, the silence grew deadlier, until, by the end of the summer, it had the hallmarks of permanence.

"Hey, you remember last year when we took the kids to the game?" said Shaughnessy. This was in the middle of August, and he was talking to Pelligrew. Sandra was away (she was away quite a bit now), he had nothing else to do, so they had gone and had dinner together.

"Yeah, I remember," said Pelligrew. "I really enjoyed that."

"We ought to do that again. We ought to make a tradition out of it."

"You mean Alex?" said Pelligrew.

"Well, sure, we'd ask Alex . . ."

"Unh-unh. I'm not going. He's been very uncharitable toward me . . ."

"Hello, Alex? This is Ted."

"Hi, Ted, how ya doin?"

"I'm fine. Hey, listen, I was talking to Don last night. He had a terrific idea—well, I told him I'd try it on you. He said let's the three of us get together and take the kids to a football game."

There was a pause. Gronsky thinking.

"He actually said that?"

"Well, yeah, more or less . . ."

There was another long silence.

Then:

"No, thanks. I can't go. Tell him I'm busy. I'm occupied. Tell him I appreciate it, but I just don't feel up to it."

Well, so much for that. At least Shaughnessy had tried. It was like trying to intervene between a couple of fighting cocks. It was silly, it was petty—it was to Shaughnessy's mind "womanish"—but he was forced to accept that there was nothing he could do about it.

And so toward September, the approach of the equinox, the newspapers fluttering with back-to-school clothing specials, the baseball homestretch, the return of Fire Islanders, and finally, toward mid-month, the onset of football weather.

It was Pelligrew first.

"I don't want to sit with him."

"With who?" said Shaughnessy.

"With *him,*" said Pelligrew. "I mean, I'm willing to go, I think Jeremy might like it, but I'm not going to sit there and have *him* shooting daggers at me."

Then Gronsky called back.

"Was that really his idea?"

"Whaddaya mean?" said Shaughnessy.

"I have to admit, that surprises me. I mean, if it was really his idea, and he's willing to forget it, I don't object. I'm not a big grudge holder . . ."

And so, to Shaughnessy's surprise, and more through need than through charity, the first steps were taken toward resuming their contact, and as the days flickered by toward the inevitable Sunday, Shaughnessy couldn't help wondering whether he had done the right thing or not.

The day dawned cloudily that unseasonably cold morning, and by the time they got there there was rain on the windshield. "Don't worry," said Shaughnessy, "they play football in anything," and they got out of the car and made their way through the parking lot.

This may or may not have been a worry to the ladies (yes, there were ladies this time; that had become unavoidable; Emmy was there wearing a beige coat and turban, Sandra wearing bloomers and a cloak with winged collars on it)—they may or may not have been concerned about field conditions and whether the game would be canceled before everyone's ribs got broken, but they accepted it stoically, they were trying to be "good guys," although Emmy made it clear that she much preferred tennis matches.

There had been several new developments on the Shaughnessy home front: He and Sandra had decided to "formalize" their partnership. Not through marriage, albeit—Shaughnessy wouldn't go that far—but through another institution that was perhaps just as mind-boggling. What they had done, they had gone out and they had purchased a co-op. They had gone to a bank, they had co-signed the mortgage papers, a benediction was said, an "amen" had been uttered, and they were forever conjoined under the aegis of tax write-offs. "Of course, it's not the Dakota," said Shaughnessy effacingly as he escorted Gronsky through the echoing labyrinth. It was on Central Park West near the corner of Seventieth, and the living room alone was about the size of a subway station. "We'd have preferred the Dakota, but we couldn't get into it. Frankly, I'm glad. This has a homier feel to it"—and Gronsky had stood there, totally amazed by the floor space, and wondering how in the hell they were going to pay for the maintenance on it.

As for Pelligrew, meanwhile—well, he was still Pelligrew. He was still on that tightrope between Emmy and her daughter. Was he screwing them both? Was he not screwing either of them? It wasn't too clear, and he was refusing to talk about it. What was a good bit more certain was that there were problems with Jeremy. Elizabeth and her lover seemed to be at the end of their tether with him. He had run away twice; he refused to eat dinner; when he bothered to address Klimefogler it was as "hey you" or "hey, chiropractor." So there was that going on—he had some typical male mid-life problems (his hair had begun thinning; it was coming out by the handfuls; he had taken to measuring between his nose and his widow's peak, and with each passing week the distance kept growing on him); he had worries about that; his bike had been stolen; he had lost another case in the appellate division; in July, for some reason, he had contracted a rash, and he had to go to a urologist, who gave him a moral lecture; he had these age and sex problems; he had problems with his motorcycle; he had problems with Gronsky, whom he had mortally offended, but other than that, he was just about the same, and in fact, all things considered, life had never been better for him.

It was the Giants and the Redskins. The wind howled angrily. The guy ropes snapped against the sides of the flag standards. In the center of the field a small pond was accumulating. When the runners took off, you could hear the sound of their feet splashing.

As Shaughnessy would confess, there had been some concerns about Jaime lately. She was a full year older—she was almost thirteen now—her auburn-haired beauty had blossomed voluptuously, and everything about her oozed sex and rebelliousness. Of course, in Shaughnessy's opinion, that was all her damn mother's fault. If Sarah were more caring, there wouldn't be this contentiousness. But no matter whose fault it was, it was certainly a problem, and it seemed to have gotten worse since the previous football outing.

Sandra, by contrast, like so many young women, had become increasingly obsessed with the idea of motherhood, so to her this young creature, this wild seed of her paramour, was a perfect lab in which to try out her nursing instincts. During the tedious drive over, sitting in the back of the Volvo, smarmily prying into all Jaime's interests, she had asked about her clothes, did she like Al Pacino, what kind of lipstick was that, had she read Judy Blume lately? To which Jaime, looking sullen, answering monosyllabically, her body slouched down, her arms crossed in front of her, said her clothes had been pilfered, Al Pacino was "sleazoid," and the only thing she had read was a Ron Rico Rum poster. Shaughnessy, of course, was acutely embarrassed—perhaps as much by Sandra as by Jaime's response to her—but it was none of his business, it was all female twaddle, and there was nothing he could do but hope that it would all go away somehow.

During the entire first quarter, Sandra persisted. "Are you warm enough, Jaime? You want to get under this blanket with me? Ted, pass me that blanket. No, not that one—the other one. Isn't that better? Would you like some hot chocolate maybe?" It was totally insufferable—even Bobby began squirming—and Jaime just sat there looking more and more petulant, until finally, unable to take it any longer, she began to strike back with the only weapon available to her:

"Why don't you leave me alone? You're not my mother!"

"I was only suggesting—"

"I don't need your suggestions! I know what you're doing. You're trying to be *pals* with me. I don't want to be *pals.* I want nothing to do with you."

Shaughnessy said nothing. Sandra just smiled at her.

"You're tired. She's just tired."

"I am *not* tired!" cried Jaime. "You wanna sleep with my father? Go ahead! Fuck it! Just leave me alone! And take this damn blanket off me!"

And with that, she stood up, clambered over the bleacher seat, half stumbled, half fell over the knees of the spectators, muttered something obscene about the hypocrisy of adults, and disappeared up the aisle and into the bowels of the concession area.

Emmy, in the meantime, was engrossed in her kvetching act. This game was so silly. It was all so—well, juvenile somehow. Like why did those players keep bashing their heads together? They had a whole field out there. There was enough room for everybody.

"For Chrissake," said Pelligrew.

"Well, I mean it. I'm serious. I have nothing against sports—I *love* Jimmie Connors. But this is so childish. It makes no sense at all to me. It's raining. It's boring. I'm freezing my tuchus off . . ."

The first quarter over. The score: six to nothing. Three interceptions, four fumbles, twelve penalty calls. Jeremy was shivering. Pelligrew was glowering. Bobby had spilled Coke all over Emmy's new stadium coat.

"I think," said Sandra, "we ought to go try to find her, Ted."

"The hell," said Shaughnessy. "You want her, *you* look for her."

"You don't mean that."

"I do too—I do *too* mean it. This is all Sarah's fault. I get sick and tired listening to it."

The second quarter started. The Redskins were leading. By now, the rain had begun to let up somewhat. In fact, Gronsky was predicting that the sun would start shining. "You just wait," he said, nodding, "they're gonna unleash their passing game . . ."

In the middle of the quarter, an usher appeared. He was followed by a cop and an unarmed security guard. Between them was Jaime. She had obviously been sulking. Her shirt was pulled out, and she had a dazed, wild-eyed look about her.

"This your kid?" said the usher.

Shaughnessy said nothing.

"She's ours," said Sandra.

"*I am not!*" cried Jaime.

"We found her outside. She was hustlin some guy out there. If she's yours, better take her. We don't want no trouble with her."

So now Jaime was back—or at least as back as she'd ever be. She was still refusing to sit next to Sandra; instead, she insisted on sitting in the aisle, where the spectators and hawkers had to keep stepping over her.

The gun went off. It was the beginning of the half time. The ladies (minus Jaime) went off to the ladies' room; Shaughnessy, who was "starved," took the boys out for hot dogs, and that left Gronsky and Pelligrew with three empty seats between them.

"You know, you can lead a horse to water, but you can't make him drink," said Shaughnessy. He had coined that this morning when he was talking to Sandra. They were sitting in their bedroom, she was putting on her stockings, and he was wondering out loud how his friends would react together. And Sandra had scowled. "I don't know why you put up with them." "Whaddaya mean?" said Shaughnessy. He had never heard that before. "Well, I know you've been friends—you were alone, they supported you—but you're not alone now, and I can't see what their charm is for you." And Shaughnessy had just sat there. He had never heard *that* before. "Are you trying to tell me I should abandon my friends, Sandra?" "I'm just trying to say that we're in a whole different stratum now. We have to think of ourselves. I'm just trying to be practical."

Well, now here was a whole different method of viewing things. An omen, perhaps? A glimpse of the future? And he had sat there staring at those long, slender legs of hers, this punk-star phenomenon with the networks all chasing her . . .

"Rotten game," said Pelligrew.

"Ungh." Gronsky nodded.

They were both facing forward, their shoulders slouched sullenly, their faces expressionless while an out-of-step marching band splashed around the field in a tribute to space travel.

"See that trap play?" said Pelligrew.

"Hmmmm." Gronsky nodded.

"That goddamn left tackle's been tricked every time on those. He goes charging in there, he gets hit by that flanker, leaves a hole in the line you could drive a Mack truck through it."

It has been argued that football is a reflection of America; that in its bigness, its violence, it symbolizes our value system; that when a man watches football he is mentally regressing, traveling backward in time toward a more violent ancestry. Could be. Who can say? It's not ours to analyze. What *can* be said, is that it brings men together somehow; that in its speed, its brutality, it unifies the gender; that its coordinated strategy makes a virtue of machoism.

"Want a drink?" said Gronsky. He pulled out a hip flask.

Pelligrew said nothing. He looked away toward the goal posts.

Gronsky unscrewed the flask, took a quick sip of vodka. He rescrewed the cap and stuck it back in his coat pocket.

They had not come together. They had arrived in two vehicles. Gronsky, of course, had brought Shaughnessy and Sandra, but when Pelligrew showed up it was in a yellow Mercedes that Emmy, one assumed, kept parked in a garage somewhere. They had nodded to each other; they had said "hi" and "how are you"; it was all quite civilized; there was no sign of conflict; but it wasn't until now, sitting alone in those bleacher seats, that they were finally coerced into coming to grips with things.

Trap plays and draw plays and end sweeps and screen passes—these are the grounds on which men can communicate. They can mentally project; they can live vicariously, they can expound and critique without having to say anything. In Pelligrew's opinion, it was the quarterback's fault. "I've been saying all year they should bench that bastard." Gronsky disagreed: It was a failure of management. "If they had a line coach in there who knew his ass from a hole in the ground . . ."

The minutes ticked by. The band kept playing. Jaime, in the aisle, was puffing a cigarette. Every so often, she would turn and glance back at them. "Well?" her eyes said. "You got something to say to me?"

Then:

"Seen Mary Anne lately?" The question was Pelligrew's. Better from him than if Gronsky had asked it, Gronsky who wanted nothing to do with that topic, to whom the mention of her name was a reminder of perfidy.

"No, not really," said Gronsky. He looked toward the scoreboard. They were announcing the scores of the Bengals' and Dolphins' games. The band was saluting the Columbia space shuttle. There was a simulated rocket. It had smoke coming out of it.

"And you?" he said finally.

"No, not really," said Pelligrew. He was still slouched down. His eyes had a brooding quality. Gronsky was suddenly reminded of all those nights they had spent together, the stories they had shared, the laughter, the intimacies . . .

The ceremony was over. The teams were returning. First the Redskins came out, and then came the Giants. The score going in had been twenty-three to three. Half the fans had gone home. There was a gull on the playing field.

"It was my fault, you know."

"Aw, c'mon, don't be silly."

"No, I mean it. It was. I get so insecure sometimes. I kept calling her up. I badgered her into it. She was interested in you. I just needed to prove something."

"It wasn't your fault. I'd have done the same thing, Don."

"No, you wouldn't. Not you. You'd have controlled yourself better."

"It makes no difference. What's over's over. To tell you the truth, I haven't given much thought to it."

The teams were lined up. There was a delay of the kickoff. Shaughnessy, with the kids, was trying to locate their box number. There was no sign of Emmy. Sandra was smiling. She was bending over Jaime, who was refusing to look at her.

"It was *my* fault," said Gronsky.

"That's absurd," said Pelligrew.

"No, it was, it was mine. I knew how she felt about you. She kept trying to warn me the first night she met me. I refused to listen. I let my heart rule my head, goddamn it . . ."

Now Shaughnessy was back. The teams were lined up again. The ref raised his arm. The clock began running. There was the inevitable "whoooo!" as the ball sailed skyward, falling end over end beyond the goal line, the end zone marker . . .

"It was *her* fault," said Pelligrew.

"How do you get that?"

"Hell, she knew what I wanted. She didn't have to come over there."

"I'd agree with you there . . ."

"I was just being myself. She knows I'm self-centered. I was just following my nature with her."

"It was her fault and my fault."

"It was mine more than your fault."

"It was all three of our faults."

"Only hers more than anybody's."

"Want a swig?" said Gronsky.

"Well, okay—maybe one . . ."

"Goddamn women," said Gronsky.

"We've learned a valuable lesson, Alex."

"That's enough!" cried Shaughnessy.

"But *why?*" whined Jaime.

"Because! It's stupid! I refuse to discuss it with you!"

"You *always* refuse!"

"You're damn right, and I'll keep refusing! You're thirteen years old! This whole thing makes me nauseated!"

The game was over. The Giants had lost. Disheartened, uncomfortable, they were on their way toward the parking lot. It had begun to sleet. Jeremy felt sick. Even Gronsky, that stalwart, had pains in his esophagus.

"You're an asshole!" cried Jaime.

"That's enough of that, missy . . ."

"Well, you are! So's *she!* So's my mother, so's everybody! I can do what I want! You don't have custody! You don't care about me! All you want is your meal ticket!"

What had occasioned this outburst was a request from Jaime (well, it was more than a request; it had a lot of demand in it) that, since the plans were for her to stay over that evening, the least they could do was let her boy friend come sleep with her.

"You're kidding," said Shaughnessy.

"Well, you sleep with *her,* don't you?"

"You're thirteen years old! There's no comparison!"

"You fuck *her!*"

"Oh, my God!" cried Shaughnessy. "This is all Sarah's fault! This is all her damn mother's doing!"

Perhaps the only good thing that had derived from this outing was that Pelligrew and Gronsky had resumed their relationship. In fact, flushed on vodka, surrounded by bickering, they felt more allied now than they had since they'd met each other.

"That goddamn Simms . . ."

"He kept throwing the ball away!"

"I keep tellin ya, Alex—they should give it to Bruner . . ."

"It was Perkins' fault . . ."

"If they had just run the option more . . ."

"Option schmoption—they oughta trade the whole team, goddamn em . . ."

Their voices echoed through the cinder-block concourse. Clusters of cops stood around looking restless. The concessions were closing. There was a boy hawking T-shirts. Emmy was wondering what the symptoms for frostbite were.

"But *why?*" cried Jaime. She was walking ahead of them. They were descending the ramp toward the stadium's mezzanine. Her jacket was open, she was turned around facing them, she was walking backward while keening her viewpoints at them.

"I am not going to argue!"

"You adults are all hypocrits! You sleep with *her!* My mom sleeps with everybody! Jesus and me, we sleep all the time together! We sleep in old cars, in motels, in the subway stations . . ."

"My mom sleeps with Ingrid."

"Never mind," said Gronsky.

"Who's Ingrid?" said Emmy.

"Who's Jesus?" said Shaughnessy.

"Our maid. She's from Sweden."

"That's enough," said Gronsky.

"How chummy," said Emmy. "Would you please hurry up, Donald?"

They came out of the stadium and into the parking lot. It was well after four, the sun was descending, what fans had remained looked dejected, bedraggled, their collars pulled up, their blankets draped over them.

"WHO IS *JESUS?*" cried Shaughnessy.

"Jesus! My boy friend!"

"Are you trying to say . . . ?"

"Oh, Gawd!" Jaime's eyes rolled. "You don't know nuthin! You pay no attention to me! Jesus Ramirez! Why don't you listen to me?"

Their cars were parked in adjacent row numbers. To the left

was the Mercedes, looking lustrous and glisteny, to the right Gronsky's Volvo, paint-chipped, deteriorated, having spent all last winter in a Thirtieth Street parking lot.

"Just a minute!" cried Shaughnessy. He stopped dead. He stood staring at her. His hair was matted. His eyes had a demon look. "Are you trying to tell me you've been fucking some spick? You're in the goddamn eighth grade, and you've had some damn P.R.'s cock in you?"

"Now, Ted—" said Sandra.

"HE IS NOT A P.R.!"

"Do you hear what she's saying?"

"HE IS NOT A P.R., DAMN IT!"

"She wants to spend the night, she wants to invite some P.R. over, she wants to screw in *my* house, and I'm supposed to stand here and listen to it!"

"Here we are," said Gronsky.

"What's P.R.?" said Jeremy.

"HE IS NOT A P.R.! HE'S FROM MONTEVIDEO!"

"From *where?*" cried Shaughnessy.

"YOU'RE A PRUDE! I HATE YOU! JUST LEAVE ME ALONE! I'M NOT GOING TO LISTEN TO YOU!"

They had reached the car. The temperature was dropping. It was only October, but it felt like January. Gronsky got in. He turned on the ignition. The engine turned over, made a cough, and then died again.

"WOULD YOU JUST GET IN?"

"I WILL NOT! YOU CAN'T MAKE ME!"

"Hurry up, Donald!"

"Jesus Christ!" cried Pelligrew.

"She's from Stockholm," said Bobby. "She sleeps with my mother. My dad used to do that, but not anymore, he doesn't."

The darkness was settling. The sleet turned to rain again. One by one, the other patrons were exiting. By now it was five, the whole lot was deserted, all that remained were two cars and eight malcontents.

"GODDAMN SWEDES!" cried Gronsky. "THEY CAN'T EVEN BUILD CARS RIGHT!"

"HE IS NOT A P.R.! HE'S FROM MONTEVIDEO!"

"I REFUSE TO EAT DINNER WITH ANY PERSON NAMED JESUS!"

"And my mother smokes hash, only I'm not supposed to talk about it."

26

"Whaddaya mean, she smokes hash?"

Bobby didn't answer. He was sitting next to Gronsky, his head on the window frame. His face was illuminated by white bars of light that flashed through the windshield, then changed into black again.

In the intervening year since the previous football outing, Bobby, Gronsky's son, had grown considerably. From Gronsky's point of view, it was like a series of stop frames, a time-lapse progression having no continuity to it. And one of the more unsettling things he had begun to notice was a certain diplomacy in Bobby's behavior now; he was like a small, neutral country that had become caught between giants, and he was quickly learning not to alienate either of them.

"Whaddaya mean, she smokes hash?"

Bobby still didn't answer. They had driven to New York, dropped off Shaughnessy & Company, and now they were heading up the Henry Hudson Parkway, the windshield wipers making a sound like a vacuum cleaner.

In fairness to Gronsky, during these past twelve months he had never pumped Bobby about his mother's behavior. This was partially, perhaps, because he was afraid of what he'd learn, but it was also because he was not like Don Pelligrew. Pelligrew, of course, was an unconscionable manipulator; he kept pulling little tidbits from an unwary Jeremy, then he'd take those tidbits and use them as wedges, driving more and more space between his son and Elizabeth. Gronsky disapproved: "You know, you better watch out, Don. You keep working on that kid, it's gonna blow up in your face someday." "Not in mine," said Pelligrew. "It isn't my fault. You don't see me spreading *my* legs for a chiropractor."

Well, that was Pelligrew. Gronsky wasn't like that. He was genuinely reluctant to use a child as a battering ram. Only now, having suffered these latest revelations, his reluctance was beginning to show signs of deteriorating.

"Come on, out with it, Bobby!"

"I'm not s'posed to talk about it!"

"Well, you did," said Gronsky, "so you can tell me the rest of it!"

"Hash! You know—*hash!* It's like pot, only better for you. At least, that's what Mom says. I'm not s'posed to say nuthin."

"Oh, my God," muttered Gronsky. They had come to a toll plaza. The rain had let up, and there were the first wisps of ground fog. He dropped in his money, the light answered "thank you." The car sped forward toward White Plains and Pleasantville.

Well, in a way, he supposed, this should have been no surprise to him; it was the logical extension of what he had witnessed a year ago: Mandy's untoward defense of almost everything libertine, her growing disapproval of his squareness, his prudishness. No, that was no news. What bothered him was Bobby—that a ten-year-old kid should have to carry the burden of it. *"My mother smokes hash . . ."* What was wrong with that woman? Boy, when he got to the house, he was going to have a few words to say . . .

Their next visitation was on the following weekend. He picked up Bobby on Saturday morning, they drove back to the city, they took in a movie, and Bobby spent the night on his new fold-down sofa bed.

Gronsky's apartment by now was beginning to shape up a bit. He had bought a bed, a "convertible," and a couple of end tables. He had a crate full of books with a television on top of it. It was not all that great, but it was becoming more livable.

"You know what?" said Bobby.

"No, what?" said Gronsky.

"You'd be a lot better off if you had a girl friend to live with you."

"Oh, yeah?" Gronsky laughed.

"Yeah—a man needs a girl friend. Well, you have to admit, you're not much of a housekeeper . . ."

The following morning was bright and sunny. They had gotten up early and had breakfast in a coffee shop. The plan was to go play some football in the park, meet Shaughnessy at noon, then have lunch up at Hanratty's. Gronsky felt good. He hadn't been feeling that good lately. For the past several days he had been suffering from heartburn. He'd take an antacid, and it would eventually pass, but he was beginning to wonder if he should go see a doctor maybe.

The fall air was bright. It was about sixty degrees out. They started out west along East Eighty-seventh Street. To their right, the road fell away into Yorkville and the unexpected sky that descended on Harlem.

They had agreed to meet Shaughnessy in the park by the football field. According to Shaughnessy, that would "work out just perfectly," because he was planning to run, and that was East Ninety-ninth Street, and he had it all figured out in terms of distance and stamina. Pelligrew couldn't come. They had invited him to come, but he had gotten a phone call from Elizabeth last evening, and he had reluctantly agreed to meet her at noon, at which time, she said, she would have a "pleasant surprise" to tell him.

"What's that all about?" The question was Gronsky's.

"Who knows?" said Shaughnessy. "Maybe she's ditching poor Klimefogler."

"Or the other way around. I can't say as I'd blame him much. It can't be much fun living with a kid who won't talk to you."

Well, whatever it was, they would have to wait and find out, and in the meantime it would just be the two of them and Bobby, and they'd play a little football, have lunch up at Hanratty's, and by then it would be time to take Bobby back home again.

They turned right on Fifth Avenue and crossed East Ninety-fourth Street. The park was to their left, luxury apartments to the right of them. When they came to Ninety-sixth, they cut in through some trees and emerged on the lea opposite Mount Sinai Hospital.

This cool autumn air was peculiarly affecting. When he was still in his thirties, Gronsky had hated fall weather: It reminded him of youth, which reminded him of failure, which in turn seemed to fill him with pangs of mortality. Now, however, with his failures more absorbed, his life having gained a certain perspective, he was better equipped to take the fall as it came: It was like a rust-colored glass through which the sun of the past shone.

"Go on out!" cried Bobby. He was waving the football at him. Gronsky nodded, took off in a dogtrot. Bobby let fire. The pass was wobbly, but he was able to spin, slam it into his belt buckle . . .

The year was 1959. They were playing Cincinnati. Nippert Stadium packed to capacity. It was the second quarter, they were behind six to nothing. It was said that the pros might be scouting the game that night. "Watch the pitchout," said Schulz. He was their captain and linebacker. It was Cincinnati's ball on Miami's twelve-yard line. Third down and seven. They were expecting a pass play. "Be careful," said Schulz. "I got a feeling on this one . . ."

"Come here," said Gronsky.

"What for?" said Bobby.

"Never mind, just come here. I want to show you a trick I learned."

Bobby came forward. There was a girl sitting watching them. She was about nineteen or twenty, wore an army fatigue jacket . . .

It was third down and seven—Gronsky at nose guard. He could still see those Bearcats coming out of their huddle, their red and black helmets glistening like space helmets, their partisan fans waving pompoms and pennants at them . . .

"It's a trick," said Gronsky. "It's called the 'pillar and post' play. At least that's what we called it—they use all different names nowadays. It's the best way I know to open a hole in a line, only you have to be careful, 'cause you can really get racked by it . . ."

U.C.'s center was huge. He weighed at least two-forty. He wore a clear plastic face guard that had been wrapped with adhesive tape. As he came up toward the line, it looked like a voodoo mask. When he bent over to hike, he was like a rock with an egg under it . . .

"Like this? You mean this?"

"No, lower," said Gronsky. Bobby's head was bent down and on a level with his belt buckle. Gronsky took him by the shoulders and placed him correctly. His elbows were spread. Gronsky positioned his feet apart . . .

The snap from center. Gronsky's forearms flew up. His elbow smashed into the big center's face mask. The center fell back. Gronsky was up and around him. Was it a trick? Some deception? Were they luring him into something? . . .

"You mean this?" said Bobby.

"Yeah, that's better," said Gronsky. "You got your head between my legs, you're pushing me backward. That's when the halfback, he slips in behind you, he uses you as a lever, he pushes me sideways . . ."

A shove to the left—and now into the backfield. Here came the tailback. Gronsky moved sideways. The quarterback spun . . . the ball spurted wildly . . . off one player's hands . . . off another's . . . a shoulder pad . . .

"Okay, toss it," said Gronsky.

Bobby fell back. The ball seemed to balance on his short stubby fingers. Gronsky ran to his right, cut back to the left. Here came the ball . . . The girl was still watching him . . .

He had the ball in his hands! He couldn't believe it! A second-string lineman from a second-rate powerhouse, the pros were all watching, he's on his own fourteen-yard line, the backfield's been scattered, he's got daylight ahead of him! . . .

"Where you goin?" cried Bobby. Gronsky had the ball. Only instead of toward Bobby, he was running away from him. Watch out for that squirrel . . . Straight-arm that trash barrel . . . C'mon, you can do it . . . Pour on the steam now . . .

He was juggling the ball—but he still had control of it. He stumbled—he lunged . . . had his knee touched that hash mark? No, he had recovered his footing, he was still moving forward, the crowd was cheering, the uproar was deafening . . .

"WHERE YOU GOIN?" cried Bobby. Gronsky kept running. He had about eighty yards to go to the fence by the soccer field. That was his goal line. No one could stop him. He cut to the right, and now off down the sideline . . .

God, how long had it been since he had actually tried running? "You know, of the three of us," said Shaughnessy, "you lead the least healthy life, Alex. I mean, I know I smoke, but at least I work out each day. What do *you* do? You sit around and watch television . . ." And Gronsky had agreed. It had a lot of validity. He should change his habits. He ought to lose twenty pounds, maybe. If he didn't like jogging, he could at least take up swimming. Swimming didn't hurt; it didn't injure your cartilage . . .

"GO, GRONSKY, GO!" The crowd was cheering. He was over the forty, he was up to the midfield stripe. Don't look back! You're a lowly lineman. "You got your line and your backfield . . . We can't all be glory boys . . ."

"I'd like you to meet Alex. He was with the old Woody Hayes outfit . . ."

"You know that's not true . . ."

"Damn it, stop thinking negatively! That's the trouble with you, Alex. There are two ways of viewing things. There's the go-getter way, and there's the way of defeatism . . ."

He was over the forty! He was down to the thirty! Only why wasn't he hearing their cleats bearing down on him? Was he really that fast? Had he left them all scattered? And what was that trill, that sound like a ref's whistle? . . .

"Oh, Alex, I'm so sorry . . ." This was Mandy's voice now. They were sitting in a bar near the U.C. campus. The game was over. Miami had lost. Gronsky sat scowling into a glassful of Wiedemann's. "It was a dumb, rotten call . . ."

"My knee didn't touch."

"I know. I believe you . . ."

"I mean, I'd know if it touched, damn it. That was the chance of my life. They had a scout from Chicago there. I run seventy-six yards, and there's nobody chasing me . . ."

The girl was still watching. Bobby was yelling at him. He had about twenty yards to go to his imaginary goal line—only this time, by God, it was going to be *real,* there'd be no flag or whistle calling him back to the scrimmage line . . .

"Did I do it right, Alex?" They were in the old Hotel Sinton. Like everything else, that's been razed and torn down now. They've torn down the Sinton, the Gibson, the Albee . . . rebuilt Fountain Square, put the fountain in backward . . . "Were you very disappointed?"

"No, of course not," said Gronsky.

Mandy rolled over. She put her head on his shoulder.

"I love you, Alex."

"Mm, and I love you, too."

"When you're down there at Quantico, will you write to me sometimes? . . ."

He had finally reached the goal line. He felt pleasantly winded. Hell, he wasn't that old. He was in the prime of his life, really. He had made some mistakes, but he had time to atone for them. He had his son, he felt good, he had pretty girls watching him . . .

On the other side of the fence there was a thin strand of trees, and beyond that the road curving south toward 100th Street. There were joggers on the road. Gronsky stood panting. He put the ball down. He stood there and looked at them.

No, life was still fine. Even his knee had stopped throbbing. He leaned against the fence and smiled toward the roadway. Such a beautiful world . . . Such wonderful colors . . . He saw the trees spin around, and then the ground rushing up at him . . .

27

Shaughnessy, like Gronsky, had risen early that morning, only in his case it wasn't because he had a ten-year-old boy with him. In his case, it was because they had left the window ajar, and the cool autumn breeze made the fronds on their palm tree rattle.

The decor of this apartment was a bit of a sore spot. Since the rooms were so large and the hallways so cavernous, Sandra had gone out and scoured the gay shops on Hudson Street, and the result was like something out of an old Lana Turner movie. There was this gigantic white palm overhanging their bedstead. The bedstead itself was of lacquered rattan. There was a blond kneehole vanity with an Art Deco mirror on it, and the telephone was white, only of pre-World War Two vintage. "What the hell is this shit?" cried Shaughnessy one evening when he came home from running to find her gay friends all clucking over it: "This is supposed to be New York, not early Santa Monica! Where'd you get all this crap, from some back lot at Paramount?" And Sandra had just smiled. "It's *kinky,*" she told him. "No, it's not—it's just sick! Look at this telephone! Only Adolph Menjou could talk on this telephone! Goddamn fag kitsch . . . I want you to get it all out of here!"

Well, they couldn't do that. It was Sandra's apartment. That was one of the things Shaughnessy was reluctant to tell people—that, although he had co-signed and it was nominally half his, it was Sandra the Sex Queen whose money was paying for it.

He sat up, wiped his nose. He took a swat at the palm fronds. "Jesus," he muttered. He looked over at Sandra. She was still asleep, her body uncovered, her face half concealed behind a sleep mask with eyelids on it.

There had been so many changes in these past few months, so many discoveries and startling turnarounds. Poor Shaughnessy, hobbled, could hardly keep up with them; it was like trying to stand up and have the waves knock you down again. There was the money, for one thing. He had never seen so much money. She had made more in a month than he could make in a year, practically: Television appearances, endorsements, two book contracts . . . who would have ever thought there was such a gold mine in health faddism? And with the money came status. This was a city of status. It didn't really matter what you had done to deserve it; all that really mattered was that you were observed as having it, and Sandra, it seemed, had a talent for doing that. They had begun eating out—not occasionally, constantly—the Odeon one night, Joanna's the next, then on down to Soho, some new place off Broadway, and "Oh, do let's have brunch at the Café des Artistes, shall we?" And Shaughnessy would go. He'd wear his corduroy sports jacket. He'd wear his faded old denims and his Field Brothers loafers, and he'd sit with his feet up (he never wore socks) and talk about art and what was wrong with our foreign policy. Because the fact of the matter was, he was as snobbish as she was. It was a trait that had long been lying in dormancy, but now, fed on lucre, it was beginning to flourish, and (in some people's opinion) he was becoming insufferable.

He got up, made some coffee. It was last night's warmed over. He wolfed down some bread, dropped his crumbs on the carpeting, put on his Nikes, climbed into his track shorts, and in another few minutes he was leaving the elevator.

There are two distinct ways you can run Central Park—you can circle the reservoir, or you can do it the Man's Way. The Man's Way, of course, is to run on the road, which loops six point two miles around the woodland's perimeter. When he had first moved up here, having forsaken McBurney's, he had gone out with Sandra and run by the reservoir, but it took so many laps, and there were so many weirdos, that he had quickly decided such endeavors were "sissified." He now ran the road. That was much more demanding. There were steep hills and dips and maniac cab drivers, and when you finished your run you really knew you had done something. You were a Rodgers, a Shorter. People looked up to you.

He entered the park up at West Seventy-second Street. Today's agenda called for two and a half laps. That was sixteen miles, which was all he was up to, then he'd go find Gronsky, have a quick drink at Hanratty's. "Oh, no," said Sandra (she had said this last night to him), "I don't mind you leaving and hanging out with your cronies, but his son's going to be there and you've got to behave yourself. Besides," she added, "remember the Antabuse."

Remember the Antabuse. He remembered the Antabuse. She had bought him this drug that was supposed to keep him off alcohol, only he'd get up every morning, flush a pill down the toilet, put back the bottle, and then go have a drink somewhere. "That's strange," said Sandra, "it's supposed to make you feel nauseated." "It *does,*" said Shaughnessy, "it's just that I have so much will power." And Sandra would scowl—he was obviously lying—but she kept buying the pills, and he kept pretending to oblige her with them.

As he entered the park, he had to make a decision: For the past several weeks he had been running it clockwise, but today he decided to reverse the direction, since it would eliminate a lap through the steep Harlem Hill section. He turned right at the drive. The road was deserted. There was a gentle slope down for the next hundred yards, then it would begin to ascend up by Bowling on the Green, then level, drop off at about West Sixty-seventh Street. His muscles felt loose. He was in excellent condition. He didn't even feel any of those marathon "highs" nowadays. When he had first begun running he used to get this euphoria, these mind-altered states in which the world opened up for him.

He had a very good reason to be out of the house today: Sandra was scheduled for a magazine interview. During the past several months there had been twelve different features on her, her shallow cleavage being exposed in each one of them. At the beginning, it was fun. He'd watchdog the interviews. He'd tell her what to say, he'd make allusions to lawsuits, he'd badger the reporters, threaten the editors, and on more than one occasion he had knocked over the camera stands. He had enjoyed doing that. At least they had paid some attention to him. The crusher had come when she was featured in *People*, and there was the inevitable picture of them lying in bed together and an anonymous reference to his being her "pad partner."

"What the hell does that mean?"

"How should I know?" said Sandra.

"I am thirty-eight years old, I have a teen-age daughter, I have a responsible position as an associate art director, and as far as they're concerned I'm just somebody's 'pad partner.'" It was a watershed experience. He would be months getting over it. He had suddenly begun to realize what a housewife must feel like. He was no longer a man, he was an escort, an end table. It was *Sandra* they wanted. *She* was top honcho here.

Down past the playground, left at the Essex House, up past the carrousel, its caliope clanging, then on toward the Mall, those great silent statues, the overarched trees marching off toward infinity . . .

It was a strange thing, this running. It had an effect on one's brain cells. It probably had to do with the intake of oxygen, but whatever it was, it erased all specifics; one's mind was left floating on a cloud of vague impressions. A few months ago, when he was running the reservoir, he had passed another runner who had asked him his phone number, and he had become so discombobulated he had forgotten his lap count and had to start all over because he was afraid he had missed something. He was feeling that now. It was just the beginning. All he could hear was the sound of his feet falling, the dry leaves rustling by the Mother Goose statue, the muffled roar of a bus down Fifth Avenue. . . .

"On Sunday," said Sandra, "we have an interview with *Us.*"

"Who's *Us?*" said Shaughnessy.

"You know—it's like *People.*"

"You mean that teeny-bopper magazine they sell at the supermarkets? Unh-unh. Count me out. I'm sick of that fan-mag stuff."

And Sandra had smiled. "Well, that may work out best, really . . ."

"Whaddaya mean, 'work out best'?"

"They'd prefer I not have you there. The word's gotten around how you act during interviews, and they say if you're there, they may cancel their story on me."

Well, now how do you like that? Shaughnessy was livid. The nerve of those guys, saying they'd cancel their story on her. He'd see about that. He'd sue the damn bastards. After all, he was Someone. He was a sex symbol's "pad partner" . . .

The road began to climb. He passed the Lake and the Boathouse. The boats were half-swamped and submerged to their gunwales. On the right, he was passing the Conservatory Pond, where on a warm August day you could see the remote-controlled sailboat races . . .

Last week (it was Thursday) she had another surprise for him: "You ought to quit that dumb job, Ted, and become my manager."

"Your *what?*" said Shaughnessy.

"Well, I can hardly keep up with it. I get so damn much mail. I've got all these demands on me . . ."

Shaughnessy was dumbstruck. What the hell was she saying to him? Did she think he didn't have any career of his own, damn it? He was an *artist.* A *specialist.* He was an *associate art director!* Should he chuck all that in just to open her fan mail for her?

Become her manager. Let him tell you about managers. He had never been to Hollywood, and he would not be caught dead there, but he had a very clear image of how that industry operated, and everything about it was corrupt and undignified. The first thing about it was that they were all parasitical. There were all these young flakes with their shirts hanging open, and they'd sit around pools calling everybody "baby," and they'd skim all the profits off the talents of other people. That was the first thing about it. The next thing was worse. They'd find some hot body, they'd take it to bed with them, they'd convince the poor thing that she actually *needed* them, and the girl, being stupid, would inevitably fall for it. Her manager, indeed. He could tell you about those guys. He'd as soon be a pimp working the street trade in Midtown. The next thing he knew, she'd have him dressed in white linen, driving around in a Porsche and wearing a chain with an ankh on it.

He was approaching the Ramble. This was the top of the hill now. After that it would fall off toward Cleopatra's Needle, then the great white-stoned Met with its Temple of Dendur, then the long gentle grade down the right near Fifth Avenue . . .

That was Sandra's Big Dream: It was the Great West Coast Fantasy. They should move to California and buy a house on some mudslide. They should have another kid, snort coke in a hot tub, and have Perrier delivered by some flaming queer house servant. Well, the hell with that bullshit. He still had some dignity. Just the thought of that life went against his morality. If they were going to move anywhere, it should be to Nantucket. Martha's Vineyard was nice. He might settle for Southampton . . .

He came to the football field opposite Mount Sinai. By now he had completed about three and a half miles. To his right, across Fifth, rose the Annenberg Building, its great rusting hulk seeming to blot out the skyline.

When he first spotted Gronsky, his mind took a turn, because it reminded him of something that had happened last Tuesday, only he had wanted to forget it, because it wasn't very pleasant and was just one more sign of all the angst he was going through.

"Whaddaya mean, he's a 'square'?"

"Well, now don't take that wrong, Ted . . ."

"I'd just like you to tell me what you have against Alex, Sandra. He's a perfectly nice guy. He's not all that brilliant, but there are good things about him . . . Well, I couldn't explain them to you . . ."

And Sandra had just sighed. He didn't have to explain them. She knew perfectly well what there was about Gronsky. It was that Gronsky had hold of Shaughnessy's alter ego. There were times when she felt she was almost competing with him.

"I suppose," she said wearily, "it's the fact he played football."

"What's the matter with that?"

"And he was in the Marine Corps."

"That's right," said Shaughnessy. "He was in the Marine Corps. I admire him for that. He's done a lot more than I have, damn it."

And Sandra had said nothing. She leaned back disgustedly. They were sitting in a restaurant called the Soho Charcuterie. She wore a white brocade jacket with a Hawaiian design on it that seemed oddly compatible with her "New Wave"-style pixie cut.

"I get so sick and tired of all this male bonding bullshit."

"You don't understand. You're a woman. You think different."

"I'm a human being! I'm the person you live with! I just think it would be nice if you had a modicum of loyalty to me! . . ."

A modicum of loyalty! . . . Jesus Christ, thought Shaughnessy. He waved at Gronsky, but Gronsky didn't see him. By the time he looked up, Shaughnessy was gone. He was rounding the bend toward 106th Street.

A modicum of loyalty! . . . What the hell was she talking about? He was the most loyal individual on the face of this planet. Why just last summer, when there was that problem with Pelligrew, hadn't he, Shaughnessy, remained true-blue to everybody?

He was into the loop now. The road became steeper. He was rounding the curve toward 110th Street. To the right, Harlem Lake lay glistening and colorless. There was a large concrete basin with the letters R-I-N-K P-O-O-L on it.

"You're just jealous," said Shaughnessy.

"Of *what?*" cried Sandra.

"Of men! Of our friendships! I've read all those articles. It drives women crazy that we men prefer men sometimes. It makes you feel cheated. It's the equivalent of penis envy!"

"Oh, my Gaaawd!" Sandra moaned. She threw down her table napkin. "That's the stupidest remark I ever heard out of anybody! Go ahead—fuck it. Go call your friend Pelligrew. See if I care. You can do what you want to, Ted . . ."

The loop bottomed out. He was approaching the hard part.

To traditionalists, like him, it was called the "Harlem Hill" agony, only recently some kids had started calling it "Heartbreak Hill," which Shaughnessy resented, because that was a Boston term . . .

He could do what he wanted . . . Well, that's right, so he could, damn it. He had avoided marriage—he had avoided commitment to her. Only how come he didn't feel free to do *anything?* How come he felt he was being swept by this undercurrent? . . .

He had just passed the field near the opposite goal line, and he had seen Gronsky crumble, his knees giving under him, but somehow he assumed it was part of the game. He kept on running. He paid no attention to it.

"DAAAD!" screamed Bobby.

Shaughnessy kept running.

"HELP!" cried Bobby.

He blinked, closed his mind to it. You must never break stride. That's the first rule of marathoning. The sky could fall in, you have to pay no attention to it.

Then:

"HELP!" screamed a voice, only this was a new voice. She had been sitting on a rock overlooking the playing field, and now she was running, her fatigue jacket flapping, approaching the road, trying to flag down a bystander.

Shaughnessy grimaced. It took a while to sink in on him. It wasn't a game—there was something all wrong here. He slowed up. He turned. He stood there panting.

"GOD! PLEASE!" screamed the girl. "WE'VE GOT A MAN AND HE'S DYING HERE!"

"It's orders, Ted."

"Yeah, yeah, yeah," said Shaughnessy.

"It's an important symposium on the calcium antagonists. It's going to be at the Waldorf, the client'll be there, and I can't go, and they need a guy from the art department . . ."

Aw, Jesus, thought Shaughnessy. He hated these functions. They were more properly the duty of the account men and copywriters, but he had agreed to go and he had sat there disinterestedly while some tight-ass M.D. droned on about angina.

But there was one good thing: They had shown a film clip. It had been created for laymen by the Heart Association, and it showed graphic dramatizations of the symptoms of coronaries, and he remembered that now as he knelt on the playing field.

"Okay . . . Take it easy . . ."

Gronsky lay motionless. He was half on his back, his legs doubled under him; his pulse was weak; his breathing was heavy; he was smiling at Shaughnessy with a look of stunned helplessness.

"GET AN AMBULANCE!" cried Shaughnessy.

Bobby just stood there.

"Goddamn it," he muttered. He stood up. He was screaming at him. "GET AN AMBULANCE, DAMN IT! DON'T JUST STAND THERE AND STARE AT ME! FLAG DOWN A CAB! THROW YOUR BODY IN FRONT OF IT!"

Bobby took off. Shaughnessy bent over Gronsky. His skin was damp. His eyes had a dazed look. "Can you hear me, Alex?"

"I'm okay . . . I'll be fine, Ted . . ."

"Yeah, sure . . . Sure, you will . . . DAMN IT, SOMEBODY *DO* SOMETHING! . . ."

"We lose one out of two serious coronary victims because of their unwillingness to recognize the earliest precursors: chest pain, dizziness, a close, tight, constricted feeling . . . Many, being men, prefer to think it's a gastric problem . . ."

"Take it easy," said Shaughnessy. He had Gronsky by the armpits. The body was heavy. He could feel the strain on his back muscles. "We're okay. We're just fine . . . That's a hospital, Alex . . . Try not to worry . . . Nothing'll happen to you . . ."

"Unfortunately, in New York the statistics are worse. The majority of victims never reach the hospital. This is partially due to traffic congestion, but it also stems from inadequate health-care service . . ."

"Okay, good . . . This is good . . ." He had Gronsky on his

back now. He was carrying him to the curb, where a taxi stood waiting. The rear door was open. Bobby was gawking. The girl in the jacket was muttering inaudibly . . .

"If the victim stops breathing, you have two to four minutes. You must immediately initiate CPR. That stands for cardiopulmonary resuscitation, and we will show this technique using computerized mannequins . . ."

Oh, God . . . This was awful . . . One of his shoes had come off. He piled Gronsky into the cab and slid in next to him. "Mount Sinai!" he shouted. He looked over at Gronsky. Gronsky said nothing. He had been dead thirty seconds now.

28

"What are you trying to tell me?"

"I thought you'd be pleased, Don."

"For Christ's sake!" cried Pelligrew. His expression was panic-stricken. She was heading toward the door, and he was moving to stop her. Behind them stood Jeremy, surrounded by suitcases.

This meeting hadn't gone quite the way he had hoped it would. When she had called him last night and said she had a "surprise" for him, he had just naturally assumed that it would be something he wanted—like her body, perhaps, or what remained of her dignity. What he hadn't quite realized was that there were other possibilities that even a man like The Phantom could not have prognosticated—such as her blithely announcing that she had just sold their house and was moving to Spain to live with her chiropractor.

"You're *what?*" cried Pelligrew.

"He's decided to retire."

"But what about *him?*" He was pointing to Jeremy.

"Oh, that's all settled. He's living with you now. He's got his jammies in there . . . He's got his clothes, all his Star Wars cards . . ."

To Pelligrew's credit—and even Elizabeth would admit this—his manner with children was both natural and mesmerizing. Why, even back in college, working summers as a camp counselor, he'd sit the kids down and regale them with Phantom stories. So when it came to being "buddies," when it came to "communicating," when it came to zeroing in on a juvenile's wavelength, there were very few men who had Pelligrew's panache—which unfortunately in this case was completely beside the point.

"I think you're forgetting—"

"My plane leaves at three, Don."

"I think you're forgetting that I can cut off your alimo—"

"No, not really. Not legally. Not as long as I'm single. Besides, Ira's rich. He's been very successful, Donald."

He's been very successful. My, wasn't that wonderful? But there were other little pitfalls he had managed to foist on her, such as Paragraph Four, Subparagraph C, which restricted her movements to a fifty-mile radius . . .

"There's Paragraph Four—"

"I wish you'd hurry this up, Don."

"THERE'S PARAGRAPH FOUR, SUBPARAGRAPH C—"

"—which is also irrelevant, because it says you'll get custody, which we're willing to grant. We've packed his toothbrush, his slot-car racers . . ."

So this was how it ended. Not in a hot flash of orgasm. Not in a fine, fiery scorn from some vendetta-bent virago. It ended in *duty.* It ended in *parenthood.* It ended in having to act like a *grown-up!*

"You know, I have to admit"—this was Shaughnessy speaking; it was on the same night that Gronsky had been trying to warn Pelligrew; they had been sitting in a bar called Fleet Street in Midtown, and Pelligrew had been grousing about Elizabeth's disloyalty to him—"you know, I have to admit, I think Alex is right, Don. What is it they say? . . . Beware what you pray for? I mean, suppose she gets tired and dumps the whole thing on you? What are you gonna do? You're hardly prepared for it." And Pelligrew had smirked. What a farfetched hypothesis! She'd have to be crazy to do something that lunatic. No, The Phantom wasn't worried. He had it all figured out. He knew how *she* worked, that simple shiksa mentality . . .

The telephone was ringing.

"Adios!" said Elizabeth.

"No! Wait!" He was scrambling. She had a ten-foot head start on him. He was trying to pursue, but there were toys strewn all over—all these board games and puzzles, all these bags with stuffed animals in them . . .

"You know, someday, Donald"—this was Mary Anne speaking; it was on that same fateful night of the Great Gronsky Insult; Gronsky had left, and Pelligrew was smiling, and Mary Anne, angry, was standing there hissing at him—"you know, someday, Donald, some woman's gonna get you. She's gonna figure out a way, and she's gonna make you suffer. I just pray to God that I'm around when that happens. That you could pull such a stunt on a man who's done nothing to you . . ." And Pelligrew had shrugged. "Whaddaya mean? What did *I* do?" "You know perfectly well. You did this whole thing on purpose. You get me to come over, you pull your same doggone number on me, then you call up Alex . . . You knew how he'd find me here . . ."

The phone was still ringing.

"FOR GOD'S SAKE . . . !" cried Pelligrew. He was slipping on marbles. Where the hell had *they* come from? Apparently, among other things, there was a large box of marbles, and in his haste to pursue, he had upset the contents of it . . .

"You keep talking about men and the supremacy of fatherhood"—this is what Elizabeth had told him last year after the football game; she had finally pried from Jeremy what Pelligrew had said to him, including the sacredness of bonds that are made from "Titanium"—"you think fatherhood's so great—you don't even know anything! Who do you think's responsible for the day-to-day scutwork, Donald? Let's see *you* do the laundry! Let's see *you* do the meal planning! Maybe *I* can have fun! Maybe *I* can go whoremongering! . . ." And Pelligrew had scoffed. That seemed so hypothetical to him. See, the thing about fathering—it was a little like masturbating. It was conducive to fantasy, it helped to ameliorate loneliness, but you'd have to be crazy to want a day-to-day diet of it . . .

"GODDAMN IT . . . !" he was shouting. She had made it to the stairwell. In another two seconds, she'd be rounding the landing. She'd be lost forever. She'd be out of his power. She'd be footloose, invulnerable, as carefree as he'd been . . .

"I'LL DO ANYTHING—PLEEEZE! . . ."

He wasn't going to make it. His foot had become lodged in a box full of Tinkertoys. Jeremy was screaming. The phone was still ringing. Elizabeth was smiling as the door slammed after her.

Shaughnessy hung up. No answer at Pelligrew's. He felt tired. He felt beaten. His hands were still trembling. He was standing in the lobby wearing his track shorts and running shoes, oblivious to the nurses who were admiring his calf muscles.

For once in Shaughnessy's life, he had acted heroically. It was a matter of instinct—it had not been premeditated. He had faced down the terror and responded with fortitude—only to learn, to his dismay, that it was too little too late, apparently.

The emergency room entrance at Mount Sinai Hospital is on Madison Avenue north of East Ninety-ninth Street. The room itself has maize-colored walls, and there's an ambulance entrance to the right of the doorway. It was here that the taxi had delivered its cargo, speeding up Madison, ignoring the stoplights, and a crew had run out carrying a stretcher on wheels, and away went Gronsky into the bowels of the hospital. It was obviously too late. The body was moribund. It had that blue, lifeless pallor, the skin growing colder; at one point, the eyes had actually rolled back. No breathing, no pulse, no warmth, no metabolism . . .

"*During cardiopulmonary resuscitation, ventilation must be kept at above eight hundred centimeters. It should rarely, if ever, exceed twelve hundred centimeters, which can force the air back down the esophagus . . .*"

Oh, God, he had flubbed it. He had been to one goddamn seminar. They had these dummies hooked up with all these wires running out of them, and there was a television monitor that was run by computer, and it would say "too much" or "too little" or "you're letting the air escape" . . . Well, how was *he* to know? You had to be an expert. How was *he* to know how much eight hundred centimeters was? No, he had done it all wrong. He had screwed up the rhythm. He had never even checked to see if the tongue was swallowed . . .

He decided to call Sandra. He had to call *some*one. "He's gone!" they had shouted as they ran down the hallway. Gronsky was lifeless, they were pounding on his chest, and the words "He's gone!" had rung down the corridor . . .

He went back to the phone. His brain wasn't functioning. He wanted to call Sandra, but he had forgotten their phone number. Was it 687, or was it 876? He stood there a moment, his hand on the push buttons . . .

"When no pulse is felt, commence cardiac compression. Fingers interlocked, one hand on the other, pressing two inches down above the notch in the sternum, fifteen compressions for every two breaths taken . . ."

And yet he thought he had seen *some*thing. He was undoubtedly mistaken. They were in the back of that cab, they were careening around corners, he couldn't find the pulse—where the hell was that artery?—and yet, for one fleeting moment, there was a flutter, a rasping sound . . .

Ah, now he remembered. It was 768. He dropped in a dime and punched out the number. All of his life he had been leaning on others, and when it's finally *his* turn, when it's *his* strength that's needed . . .

"Hello, Sandra?" He paused.

When it's *his* strength that's needed . . .

He closed his eyes. It was all closing in on him.

"Ted? Is that you?"

And suddenly he was sobbing. "He's dead. I killed him. I did everything wrong, Sandra."

The Annenberg Building faces upper Central Park in the middle of a quadrangle called Nathan Cummings Plaza. It's a tall brown highrise made of oxidized metal and was originally intended for administrative purposes. The eighth floor of Annenberg has a cardiac care unit. It's here that one goes after emergency treatment. It's at the end of a corridor, it's crowded, it's shopworn; it has the scuff-marked appearance of an army enlistment center.

"About through?" said the voice.

Mandy didn't answer. Since there was no place to sit, she had retired to the ladies' room. At least she had assumed it was that. Apparently it wasn't. The voice at the door was between tenor and baritone.

These past several hours had been a nightmare for Mandy. The call had come in from a stranger named Pelligrew, and she had jumped in the car, her hair still in curlers, speeding thirty-five miles down the 684 Interstate. It had been such a long time since she had driven to the city. She had become completely confused near the Hutchinson Parkway, and she had almost landed on the Whitestone Bridge, which might have led somewhere, but not to Mount Sinai.

"Mr. Gronsky—where is he?"

The receptionist stared at her.

"I'm his wife. He's a patient. You just brought him in here."

"Is that G, as in gopher?"

Oh, my God, this was awful. Her hair was a mess . . . she had brought the wrong color lipstick with her . . .

Perhaps here it should be said that in any relationship there are two obverse sides, two points of infinity, and the Gronskys' story was no exception, although neither would have accepted the other's approach to it. From Mandy's point of view it had begun one morning when she was readying a bundle for the Bedford Hills Thrift Shop and, in the course of emptying her husband's pockets, found a scrap of paper that would turn her life around. It was a love note, quite passionate, from a girl named Maureen. It was obvious that Gronsky had been having an affair with her. It was youthful, exuberant, and not very prudent; it had apparently been sent through the interoffice mail system.

Mandy was distraught. The betrayal was twofold. It was a betrayal of the heart and a betrayal of philosophy. Because Gronsky, after all, was a champion of conservatism, a man who had always detested disloyalty.

The first thing she had done was to see that Maureen got dismissed. That was no problem, she simply called up her father, and the next day Maureen had a note on her desk telling her to be out by that night and giving her two weeks' severance.

But revenge against Maureen was a pyrrhic victory. Mandy felt abused—she was not getting any younger. Her housework suffered. She began pampering herself. She took up tennis. She became more petulant.

When Ingrid came along, it was like a jolt of electricity: "Vy do you Americans put up viss ziss nonsense? Look at how you liff, all ziss bourgeois morality. In Sveeden, vee know. It iss emotionally unhealthy for you." And Mandy had listened. She was not unattractive. She was still in her thirties, she had the beginnings of crow's feet, she had put on some weight, she had a slight touch of cellulite, but when she moved, when she smiled, when she was dressed in her tennis outfit . . .

She had an affair at the club. That was Experience Number One. It was the first time she had ever known anyone but Gronsky. He was lean and athletic, and for a while she was captivated. If she could just have some time, if she could just get her head together . . .

"Haff you neffer smoked pot?" This was Experience Number Two. "Here," said Ingrid, "I sink you should try some"—and they had sat, those two women, watching clothes in the clothes drier, feeling that cool distant high that all the headlines had talked about.

Experience Number Three came late in November, after Gronsky was gone and there were the first signs of loneliness, and Mandy, in a bathrobe, was sitting on the bed, and Ingrid, half-naked, was combing her hair for her. "You haff beautiful hair." The strokes grew more languorous. "I sink," said Ingrid, "it is time now vee graduate," and she had taken Mandy's hand and placed it on her breast while with her own narrow fingers she probed the folds in that terry cloth . . .

By early December, Mandy knew what was happening, but for the life of her she didn't know how to get out of it. They had begun sleeping together, at first surreptitiously, but later more openly, sometimes leaving the door ajar. There was a *ménage à trois.* It was with a man who plowed driveways. "Men," explained Ingrid, "add a spice of variety." The drugs grew stronger. The orgies grew headier. There was talk at the club. She sensed Bobby withdrawing from her.

It had erupted last summer in an unfortunate incident, which, had Gronsky found out, would have been the end of everything. Ingrid had been baking some "experimental brownies," and Bobby had come home and found some and eaten them. Mandy felt panicked. There was a rush to the hospital. Bobby's stomach was pumped, and he was released the next morning, but that was the end, she had had enough "freedom," and all she wanted now was to get Gronsky back home again.

"You all right?" said the voice.

"Just a minute!" She grimaced. She was standing at the mirror, trying to put on some eye makeup. She had a Max Factor blusher and an Ultima II eye shadow. She fretted at the lines that seemed to multiply daily now.

Like so many women who have spent their lives in the suburbs, Mandy's view of Manhattan was severely distorted. It was a frightening place, even the people were frightening, and often she had wondered how her husband survived down here. "Iss simple—he fucks." That's what Ingrid had told her, and Mandy, feeling vulnerable, was prone to accept that. That's what men do. When they're married, they're docile; as soon as they're free, as soon as your back is turned . . .

She unlocked the door and came out of the bathroom. There was a man standing there along with a boy about Bobby's age. She nodded, smiled awkwardly. The boy went in after her. She turned and walked slowly toward the chief cardiologist's office . . .

"Will he be all right?"

"We don't know," said the doctor. "He's been fibrillating badly. You know, he actually died this morning. If it weren't for his friend, that guy—what's his name, Shaughnessy? Did he tell you what happened? They were in the back of this taxicab . . ."

There was a small vinyl bench outside the cardiac care unit.

She went over, sat down, looked around at the other people. They all looked so young. She had never met any of them. She had the uncomfortable feeling that they all disapproved of her.

"Excuse me. I'm sorry—are you Alex's wife?"

Mandy blinked, tried to smile. One cheek had mascara on it.

"Have they told you what's happening? They won't tell us anything. They say only his wife is allowed to be in there with him."

She was an extremely young woman and, in her own way, quite pretty. She had raven-black hair and an aquiline nose structure. One of Alex's girl friends. Some babe he'd been sleeping with. Chucky little chin . . . the big bosoms that men like . . .

"I'm not sure," said Mandy. "They say he's been fibrillating."

"They say he's what?"

"I don't know. They just told me that."

"It means spasms," said Shaughnessy. "Excuse me, I'm Ted. You got your heart—it's like this—you got your muscles fucked up in there . . ."

Mandy closed her eyes. This was all so confusing. For seventeen years she had known everything about him. She knew his friends, his associates, the men he'd played golf with . . . Who *were* these people? What did *they* know about him?

"Oh, Ted, do be quiet."

"Well, I'm trying to explain it . . ."

"The doctor'll explain it. Excuse me, I'm Sandra. I'm terribly sorry. We've all been so fond of him. I've been saying to Ted, 'That man is so dear to me' . . ."

"FOR CHRIST'S SAKE!" cried Pelligrew.

"WELL, I CAN'T GET IT OPEN!"

"WELL, TURN THE LOCK, DAMN IT! I'M GONNA PEE IN MY PANTS OUT HERE!" That was the man down the hall. He had been waiting for the bathroom. Apparently his child had managed to lock himself in somehow.

"I'm Mary Anne Delucci."

"How do you do," said Mandy.

"I just hope he's all right. I got a call, he was asking for me . . ."

"Excuse me—Mrs. Gronsky?" It was a man in a surgeon's gown. "He's coming around. I think you might want to see him now."

29

Gronsky blinked, tried to focus. dSՈ . . . He twisted his face. That didn't make sense. dSՈ ˙ɾuI əsoɹʇxəᗡ %ς lɯ 00ς˙ What the hell did *that* mean? Must be some sort of code or something.

When he finally regained consciousness at about seven in the evening, he was lying in a room that had no front wall on it. It was a three-sided cube that opened out on an anteroom, from the ceiling of which hung a strange-looking television set. He stared at the picture. It was a strange-looking picture. It seemed to be a program on how to draw sales charts. There were these zigzaggy lines, and they'd start at the left, then they'd move to the right, then they'd start in all over again.

"He's awake," said the echo. That was the first thing that reached him. He had no idea who or what they were talking about. "He's awake . . . he's awake . . ." It came down through a canyon at him. He tried to inhale, but there was a stake through his midsection.

Once, long ago (but how long? and where was this?) he had been walking down a street, and there was a tall open window, and the window looked in on a room with high bookshelves where a middle-aged woman stood aloft on a stepladder. There was something about her. She wore a gray buttoned sweater. Her body was frail, and her hair had white streaks in it. She was standing on the ladder, and she was examining a volume, and when he said something to her, she smiled, she looked up at him . . .

That was at seven. He'd try again later. He wanted to get back to this place he had been earlier. He had been standing in a hall, and there was a door at the end, and the door was ajar, and there was a room, it was beckoning to him . . .

When he awoke about ten, his mind was more conscious. The bottle, he now realized, had a tube running out of it. The tube disappeared into the folds of his bedsheet, and when he tried to move his arm it seemed to jiggle the bottle contents. All these sights and odd sounds. There was a thump, like a heartbeat. It seemed to be coming from a pump where the bottle hung. To his right, out of view, there was a low, gaseous gurgling, only he couldn't turn around because of the stake through his midsection.

"How you feel?" said the echo. A hand touched his forehead. He tried to look up, but there was a clamp in his nostrils. There was some sort of prong, and it was stuck up his nose, and when he tried to turn his head, it seemed to tug at his face muscles.

"Oh, my Alex . . . poor Alex . . ."

Gronsky didn't comment. He felt totally indifferent to whoever "poor Alex" was. Forget about Alex—what about *him?* He had a prong up his nose, he had a stake through his midsection . . .

As the hours wore on, he'd have this new world to interest him. It was a small, timeless world full of bedpans and bottle labels. And words. God, the *words!* They seemed to eat through his brain cells: arrhythmia . . . bretylium . . . defibrillator . . . lidocaine . . .

"You're a very lucky man"—so the doctor had said to him. "It isn't every man who gets to die and come back again. You have your friend Ted Shaughnessy to thank for that miracle. He goes to one seminar, and he's as good as our ambulance driver . . ."

"Here's a myocardial infarction of the inferior wall complicated by recurrent ventricular fibrillation. We have the antipated areas of hypokinesis, but overall normal left ventricular function." The exchange students nodded. There was a Korean, two Indians. They wore long cotton coats, and their pockets had snakes in them. They took out the snakes and held them to his chest. They talked among themselves in a garbled vocabulary . . .

For the first couple of days, only Mandy could see him. He

caught a quick glimpse of Bobby when a door was left open, but it was Mandy who stayed, Mandy who soothed him, Mandy who ran and got a nurse when he needed one. He familiarized himself with his three-sided cube. The wall to his left had red and white candy stripes. On a shelf by his bed there was an array of electronics, including an EKG monitor and an electric defibrillator. But always, in the end, he'd return to that hallway with the door left ajar and the room beyond beckoning, and the woman (which woman?) who'd be standing there smiling, saying, "Whenever you're ready. I'm right here—I'm just waiting for you . . ."

"I suppose you heard?" This was Pelligrew speaking. They were now in day three, and he could receive a few visitors. Pelligrew had arrived wearing a blazer and a pea cap, and he stood around scowling at the IVs and pulse monitors.

Gronsky said nothing. He hadn't heard anything.

"It was just like you said. She did a real number on me. Flew off with that clown, left me stranded with Jeremy. Can you imagine such a thing? After the affection I poured on her . . ."

"I brought you something." This was from Mandy. She had arrived after lunch carrying a package from Gimbels. It contained a razor, a toothbrush, and a new pair of bedroom slippers. "For later," she said. "When you're up and around maybe . . ."

"Okay, just relax." This was one of the interns. He had a needle and a tube, and there was some sort of dye in it. Gronsky looked on while the dye disappeared, flowing up through his arm, making traces for x rays . . .

In the late afternoon, another doctor appeared. He was tall, very thin, and had a lopsided moustache. "You know which is yours?" He glanced at the television. "Second from the left. That'll save you from asking later . . ."

"How ya feeling?" said Shaughnessy.

Gronsky didn't answer.

"I brought you some books. Coupla Agatha Christies." He unwrapped the books and laid them on the radiator. There was the same discomfort Gronsky had noticed in Pelligrew.

Thanks. Gronsky nodded.

Shaughnessy just stood there.

THANKS! Gronsky blinked. He touched Shaughnessy's forearm.

Shaughnessy said nothing. His eyes looked frightened. "See ya later," he said—and abruptly he left again.

End of day four. Condition less critical. By now he had become interested in his chart on that television. He couldn't help wondering if he could control its activity. Mind over matter. Sort of a reverse biofeedback, maybe . . .

"Who's Mary Anne Delucci?" The question was Mandy's. They were into day five, and she was pouring some water for him. The room was subdued except for a crack in the blind slats. He couldn't help noticing how tired and alone she looked. "Are you in love with her, Alex? Is that why you asked for her?" Gronsky said nothing. She held out the glass for him. "It's all right—I forgive you. We've both had experiences." She lifted his head. She tilted the glass for him . . .

"My name's Alex." He smiled.

"Yes, I know. You're the football player."

They were climbing some stairs, and he was studying her backside. He had a baby in his arms, and at the top of the stairs she turned, she smiled, their fingers touched briefly . . .

"Can you forgive me, Alex?" Who was this talking? He had opened his eyes thinking it was probably Mandy, only that's not who it was, it was Mary Anne Delucci, and she was sitting by the bed, her eyes smiling moistly at him. "Oh, Alex, I'm sorry. I should never have trusted him. God knows, I was dumb. He was just playing a game with me. And the silly part is, I didn't even want him. It's hard to explain, but you seemed so remote to me . . ."

"You're in love with her, aren't you?" Now Mandy looked sterner. It was evening again, and the sunlight was fading. Where was his doctor? He wanted his doctor. He had a question to ask about his graph on that television. "Oh, Alex, grow up. She's too young—she's a *child,* Alex. I suppose she's sexy. Is that all you're after? We've had seventeen years. Don't just throw them away. I'll admit I was wrong, but I don't want to lose you for it . . ."

"I quit my job." This statement was Shaughnessy's. They were now in day six, and it was the middle of the morning. A nurse had come in and looked askance at Shaughnessy because he had almost knocked over another patient's IV bottle. "I quit. I said fuck it. All they want's a damn bureaucrat. I got better things to do than draw gall stones and sinus cavities. Besides . . ." He paused. His head lowered slightly. "Well, I've been talking to Sandra, and she does need a manager . . ."

"I've decided to get married." This was from Pelligrew. They were now in day seven, and he had arrived looking haggard. Apparently Jeremy had been taking his toll on him, what with the laundry and the cooking and getting him up and to school each morning. "Well, what else is there? The kid needs a mother. You have no idea. You can't imagine the hardship on me. The only problem is, there's no woman who'll have me. I've called eight different women. You wanna hear what they say to me? . . ."

At the end of day seven, he was released from Annenberg and wheeled on a cart to the Klingenstein Center. This was an adjacent building containing hospital wards, and he was allowed to see visitors on a more normal basis now.

"Well, aren't you going to ask?" Her name was Nurse Selridge. It was the beginning of day nine, and he was feeling much better. He could read, take some solids, lie and stare at the television. And he could think. Ah, yes, that. He had become quite good at thinking now.

"Well, aren't you going to ask?" She was taking his temperature. She was a piano-legged woman with an enormously large bustline. For some strange reason, she seemed to have taken a liking to him, and she was constantly fussing and rearranging his pillows for him.

"What should I ask?"

"Oh, come on, don't be bashful. All you men are alike. There's only one thing you think about. As soon as it's the heart, you say, 'Tell me the truth, Nurse. Can I still get it up? I'm not gonna die in the saddle, am I?' . . ."

At the end of day ten, he was able to "dangle." Mandy had come in, and she had brought a new deck of playing cards. They were playing gin rummy. He was sitting in his ward gown. The predominant sound was of the cards slapping bed linen. "Oh, Alex . . ." She smiled. Her eyelids grew laugh lines. Her lips turned up as she began moving her cards around. "Do you remember"—she blinked—"do you remember that day when we took Bobby to Pound Ridge and you tried to get that darned kite up for him?" Gronsky didn't answer. He examined his gin hand. "That was such a good time. I got so hysterical. You had the string all fouled up, and the kite wouldn't fly, and it kept smashing into trees, and you got so darned infuriated . . ."

"Gin," said Gronsky.

"Do you remember that, Alex?"

"I got gin," he said. He looked away toward the window. From somewhere in the distance there was the sound of a jackhammer. Another new building. Another renewal project.

"You're going back to her, aren't you?" He was now in day twelve. He was able to walk, use the john, stroll the hallways. They had given him some pills—some drug called propranolol—and he'd be taking those pills every day from now on, they told him. Mary Anne scowled. They were sitting in the visitors' lounge. There was another man there, and he was smoking a cigarette. Oh, God, that smelled good! He'd give anything to have one. When Shaughnessy arrived, maybe he could filch a few puffs off him. "You don't have to tell me. I already know. I kept saying to myself, 'Don't you dare get too close to him. He's not really free. He's got all that darned baggage. The minute she calls, he's gonna run right back home again' . . ."

"I've decided to ask Emmy." This was Pelligrew talking. It was the thirteenth day, and Gronsky felt stronger now. They were strolling through the halls, it was about eight in the evening, and Pelligrew had been itching to try this new concept on him. "I want your opinion. I'm gonna ask her to marry me. I mean, why the hell not? She's the only one left, damn it. Of course, it's a little uncomfortable—I'd be in love with my stepdaughter—but I think it could work. I think I could cope with it . . ."

And meanwhile those dreams . . . the woman on the staircase . . . the lady on the ladder looking down through the window at him . . . What did they mean? Were they some sort of omen? And how was he going to explain the course of action he had decided upon?

30

"So if you'd like—" said Pelligrew.

"I'm sorry," said Emmy. "Donald, could you excuse us while we go to the powder room? This is all so exciting, and I want to continue it, but all this wine, all this coffee . . . We won't be but a second, darling . . ."

It was the very next evening, it was about quarter after ten, and the crowd at the Four Seasons was beginning to thin out a bit. This being November, they were into their autumn mode. The warm air moved softly through the metallic link window hangings.

Ah, the heartaches of a Phantom! Things weren't going too well for him. His practice was suffering. His apartment was a shambles. The school had called yesterday to say Jeremy was sick, and they were sending him home with a 102 temperature. He had nowhere to turn. He had run out of resources. What else could he do but try to cash in on Emmy? Emmy had money. Emmy had living space. Not to mention sweet Lilah, who'd be Jeremy's half sister now.

Once, late last year, when it was playing the rerun houses, he had gone by himself to see *Kramer vs. Kramer.* He loved that movie—it had so much insight!—the persecution of men, the injustice of matriarchy. And he had come out of the theater feeling vengeful, rapacious. That a woman would actually walk out on a kid that way! And later that night, he had picked up a barfly, and he had taken her home, where he had pounced on her angrily . . .

See, when all was said and done, it was a matter of protest; a matter of hurling one's bones into the clockwork of history; for he was not unaware; he did not live in a vacuum; he knew perfectly well that this was the Age of the Heroine. Nevertheless, a man does have validity. There are only two sexes, and you can't ignore one of them. And since Emmy seemed to like him and had the means to take care of him, he saw nothing immoral about proposing a partnership with her.

"Tell you what," was her answer, "let's have dinner and talk about it. We'll go to the Four Seasons—I happen to know the two owners there. Just you, me, and Lilah—we'll make a wonderful night of it. And you can tell me about Jeremy, then we'll tell you what *we're* thinking . . ."

The Four Seasons Restaurant, at Park and Fifty-second, is by no means New York's most expensive eatery. There must be half a dozen others of similar caliber where two can dine comfortably for the price of a cruise-ship ticket. Pelligrew, however, had never had dinner there. He had had drinks in the bar—he had nibbled cheese in the Grill Room once; but dinner was a treat that exceeded his resources, so he considered himself lucky that Emmy was paying for it.

To go back and unravel the skeins of this relationship: The truth of the matter was, Lilah had never succumbed to him. Even that night when they had lain there in bed together, he had found her so "challenging" that he had come prematurely somehow. And ever since then, she had grown increasingly skittish. "Oh, come on," she kept saying, "you're not really that interested"—and night after night he'd keep wrestling with her mother while that photo on the bed stand kept mocking and jeering at him.

Here's how he saw it: He was going to marry Emmy (never mind the fact that Gronsky had said he was crazy), he was going to tie the knot, move into her apartment, and let these two East Side Princesses share the privilege of baby-sitting. They'd enjoy doing that. They'd consider it an honor. They'd not only have him, they'd have his clone, little Jeremy, and he'd come home every night, and Emmy's maid would cook dinner, then they'd wile away the evenings discussing topics like—well, incest, maybe. That was not so insane. In fact, to him it seemed logical.

Hell, they couldn't expect The Phantom to live by middle-class values, could they? And if it didn't work out—well, he could always divorce them, having first found a way to get a slice of their assets, naturally . . .

"You're late," said Emmy, when he arrived at the restaurant. She was sitting downstairs wearing a full-length black sable. Lilah looked sultry in a black leather trench coat. Pelligrew was dressed in his best three-piece "court outfit."

"I couldn't get a sitter."

"Ah, poor Donald," said Emmy.

"No, I mean it. I'm serious. You don't know what it's like, goddamn it. I asked four different women—all of them were busy. I finally had to leave him with my neighbor—you've met her, maybe . . ."

They mounted the stairs and turned left toward the Pool Room. Emmy looked prettier than he had ever seen her. There was a light in her eyes, a kind of inner effulgence, as if some long-sought desire was about to come true for her.

"Shall we order some wine?"

"Sure, why not?" said Pelligrew. They had been shown to a table to the left of the reflecting pool. A wine list was passed, and Emmy selected—a Pomerol, Château Petrus, one of the late 1960s vintages.

It was one of the inestimable Pelligrew's more deeply held tenets that a man should never offer to pay for anything. This was not only an extension of his sixties upbringing, it was ideologically compatible with the dictates of feminism. In fact, he had once gone so far as to write a ten-page monograph—a wild, hostile diatribe about who gets the dinner check—which, in an ill-advised moment, he had fired off to *Ms.* under the misconceived notion that they would see things as he did. When the piece was returned, he was genuinely baffled. Were they really too dense to see that he was on *their* side? "Dear Ms. Steinem," he wrote, "You are a fool and a hypocrite—which is not to imply that I'm not physically attracted to you . . ."

The headwaiter appeared. Emmy decided on lamb. "Make that very, very rare, and no potatoes on the side, please." "Oui, madame," said the waiter, and he made a notation, although he felt constrained to inform her that potatoes were included with it.

Lilah ordered fish. "I'll have a slice of smoked salmon. Are there potatoes with that?" "As you wish," said the waiter. "Good. Then I'll have potatoes. Only no Sarlandaise sauce. I can't stand Sarlandaise. I'll have them *à la Provençale,* please."

Pelligrew just sat there. He didn't know all these niceties. He knew his basic James Beard and his *New York Times Cookbook* favorites, but when it came to ordering, say, Steak Occitane, he hadn't the foggiest idea what the hell its ingredients were.

"So anyway—" he said.

"Excuse me—waiter!" said Emmy. She raised her hand, and the waiter came back again. "You do understand that I want that lamb rare, don't you? I won't eat well-done lamb. I want it pink, with the juices in it."

"Oui, madame," said the waiter.

"Oh, and waiter—" said Lilah. The waiter returned. "Take this bread from the table, will you? I've ordered potatoes—that's enough carbohydrate. No, wait—leave the butter. You don't have any Ry-Krisps, do you?"

As has been noted by others, there is a politics to ordering, an assertion of power that takes place during menu reading, whereby tartar sauce, say, is demanded for hamburgers and drinks are returned because the tonic seems flat-tasting. That was not new to him. He liked to do it himself sometimes. He'd have some hapless young waitress bouncing back like a yo-yo, adding quirk upon quirk, fetish to fetish, until finally, progressively, he had psychologically sodomized her.

"You were saying—" said Emmy.

"Excuse me," said Lilah. The wine had been brought, and she had taken a sip of it. Her lips were drawn up in a vinegary smile. Her hand was at her throat, and she was making dry rasping noises.

"I was saying—" said Pelligrew.

"Ugh! Forgive me—I'm sorry. Is it my imagination, or does this wine taste funny?" She held out the glass. "I don't know, it tastes funny to me. You taste it, Donald. I have the feeling it's turned or something."

It was Emmy's turn next. She had begun staring at her appetizer. It was caviar from Oregon—thirty-two bucks worth. She had already downed half, but now she was scowling. She would have preferred to have beluga, which cost twelve dollars more than that.

When the lamb finally came, it had potatoes on the side.

"Ahem!" said Emmy. She scowled at the waiter.

"Oui, madame," said the waiter, "it is the fault of the kitchen, although if I may be so bold, madame might wish to leave them there . . ."

Lilah interjected. She was picking at her salmon. "This doesn't taste fresh."

"I beg your pardon?" said the waiter.

"It tastes metallic or something. It tastes like it's frozen. I've changed my mind. I think I'll order the sweetbreads, maybe . . ."

Pelligrew said nothing. He had been staring at his steak, but so far neither woman had even settled her entrée problem. The lamb had gone back, the salmon was fleeing, and, having rejected two wines, they were now sampling Beaujolais.

"So I was thinking—" said Pelligrew.

Hold it—here came the lamb again. The potatoes were gone —it was just lamb with some parsley on it—but it still wasn't right because it had been allowed to grow cold, and we all know what happens when a Princess's food's not piping.

"How's your steak?" said Lilah.

"I'm not sure," said Pelligrew.

"Don't wait for us."

"No, good heavens!" said Emmy, and neither would rest until he at last began eating, at which point they smiled, although their eyes had starvation in them.

When the lamb came back in, it had steam pouring out of it. There weren't any potatoes—it was just the way she had ordered it—only when she poked it with her knife it still wasn't right, because in the course of reheating it had lost all its pinkish color.

"I can't eat brown lamb."

"You should have kept the potatoes."

"I cannot stand potatoes, and I cannot stand brown lamb, damn it! I've changed my mind. Let me look at the menu. They'll have to take all this back. I think I'll try the roast partridge, maybe . . ."

And so on and so forth. The evening dragged on. Once the partridge came in, they had to change all their wine orders, so that by the time they were through they had gone through six different vintages, five different entrées, and an inevitable dessert squabble.

"Dear Ms. Steinem," he had written (this was a couple of years earlier; he had sent her three letters, and she had never replied to them; by then he had become convinced that they were bugging his telephone and posting their operatives on adjoining rooftops)—"Dear Ms. Steinem," he had written, "When you reinvent the female, please be sure to include room for an auxiliary urine holder. The present-day models have these teensy-weensy bladders that inevitably become full just as soon as the check arrives . . ."

He tapped on the table. It was now ten-thirty. The check was by his saucer, but he was trying to ignore it. If the women should return and see him glancing at the total, they might erroneously conclude that he was offering to pay for it.

Ah, Elizabeth, he thought. She had been preying on his mind lately. Where the hell was she living? Torremolinos or someplace? "You know, someday," she had said, "you're gonna get your comeuppance, and it'll serve you right, you're such a first-class son of a bitch . . ."

It was now ten-forty. He was looking at the dinner check. It was the most enormous total sum he had ever seen on a restaurant tab. It had these three giant digits to the left of the decimal point, and under that was the tax, then a space for gratuities . . .

At about ten to eleven the truth began to dawn. He asked the headwaiter if they could check out the rest rooms for him. "Oui, monsieur," said the waiter, and he went off in that direction, only when he came back later he was alone, there were no women with him.

The minutes ticked by. The truth became clearer. He felt the cold edge of panic rising up from his solar plexus. And that's when it happened. They gave him The Letter. "Dear Donald," it began—and it spelled out everything.

31

"Are you sure?" said the woman.

Gronsky didn't answer. He was standing by the bed tray buttoning his shirt front. He was about fifteen pounds lighter, his street clothes were baggy, but other than that he looked surprisingly vigorous.

It's amazing the effect that a confinement can have on one. There's a magic about it; it's like a feeling of rebirth. It may have something to do with the asepsis, the solitude; it's like living in a womb in which the past is eradicated. "You're a totally new man"—that's what the doctor had told him. "You have a little dead tissue—we call that necrosis—but there's really no reason you can't live to be eighty. The only question is, will you be willing to change yourself?" And Gronsky had blinked. He wasn't sure he quite got that. "I mean," said the doctor, "that there's a question of will involved. We can patch up your heart, but we can't cure your life for you. Unless you're willing to change, you're going to be back where you started from."

The night before last, Gronsky had had a series of "insights." They were of the "REM period" type, such as one has on awakening, and although in and of themselves they didn't make too much sense, when he opened his eyes, they all seemed of a pattern to him. There was a woman on a staircase. She seemed calm, rather confident. He had the distinct impression that she was of a higher evolution. "You're not ready," she had said, and she had turned, walked away, and when he had tried to pursue, her possessions rejected him. There was a woman on a ladder.

She looked lonely but contented. She had an expensive-looking brownstone with a book-lined study, and although she was older, she seemed sexually attractive, only he couldn't figure out any way to get in to her. What had followed after that was a series of phantasms, some sexual, some guilty, some vaguely nostalgic, but all of them centering around one nagging question: What is it I want, and how do I get to it?

"The course of true love"—was it Shakespeare who said this? —"the course of true love never did run smooth"—and he had thought about that, and he had lain there scowling, because it didn't make sense. People have got it all backward, damn it!

"Are you sure?" said the woman. She looked at him quizzically. There was a slight trace of doubt, a modicum of wonderment. He was buckling his belt. He laced up his shoes. "Are you coming?" he said. He didn't wait for an answer from her.

"You do understand?" "I'm not sure," said Bobby. He had asked to see Bobby without benefit of Mandy there, and he had sat his son down and tried to explain it, using whatever analogies might get through to a ten-year-old. "The important thing is, I'll still be your father." "Yeah, sure"—Bobby smiled—"and will you still come to visit me?" "You bet. Every week. That's a solemn promise. And if someday you're older, you want to try out this city life . . ."

At the cashier's office, he ran into Mandy. Of course, he had talked to her, too; she was the first he had talked to. "I just hope," she had told him, "that you know what you're doing." And he had nodded. He did. He hadn't the shadow of a doubt about it.

In the hallway outside, Mary Anne stood and waited for him. He supposed he might have managed a less embarrassing leave-taking. It wasn't too cool having one's past and one's future both standing around while you fill out insurance forms. Although in a way, he supposed, even that made no difference. Mandy would survive. These women are tough nowadays. It's the men you have to watch. We're so suddenly delicate. It's as if our topsy-turvy age has unmasked all the frailties in us.

Outside, it was gray. There was a forecast of snow flurries. The city lay coiled against the onrush of shopping season. A cab rolled by. "Shall we take it?" he said.

Mary Anne smiled. "I'd rather walk it, if you would."

EPILOGUE

Once upon a time, back when Shaughnessy was single, he had happened to read an article about a popular screenwriter. A New Yorker by birth who had produced a best seller, the man had been lured by the Sirens of Hollywood. The gist of the article was that he was not very happy. He was like a fish out of water—he missed his old neighborhood; so he had rented a plane, a huge 747, and he had paid to have his neighborhood shipped out to L.A. with him.

Well, if Shaughnessy so chose, he could do something that frivolous. He could punch out a number on one of these telephones; he could charter a plane, send a telegram east, pick up Gronsky and Pelligrew and have them come spend the weekend with him. He'd enjoy doing that. They could sit and get shlonkered. That was the trouble out here; you couldn't sit and get shlonkered properly. You could sit and get stoned. You could sit and get addled. But shlonkered? No way. It would have seemed un-Californian somehow.

The Brown Jordan deck chair that he had been sitting on all morning had begun to heat up, so he draped it with a bath towel. The sun was ferocious. It made mirrors of his sunglass lenses. He sat up, turned around, rubbed his shoulders with baby oil.

It had been almost two years since they had moved to this paradise. He looked a little older now; his sideburns were graying; last year, around Christmas, he had decided to grow a beard, but it had come in all mottled, so he had shaved it off again. He was still in good shape. His body was suntanned. He ran ten miles a day, most of it on sand, and in the evening he'd go down and work out in their gymnasium, which was really a gazebo between the pool and the tennis court.

On the table, by the pool, there were six Princess telephones. They were the mandatory white, and they were connected to an intercom. One or another phone seemed to be ringing incessantly—some producer, some agent, some v.p. from Lorimar, maybe. And Shaughnessy would answer. That was what Shaughnessy did nowadays. He'd sit there by the pool and he'd answer the telephone. "Hey, Lenny, how are ya? . . . That's fabulous—beautiful! . . . Just a minute, I'll call her . . . Naw, no trouble, I'll ask her, Lenny . . ."

As a matter of fact, there was a phone ringing now. Since it was their houseboy's day off, he had to get up to answer it. Yes, he had lost that fight, too—they had their very own houseboy, and when he minced around the deck his little tushy made wiggling movements . . .

Out beyond the pool deck with its flowering hibiscus, out beyond the Jacuzzi, the bathhouse, the hot tub, there was a solitary speck about the size of a water bug; he could see its arms wheeling through the trough of a ground swell. That would be Sandra. She'd be doing her exercises. Madonna and child, one within the other, a child to take the place of that rebel named Jaime, who had ended up pregnant and was now living in Florida somewhere . . .

As he picked up the phone and looked out toward the water he couldn't help thinking that this was better than Nantucket. The East was so cold. It was—well, so behind-the-times. He fingered his ankh. "Hello, Sandra Silk's residence . . ."

"Target turning right, heading west toward von Furstenberg." He retracted his antenna, turned his face toward a wall poster. Mirrored ceilings looked down on a vast sea of narcissism. It was springtime at "Bloomie's," and "Bway" was crawling with it.

In the intervening years since the Jeremy debacle, time had taken its toll on the outward Don Pelligrew. He was heavier now; his face was more jowly; his bare scalp was visible through what remained of his hair follicles. But he was still rather handsome.

He had the same deep-set eyes; he had the same way of talking —elliptically, startlingly—and when the girls called him "sir," which seemed to happen more frequently, he'd just smile, shrug it off, mutter something outlandish to them.

"For Christ's sake," said Gronsky one night about a year ago when they were in Gronsky's new home and they were talking about women; it seemed that everyone he knew was becoming more and more settled, and the happier they looked, the less in common he felt with them—"For Christ's sake," said Gronsky, "why don't you act your damn age, Don? I've been listening to this bullshit for the past umpteen years, damn it. Another 'perfect woman'—another 'relationship.' You oughta go see a shrink. It's getting boring just listening to it." And Pelligrew had scowled. They were sitting at the table—Gronsky's new wife was there, they had just started dinner—and he had suddenly stood up, he had tossed down his napkin, said, "Excuse me—I'm leaving," and he had never gone back again.

That had happened last year, and it was the end of their relationship. Which was all right with him—he didn't like Gronsky anyway, that holier-than-thou mensh with his midwestern stodginess, his inability to grasp any of life's subtler nuances . . .

Take a left at Lauren, a quick spin through Sheseido, now on toward Chanel, Alexandra de Markhoff, and in another few minutes they'd be rounding the stairs, heading down toward brassieres, toward those panties with "Bloomie's" on them . . .

What had initially attracted him to this particular victim was that she was older than the others—in her mid- to late thirties, maybe—and there was an expression on her face, a kind of broken-souled quality, that said, "Take me—I'm easy. Do whatever you want to with me." She was also not Jewish. That was definitely a virtue. He'd take Irish girls, Swedes, he'd take German girls, Dutch girls even, but he had sworn off all Jews, he would have nothing to do with them, they were an immoral lot, and his heart winced in terror of them.

"Dear Donald," she had written. It had been delivered by a waiter, and Pelligrew, puzzled, had opened it tentatively. It had obviously been composed in advance of the dinner, and she had handed it to the captain on the way to the ladies' room. "Dear Donald," it said, "Please accept our apologies. This is a little trick you taught us up at P. J. Clarke's once. You're an amusing sort of soul, and we've enjoyed your company, but as I've told you so often, every man has his use, sweetie . . ." It went on to define "use" as it pertained to Pelligrew: "I am so terribly carnal —poor Levi used to say that—and if it weren't for your ability to keep me well serviced, I daresay, dear Donald, I would have ended this months ago . . ." Attached to the note was a packet of documents. The first was a letter to the New York State Bar Association. The date was left blank—she had obviously not mailed it—but it was meant as a reminder of what might subsequently happen to him. The next was a copy of her late husband's codicil. It was the original sheet on which he had made his amendments, and there was a signed affidavit from a handwriting expert saying that the scratches were Pelligrew's and there was evidence of will tampering. Finally, under everything, there was a copy of a photograph. Across it, in lipstick, were scrawled the words " 'Bye, 'bye," and when he tried to erase them, they wouldn't come off, they just smeared like a stain all over Lilah's young mammary glands.

So after lo these many years, he had finally been bested. He had been brought to his knees by an aging ex-Princess type. It was a horrible retribution, and it was amazing he had endured it. Lucky for him he had been wearing his Phantom cape . . .

"Sandra Silk's residence."

"Hello, Ted? This is Alex."

There was a moment's hesitation—then, "Hey, Alex!" cried Shaughnessy.

"How you been, you old bugger?"

"Where the hell are you calling from? I was just thinking about you. You must have, what, ESP or sump'n . . ."

The ad director's office, which was next to the publisher's, wasn't quite so impressive—it was just a large rectangle—but it was nicely appointed with a black walnut desk, a red leather sofa, and a mahogany end table. Gronsky leaned back. He put his feet on the desk top. He was considerably thinner—he had lost twenty pounds or more—his once broad face looked craggier, handsomer; there was a color in his cheeks that hadn't been there three years ago.

It had been almost that long since he had gotten his promotion. It had happened soon after he had left the hospital. The economy had soured, then the revenues had fallen, and eventually there were threats of paper cancellations. "Well, what can I tell you? You were right, he was wrong, Alex." This was from Eastman after he had fired Karpeghian. Since Mandy had announced that she was dating a real estate broker, Eastman's attitude toward Gronsky seemed to have picked up considerably. "But then what would life be if we didn't make mistakes, huh?" and his cheeks had turned red, and he had offered Gronsky a cigar, and Gronsky had smiled—he was tempted to take it—but of course he couldn't, he had given up smoking now.

"The course of true love"—yes, it was out of Shakespeare, and it had been spoken by a courtier who knew nothing about living, and that was way back when, and people still hadn't caught it, they continued in the illusion that it must all be made complicated: "The course of true love never did run smooth," and it was preceded by a line that that's what you read in romances, only this wasn't a romance, it was life, it was real, and any life, when it's real, can't be tidily formulated.

After he had left the hospital and gone back to his apartment, Mary Anne had come with him because he seemed genuinely to want her now, and they had made love soon after, and it was as good as he had fantasized, and for the next several months their desires were insatiable. But problems did arise. She was young, she was callow. What to her was discovery was to Gronsky mere prelude, and as the novelty wore off and their desires began waning, the hiatus between them grew more and more threatening.

"I want to have a baby." That's what Mary Anne had told him. It was a subject of discussion that had become increasingly wearisome to him. He was now forty-five. He had suffered a heart attack. Just the thought of a baby—all those feedings, those diaper changes . . . "You think it sounds silly. I am twenty-six years old, Alex. I was born in the Bronx. My family's Italian. I want to have a baby. I want to get married. That is not so absurd. I don't like you laughing at it . . ."

So eventually she left—she had found someone younger—and again he felt lonely, only now it was easier, and he had met other women, had affairs with a couple, and when Sandra got pregnant they had named him as godfather . . .

It was on a warm July night, and he happened to be at Pelligrew's—this was before the argument that terminated their friendship—and he had gone out to buy ice, and he had just come back in, and a familiar voice called down from the landing at him:

"Could you shut the door, please?"

It was a command, but a polite one. She was standing by the railing, one hand on the newel post.

"Oh, yeah. Sure—I'm sorry . . ." and he went back down the stairs, and he kicked the door shut and shouldered his weight against it.

She had aged only slightly since the last time he had seen her. Her hair was more silver, her neck had some creases in it, but, all things considered, she was the same slender woman who several years earlier had left an impression on him.

"My name's Alex." He smiled.

"Yes, I know. You're the football player."

He was mounting the stairs. The ice had begun melting. "And you're Linda Cauthen." Since he had taken up swimming, he could bound up those stairs with a whole lot less effort now.

She wore blue jeans, a tank top, and a pair of blue tennis shoes. The glasses were gone—she had apparently bought contacts—but her smile was the same, there was the same sense of confidence, there was the same lonely air that said, "Why aren't you ready for me?"

So that's how it started. It was like a meeting of the spirits—two aging Midwesterners, two battle-scarred sex veterans, and when the planes converged it was hardly momentous, just a man and a woman trading smiles on a stair landing.

Gronsky asked her out. She said, "Sure"—that was easy. They went out for a drink. They took in a picture show. She told him about her job: She was a v.p. in marketing. He told her about *Focus:* "I've reached my level of incompetence, probably." And in the evenings to come, he would learn more about her. She had been born in Iowa, she had majored in business, she liked dancing and sewing, she didn't like cooking, she had lived for some years with a Lufthansa Airlines pilot. There was nothing very special. She was hardly seductive. "I just never caught the knack of batting my eyes," she told him. But it was as Shaughnessy had forecast—it was a matter of temperament. It was like discovering a friend who had spent her whole life just waiting for you.

They got married on a weekend. They didn't take a honeymoon. For the first several months, they lived in her apartment. Then one night, at dinner, she said, "Alex, guess what? I saw the cutest little brownstone, and the idea occurred to me . . ."

So that's where they were living. It was on East Seventy-third Street. It had a front-facing library with tall casement windows, and in the evening they'd go out, and she'd cling to Gronsky's arm and say, "How quiet it is! You almost never hear jackhammers . . ."

Had Gronsky found happiness? Look at how he's beaming. Look at how he's laughing with his old friend Shaughnessy. He has a wife he adores. He has a son he gets to see. With the help of some pills, he has a reasonable life expectancy. Has Gronsky found happiness? It depends on one's viewpoint. He still looks at girls. He still likes to drink too much. It's a relative thing. He might have done better. He might have stayed dead and been living in paradise.